I continued to rage silently downstairs. If I had seen his face in the window, I would have found my gun and put a bullet in his head. I was convinced that this lunatic was somehow, for some reason, after me. He wanted to scare me to death, drive me insane, or something. I knew in my heart that he was crazy. And I felt I had to nail him. It was a survival instinct. . . .

"Horrifying . . . This spine-tingling psychothriller will strike a chord with single women everywhere."
—*Booklist*

"A seamless suspense novel that guarantees readers edge-of-the-seat drama . . . A knockout!"
—*Publishers Weekly*

"Robyn Carr knows why you read the psychothriller: for the primal scream of terror."
—*Philadelphia Inquirer*

"Once you pick it up, there's no putting it aside . . . Resonates because it taps into all women's vulnerability and raises issues as hot as the latest session with 'Donahue.' "
—*New Woman*

"Move over Hannibal Lecter . . . A chilling, gripping piece about a cunning psychopathic serial killer . . . Fascinating!"
—*Rapport News*, Los Angeles, CA.

MIND TRYST

ROBYN CARR

ST. MARTIN'S PAPERBACKS

This novel is a work of fiction. All of the events, characters, names, and places depicted in this novel are entirely fictitious or are used fictitiously.

MIND TRYST

Copyright © 1992 by Robyn Carr.

Cover photograph by Herman Estevez. Cover design by Tony Greco.

Library of Congress Catalog Card Number: 90-27870

ISBN: 0-312-92932-3

Printed in the United States of America

St. Martin's Press hardcover edition/February 1992
St. Martin's Paperbacks edition/February 1993

10 9 8 7 6 5 4 3 2 1

For Stephen Crandall and
Charlie Ryan—my best guy pals.

I would like to express my gratitude to my early readers and technical guides. First, Nancy Higgenbotham and her razor-sharp eye helped me to define a couple of key characters and pick up a couple of loose threads, not to mention giving me tremendous moral support during the writing. Kim Seller Garza, who has read early drafts for me in the past, is always a tremendous help and good friend. Also, she reminds me, she ends up always being right. Thanks to Geraldine Rose for helping me understand and appreciate the specialness of the practice of law in a small town. And finally, thank you to Police Detective Ricardo Garza; his technical advice was extremely important to the completion of this novel.

1

THE truth matters. To my mind the first symptom of evil or derangement exists in the lie. How evil, how deranged depends on the magnitude of the lies. I think of that as I look around my house, partially remodeled, filled with boxes packed for moving. Again. I've been here a year. It took a year for the lies to build to a climax that could have cost me my life.

In my work, in family law, I expect exaggerations. I expect an extraordinary bias. Clients do not admit that they're jealous of their ex-spouse's new partner as they ask to change the custodial guardianship or visitation. I have never had a client confess that he or she is molesting the child. I sometimes rely on gut feelings.

I have been heard to preach on the subject of lies, especially to my son, Sheffie, who has been dead three years now. He was only eleven when I lost him; he stays an eleven-year-old in my dreams and imagination, though I desire to imagine him at fourteen. I would say things like "You cannot know the power of a lie, no matter how small." And "If it isn't the whole truth, it's a lie."

When I moved here to this small Colorado town, to practice family law, one of the first things I did was consider the creation of a partial lie. I came to work for and with Roberta Musetta, a sixty-year-old attorney who had practiced in this town for thirty years. I was willing for Roberta to know the details of my personal life but was not willing for everyone to know everything. "Let's say never married, no children."

She looked at me levelly, her brown eyes hovering over the rim of her glasses. "I think I can understand the 'no children,' but why 'never married'?"

"I was only married for a year, Sheppard is my maiden name, and often when I say I am divorced people feel compelled to ask me if I have children. It's painful for me to say that I had a son and he is dead. It's a kindness, if you think about it, because no one knows what to say next. No one."

"How did he die?" she asked.

"Or they say *that*."

Roberta was not intimidated by anything and she hadn't been then, either. I could be so damned defensive about it sometimes. "He was on his bike in an intersection and was hit by an armored car. Witnesses said he was crossing against the light. He died instantly. He was eleven."

"I'm sorry for your loss."

"Thank you, Roberta. I *can* talk about it; it's talking about it with *everybody* that bothers me. One of the reasons I've come here is for a complete change of scenery, lifestyle, a new beginning. When a single mother loses an only child, there is a devastating kind of aloneness. It terrifies people and makes them behave more strangely than the bereaved. I couldn't deal with the reaction anymore."

"I see," Roberta said. But she couldn't come close

without the details. The zenith of the events was when a close friend, Chelsea, broke into my house when I refused to answer the phone and door one Saturday for reasons that had nothing to do with grief. I was avoiding a man determined to date me, I'd had a brutal week in court, I had drunk too much the night before and had a vicious headache, and I wasn't expecting anyone. I unplugged my answering machine and phone so I wouldn't be tempted. I turned up the stereo so I could hear it all the way to the bathroom and filled up the tub. The loud music drowned out the doorbell. I thought about gardening later; I thought of trying a good book. Imagine my delight when a young policeman entered my bathroom with my friend.

I can't criticize Chelsea; she is a dedicated caretaker. I had been depressed, overworked, and impatient; I had not left my answering machine on, my car was in the garage, and the stereo was blasting. Clearly I had hanged myself or taken an overdose of pills.

I was determined to change things. I couldn't stand the pity and I couldn't stand being watched so carefully.

"I shouldn't ask you to lie for me," I had said to Roberta. "I suppose I could try changing the subject or refusing to answer."

"It'll be over quicker," Roberta replied, "if you just say to anyone else what you said to me. I, for one, am unwilling to elaborate on the personal lives of friends and coworkers."

A part of me embraced what she said. Speaking of Sheffie's death caused me pain, but his life had given me great joy. By erasing him, I would rob myself of that pleasure. He lived in my heart and mind; I couldn't wish him away with a lie. Not even to save myself from some pain. Still, another part of me held reservations about revealing too much too soon.

My task, in telling what happened to me here in Coleman, is to explain how a woman sensitive to liars, experienced in dealing with them, and intelligent can end up in grave danger. End up nearly dead. My sanity abandoned me; my clear head, steady hand, and sound instincts were buried under an avalanche of lies and manipulations. For a while I couldn't distinguish between the rational and irrational.

It's easy to find the beginning. I was sitting right here, in this room, on this curved white sofa. My knee was raised, as it is now, and I held a cup of coffee with both hands. The bookshelves were not there and the walls weren't painted. There were boxes scattered around the room because I didn't have the strength to unpack. I was depressed, and surprised to be. I had made a major change in my circumstances, and all the while I prepared to leave Los Angeles, I had been excited and optimistic for the first time in years.

I had traveled to Coleman several times. A sleepy old mining and lumber town southwest of Denver, it's in a pleasant valley with no highway. There is little mining now and timber is seasonal work; there's ranching, some farming, hunting, camping, skiing, tourism. Coleman is one of several small towns nestled in what is called the Wet Mountain Valley; there's the Silver Springs Bar and Restaurant, a refurbished hotel that's one hundred and twenty years old, some raised sidewalks, and an old scenic-rail service.

The town has been rediscovered by the baby boomers; young professionals who have opted to trade materialism for an atmosphere of safety and tranquillity have come here. You can get your teeth crowned cheap—we have several young dentists. In the past fifteen years, I'd been told, the town had sprouted some bed-and-breakfast inns, an herb-tea manufacturer, organic farmers, and even a women's shelter. The population is under one thousand, with another thousand in surrounding rural areas who would claim Coleman as their town. It's one of the bigger unincorporated towns that speckle the large valley. Pueblo is the closest city, with a population of forty thousand. Denver and Colorado Springs are not out of reach to anyone willing to make the one-to two-hour drive. Most of our services—sheriff, hospital, social services, et cetera—come from the Henderson County seat in Pleasure, some thirty miles up the road. Coleman does have its own fire truck and ambulance now, with an active volunteer fire department and auxiliary. There's a great high-school football team, a major real-estate conglomerate, and a charming combination of the old and the new.

Since I had somehow managed to buy a newly built tract house in Southern California, I chose a house in Coleman that was sixty years old. I was doing everything differently. I hoped to do much of the renovation of this old house myself.

That day that comes to mind found me immobilized by depression. I had suddenly felt as though I had abandoned my son by leaving L.A. He had been dead two years already, but he was so much on my mind that I couldn't function. I couldn't unpack the boxes, put on my makeup, or make conversation. I had hired someone Roberta suggested could help me, a handyman-builder by the name of Tom Wahl. He was an average-looking, not unhandsome, friendly man. He had dark-brown hair, brown eyes, and a nose with a bony bump on its bridge. Like most men who did heavy work, he had large, callused hands and strong shoulders. He wasn't a great big guy, five ten or so, with a rather thick torso. He measured my wall for shelves, making small talk about how much personality these old houses had— each one different—and I looked as though I should be put to bed.

I was preoccupied, sitting on the curving sofa I'd been so proud of, wishing I had sold it along with the other things I had decided to leave behind. I had saved for two years to buy it, and because of its white, sterile appearance, I kept it covered so Sheffie wouldn't soil it. What I was remembering was the number of nights he had fallen asleep on it and I had either carried him or directed him sleepily to his bed. Damn. It could happen to me like that, without provocation. I didn't need a photo or favorite toy to be jarred into that sense of loss. I was overcome with longing for my child. There were times I thought I was doing so well; then other times I thought I'd never recover.

Add to that the fact that I've never had a robust appearance. Up until Sheffie died my friends would claim to be jealous of the fact that stress takes weight off me rather than induces me to eat and plump out. I have one of those pale, anemic complexions—if I cry briefly, I look as though I've cried for days. The suggestion of tears causes the rims of my eyes to become red, my nose gets watery and pink, and I splotch. I get hives and rashes easily. My hair is strawberry blond, enhanced by a rinse which became my prerogative at thirty-seven when I arrived in Coleman. Sitting there in old wrinkled clothes, holding coffee, looking pink around the gills, and being in that dismal, remote mood, I must have given Tom the impression I was a sad case.

"Miss Sheppard?" he asked. "Who, ah, painted that wall?"

"I did," I said defensively. I remembered thinking that anyone can paint a wall. Not true. I had made it look far worse than it had—streaked and gloppy. It looked like a window that had been cleaned with a wet paper towel that only smeared the dirt around.

"It could use a little touching up, don't you think?"

I looked away from the wall, not answering. It was a stupid question.

"I could paint it for you," he suggested.

"No, thanks. For right now let's just stick to the shelves."

"I wasn't going to charge you."

That always gets my attention. I am suspicious of freebies. "Why would you do that?"

"Well, you'd have to buy the paint. You need primer, too. I could write it down for you, tell you what to get."

"But why?"

"Why not? I have the time and it looks like you could use the help. Roberta says you're planning to do extensive work on the house."

I have no trouble getting right to the point. "So, you would paint that wall for me and then I would be sure to call you when I'm ready to start on the kitchen and bathrooms?"

He was scribbling a measurement on his white notepad. When he had finished, he looked at me and laughed. "I don't care whether you call me or not, Jackie. I don't need the work. I was just trying to help."

"And I'm just trying to find out why." I was sounding more and more difficult, more and more bitchy. It was as if I was challenging him: Don't try to like me; I won't be liked. But it was more than that; I knew there had to be a straight answer in there somewhere.

"Because you're going to have to call someone; it appears you can't do it. And you look worn out. And you're a friend of Roberta's, who is a friend of mine. Though you might not be used to it, the people in this town help each other out when they can. The permanents, anyway. Where are you from?"

"Los Angeles."

His tape measure sang as he extended it. "That explains it."

"Oh?"

"L.A. is a different kind of place. I lived there for a few years myself. This kind of thing never happens in L.A. At least not without a catch. It happens all the time here."

"What did you do in L.A.?" I asked. I know I asked that right away and I also know that he didn't give a sign of being uncomfortable with the question.

"Paperwork," he said, his back to me. "And I never liked it. I'm from the Midwest . . . suburb of Chicago. After a few years in Los Angeles I started looking for places outside of the city where I could get out of the smog and noise. I had tried northern California, Oregon, Washington, and it ended up I fell in love with Colorado. I don't ski; I like to camp, hike, fish. . . . I like it better in summer—one year I bought some land. I started to build on it, and without any concrete plans to, I had settled here." He said all this while he was measuring. And writing numbers down.

"We can put some shelves around the fireplace,

like so," he said, gesturing with one hand. "I think you'd like the look if I removed this old oak mantel and replaced it with bleached pine like the shelves. Let me draw you a picture first. Then I'll write up a materials list and estimate."

"What did you do in Los Angeles?" I asked again, relentless as a typical litigator.

"I wasn't a carpenter, that's for sure. Everything in L.A. is prefab. I worked for the state in the social-services department. Becoming a carpenter by trade was an accident. When I came out here permanently and started building my house, I met everyone connected with selling me my supplies and people started paying me to help them with their building and woodworking."

"Social services," I said. "I'm in family law."

"Really? Oh, wow," he said, laughing. "You're a lawyer?"

"Yes."

He laughed some more. "Figures."

"Figures, how?"

"Oh, I feel embarrassed for myself. Roberta told me you'd be working in her office, and being the male chauvinist I am, I figured you were a secretary. Sorry," he added sheepishly. "Even with Roberta being here most of her life, some of us are still not used to women lawyers, women doctors, and that." The "and that" was pure Chicago, a regional speech habit like the "ay?" of Canadians. He put his pencil in the pocket of his plaid flannel shirt. "Good for you," he said.

I tend to forgive people like carpenters for having sexist notions and am impressed when a laborer knows that much about his values and conditioning. I'm easily charmed by men who seem to want to be better men.

"I'll make a drawing for you. It'll take me a few days."

"Thanks," I told him, following him to the door.

I didn't think about him again that week, except for the fleeting thought that this was a nice guy. The town, in fact, seemed dominated by nice men. I met some in the office—Roberta making introductions—or in this or that store. Those who hadn't been introduced nodded on the street. The school crossing guards waved; the postman always had time to chat.

That first week in Coleman it took all my energy to behave as though I weren't deeply troubled by thoughts of Sheffie. First the sight of the sofa filled me with memories that made me cry. Next, as I was looking at that damned wall, I remembered part of an argument we had when he colored on the wallpaper. He'd been a good kid, never before did things like that, and it was a milestone of mine—wallpaper.

Do you know how much this wallpaper cost? How I had to scrimp to buy it?

I didn't mean to.

You did mean to; you had to mean to—you did it.

He had gotten one of his rare spankings then. I had cried as I stripped off a section of wallpaper and replaced it. I found I could afford the time and expense of the repair; I had overreacted. In those pre–child support, post–law school days, I had indulged in so few luxuries and held each one dear.

I have an ex-husband, Mike. I have to struggle to remember how it was I accidentally married him. Those reasons wouldn't snag me now: He was reckless, sexy, and somewhat arrogant. I was right out of college when we met. He was in his second year of college after four years in the Air Force as an enlisted man. In retrospect, he wasn't even a particularly good date, much less husband. He had been an awful husband—inattentive, self-centered, restless. He was going to school on the G.I. Bill; I was working as a secretary in a law office, hoping to train as a paralegal. My income was not enough to support us, and Mike had to work part-time in addition to school.

His name is Michael Alexander, and he began to step out on me, I suspect, in the first three months we were married. I didn't know it at the time, of course. I began to suspect him of affairs, if not just carousing, before our anniversary.

We argued constantly, didn't like any of the same things or people, couldn't agree on room temperature, lighting requirements, or television shows. After three or four months I began to have dinner out with my friends and he went to sporting events or played poker with his. We accomplished one amiable discussion in our marriage, about our divorce.

One Saturday, when I was cleaning and doing laundry and he was working on a paper for school while simultaneously watching a football game, I said to him, "It just isn't working, is it?"

He stared at me for a minute, got up and turned off the TV for the first time since we'd married, and then said, "No, Jack, I guess it isn't working." He is the only person who ever called me Jack.

"Maybe we ought to talk about ending it rather than fight about who's right and who's wrong."

And we had. We were far more civilized in our divorce than we had ever been in marriage. It seemed we'd finally found something we could do together amicably. The little house we occupied was leased and I could afford the rent, utilities, car payment, and insurance for at least the rest of the year without alimony. Mike had friends he could move in with.

Alimony had not occurred to me; he was a starving student. We agreed to separate and divorce sans war; we hadn't had a good time together anyway. Parting was the only thing we did that made sense.

I was twenty-three at the time. Now that I'm older, I realize how many times I have liked someone without loving him, or loved without liking. Mike I had briefly loved. I didn't like anything about him. Now, though I'm not in love with him, I'm growing to like him. He has become admirable in my eyes.

We separated and I felt instant relief. Then I missed a period. Then two. My pregnancy was a complete accident that resulted from one of our rare sexual encounters.

My fear at the time was that he'd demand to move back in and stop the divorce proceedings. Or insist I have an abortion. Although I doubted the soundness of my decision, I had instantly decided I would have my child and raise him. My reasons were murky; I wasn't sure this sort of thing would happen to me again. I hadn't dated extensively; I didn't have my sights set on love, marriage, and family. I was solitary, a trait of only children, and independent. I had learned I couldn't live with Mike Alexander, but I was certain I could live with his child.

As self-centered as he was in those days, he let me have my way as long as it didn't cost him anything. I called him from the hospital the day after Sheffie was born, and despite the fact that my parents were enormously rude to him, he was civil and thanked me for letting him look at his son. He asked if he could visit him once in a while and I said sure.

"I'm naming him Sheppard Michael Alexander," I said. "I'm going to have my maiden name again. He will be Sheppard Alexander and I will be Jacqueline Sheppard." He thanked me for giving the baby his name. Mike visited twice that first year, if I remember.

I was lonely in those first few months after Sheffie was born, but I loved him so devotedly and felt so needed that I didn't indulge the self-pity.

Years of building myself up into my idea of success followed Sheffie's birth. I moved back in with my parents to save money and have my mom's help with the baby. I worked ferociously and ambitiously. After three years with the firm and a two-year-old child, I managed to get a scholarship to law school. Why settle for being a paralegal when I was smart enough to pass the bar?

I was completely unprepared for the demands of law school, though I had been warned by the attorneys in the firm I had worked for. The constant encouragement and even tutoring from lawyers I had once typed for helped me get through. They let me clerk in the summers and offered me my first job when I passed the bar. There I was, a brand-new, freckle-faced, single-mother lawyer with a five-year-old son. I was back out on my own, settled with my child in a little tract house, practicing law.

I was one of those late babies; my mother was over thirty-five when I came along and my father was older still. I had only a year in the firm when my mom, then sixty-five years old, had a heart attack and died. Her death devastated me; there were no brothers or sisters, and my father, twelve years older than my mother, was not well. We had always expected to lose him first. In addition to dealing with my loss, I had to begin to take care of my father. Had I not had Sheffie, I might have crumbled. The arms of a small, loving child can do more than penicillin for what ails you.

This is when Michael Alexander came back into

my life as, get this, a model ex-husband. He had remarried, a woman named Chelsea whom I would eventually choose for a best friend even with Mike betwixt us. Chelsea was ideal for us both. She quickly gave him two daughters and pushed him back into his son's life, child support and all. He couldn't be argued into back support, but he became generous with his time and his money.

I remember that Sheffie was stunned at first, and suspicious. He soon settled into the weekend routine, which gave us both something good. Sheffie, who was losing his grandpa, had a dad, and I had valuable time to myself. I owe Chelsea. It was Chelsea's doing that Mike and I were able to forge a friendship that came as a minor relief when our son died. Mike told me it was Chelsea who said to her husband, "What do you mean you're not paying any child support? Is that how you plan to demonstrate responsibility to our daughters? And what about their right to know their brother?"

Chelsea Alexander made of Mike something I could not have managed. She somehow found potential in this playful jerk; she encouraged his dreams, his performance, his fidelity. He had majored in criminology, and became a cop. He developed a more sensitive nature because of Chelsea, fathering daughters, and working with women. His partner, I learned by accident, was a woman. I never would have fallen in love with him, but I began to respect him. I do respect him. I owe him my life. Regardless of what all the pop-psych books say—that it is impossible to change another person—Chelsea fixed Mike. She entered his life and molded him into a husband and family man. Somehow he had reached an age and maturity to know a valuable woman when he had one—and Chelsea was it.

All these things and people combined to bring me here. My father, who suffered from hardening of the arteries, was diagnosed as having that tragic thief of the mind, Alzheimer's. He had to be placed in a nursing home, and when Sheffie was killed, Dad wasn't able to comprehend it. My father was the last thread that tied me to Los Angeles. When he died it was time, I thought, for a big change. I had come to realize that I would always be plagued by a certain sadness from my losses, but in a new town I needn't be reminded by friends and acquaintances that I had once been so positive.

I set about making new friends. In a place like Coleman, a small-town civility abounds, yet conceals standoffishness. At first glance it appears friendship will be easy. I found a group of men who had coffee and cigarettes every morning at the café; after stopping there for a muffin-to-go three days in a row, I had become a regular and one of their acquaintances. I purposely lingered to stretch the truth with them every day. Two ranchers, a telephone lineman, a county surveyor, the hardware-store owner, and Harry Musetta, Roberta's husband. They seemed to enjoy teasing me about the time—all of eight thirty A.M.—and the fact that they had already worked half a day.

That was where I first met Billy Valenzuela, a forty-five-year-old man who had suffered brain damage in an auto accident when he was in his late twenties. From the time he had recovered enough to begin to function, town people gave him little jobs like yard work, dog sitting, deliveries. He was sweet and shy and had the mental capacity of a ten-year-old. He was large—six feet and two hundred pounds—with a kind and gentle disposition. He drove around town in his beat-up old pickup with his dog, Lucy, and he lived alone at the edge of town in a tiny two-room house that he had shared with his mother until her death. Now the town took care of Billy, in a way, keeping him in enough cash to get by.

One morning in the café I ran into Tom Wahl while I was getting my muffin. He was not sitting at the long table with the men; he seemed to be adjacent to them, at his own table talking to one of the guys on the end. As if I were being reacquainted with an old friend, I gave him a big hello.

"You should watch the company you keep, Tom. These old liars are going to get you into trouble," I teased.

"Lady lawyers," Harry said, "are what get you into trouble. You can trust me on that one."

"Roberta files her briefs at work, washes Harry's briefs at home," someone joked.

"I wash all the briefs," Harry said. "They call it retirement," he added.

"I'm hanging around here waiting for you," Tom said. "I have that drawing and materials list."

"Great," I said. He passed an envelope to me and I slid it into my purse.

"Think you'll have time to look it over this morning?" he asked.

"Sure. Can I call you later?"

"I don't know where I'll be today. If I am around home, I might have the saw or drill running. I'll call you."

From that point on, I guess, I thought about Tom most of the time. And will, I suppose, for the rest of my life.

2

I CHOSE Saturday for Tom to come to the house to install the finished living-room bookcases. Oh, the drawing impressed me, as did the list that broke down the materials and labor costs. We firmed things up when he dropped by Roberta's office with his contract, spelling out that he would do the work and be paid the sum of $457.

"Labor is only one hundred forty-two," I said. "You can't be making much of a living at this rate."

"Believe me, I get along fine. You want to give me a tip?"

"That isn't what I had in mind," I said. "I'm surprised, but pleasantly so. Don't press your luck. I might decide to try to build the shelves myself."

When he finished laughing, he said he'd see me on Saturday at about nine. It was going to take him all day to do the work.

I found myself looking forward to the day. The people of Coleman were cordial, but until you've entered a small town as a newcomer and tried to wedge your way in, it's difficult to understand the kind of resistance there is to a new resident. It feels like hesitancy. I wondered if it was suspicion or timidity. The old-timers in the café were great joke-sters, but I was not invited to the town picnic or the Chamberses' potluck supper. The women in the beauty shop were likewise friendly, fun in a down-home kind of way. There were no invitations for dinner.

And there was Billy; large, klutzy, sweet Billy, who cleaned up my yard every Friday. Billy ran errands and made deliveries for Roberta twice a week. For me, he did mowing, raking, and trimming. He did not qualify as a gardener; his work was mediocre and he left things undone: a tuft of unmowed grass here, a forgotten pile of cuttings there. Plus, he needed constant encouragement to do it at all. For fifteen bucks a week I found him a value, but he was not a conversationalist.

My relationship with Roberta was warming up; we were developing a kind of mutual respect, but there wasn't any of that "Come out to the house to eat with Harry and me." I could see the potential for that more from Harry than her. Nothing about settling into Coleman was quick for me.

Then there were the summer transients: vacation-ers, those passing through, and some part-time resi-dents. It takes months to know which faces are here for a day, a week or two, a season, or permanently. Sometimes you find a long-term resident or perma-nent resident when they find you—in the grocery store or in front of the post office. "Hey, are you the lawyer? Let me ask you something." Those acquain-tances don't offer camaraderie or amusement either, and if they do, it's usually for free legal advice.

I made do on long distance—I didn't have to look at my old friends' pitying eyes and was able to cover any tones of my own depression over the phone. Or not talk. A trick I had learned was to use my cheeriest voice to say, "Doggone it! I was on my way out. Let me call you back later." Later, when any symptom of the blues passed, I could pick up the phone.

Roberta Musetta is a whole story in herself. She was sixty and dyed her hair brown, but I never got the impression she had an ounce of vanity. She was about thirty pounds overweight and heavily bosomed; she might have had a grandmotherly appearance for anyone not acquainted with her rough edges, stern, humorless nature, and pigheadedness. She had glasses for reading, but was either uncomfortable wearing them or used them to emphasize her reaction to statements. She kept track of them with one of those chains around her neck; I knew, instinctively, she had worn that long before it became chic.

Despite the community's reticence, it was with Roberta that I felt both needed and respected. She was overworked, though there were some other lawyers in town and several in Henderson County. We had one secretary, Peggy, whom Roberta snidely referred to as "part-time" although she was meant to be fulltime. She arrived late, often left early, and did as little typing and filing as possible. Roberta's office— our office—was a disaster. Files were stacked everywhere; ashtrays remained full until they overflowed. She had a caseload that appeared impossible for a lone attorney. Her memory for details was astonishing. There were more civil suits per capita in Coleman than in large cities like Denver or Colorado Springs. People are going to see one another for decades; they require more legal closure on their arguments.

During that first week, when Roberta was going through some of the cases pending, lifting a file, explaining it, putting it down on the other side of the desk, my first reaction was to say "Jeez." I was more in awe of the clutter than of the work.

"You aren't going to try to organize me, are you?" she asked unkindly.

"Not unless you ask me to."

"I am not only not asking you to, I am ordering you not to. Though it may not appear so, I have a system and I know what I'm doing. If you want a challenge, work on Peggy," she suggested. Peggy was down at the store buying snacks, something that happened several times a day. Peggy had a genuine weight problem, about one hundred extra pounds. "If you can get the Chee-tos stains off my paperwork and get her to empty the trash or wash up the cups, I'll give you a Christmas bonus."

"You have no objection to my being neat, do you?" I asked.

She leveled a stare at me with those hard eyes of hers, looming over the rim of her glasses. Surely there was a sense of humor in there somewhere, I thought. Then it came. There was a deepening of the lines at the corners of her eyes and around her thin lips; there was a slight twitch in the mouth. "Whatever blows your skirt up, dear," she said evenly.

Roberta worked at being a pain in the ass. She might not have been frivolous or forthcoming, but she had many traits I admire in successful, older women. She worked like a farm animal, for one thing. She didn't seem to be easily manipulated into doing anything other than what she had planned. Harry seemed equally autonomous; he didn't pester her for any of the wifely duties that I could see. She called him an old fart.

"Although your background is in family law and most of the cases I'd like you involved in are areas in which you're already experienced, I don't want you to get the idea you can specialize in a place like Coleman. You're going to have to get your feet wet in some other areas as well: property closures, historical water rights, change of easements, tax law, corporate law, et cetera. I'll be able to help you with most of that."

"You don't think I'll be a handicap, do you?"

"You wouldn't be here if I thought so." She could be so matter-of-fact; there was the merest hint of a compliment in there. I had no trouble at all getting used to that aspect of her personality. I like the straight shot. "As it happens, there is more of the kind of thing you're used to going on here all the time. Divorce, property settlement, social-services work like foster care, adoptions, custody disputes, restraining orders . . . a sad amount of domestic violence. I don't mean to imply that these circumstances are new; hardly that. These people have only recently discovered law. Many are still settling things behind the barn with fists or guns."

In small towns that survive on seasonal work there is economic dislocation that lends itself to domestic disharmony. Translated: A man works timber all spring, summer, and fall. He is laid off and collects unemployment, sits around the house and drinks beer all winter. Ninety percent of our domestic abuse, restraining orders, and divorce filings takes place between Christmas and the end of March.

"Here's one for you," she said, handing me a folder. "You can run over to the county seat and file for a restraining order—in pro per—not in Family Court, in Superior Court. We need to keep the live-in man away from his girlfriend's mother."

I took the file and saw that a grandmother was trying to get custody or long-term foster care for a grandchild she felt was in jeopardy. I scanned through: possible child abuse, drug-related difficulties with the cohabiting couple; the child had been removed to foster care and the mother had been ordered by Henderson County Social Services to get family counseling. At first glance it looked like the major problem was the live-in man, possibly the child's father.

"How do things like this generally go in a place like Coleman?"

"It might go away before it gets to court—people enjoy their family fights, but they like them at home. The grandmother may work her own deal to be primary caretaker of the child, often negotiated in a huge family quarrel. There could be years of back-and-forth nonsense until the poor kid reaches thirteen or so. Eventually, this whole scenario will probably repeat over and over." She shrugged, a gesture more helpless than anything. "So it goes."

"Won't the state get involved?"

"County. This is their involvement, modest though it seems. These people can't manage separation. Since we don't send kids out of town to foster homes, they are always connected to the same group of people. This county-appointed foster home? This grandchild is now the second generation to be cared for there. The same problems crossing generations. Physical abuse, alcohol abuse, long-term family troubles, and tripe."

"Tripe?"

"Bullshit."

"I bet you can see the case coming before it comes," I suggested.

"Much of the time. I've known these people most of my life. We have our town hotshots, our town trash, and our town nobles. The names rarely change, although there have been some nice surprise

22

successes over the years. It's much of the same stuff you're used to dealing with, except here it all has a different flavor. We seldom solve problems in this office—we mainly change the rules temporarily. You'll see."

"Does counseling ever work for these people?"

"It could with some education and separation, but as long as they keep flunking out of school and running away and coming back to the same inadequate family system, what's the use?"

"How do you stand it?" I asked her.

"I'm doing a good job for these people," she said. "I stand it fine. Aside from the purchase of a ranch or the making of a will, not many people drop in here to share their good news." She pulled off her glasses. "Surely you understand that."

Small-town law. In L.A. I did have the illusion of occasionally winning something for someone. Once their adoption or divorce was finalized, I didn't see them again. Roberta, on the other hand, would be running into clients at the beauty shop or drugstore for the next twenty years, as she had for the last thirty. We did more business in stores, on the street, and in the café than we did at the office. Clients rarely made appointments unless it was for one of us to go to them. They hung out and waited for one of us to stumble by; we billed them whenever we filed or wrote something. For several weeks I had to carry a list of charges in my purse to quote Roberta's fees for services I was asked about. Roberta said she didn't think it would matter one way or the other; sometimes disputed invoices became favors. All this makes the practice of law in a town this size sometimes oppressive. Bleak. Often predictable.

I met the Honorable Bud Wilcox, Superior Court judge, in Roberta's office. He was fiftyish, classically handsome, and he possessed a stylishness that spoke more of Washington, D.C., than Coleman. Well-built and tanned, he had a finely chiseled nose, square jaw, thick gray hair, and intelligent blue eyes. He wore expensive clothes: pleated pants of fine wool; Florsheims; starched, monogrammed shirts; a cashmere sweater. Also, a Rolex.

And he was clumsily flirtatious. He had an eye-twinkling come-on that included showing off his watch. "Well, Miss Sheppard, it looks as though the bar has raised its standards. It certainly will be a pleasant change in my courtroom; I can tell already that it'll be hard to be objective." Flick, flick . . . check the time. "I hope we'll run into each other outside of work as well."

Ugh. I found out from Peggy that he was a known flirt; he had a fat, unhappy wife and two teenagers who had frequent scrapes of trouble. His son, now a college freshman, had gotten speeding tickets and been drunk at high-school parties, and was arguing that he was not the father of a cheerleader's child. Bud's sixteen-year-old daughter, gossip said, had had two abortions, dabbled in recreational drugs and had already been in treatment, and had run away from home at least once. I cringed at the prospect of a womanizing judge from a dysfunctional family.

It was in that frame of mind that I faced Saturday, and met Tom as though he were my only friend and a long-time friend at that. He wasn't as eccentric in those small-town ways as the rest of them; he was more like me, being a big-city person who had escaped to a small town. He seemed equally glad to see me. In the back of his truck he had the finished shelves and cans of paint and primer for the wall.

"You couldn't resist," I said. "No willpower?"

"I thought I'd put you to work on the wall while I install the shelves, if you feel like it."

"And you're going to add the cost of the paint to your bill?"

"Since you didn't ask for the paint, Jackie, I can't charge you. If you decide you want to pay for it, here's the receipt."

"I want to pay for it," I said, secretly delighted. Is it too cynical for me to admit that I had never experienced the kindness of strangers before? Friends in whom I had invested time and favors, yes . . . but not strangers. Of course, Tom never seemed like a stranger at all. Not even in the beginning.

We worked together smoothly and comfortably. I had questions about the townspeople, about the renovating I wanted to do on the house, about him.

"What was it that drove you out of L.A.?" I wanted to know.

"The way no one trusted anyone. And for good reason. Crime was getting terrible, pollution was already catastrophic and getting worse, and there was such an emphasis on materialism. I don't want to sound like some new-wave guru, but here in the mountains you usually know right away which people are decent folks, or if they're eccentric but harmless, and which ones are no damned good. The no-damned-good ones are rare and stay among themselves. We have the Bledsoes, the Travises, the Gillises—a batch of hoodlums who stay drunk and pregnant, who fight, race their cars and trucks, and keep the bunks in the county jail warm. And we have a bunch of terrific people here—Roberta and Harry, the Trumans, Andersons, Talleys, Rawlingses, and more. Honest, hardworking people." He spoke while he fitted finished boards together. Then he looked at me. Well, he looked at my back, because I was priming the wall. "What about you?"

"Me? Oh." I thought for a second; I chose my answer. Though I had rehearsed it many times, the one I rehearsed didn't come out. As I said, I had trouble with lies. I could avoid the whole truth . . . for how long, I wasn't yet sure. I had a feeling that it wouldn't be long with Tom. I proceeded with a sigh. "I was suddenly alone. I was an only child and my mother died a few years back. My dad was already doing poorly: hardening of the arteries. He had to be put into a nursing home because it was evident that he was more out of reality than in and had to be watched around the clock. He got lost a couple of times when he was on his own. It was Alzheimer's. When he died there wasn't any reason for me to stay in the same place, doing the same thing."

"Pretty strange . . . you not being married."

"That isn't strange at all," I said defensively, then made a joke of it: "I had a couple of near misses. When you think about someone my age involved in law school and then involved in law, it's not unusual. Marriage takes time and energy." So far I had not lied; I had evaded expertly.

"You must have left behind a lot of friends. You can't be that much alone."

"I do have some close friends," I said, knowing that my voice must sound wistful. I was beginning to miss some of them terribly. I missed the ones I had lost as much as the ones who had driven me away. With death and divorce, some gutless wonders tend to disappear; they can't bear the helplessness. Others, the hard-core codependents, damn near move in. I was lonely for both types. "I'll have a big phone bill until I make some more new friends . . .

and I know I'm going to have plenty of company come ski season. I plan to learn to ski now that I'm here."

"What kind of friends does someone like you have?" he asked.

"I don't know what you mean," I returned honestly.

"You know. Like lawyers, cops, judges."

He couldn't know how dull that sounded to someone in my field, especially since I'd just met Bud Wilcox, the gold-fettered judge. "No, although I have acquaintances among the above. No, my closest friend is Chelsea, a housewife and mother of two little girls. Then there's Barb, an RN; one friend from high school, who is a teacher; Janice, the secretary from my old law office; and one friend who's an actress and model."

"You didn't want kids?"

I shrugged my shoulders and looked away. I wasn't ready yet to share those details with him. "I find myself envious of my friends with children. Sometimes I wonder if all this hard work and this big-deal career is my first choice, or something that just happened to me. I'm thirty-seven; I won't start a family now."

Mike Alexander hadn't been my only adult relationship. I had a fairly sad one at the time of Sheffie's death. I had been seriously dating a guy named Bruce. He was an insurance agent who specialized in the entertainment industry. Bruce was fun; Sheffie loved him. We'd dated for six months, had begun to talk about the possibility of getting married, and then my loss happened to us. He was supportive and loving during the worst of my grief. He was likewise grieved—he loved Sheffie. We were torn apart by it. It was no one's fault, but my life turned into one big depressing liability. When he started edging away, I set him free. Bless him, he checked up on me from time to time after that. He found someone else, a woman who could not only make him happy, but be happy herself. I had to redefine the word.

Thinking about Bruce made me feel sad. For us all. Things would have been different had I come back to life before he was committed elsewhere.

I didn't realize that I was daydreaming; I had become remote in that remembering.

"You just went away for a while," Tom said, his voice gentle.

"I know. Sorry. Your questions jarred my memory. I want to enjoy Coleman . . . but you remind me of all the people I had to leave behind. Ever wonder if you've made the right choices?"

"All the time," he said. "Some of them made me, though. I do the best I can."

"Who are your good friends here?"

"All my good friends are still acquaintances. I've been here four years now and I'm still a newcomer."

"That doesn't sound promising."

He grinned broadly, suggestively. It might have been at that moment that I first considered the possibility that Tom and I could be more than friends. "It looks like the new newcomers are promising."

At the end of that workday I wrote him a check, and that evening I relaxed while I became acclimated to my new living room. I put my books, stereo, knick-knacks, and things on new shelves. I daringly hung my favorite painting over the sofa on my new wall; I did no damage, thank God. I should stay away from hammers and screwdrivers and paintbrushes. Then I sat there, my favorite tape playing, my lamps plugged in, and sipped a glass of white wine. I had had a good day, made progress on the house, and felt that I'd done the right thing in moving. I slept well that night and the next afternoon I wasn't completely surprised when Tom dropped by.

"I should have called," he said, apologetic. "I thought about stopping by to see how the room looked with everything put away and realized I didn't have your home phone number."

"That's all right," I told him cheerfully. This was a sign of how lonely I was; I tended to mind unannounced visits very much. Dropping in, since the bathtub scene with the policeman, was an unwelcome presumption in my book. This once I was delighted that Tom had taken the chance, followed his instincts.

We admired the wall and shelves together and I took him upstairs to look at some of the other rooms I wanted to renovate. The upstairs bathroom was a horror story I knew I couldn't handle alone: The tiles were half broken, the other half chipped. I wanted new windows, I wanted to strip the crud off what could be beautiful wood floors, I wanted bigger, more attractive, louvered closet doors.

After about three hours of my wishing and wanting, Tom putting in his ideas here and there, we went out for a bite to eat together. Everyone knew Tom, it seemed. I was beginning to see the difference between being an old-timer, a newcomer, and a new newcomer. While the gas station attendant, waitress, and locals we passed on the sidewalk said their hellos, there is a difference between friendliness and familiarity. He was liked; he wasn't necessarily one of them. That gave us something in common. I was needing a friend. Independent as I am, I am made vulnerable by loneliness.

We made a date to begin tearing tiles out of the

bathroom the next weekend. "Are you sure?" I asked him. "You must have some kind of social life I'm interfering with."

He laughed in such an engaging way. Tom had a twinkle in his eye that wasn't an aggressive come-on, although there seemed to be the right amount of innuendo. "Jackie, this *is* my social life."

"That doesn't sound good. You're in worse shape than I am."

"That's very likely."

I didn't hear from him all week. I thought about calling him a couple of times, though. I made long-distance calls instead. It was about Thursday, I guess, when I began looking forward to Saturday. Out of a lawyer's hard-to-break investigative habit, I asked Roberta about him. "What do you know about Tom Wahl?"

"Why?" she wanted to know.

"He's helping me with my house. He's coming over this weekend to start work on the bathroom."

"So? What do you want to know?"

"What you know about him."

"That's a broad request. Be more specific." She didn't look up from her work while she fired back at me.

"Okay, specifically, would you let him grout your tiles?"

"Yes," she replied, humorlessly.

"Jesus Christ, Roberta. You do make a person work hard. Does he have any legal history with you?"

"He was thinking of filing a lawsuit against the State of California. It was bigger than I was; he chose to drop it."

My rear end found the nearest chair without benefit of my eyes. "Oh?" I asked, intrigued.

"I can think of no reason to discuss it with you," she went on.

"I see. Do so anyway, if you please." Although I wasn't initially irritated with Roberta's attitude, I found I had to be as tough as she in order to work with her, for her. This was still her law office. There had never been any talk of partnership—it was an assumption I had that, in time, I would be invited in. I was not going to have partial involvement here. I could either be fully trusted, or not trusted to work here.

"I think it would be better if you got it from him, but the files are not locked, as you know."

"Look, let me be up-front."

She finally gave me the benefit of her attention. Off came the glasses. "That would be a delightful change."

I looked skyward and shook my head, showing my exasperation. "I've spent more time with Tom than anyone else in this town and I enjoy his company, so far. If he's going to be working in my house, we'll be spending time together. I have a feeling he's going to ask me for a date. I'm not looking for dates and I'm not looking for a serious relationship, but he seems like a nice guy and you know all the local registered rapists. Mind giving me some motherly advice?"

"Oh Lord," she grumbled. "Look, I'm not much for advice to young women on dating. . . . I was born married to Harry. Tom is all right, he hasn't been in any trouble around here that I know of, and I could safely recommend his carpentry. If I were you, I might want to date him. From my perspective, however, he is undatable because of his personal problems."

"Which are?"

"Touchy stuff, Jackie," she said, and her voice lowered as she became sincere. "I tend to stay away from people who have been through the grinder, and that poor guy has had more than his share. He is, in actuality, a psychologist who worked for the Department of Social Services in Los Angeles, your hometown. It's so long ago now, I doubt you would ever have crossed paths. When he was about thirty—ten or twelve years ago—he was a court-appointed Ph.D. in a case involving a man indicted on murder charges. Tom testified that the man was not psychotic or mentally incompetent and should stand trial. He was overruled by the court and by defense testimony; the alleged murderer was hospitalized rather than jailed, and he began to terrorize Tom and his family. Tom's wife and daughter were murdered while Tom was away one night."

"The accused who was hospitalized? Had he been furloughed or something?"

"I don't remember all the details—it's been years since he told me the story. Tom believes the man he testified against murdered his family. He believes this unequivocally. He had something he regarded as strong evidence or proof. . . . I'm afraid I can't remember. The man was questioned, the D.A. didn't concur with Tom. There were several recorded messages on Tom's answering machine that were frightening. After a fruitless battle for justice, Tom came here, where he lives a low-profile life and does not practice his trade any longer."

I was fascinated; the complexity of this story held me still and intrigued. "What was the basis of his suit against the state?" I finally asked.

"Strictly punitive; the criminal was the benefactor of the state's indeterminate-sentencing law. If you're guilty of a crime, you can be sentenced to jail for a determined period of time. If you're crazy or of diminished capacity, as the accused claimed and was found to be, you cannot be insane for a determined period of time. You're sick until you're well; that could be six months. Tom wondered if the suit could have any effect on the changing of the law."

"And the case against the guy?"

"I'm afraid I don't know. I don't know if there finally *was* a case. All I know is what Tom has told me; he claims that a close psychological evaluation showed the man had a long history of criminal behavior. Tom believed him capable of remorseless killing. There was no evidence to link him to the murder of Tom's family. But remember, he had been indicted on a murder charge initially."

"The murder Tom evaluated him for?"

"Of which he was found not guilty by reason of insanity. You would have to ask Tom for any more details."

I sat back in my chair. Roberta looked back at the challenging mess on her desk while I solemnly absorbed this. I had gotten no vibes of lurking trauma or misery from Tom. I tried to imagine what he might be going through. Could he feel he had had a hand in his wife's and daughter's deaths by failing to convince the court to prosecute the murderer?

"It's going to be hard to pretend I don't know about that," I finally said. "It's going to be hard to decide what to do."

"If I were you, I'd be cautious about relationships filled with complications. It would be tempting, I think, for you to draw the conclusion that you share loss. I think that's inaccurate."

"What do you recommend, Roberta? It's painfully quiet around my house, if you know what I mean."

"I know exactly what you mean. Let your friends know it's time for a visit. Remember what motivated you to come here. I'll tell you this much; if you have more than two dates with Tom, you'll have a dozen . . . and if you have a dozen, you two will become a couple. All that sort of thing happens around here just because there are few people free to couple. And once you've become a couple, you'll have a relationship. Then, in order to do anything different—see a movie alone, date another man—you end up having to alter or end the relationship. It's different when you see all the same people at all the same places all the damn time."

"Has he dated anyone around here?"

"He dated a woman named Elaine for a while. She was a decorator; her business wasn't profitable and she moved away. They were steadies, I guess you'd say. Tom didn't seem traumatized by her departure, that I noticed."

It didn't seem to bother Roberta that I sat motionless in the chair, thinking. I could barely deal with my own catastrophic losses, much less take on someone else's. Alternatively, if I entered this friendship or whatever it was going to be, couldn't I count on a superior level of understanding for my darker moods?

"So, you don't advise getting involved with people who have a lot of ugly baggage to drag around, right?"

"I didn't say 'advise.' I said I wouldn't."

"The same statement could be made about me. You know my circumstances. I'm dragging around a real dung bucket that some poor unsuspecting fool wouldn't want to have to deal with."

Again I got her eyes. Her glasses came all the way off, a sure sign of wishing to be heard. "Your situation isn't the same, Jackie. You were the victim of terrible timing and rotten luck. In Tom's case, he is the victim of an intentional, horrendous, violent crime. There's a deep, psychological difference. You look both ways; you maybe don't trust armored cars. What changes do you suppose he's made in his behavior after a client murdered his family? What barriers do you think he's built up? What personality disorders could exist?"

"Answer me one question. Do you like him?"

She made an unpleasant face.

"He thinks of you as one of his friends," I pointed out.

"I don't dislike him," she said. "I have very few real friends; I wouldn't count Tom Wahl among them."

"Do you think he's telling the truth about what happened to him?"

"I know he is. I looked through some of the newspaper clippings he saved from the original court case. It's not a question, in my mind, whether he's telling the truth. It's a question as to how screwed up he is because of it." She put her glasses on. "Go slowly." Then, after looking at me for a second, she lowered her gaze and muttered, "Figures."

I thought I knew what she meant by that last freezing statement. I assumed she decided she had misjudged my need for sex. Strangely, sex hadn't figured in this at all. That was still a long way off for me.

"I'm not going to tell him I know about this," I announced.

She didn't respond. It wasn't as though Roberta were going to be gossiping about it. Getting her to discuss it at all had required perseverance.

For the next few weeks, while I worked beside Tom as we tore out and replaced bathroom tiles and linoleum, and sanded down oak floors, I damned my luck. He laughed so easily; he was so pleasant to be around. He made flattering but not suggestive comments. "That's your color—yellow." "I brought burgers and guessed you would want a shake." "When we're finished, this place is going to feel as sophisticated and yet as warm as you are."

We didn't talk about deeply personal things, and in all truth he was the only companionship I had. I'm cautious. I didn't invite any deeper relationship. And he didn't ask.

I did read the brief file that Roberta had initiated on his proposed lawsuit. There were no newspaper clippings in the file and Roberta had prepared a standard intake report. It described the event as Roberta had, with one additional piece of information. Tom's name was Tom Lawler. Since the California incident he had changed it to Wahl.

I made a close study of his behavior; I was looking for a sign of depression or guilt. Nothing could be further from his character. He wasn't verbose; he seemed to choose his words carefully and spoke with sincerity. I began to get glimmers of his counseling experience. He would say things like "How do you feel about that?" "Would that feel good if you did it that way?" And "I hear you." He seemed, if anything, more sensitive than the average guy.

I had no prejudice against a person who had had troubles. How could I when I didn't want to be avoided because of the tragedies I had endured? I don't mean to hint at the concept of silver linings. However, people who have endured great hardship tend to be stronger, more resilient.

That's what I thought I saw in Tom. Recovery.

I had been a resident in Coleman for three months before anything that resembled a date came up. We had worked together for weeks. It was late August and we had finished the master bath, hung new closet doors, and sanded down all the upstairs floors. We were finished and not planning another weekend of work.

"I'm a half-decent cook," he said. "Why don't I make you dinner next Saturday night?"

"What a nice thought," I replied sincerely. I had begun to wonder if Tom's only problem was hesitancy. "Unfortunately, I'm not going to be here. I'm treating myself to a quick trip to L.A. to visit friends. I'll leave Thursday evening and be back late Sunday."

"Oh," he said, becoming morose instantly. He was quiet for a minute. "I suppose there's a guy back there—"

"Oh no," I hastened to assure him. "No, Tom, I'm not dating anyone."

"Are you sure? Because I don't want to get in the way of anything. I don't want to— Ah, hell."

"Were you thinking of us having more than one dinner together?" I asked. Blunt has always been more natural for me.

"I'd like that . . . and don't get me wrong, I'm not suggesting anything serious, permanent, or anything like that. Don't think the wrong thing. If you're dating someone, that's no big deal. We can have dinner, be friends . . ." He shrugged his shoulders, appearing almost shy. "Friendship would be welcome. I don't want any complications in my life."

"I think I understand," I said, though I wasn't sure I did. It must have shown in my eyes or been carried in my tone.

"I was dating a woman who came here to start a decorating business," he quickly went on. "I was starting to enjoy myself and so was she and then all of a sudden she admitted she had left a long-term relationship for a breather. A breather, she told me, because they had run into trouble. The whole time we were dating, she was keeping this other relationship alive, by phone, letters, visits. She was also keeping it a secret from me. And she decided to go back. That's something I would have expected to hear about early on in our dating."

"I'm sorry," I said. That sort of thing happens to people like us, people who have never had a relationship go the whole distance. The same thing had happened to me. In law school I dated a man, though time with him was rare because of my work load. He had broken up, he said. Over, he said. It wasn't over in the least. He had managed to keep two busy women lurching over their schedules to fit him in.

"I don't want to sound like a wimp," Tom explained. "It's not like it ruined my life. It was disappointing. It would have all turned out different if she had told me from the beginning that she wasn't completely sure about the guy she left behind. All the same things would have happened, I'm sure, except my perspective might have been different."

"You felt she lied to you?" I asked.

"Well, Jackie, she did lie to me," he said. "She told me right off that she had no commitments and nothing going on. Then later she amended that and said she had recently come out of a serious relationship. And still later, the truth—that they'd separated to see if they should give it up or try to work it out. They'd been in touch all along." He shook his head. "I wish she had told me she couldn't talk about it, or it was none of my business. I'm stodgy. Old-fashioned. I have a problem with games and manipulations. I don't lie, I don't like lies."

"I don't either," I said, somewhat emphatically. "And I am not fresh from a breakup, I'm not seeing anyone, and although I am definitely not looking for a serious relationship at this point in my life, I don't think dinner would be risky at all." I tried to give him a reassuring smile, though I sensed that he was putting too much pressure on us both when only a dinner together was at issue. For some reason I excused this idiosyncrasy. I did wrap it up and tie a knot on it. "So, let's make sure there aren't major expectations on this." It wasn't him I was trying to avoid or keep at bay, it was how the two dates become twelve, et cetera. "Friendship would be welcome, but let's not get radical."

"Radical." He grinned. "The kids say that all the time." He laughed, sounding more comfortable. "Good. Dinner is all I have in mind. I don't want to load up on expectations. You're not opposed to seeing where our friendship goes if I'm a halfway good cook?"

"Oh, definitely not," I said.

"Good. I'll call you when you get back."

3

My reason for going to Los Angeles on Thursday evening had to do with my desire to have Friday, a workday, to drop in to the law office that had employed me. My old colleagues fawned over me; some of them took me to lunch and I entertained them with homespun small-town tales. I told of the cousins who shared water rights and a long-term family feud, intermarriage, and fistfights, and had graduated to drag racing along country roads. I had heard their properties were strewn with car parts and rusting kitchen appliances, and there was usually one family member in trouble with the law at all times.

And on the upscale side, I told them about the artists' commune twenty miles up the road, where the most wonderful pots, sculptures, paintings, and bric-a-brac could be had at a bargain. And about the heiress to a multimillion-dollar candy company who turned her back on the huge family enterprise, escaped her corporate roots to operate a country-style bed-and-breakfast on land where she also grew organic vegetables and herbs.

They complimented my color, my twinkling eyes,

my healthy appearance, my restored humor, and I inhaled these remarks like a person long without breath. People said things like "Colorado is good for you" and "All that mountain air must be what you needed." What they meant was they thought I was coming out the other end of the long dark tunnel of pain. I sensed a perverse relief among some of them, particularly the other women, who must have been secretly relieved when I took myself, my practice, and my enormous grief away from their scrutiny. Women, nurturers all whether high-powered execs or maids, feel innately responsible for each other. My pain was their pain on some level. I returned like the girl who had gone off to college and made good. I returned restored. It was my secret that I was the same person.

I got the gossip and gave it. I spent the weekend with Barb, one of my few single friends, while visiting others. I wasn't closest to Barb, but her lack of additional family meant that my coming and going did not disrupt her lifestyle. She armed me with a house key and I traveled around in my rented car, returning late at night to her town house and spare room. It was so successful a trip that I never thought about the one piece of suspicious news dropped on me.

"I trust you had no trouble getting your furniture," Janice, secretary to the senior partner, said.

"What furniture? My furniture arrived with no problem."

"No, the furniture you were financing. Coleman Home Finance called here to check on your past employment."

"Who?"

"Coleman. I'm sure it was Coleman Home Finance Company."

"I didn't apply for any financing. What did they want to know?"

"Whether you had been gainfully employed here prior to moving to Coleman."

"My salary? My marital status? What?"

Jan shook her head. "You know I wouldn't give out any personal information. There was nothing suspicious at all; I would have contacted you if there had been. The call seemed routine. The guy had your phone number, address, work number, et cetera. Merely a credit-card check, I guess."

"Except I didn't apply for any credit," I said, unnerved by that.

"You know what happens when you move into a new house," she said. "I had calls from carpet cleaners and water-softener salesmen, and dozens of free gifts, none of which were free at all. I'll bet a local business was trying to check you out to see if you were approachable for credit. Or maybe it was the lawyer you work for; could she have done that?"

"Roberta? Her manner is much more direct. She wouldn't disguise her questions. Are you sure that's all they wanted to know?"

"Employment verification. The caller provided the address. Maybe it was your local homeowner's-insurance guy. I would have called you immediately had it been the least bit unusual."

I dismissed it from my mind then. I'll never know who made that call. Jan easily calmed me; I do remember, from when I bought my little house in L.A., the number of leading phone calls searching for information. "Can we do a run-down on the basic security of your home as a free gift?" What do they expect you to say? "No thanks, I have four Dobermans and a Magnum"? Then, I guess, they can cross you off their list of people to burgle. This is so much an L.A.

or New York mindset, I decided then and there to let the phone call go. It didn't even cross my mind later, when I got home and had a legitimate concern.

Another thing we talked about, briefly, did come to mind later—though it was over a week before I recalled it. When Janice asked me if I'd met any potentially datable single men, I mentioned Tom. I said he'd come from L.A., where he'd experienced a terrible tragedy and lost his family. We had this in common; it was unnecessary to draw the common lines for Janice. I did say his old name and his new name.

I don't consider myself a 'fraidy cat. I'm not big and I'm not strong, but I'm clever and I've never been easily upset. Things bumping in the night can always be attributed to the house settling or the cat. I had only called the police twice—once when a jogger stopped jogging in front of my house and seemed to be loitering there and once when I got home to find the door standing open. I say this because my reaction to what I found at home was to panic and feel seized by helplessness.

Back in Coleman, when I got in the door, flipped on the lights, and saw my lovely, warm, remodeled living room, I was elated to be home. Home. That felt good to me; I had left wondering if I would ever feel that way about this old house in a town where I had clients and acquaintances but no friends. I left my bags and purse sitting inside the front door and kicked off my shoes. I went straight to the stereo and flipped on my "easy listening" channel, then rummaged about in the kitchen for a glass of wine and a plate of crackers. I sat there for thirty minutes, enjoying the solitude and comfyness of my little house, plagued by nothing. The phone rang.

"Good, you made it back safe and sound," Chelsea Alexander said.

I fought an irritated grunt. Checking up on me, I thought. "I was unwinding with a glass of wine. I had fun, but I'm exhausted. You really didn't have to call."

"Oh, don't get your undies in a bunch, sweet pea. I know I don't have to. You're so goddamn defensive sometimes. I'm not worried about you, Jackie, and if you hadn't answered the phone, I would have tried later or tomorrow. There is nothing wrong with someone knowing where you are. It's different from someone telling you where you're supposed to be."

To avoid getting into that whole argument, I changed the subject to my flight, which was uneventful, and the long drive southwest from Denver, over sixty miles through and around the Pike National Forest. It took me two hours from the airport and was enough trouble to keep me from running back to L.A. every time I grew lonely.

Mike got on the phone very briefly; I had seen Chelsea and the girls in L.A., but Mike had been working. "Jack," he said.

"Mike," said I.

"You doin' fine?"

"Fine. You?"

"Okay. So, when you coming back?"

"I don't know. Come here. Learn to ski."

"Aw . . . maybe the girls. Me? I'm lucky I learned to walk."

I didn't let him hear me laugh. He was the luckiest man alive and I wasn't sure he deserved us, Chelsea and me. Nothing in his character should have landed him Chelsea, the most stable, rock-solid, nurturing, dedicated person alive. She came back on the phone.

"So, baby-cakes, you glad to be in your new-old house?"

"As a matter of fact, I am," I said, sounding surprised.

"I suppose even the towels are matched already?"

"No, they're not, but I'm ready for you and that asshole . . . I mean you and Mike and your doll-babies to come see me and learn to ski."

Chelsea, who never called him an asshole, loved it when I did. She laughed. "I'll bring the little dolls out and see you this winter, when there's snow . . . if you're sure."

"Oh, kiddo, am I sure. I'm settling in, meeting people slowly. I think I did the right thing in moving here. It's so peaceful and wholesome. I'd love to share it with you."

We talked on—did a partial postmortem on my visit. I had been lulled into a kind of serenity—my new-old house around me, the wine hitting my gut, Chelsea's humorous and warm voice on the phone. I felt relaxed; tired and rested all at once. An hour had passed from the time I got home until I trudged upstairs with purse, hang-up bag, and suitcase.

I dropped the purse, hung up the hang-up bag, and was just about to toss the suitcase on the bed for unpacking when I stopped short. There was an impression on the bed—an indentation from the pillow to the foot. I had made the bed, smoothing the thin, patterned chenille spread flat, and there was a dip and ripple down the bed the length of a body. The spread was old and fragile and white; it had been my mom's. Someone had lain down on my bed while I was away.

I did a cursory check of my memory; I knew perfectly well I had not made that imprint. I reconsidered how I had packed, what I had done prior to leaving, whether I sat down to answer the phone. My memory for details is sound. I had had no last-minute phone calls and had made up the bed after taking my bags downstairs and leaving them by the front door. I knew this because I have a travel habit that hasn't been broken in years. I get everything ready to go and then I make a run through the house to put dirty dishes in the dishwasher, hang up fresh towels, pick up dirty clothes, change sheets, et cetera. I am always tired when I return from a trip and find a neat, clean house and cold, crisp sheets to be a welcome creature comfort.

I had not made the impression on the bed.

My pulse picked up and I started to get a peculiar feeling. The front door had been locked; nothing was out of place downstairs. My curtains were open in the living room and I hadn't noticed any open windows on the ground floor. I hadn't checked the back door to see if it was locked, though I had noticed it was closed. My house is compact; if the VCR, stereo, and TV weren't taken, if drawers weren't opened, then nothing had been disturbed. Down the upstairs hall were two other bedrooms and another bath—the doors were all closed. I planned to turn one room into a guest room and one into an office. There were only boxes in them now.

Before I thought further, my mother-blinker, still functional, went off and thoughts of danger went out of my head as I rushed to the room in which I kept two small boxes of things that had been Sheffie's. I opened the door to that spare room and saw the boxes, still taped shut, sitting against the far wall. They looked lonely; they were undisturbed.

Shaking, I went back to the bedroom and into my new, beautiful bathroom. I opened the linen closet; nothing appeared touched. I stood on the lowest shelf to reach the top shelf, and pulled my gun from behind the towels. When at home I kept it in the bedside stand, in the drawer under my pink angora sweater. When I left town, I hid it farther away so that if I was ever robbed, I would not be providing a gun to a criminal. It's a small, handy, .25-caliber handgun. Pretty, silver, and loaded. I'd never needed to defend myself with it, having only had one or two spooky clients in my ten years of practice. I believed that I would shoot it if necessary. Women are inherently unsafe in this world; this is a fact of life. It is one of the things that propelled me into family law. I took the gun with me.

I went downstairs, checked around and closed the blinds, and sat down and cried, my gun in my hand, in my lap. I felt a combination of emotions that maybe only the mother of a dead child could understand. I was disturbed by the imprint on the bed and unsure what to do about it; I was more jarred by my alarm for the two boxes holding Sheffie's memorabilia—school photos, blue ribbons, drawings, precious junk. I knew I had to have the stuff, though I had no plans to pick through it. The sharp panic that something had happened to them was too familiar; identical to the way your heart and stomach slam together when your child is playing in the front of the house and you hear the sound of screeching tires. Or dead silence in the bathroom when he's in the tub. Or no more splashing in the backyard pool.

I was overwhelmed with some emotions I had no idea how to handle. He was gone, yet with me every moment. That instant flash of fright is like a gasp of the soul.

When the phone next to me rang, I gave a slight shriek. I let it ring three times. I picked it up hesitantly.

"Hi, you're back," Tom cheerfully intoned.

"Tom." I sighed, trying to slow my heart rate.

"Was it fun? Did you have a good time?"

"Ah," I started. I coughed. "Ah, hold on," I said, not knowing what to do. I took a couple of deep breaths. "Tom," I said, trying to sound all right if nothing else. "Yes, thanks, I had a good time."

"Good. I didn't know what to do with myself all weekend now that the bathroom and stuff's all done."

"Listen, Tom, could we talk tomorrow? I'm kind of . . . well, bushed."

"Oh Jackie, I'm sorry. You okay? Did you hate leaving your friends?"

"No . . . no . . . it's just that . . . I'm kind of . . ."

"It's okay, I can call you at work tomorrow. If you're sure you're okay."

"I'm not sure," I said, my voice beginning to tremble. I'm coming apart, I thought. I need time to think this through, come up with an answer as to how this happened. I was shaken, and aside from Roberta, there was no one else to tell. "I have a suspicion that someone might have been in my house while I was gone."

"Oh? Have you been robbed?"

"No. Everything seems to be fine," I said, looking around as I said this. "But . . . oh jeez, you're going to think I'm out of my head . . . I think someone laid down on my bed."

"What?"

I was momentarily embarrassed. "There must be an explanation . . . something I forgot . . . like maybe I laid down for a minute before I left town." Except that the imprint wasn't on the side I use, the side where the phone and clock-radio are.

"Maybe you should call the sheriff," he suggested.

"And tell them what? That someone—"

"Yes. Yes, Jackie. If that's what you think happened, call the sheriff, let them send someone out to check the house."

"No, I—"

"Listen, you sound rattled and I'll come over, but I think you should call the sheriff's office. It's their job to check possible break-ins, and it can't do any harm. Better you call them right now and I'll come over to lend moral support."

"I feel stupid," I said, a large tear spilling over.

"You're sure nothing's missing?"

"So far. I haven't looked thoroughly. . . ."

There was silence for a moment, as though he were thinking. "Call them. Be safe instead of sorry. I'm coming over, but it'll take me a while to get there. I'm about thirty minutes away."

"Listen, you don't have to—"

"I won't stay. Let's get you locked up tight, feeling secure, then I'll leave."

All I needed was someone to talk me into it. I know I'm not a flake. I was projecting what I thought Tom, or the police, might think. Much of my anxiety revolved around the idea of someone looking at my life, my boxes of stuff that had been Sheffie's, my neatness, which isn't compulsive except when I'm leaving town. I had the urge to go back upstairs and see if my underwear drawer was in disarray, but I knew better than to go back upstairs. Besides, my underwear was always in disarray. Reasonably, there was no one in my house. It wasn't as though I had come in and disturbed a thief. I had been in the kitchen and on the phone for over an hour. If I were going to get attacked, I had the most unmotivated attacker in the state.

I took the offensive, unnecessarily, with the cops.

"This is Jackie Sheppard, 449 Apache Drive, and I've returned home from a trip to find that someone was in my house while I was gone. Please send a patrol car." And then I was pushed into saying that nothing was broken, stolen, or disturbed, except for the imprint on the bed. I finally hedged, asking them to please check the house for me so I could relax. I sounded to myself as though I were making excuses. The dispatcher said it would be done and tried to establish that it was not an emergency.

Then I looked around. Gun in hand, not expecting to find anything, I walked through the downstairs. I opened the louvered doors that separated the kitchen from the dining room. Nothing. I opened the front hall closet in the entry. Nothing. Behind the kitchen in the back of the house was a small enclosed back porch that served as a pantry and laundry room. I hoped to enlarge and renovate it into a larger room, create a sunroom that would extend the length of the house. It had a back door with steps that went down into the backyard. I could see that the dead bolt was unlocked. There it was. I remembered locking that damn door. As I threw the bolt, I had thought how doing so reflected such an L.A. mindset; I believed few people in Coleman felt compelled to lock their doors. I had considered becoming more complacent about this ritual. The door had been unlocked in my absence. Whoever entered my domain and lay down on my bed in my bedroom had used the back door.

Now, what the hell does something like that mean? What would the motivation be? Who would go to the trouble, for what purpose? Since I had found what I was looking for, I looked no further without someone in uniform. I also had an unfinished basement, a cellar. There was a furnace down there, and mouse droppings. The door was in the pantry. I had it pad-locked; I had the only key on my key chain. I wasn't going to go down there with or without protection.

When the doorbell rang I walked briskly to the kitchen, opened the fridge, and placed my loaded pistol in the vegetable crisper. I had only twice told of my firearm possession—I educated Sheffie, and I told Chelsea, who told Mike, and then I lectured them; the gun was registered, but no one was to have knowledge of it. An innocent comment, an ill-timed joke about the little pistol-packing mama . . . these were the sort of thing that got people robbed and killed. Fact: Most assaults, rapes, and murders are committed among acquaintances.

Bodge Scully was the sheriff. *Is* the sheriff. It was Bodge himself, in what I suppose were hastily drawn-up drawers and a wrinkled shirt with stale, dried perspiration stains under the arms, who stood at the door. I was impressed; it had been less than a half hour since I called.

Where a name like Bodge came from is a mystery. The man happens to be kind-hearted and an excellent small-town sheriff. Around fifty, over six feet tall and thirty belly-pounds overweight, he was a homely man. His face was pocked, his sand-colored hair strung with silver, and his eyes almost raccoonlike in their dark circles and folds of flesh. He had the worst nose; it must have been broken a hundred times, it was so bent and bumped. His eyebrows could have used a trim. Bodge had a bright, crooked, white smile full of crowded teeth that added to his comforting, cozy manner.

I had met him twice in Roberta's office and found him affable. Roberta, who was not a fountain of easy praise, said Bodge was damn good. "Oh, Bodge, I got you up for this, didn't I?"

"I live right on the edge of town," he said, "and it would have taken forever for a car to come out from the county station; there's a patrol car in Coleman tonight—but he went out Driscoll way to calm down some hard-partying Driscolls, so I figured you'd have to wait a long time for him. I thought I'd come on over."

Past him I could see the official car on the street. My front door was up a small hill, with about fifteen concrete steps. "I appreciate it, Bodge. Come in."

"What's going on?"

"I want you to know that I'm no flake, Bodge. I've managed my share of suspicious people over the years; we have a few more of them in L.A. than you have in Coleman."

"Don't count on it," he said, his voice gravelly and his speech unhurried and quaint. He was walking in my house, looking around as he moved into the living room, seeming to head for the kitchen without being directed. I was therefore talking to his back.

"What I'd like you to understand is that I can handle myself fine and I don't get upset over little things; sometimes I don't get myself worked up over the big things. This—"

"Whether or not you get worked up is nothing to me. Even hysterical people have real incidents." He turned and looked at me.

"Someone came into my house while I was out of town and laid down on my bed. As far as I know, nothing was taken or disturbed; the dead bolt on the back door is open and I haven't checked yet to see if it was damaged. I am certain I locked it."

"Where do you keep the liquor?"

"That cupboard," I said, pointing. "Wine in the fridge. Jug wine, cheap kind." I laughed in mock embarrassment. He opened the cupboard and looked. There were only three bottles, two unopened and one, the scotch, half full. That's the only thing other than wine that I like and I don't overindulge.

"All here? I've known kids to break into houses that they know are empty and pick up loose change and booze."

"It looks all there. I haven't checked everything closely yet. Drawers and things."

He walked past me to the back door and opened it. He made the dead bolt go back and forth in an easy slide.

"Aren't you going to be careful for fingerprints?" I asked.

He looked at me closely and smiled. "What would the charge be?"

"Breaking and entering? Trespassing?"

"I think if you're right and it was locked, it's a clean pick, Jackie. No damage. Might have been a key."

"There are no other keys out."

"Last owner?"

"The house was empty for a long time. Real-estate agent?"

"Let's look at the bedroom," he said. "You haven't touched anything?"

"No." I wouldn't elaborate about the gun. "I came home, had a glass of wine and some crackers, and talked on the phone for about a half-hour. A friend from L.A. I was in L.A. over the weekend and a friend called to make sure I got back all right." Funny, now it was sounding good to me—having somebody check on me.

Fortunately, the imprint on the bed was unmistakable; it wasn't as though I could have imagined it. A large, heavy person whose head was on the pillow and whose legs were long had left a few wrinkles and dents on the bed.

"I know I didn't do it because I have this eccentric ritual about leaving the house perfect when I'm out of town. I'm not a breezy traveler; travel is work for me and I love to come home to a clean house, clean sheets, all that."

He pulled down the spread and examined the covers. "Look like the way you fixed it? Left it?"

"Yes," I said. The sheets were smooth; no one had been under the covers. I hadn't even considered someone getting *in* the bed. I sighed in relief. After he yanked the spread up again and I smoothed it, all trace of that body was instantly gone. I immediately felt better; I immediately felt foolish. I began to wish I'd done that, made it go away.

Bodge walked through the rest of the upstairs and opened all the closet doors. I followed around behind him. "You tell me if you see something out of place."

"Okay," I said. I was beginning to feel silly. Not that I'd been mistaken, because that was impossible. It was the idea that he was here, looking around, and there was no real crime, no serious misdeed. There was nothing.

Back in the master bedroom, I opened the dresser drawers and checked the small jewelry box. I don't keep the kind of meticulous drawers that would show a sock had been touched. They looked like they always looked; full and jumbled.

"Well . . . Jackie . . ."

"I know. What can you do?"

"Go to the bathroom since you've been home?"

"I went in the bathroom—I didn't . . ."

"You have a male visitor that spends time here?"

"A man? As in someone I date? As in someone who might come in here or have a key or something?"

"No . . . as in might lift the seat when he urinates."

I was momentarily confused and then my eyes

widened. I shot to the bathroom door and looked in; the seat was up. "Damn," I muttered, looking back at Bodge. "Now, I know I didn't leave it like that—it's only up to be cleaned and I didn't clean the toilet before I left. I would remember."

"Okay. Well, I can brush it, but—to tell you the truth, Jackie, unless you find something damaged or missing or some other thing that stands out, we don't have anything here. Why don't I get you locked up tight and I'll radio Sweeney to do a couple of drive-bys during the night. Unless you're scared and you don't want to stay here."

"He peed here," I said, both shocked and insulted. "Some creep came in here to lay down on my bed and pee. What the hell does that mean?"

"You could call Roberta Musetta, couldn't you?"

"No," I said, somewhat exasperated. "Tom Wahl called me a while ago. He was the one who said I should call you if I thought this was spooky. He's going to come over to give me moral support. I'm sorry I bothered you."

"Don't be, Jackie, it's fine. There was someone in your house—for whatever reason. You know Tom pretty well?"

"He did the shelves, painting, floors, and renovated the bathroom. I haven't dated him or anything like that. I guess you could say we've become friends."

"If he's on his way over, you're in good hands. He's strong and able; not many people would want to go through Tom to get anything. All that building, I guess." He rubbed his hands over his paunch. "I should do something like that, get in shape." He left the room and went toward the stairs, me taking up the rear. "I'm going to get the flashlight and walk around the yard. I'll check in with you before I leave."

"Thanks, Bodge," I said. I wanted something; I wanted reassurance or, at the least, an explanation. "Ever been called out for something like this before?" I asked.

"Nope."

"Do you think it's weird?"

He shrugged. "You might remember something later, come up with a reason or explanation."

"And if I don't—then do you think it's weird?"

"Different, anyway. It doesn't seem like you're in any danger. Leave a light on downstairs tonight; make the place look occupied."

"Yeah," I said. I felt exhausted and knew I wouldn't be able to sleep as usual.

In the end I did, though, because of Tom. He was warm, generous, and humorous. He shook hands with Bodge and they talked about things that had nothing to do with my "incident." Tom asked Bodge how the rumpus room was coming along and later told me that Bodge had started building on a room for the kids when his oldest was in high school and now was hoping to finish before the grandchildren were all grown up. This familiarity helped me; if Bodge was friendly with Tom, I felt I had the next best thing to a deputy. And then Tom listened patiently as I trilled about what kind of a nut would leave these hints of his presence and yet have no reason to come into my domain other than to be sure I knew he was there.

This was when I was initially introduced to his counseling skills; I was fairly wound up. I was talking fast, moving my hands, running the gamut of emotions, and he sat there, calm, patient, listening, until I wore myself out.

"How about another glass of wine?" he suggested.

"Want one?" I asked.

"I'd rather have a beer, but wine is okay. I'll stay here if you want. On the couch."

"Oh God, I hate for you to have to do that. It's such an inconvenience."

"Jackie, look at the time. We're past the inconvenient part."

I had gotten in at nine. Tom had called at about nine forty-five. Bodge had taken another half-hour or more. "Jesus, it's eleven. I'm sorry."

"You didn't do it to me—and I offered. You're all worked up and won't sleep if you're here alone. I might as well."

I handed him a glass and sat on the short end of the L-shaped sofa with mine. "What if you're the one who laid down on my bed and peed in my toilet?" I joked. It never occurred to me for a second that he'd do that. Bogeymen are always unknown characters even when you know the statistics: They're usually someone you know.

"I'd do that on invitation, but I'm a bit too busy to be doing it for sport."

"You're not protecting me to get in my pants, are you?"

"Actually, I was thinking of cooking you dinner to get into your pants—this is less work."

"Are you always this blunt?"

"Hell, no; you're the blunt one. You started this."

"I did. This is such a strange event. You're not invited to sleep with me."

"That's okay. I'll still sleep on the couch; I have to leave early, though. I've got horses to feed."

"You have horses?"

"Two. I'll introduce you sometime." He lifted an eyebrow and peered at me. "Feeling better now?"

"What kind of thing is this, do you think? Why would something like this happen?"

"I don't know." He shrugged. "I knew a guy once who used to go sit in people's cars in parking lots at night and go through the glove box. Sometimes he'd smoke a cigarette or leave his underwear behind. He occasionally urinated."

"Come on!"

He laughed. "It's true."

"Who was that?"

"You want his name?" he asked, as if aghast. "You must have asked Roberta about me; that's what I figured you'd do. Did you?"

"I asked her about you and she tried to tell me, briefly, what your legal history with her was. . . . Which you must understand is what happens in a law office. We weren't gossiping about you. I know about your case and that you dropped it. I don't know the details."

"The details are shitty, Jackie, and if you don't mind, I wish you wouldn't tell anyone. I don't want it to get around. I've been trying to leave it back there. So, then you know that I was a practicing psychologist in L.A. I had a heavy caseload and got to meet some of the more notable characters in town. I wonder what that parking-lot guy is into now."

I sat on the edge of the sofa a bit. "What was wrong with him?"

"Borderline personality," he said with a slight shrug. "That's a grab bag. His parents were secretive and abusive and he got off on sneaking into people's vehicles late at night while they were having drinks or dinner or seeing movies. He wanted to see what they had. He wanted to be in their space and look around. He claimed he didn't go in houses."

"Got off? Literally?"

"Sometimes . . ."

"Blllkkkk!"

"He also got beat up a couple of times when guys came out of the bar and found him. Usually, if he got caught he ran and they ran—suspecting they'd scared off a car thief. Most of the time no one knew. He claimed. He seemed like an average, normal guy. He had an accounting business, a wife and two kids, and went to church. I saw him because he got arrested."

"Whew."

"People have intense personal lives and lots of secrets. You must have run into a lot of that in family law in Los Angeles. Huh?"

"Well . . . not any clients I suspected were sick. I focused on domestic law—divorce, custody, trusts, wills, and now the famous prenuptial agreement. Domestic situations can make normal people act crazy, but they're not mentally ill. I did have a client once whose ex-husband dressed up in her clothes on the weekends . . . but that's about as bizarre as it ever got. I had a couple of scary people, violent types who beat up their wives and kids. Was your specialty abnormal psychology?"

"No, although I was headed in the direction of forensics. Then it came too close to home. A client killed my family. I think he was after me; I'll never know for sure. I think he thought I would be home. I should have been home—it was late. My wife and daughter were in bed. I'm sorry," he said suddenly. "I didn't mean to lay that one on you. I know how heavy it is. That's what happened and how I ended up leaving L.A. and my profession. I wasn't scared, see. It made me sick. And the police couldn't nail him. He got nailed later, though."

"Where is he now?"

"Now? No telling. He got in some trouble later, got locked up for a while. Then he got paroled and I believe he followed me to Oregon, where I went before coming to Coleman. I never saw him—this was about three or so years after my wife and daughter . . . Anyway, I'll never forget his voice, especially since I have it on tape. He called me and told me he passed right by me when I was coming out of a fast-food place; he said he watched me go to the library and the dry cleaner. One call, one time, and I never saw him. As if he wanted me to know he's out there and in control; I'm the vulnerable one. He could be anywhere."

I shuddered at the thought.

"Wouldn't you have recognized him?"

"Sure, if he looked as he had looked. He could have been dressed up like a fat old woman for all I know. Or he could have altered his appearance somehow.

"My name isn't Tom Wahl, but Tom Lawler. On the off chance anyone around here is reading psychiatric journals or following old cases—this one is written about heavily. I don't relish explaining all this to people I don't consider close friends. It's not that I can't or won't. It isn't how I want to be known. I prefer to be known for building. Besides Roberta, you're the only one I've talked to about this."

"Okay," I said. "I'm sorry that happened."

"It was raining shit there for a while. I testified that the guy was mentally competent to stand trial, which he was. That's the bone he felt he had to pick with me; I was a witness for the prosecution. . . . He was after hospitalization in lieu of imprisonment, and he got it. The court found him crazy. He might be brilliant, though I couldn't be sure—he sure tested high; I gave him a full battery of psychological tests. He said he never went to school a day in his life. He was just a real badass."

"What's the psychological term for 'badass'?"

"Psychopath, sociopath. His game, his rules, his logic. Childlike in his self-centered logic. 'I hit her because she was bad.' He sounded guilt-free—even as he admitted his crime. A sociopath's behavior is not moderated by consequences; punishment has no impact and does not cause them to behave in a more socially acceptable way. He was being evaluated after killing a woman— domestic abuse; they lived together. And he said he felt bad about the fact that he'd had to take such radical action; he was sorry that she had been so bad." Tom shook his head. "It did not occur to him for one second that he was wrong; he felt he had to handle the situation himself."

"Sounds psychotic to me," I said.

"No, not a bit. He was in reality—his reality. He didn't hear voices, get visits, or anything like that. Psychotics are driven out of control and out of reality by their particular mental incapacity; they're hallucinating much of the time. This guy was not hallucinating. He didn't value any other person and didn't value himself. That TV jazz you see where the murderer breaks down and begs for his life when he's finally cornered is TV jazz. This guy wouldn't have broken. I got the impression he might welcome any pain."

"Do you ever worry that he'd come after you again?"

"You mean am I paranoid?" he asked. "Yeah, though I shouldn't be anymore. There's been no contact, nothing suspicious, and I did change my name and all. I'd love that son of a bitch to come after me. I have all the requisite murderous feelings where that asshole is concerned. I'm not normally homicidal, but there are circumstances for every human being in which murder is relatively logical.

"Problem is," he went on, "I'll never be sure if he wanted to kill me or intended to wipe out people I cared about so my suffering would be worse. Maybe his motive was to kill my family and then have me live in the terror of wondering when he'd finally get around to killing me. I couldn't live through another ordeal like that, finding the bodies of loved ones. Because of that possibility, I don't go looking for him; I've sacrificed the great pleasure it would give me to kill the motherfucker. I don't think I could kill him enough anyway."

I asked him how his wife and daughter were killed.

Strangled, he said. No blood. It was a grisly scene. Twelve years ago.

"He chased you out of your profession. You gave up your own name."

"I was next thing to crazy for a few years; I tracked him for a while, which is how I know he was arrested again and did some time. After I left L.A., I went to Oregon and worked in a mental-health clinic—but I had lost the ability to reason; I reacted to situations with emotion rather than interest, fascination, or professionalism. And then there's guilt, naturally— I took a lot of responsibility for the deaths connected to him. It occurred to me that I wasn't treating clients. Finally," he said, shrugging lamely, "the bottom line was I couldn't do the job anymore. It's like a job injury. I was disabled."

"Do you like your life now? Do you still feel disabled?" I asked. I had personal reasons for asking. Can you go away, build a new life and new identity, and have it work? Succeed?

"It's missing a few things. I used to be gregarious

and now I'm not. I used to have women friends and lovers and had, at one point, a keen interest in family life and more children. Now I don't know if that'll happen. I'm forty-two, too old to be making babies. I'm not as connected to people as I was before this damage happened; I may never be again. I've learned to like being solitary. Years past I was a party boy— unfortunately, even when I was married. I went to a lot of ball games, bars, parties; now I fish and sometimes hunt. It's a big switch. I guess I'd have to say my life works. I have regrets; I can't think what I could have changed."

I thought he made good sense. He appeared stable for someone who had undergone such trauma and made such an enormous life change. "Think you'll ever again want city life?"

He laughed. "You know, even if that maniac hadn't driven me out, just knowing about guys who leave their underwear in cars is enough to make you appreciate Coleman. I know there are some kooks here; I'm relieved not to be treating them. People seem safe and normal. This is a good place; I think people like me and accept me."

"You don't get close."

"There's no one to get close to, Jackie."

"That woman . . . the one you talked about before."

"Elaine Broussard . . . yeah, there you go. See, I thought I was getting close to her. Don't laugh now, I thought the biggest problem I had was that I wasn't as in love with her as she was with me, and I was thinking about asking her to marry me anyway. She was crazy about me: aggressive and too possessive. She was youngish—around thirty-three—attractive, kind-hearted and good. Generous, that was her big feature. She liked to help all the time. I wrestled with this idea that she wasn't my everything. She was what I thought most men wanted in a woman." He laughed a bit uncomfortably. "I was faced with the dilemma of settling for a little less than I wanted or breaking the poor woman's heart."

I sipped my wine.

"What an arrogant idiot, huh? She left me. Told me one day that there was this guy she had broken up with and . . . well, they'd been in touch all along, and it looked like she wasn't going to be happy without him. Beat that. I got all the wrong signals. Well, she gave all the wrong signals."

"What's 'too possessive'?"

"She wanted me to call her at work, make plans for every evening, move in together. She made me things all the time— cakes, casseroles, curtains. She did her own decorating things, like wall hangings and baskets and stuff. . . . She had me so loaded up with those kinds of things, I felt like I was living in Grandma's cottage. I didn't reciprocate, and I was convinced that Elaine was determined to get me to marry her."

"No kidding? Her attention never slacked off?"

"Not for a day. I figure she was compulsive. It might have been why her primary relationship was failing—suffocation. She also left her partner high and dry, too. Never mentioned this guy to her partner, Beth. She said she had to go back up north to work because she couldn't make it in this little town. She cleaned out the bank account and sold their stock."

"You don't seem to miss her."

"I miss some of the more comfortable aspects of having a steady." His eyes twinkled.

I was conscious of the fact that he'd been honest and revealing whereas I held back. I hadn't offered any details of my life before coming to Coleman.

"Maybe we'll talk about those things over dinner. Let me ask you something. It's late. Do you think I'm safe here?"

"Yeah, I do."

"Then, I don't mean to be inhospitable, but I'm bushed, I feel safer now, and I'd like to be alone in the morning when I am at my most repulsive."

"Sure?"

"I'm sure. You've been a big help."

He left then, very agreeably. No hedging, stalling, or innuendo. "How about if I give you a call at work tomorrow?" he asked. "Would that be hovering?"

"No," I said, "I'd like that."

4

It isn't routine for me to check out potential boyfriends. Maybe it should be. But they've all emerged from such reliable places. And there weren't many. I met Bruce, that one serious relationship six months prior to Sheffie's death, at his place of employment. We learned we had many mutual friends; I met his family—a father, stepmother, two sisters—after our third platonic date. Over the years of my single motherhood, I didn't consider mine an active sex life. I remember that Mike accused me of not being thrilled by sex. I accused him of being unthrilling. I like sex. It's fun and it feels good. I am not willing to risk any other aspect of my humanity for it. I won't take a health risk, career risk, or parenting risk; I won't risk my state of mind and emotions.

Sometimes those things have been compromised despite my caution. I once contracted chlamydia and had to take antibiotics; it was my sexual partner who diagnosed and treated me. Also, he gave it to me— it was my single experience of having a physician for a lover. I thought contracting a sexually transmitted disease from a doctor the most remote possibility imaginable. Thus, my notion of M-Deity collapsed.

I slept with one of the married partners once; we had been on a long, messy case together and it happened. Neither of us planned it and both of us had regrets. The career discomfort for the next entire year was prickling and corrosive; we somehow got past it. I had a brief affair with a police detective who hated kids, and Sheffie's peace of mind—he was six at the time—was stressed. And, not surprisingly, I have shed tears over men who left me. Even when I knew it was best.

In short, I was thirty-seven when I moved to Coleman; I had been married once for only a year (technically), and have had more lovers than I wish. Add up the numbers and the numbers add up. Divide them, and the average would be one significant relationship of insignificant intensity about every other year. Ten men in twenty years. That seems typical and even conservative for single women my age. I choose to think so, anyway.

I didn't anticipate finding a man in Coleman. It wasn't on my agenda. When I considered men and sex after Sheffie's death, I couldn't categorize their potential place in my life. As an escape from my reality, which was painful? As a means of attaching myself to another human being to lessen my grief? As a path to beginning again and reestablishing the sense of family I had lost? These possibilities seemed not to work for me; I couldn't rise out of my despair and grief long enough to notice a man or think of romance.

Finding myself attracted to Tom was unexpected.

Then on Monday afternoon Janice Whitcomb from Cook, Connally, and Emory called me at work. She had been in the law office for fifteen years and was as much a fixture as the desk at which she worked. Janice was that rare being who had found her niche and strived to be the best legal secretary on the planet; she had achieved the position of office manager as well. She had no ambition to become a lawyer; she kept a ruthless grip on office efficiency. Also, she was my friend. One of my more overprotective friends.

"I vaguely remember reading about this guy . . . this psychologist whose family was killed by a patient," she said. "I had to go to the newspaper library anyway, and I went through the microfile on that case. Let me ask you something. Are you thinking of getting serious with this guy?"

"Why?" I wondered aloud.

"Well, it's none of my business, but the murder of the wife and child is sloppy, according to the press. I looked at two brief pieces on the subject and there were no arrests. The man who Lawler insists did it was hospitalized at the time. Maximum-security hospital. The one who had a hard time coming up with an alibi was Lawler."

Something seemed to hit the pit of my stomach. I might have groaned.

"What's he like?" Janice asked me.

"He seems gentle, sincere," I said. "He's not practicing anymore, which is easy to understand. He's quiet about it around here; he doesn't want anyone to know. He says he doesn't want to explain it all to people he doesn't consider close friends. Also understandable."

"What's he told you about the crime?"

"The bare facts. He testified against the defendant, the defendant was remanded to a mental-health facility from which he harassed Tom, and Tom's family was killed. He wasn't released? The defendant?"

"Not at the time of the murders. I could find out when. What's your stake in this?"

"I'm thinking of dating him."

She laughed in a subdued sort of way. "Tell me, Jackie, what sort of dates does one do in Coleman? Town picnic? Trail ride? Hay ride?"

I stiffened while on the phone, which of course she couldn't see. She could hear it in my voice, however. "Well, he offered to cook dinner for me."

"Ah, dinner. Good-looking?"

"Yes, in a way. He seems honest, straightforward. Mostly, he's engaging; he seems to have a good sense of humor and a compassionate nature. He seems solid. . . . But jeez, what he's been through. I don't know what to think."

"You're thinking of sleeping with him."

It was a possibility; why else would any of this matter? What I was thinking was that I liked him and he was making himself available to me. A friendship that wasn't strictly superficial had begun to appeal to me, since I was feeling lonely in my new town. I had stumbled upon him. Had I not happened upon a man who was intelligent, sensitive, attractive, and entertaining, I wouldn't be looking for someone to sleep with. Tom was, however, those things. I didn't need a relationship—I didn't need to not have one.

"He's a carpenter now," I told Janice. "A builder of sorts who has been helping me with some of the renovations on my house. Not for free, mind you— I hired him. He's the only unmarried man I've met here. I've known him over three months now, so he's not exactly giving me the rush. He moves slowly, carefully. I haven't even held hands with him."

"Does anything about him bother you?"

"Him? No. His 'case' bothers me, though. I'm curious to know how he's been affected. Being the victim of a violent crime can be a diseased situation."

"I could get some details on this for you, before you get, you know, more involved. I could get court stuff and police stuff."

"I don't know if that'll be necessary. I feel like I'm peeking in someone's windows."

"Well, Jackie, you're thinking of dating a guy with a bizarre and complicated past; you ought to at least know what's in it. Huh?"

"Okay," I said reluctantly. I had a pang of guilt. I would hate being checked out. My need to know the facts was greater than the guilt. "Let me know what press you find."

"You going to cool it until I have something?" she asked.

"There's not a big rush. Listen . . . I don't need this talked about. Don't build this into a serious investigation. This guy has apparently had a safe, quiet, anonymous life here in Coleman; I don't want to cause him any trouble."

"Sure, fine."

I was glad, later, that Janice had taken that on. I think the big inner battle I was fighting was that maybe I didn't want to know. Was it possible to have an ordinary, pleasant friendship with a guy and not dredge up the past? I couldn't find a rational argument for turning down information. Ignorance might be bliss, but it's irresponsible and dangerous too.

Tom and I were both scarcely known in Coleman. Neither of us had a single other intimate friend. I realized I was being romantically pursued by a man with a short history. All the long-term checkpoints—family, friends, job—were inaccessible. All I knew of him was what he told me.

What I had wanted, I realized, was to be told he was all right. That it was perfectly safe to get to know him better.

As I left my house the next morning, I found a bunch of flowers on my back step. Not a vase, not a floral arrangement. A bunch, tied with a shoelace. No note. I had begun using my back door to enter and leave the house because it was more convenient to the driveway. Sometime between my return from work at seven the previous night and seven in the morning, someone had been in my backyard, at my back door. While I was home. No knock. I hated this. I took the flowers to work with me and, not knowing what else to do, stuck them in a coffee cup.

"Bodge said he was out at your place Sunday night," Roberta mentioned. It was only Tuesday. If I could tap the Coleman hotline, I could get what I wanted fast. I still didn't know how that was done.

"What a big mouth," I said, still writing. "Did he tell you why?"

"He said you thought you had someone in your house while you were gone."

"I did have," I said, putting down my pencil. "Someone had lifted the toilet seat and left an imprint on my bed. Tell me the truth, Roberta—did Bodge ask you if I was a flake?"

"No."

"You mean he just mentioned that I called him and thought I had someone in my house and didn't say anything else?"

She took off her glasses. "That's right," she said. "And I told him that if you thought you had, you had."

I was temporarily quieted. "Thanks," I finally said. I expected her to have some comment for me, but she didn't say anything more.

"See these flowers?" I asked her.

She lifted her specs and made a face. "Homey touch."

"They were on my back step this morning. Tied with a shoelace. No note."

There was a long silence. She looked back at her work before she asked, "Secret admirer?"

"Beats the hell out of me. Is Billy capable of anything like leaving flowers? Going in my house? Either or both of those things?"

"I don't think so," she said thoughtfully. "Billy is not the least bit secretive or sneaky, and he's shy. I've never heard of him acting like that around anyone else."

"What if he has a crush on me or something?" I asked.

"You could do worse," she said, closing the subject. She had nothing more to say. She didn't ask me if I was nervous about this, if I had discovered anything more, or if I needed advice.

We locked up at six o'clock and stood on the sidewalk outside the office. She asked, "You *have* had the locks changed?"

"Yes. Yesterday."

"Good."

"It's strange, isn't it?"

"Yes, strange. There are stranger things around here that after time we come to accept as typical rather than unusual. Idiosyncratic or eccentric. Elizabeth Trewell is agoraphobic and hasn't been out of her house in seven years—and we all know about it, do nothing about it, and enable it. She's generous and helpful; when the community needs something like volunteer work, donations, whatever, we go politely to her door, do not enter, do not expect her to exit, and ask her a favor that she can fulfill without leaving the house, which she good-naturedly does. Now, that's strange.

"George Stiller's father goes for long walks in the middle of the night in his nightshirt. He's eighty and he's been doing this for years. He's not a sleepwalker, he isn't a pervert, and he doesn't drink. He's been chauffeured home by the sheriff from the cemetery, the park, and various street corners, and has never given a single explanation other than he's getting some air. That's strange. I wonder if he's gotten into lying down on people's beds.

"And of course there's Billy, who is brain-damaged and can be a burden to us sometimes; we all watch out for Billy. We've learned to accept most of his childlike behavior, but he has been known to give people who don't know him the creeps. He likes babies; he's upset a young mother or two by staring too closely at the babies. Some of the kids are terrible to him, running from him screaming, teasing him, having their laughs over his clumsiness and mistakes. Poor Billy; he takes it so well. He's become another strange fixture around here. He's never done an aggressive thing in twenty years, so if he's your admirer, feel complimented."

She lit a long, slim, brown cigarette. She is the worst chain-smoker in the world. Her voice, deep and masculine, evidences years of this abuse.

"What about His Honor—Bud?"

"Oh, there's nothing wrong with Bud. He's got a come-on for the young women, but he's harmless. I've never known him to act on his flirtations. He even invites Peggy out to lunch now and then; maybe he has a thing for chubby women."

"He's obnoxious. Obvious."

"Not in court," she said, which was true. Dress

Bud in his robes and he turned into an authentic judge.

"Strange things somehow become commonplace by virtue of the entire town's awareness of them. We have hermits, drunkards, incestuous families, and—"

"Incestuous families?" I interrupted.

"I told you—the Driscolls have been intermarrying for years, for generations. Well, that's not true. I don't think they have had a legal wedding. There are plenty of kids and you can't tell who's whose. Elvin and Polly Driscoll are actually brother and sister."

"God. I guess I thought they were intermarrying cousins."

"Not cousins. Aunts and nephews; uncles and nieces; brothers and sisters; fathers, stepfathers, et cetera, and anyone."

"Doesn't the law step into a situation like that? That's disgraceful!"

Roberta gave a hoot of laughter. "You've brought all this commendable social order from Los Angeles; how tidy. Yes, the law has been to visit, as have the country social welfare and a state agency or two. They've been separated, reprimanded, and once one of them even went to jail for a while. Nothing changes. There's no complaint other than the fact that there's low IQ running rampant through that family because of the inbreeding. Why don't you run out there to their trailer park and stand guard to keep them from screwing each other?"

"Blllkkk," I said. Roberta laughed harder, coughing at the same time. Her laugh *was* a cough.

"You really ought to see the compound," she chuckled, inhaling. "It's about six trailers surrounding a garbage pit that's decorated with a lot of auto parts and various appliances."

"What do any of them do for a living?"

"Piecework. Construction gangs, road-crew work now and then, seasonal stuff, sell off junk, maybe they steal. They don't bother Coleman people because Bodge won't tolerate any infraction in his town. He might be a county sheriff, but Coleman is his home. They're all on welfare and they know that Bodge can get the dole yanked."

"Nice little town," I said. Sounded to me like beyond the trees there were a bunch of degenerates who lived like animals. Yet my experience had substantiated that any social class in Los Angeles could produce such lifestyles as easily. The emotions with which we accompanied these finds in the big city were shock, distaste, and abomination. Roberta sounded mildly amused and generally unflapped.

"It *is* a nice little town," she said, refusing to be baited into extolling its virtues. Some of them I knew. Great football team. Some interesting, affluent residents—a couple of 747 captains with big homes up on the ridge; a novelist who lived here half of every year; Eagle Scouts, family softball league, clean air, and beauty that I found rapturous.

"Bodge told me something else. Some hunters found a decomposed body near the gorge by Canon City."

"Where's Canon City?"

"South of here. It's off the freeway west of Pueblo. He got it on teletype—thinks there's a chance it's a resident of Coleman who's been missing for about four years now. A woman who left her husband and two kids and was suspected of running off with an old boyfriend, except that the boyfriend turned up in Denver and . . . Oh, long story. All gossip. Long and short—she disappeared. The teletype describes a woman who could be her. I didn't know her."

"Cause of death?" I asked.

"I don't know," Roberta said. "Driscolls notwithstanding, we haven't had a good crime around here in twenty years. Nothing but little shit. I find this discovery frightening. Ominous." She tossed her cigarette butt onto the sidewalk and ground it with her old, box-shaped leather shoe. "There are a lot of unlit, potholed country roads around here. Make sure your car is in good running order.

"Tomorrow I'm going into Colorado Springs to see a client about defending him in a personal-injury suit filed against his auto-parts franchise. Why don't you come with me? Get your feet wet. Get out of here for a day."

"All right," I said. There wasn't anything urgent to keep me in Coleman. "Want me to drive?"

"You probably don't allow smoking in your car," she said.

"Fine, you drive."

The woman's name was Katherine Sullivan Porter and she was twenty-nine years old at the time of her death. Her children were seven and four when she disappeared. Her husband, Bob Porter, an active high-school teacher and basketball coach, had reported to Bodge that his wife was missing and she had not contacted anyone in her extended family. He could think of only one person she might have left with, an old boyfriend from Denver.

Bob had met Kathy in Denver, married her, and brought her back to Coleman, where she was a housewife and he was a teacher. They had experienced only the typical, short-term marital scraps. She had confided in a friend, a few days prior to her disappearance, that she found her personal life lacking in excitement and romance. Bob Porter's suspicion had not been aroused, as Kathy had had such symptoms every spring since they married.

She had been strangled—the hyoid cartilage was fractured—her hands were bound behind her back with twine, and a clear plastic bag was tied over her head. Whatever else had happened to her, the coroner said, was impossible to determine from skeletal remains that were four years old.

What made this case most interesting to Bodge were the things that hadn't happened. Her body was clothed, her clothing was intact and undamaged, her wedding and engagement rings were on her finger, and she still had barrettes in her hair. She had been buried, not dumped. Hunters discovered her eroded gravesite. There was no evidence of a struggle. This smelled premeditated, personal; the most reasonable motivations for such a crime were limited to issues of domestic violence, acquisition of insurance, or revenge. Such issues did not fit with Kathy Porter's life. Her marriage had been typical if not exciting; there was a small insurance policy, no substantial property, nothing to be gained. And Kathy was well liked, though not well known. She was quiet, domestic, and shy.

When Bodge came to tell Roberta what he knew about this, I listened in with rapt interest. Bodge had taken the disappearance seriously because Kathy seemed to have been lifted off the earth into thin air. Her death and burial were horrifying.

"Well, I sure didn't know who she was," Roberta said in her deadpan way.

"Who were her friends?" I asked.

"She was well known in her neighborhood. Her closest friend was the woman down the block, who had children the same age. They were both involved in the co-op preschool," Bodge said. "Thing is, her girlfriend wondered if she'd been having an affair, but she didn't wonder that out loud till after Kathy was gone. We were able to establish without any difficulty that she wasn't with the guy her husband knew of in Denver. Bob contacted him, found him uncooperative, and we stepped in. He hadn't heard from her since they broke up and he was covered at the time of her disappearance. Phone records didn't show any phone calls, long distance or otherwise; she wasn't planning anything that we can see. Nothing was missing. Nothing was left behind by whoever took her away."

"What about the husband?"

"Bob was devastated. We never found him suspect and so we checked out the affair angle. Bob was unaware of any discontent, any withdrawal, or increasing domestic arguments at the time. After he talked to her girlfriend, Leah, he remembered only minor complaints. The old boyfriend came to mind, but Bob doubted even that. Leah came up with this idea of an affair because Kathy stopped spending time on the phone with women for a couple of weeks before she disappeared, which might have indicated that she was busy in some other way. And she did some complaining about Bob's inattentiveness with comparison to the kind of attentiveness she wanted . . . or was getting.

"Bob conducted as much of the search as we did, if not more. He's the one who has thought from the beginning that there was foul play. She was seen dropping her son off at preschool and failed to pick him up three hours later. Bob was with his students all that morning."

Bodge pulled a beat-up pack of cigarettes out of his shirt pocket. "I'm nowhere." He lit one and took a long draw. "The coroner doesn't think she was raped or mutilated, unless her attacker raped her without hurting her clothes and dressed her after she was dead. There's no blood on her clothes. It's like she was hitchhiking and got picked up. No one can imagine Kathy getting into a car with a stranger; she was cautious to a fault. Overprotective mother. More like someone she knew took her quietly out of town, killed her, and disposed of her."

"Was she pretty?" I asked.

"No, I didn't think so. Ordinary. Her picture is going to run in tomorrow's paper—she was five-four, fair, blue-eyed, slight bone structure. She wore her hair plain," he said, moving his hands to indicate a nondescript ponytail. "I need some new information."

"Some will certainly develop," Roberta cynically predicted. Because, as Roberta must have guessed, the town glommed onto this scandalous, scary incident and worked it worse than a hangnail.

Speaking of which, I decided upon manicures at this time. I have trouble sitting still for an hour while someone plays with my hands and talks nonstop about little or nothing, but I wondered if I might find the Coleman grapevine in Nicole's Beauty Parlor. I hit pay dirt. It was a hotbed of gossip that was considered reliable by few. Nicole's was like the *National Enquirer*; no one necessarily believed all that stuff—but they listened to every last word.

"Everyone figures she wasn't seeing no one around here. She must have somehow got herself someone a ways away," said Nicole, who was a woman of forty and had a little Indian heritage.

"How did you come up with that?" I asked.

"Well, by the way Leah—that's her best girlfriend—Leah says she started doing her housework at night. See, she used to drop her boy off at nursery and then either shop, do housework, or have coffee with Leah. Then, afternoons, when they could, their boys would play together at one or the other house. This gave 'em extra time off from the kids. I did that with mine when they was small."

"So, how do you figure it was someone far away? I mean a ways away?"

"Because she'd say she was going shopping and then didn't have no shopping to talk about. And she'd be gone in the car, but no one ever seen her car at houses or stores or hotels or diners around here. And she didn't use those mornings or afternoons to get her stuff done, because just before her husband came home she was all busy trying to get everything done."

"Maybe she watched the soaps," I joked.

"She fell behind on the soaps, Leah said."

"Wow," I said. "That *is* something." I was being wholly sincere. My mom watched the soaps. If she felt unwell, she fell behind on the soaps. It was a symptom of a major problem. "Did you tell Bodge all this?"

"Bodge knows all that stuff—it don't make it easier to find out who she was playing around with. Somebody real special, I guaran-damn-tee."

"Special, how?"

"Listen, you got girlfriends?"

"Well, yeah, I have some good—"

"Women all of a sudden get themselves a man that takes their mind off everything—everything—kids, husbands, shopping, soaps, friends—and they say things. They lose weight because they all at once feel great and feel terrible. . . . They always say things. I mean, in March she's trading babysitting, shopping coupons, soaps, menus. . . . and in April she's all closed up and don't have time for anybody, can't be on the phone, don't shop with Leah, and she's out every morning. Maybe she's having a little daylight dee-light with somebody so illegal she can't even hint about what's happening."

Nicole dragged it out as though she'd been thinking about it for years. "She's talking about how all these years she ain't that happy with Bob. Bob's a good man and he don't drink. Bob's a fine daddy, he don't hit the kids, and he makes a decent living. She asks Leah if she and her husband ever made love in the daylight or if Leah's husband ever took her to the bedroom and had a nightie laid out there that he'd just like to see her in. And she says that's the sort of thing a woman just can't hardly say no to."

"I don't get it," I admitted.

"Look, she doesn't say Joe Schmoe is sure good-lookin' and she doesn't say, even to Leah, 'You can't tell a soul.' Nothing. But she's got these things she couldn't resist and she don't smile at no one at the PTA or the church or anything. Whoever had her had her good and kept her quiet. Whoever that was, he killed her—you know it."

I couldn't think of a good rebuttal. "What do you mean by a guy 'so illegal'?"

"I don't know. Married? Preacher? The governor? Like he's the mayor or the sheriff or something."

I laughed in spite of myself. Bodge? Who could fall in love with him that fast, that hard? Then I thought of Bud Wilcox and forced my thoughts away from him. I was getting that skittish feeling one gets when there's a crime too close to home; everyone becomes stranger than they already are.

"So," Nicole said, "I figure Kathy had herself a man who promised her, 'Don't say anything to anyone—and when we can, we'll run away together. It's the only way; we could never stay in this town.' And then what he did was kill her because she wouldn't run away and he didn't believe she'd keep quiet."

Sounded to me like Nicole had him cold—or had a good soap opera. "How does a guy get hold over a woman like that?"

Nicole smiled. She had deep dimples in her round cheeks. "Now, I coulda sworn you'd know how . . . but then maybe you're just an innocent."

"Come on," I laughed, "who's that good?"

She sobered. "I sure as hell would like to know."

I got my call from Janice. It was bad news and I chose to confront it head-on. I couldn't avoid Tom forever, and I suspected there was more to the story than Janice had told me. I left a message on his machine, he called me at work, and I asked him to drop by for a beer. I told him there was something I needed to discuss with him and I allowed my attorney's voice to convey the gravity. I had to buy the beer, of course.

His appearance had changed since I first met him. He called it his winter growth. His hair was shorter on top and he grew a beard that enhanced his mountain-man appearance. His dark hair, dark beard, and hooded eyes made him look sinister when he was serious, but when he smiled and his brown eyes twinkled, he looked more handsome than he actually was. His beard, still short and trim, made him appear larger.

"What's up? You sounded so serious."

He came in and followed me to the kitchen. I handed him a cold bottle of beer and went back to the living room, where I had a glass of wine on the coffee table. I didn't sit down. I stood to talk to him. "I want to ask you something and it *is* serious. I happened to be talking to one of my friends back at

Cook, Connally, and Emory and she remembered hearing about your incident—the domestic homicide, the coroner's inquest, and the murders of your wife and daughter. She remembered something you didn't mention. You were the only suspect in the murders of your wife and daughter."

Shock widened his eyes. His mouth stood open and he stared at me as though I'd shot him a fist to the gut.

"True?" I asked, wanting to get this over with fast.

"God," he said, breathless. He ran a hand through his hair, short on top, longer in back. "God, Jackie. True. Jesus, I wasn't charged. Did your friend happen to tell you how it was I became the only suspect?"

"No. Was that psychopath charged? Was anyone ever charged? It's creepy. I'd love it if you'd explain."

"You didn't tell anyone about this, did you?"

My chin went up; I was suddenly afraid to be targeted as the only one who knew. I wanted backup. "My friend knows, Janice Whitcomb, at the firm. She told me. Why?"

"Well, damn, because I sure as hell don't want some character assassination like that going around here. Christ, I didn't kill my own family; how could I do that? I know who killed them."

"Jason Devalian?" I asked. I had the facts now.

He stared at me for a long moment. "She just happened to remember the name of the murderer, too? Come on, why don't you admit it—you checked me out. You always do that when someone appeals to you?"

I shrugged. I'm not that tough, but I can look tough if I have to. "I mentioned your name when I was visiting in L.A., Tom. That's all. You told me this story, it happened in the city I had lived in and where

I still have friends, and no one around here knows anything about it. Janice picked up on it, remembered it vaguely, and looked through a newspaper file. I didn't ask her to—"

"Roberta knows," he said, raising his voice. "Why didn't you ask Roberta?"

"Don't shout at me, please. Why don't you stay cool and tell me what happened. I don't know you and it's reasonable that I should get the facts and the truth about you. And I did ask Roberta about you before I even let you grout my bathroom tiles. She said she thought you were a nice guy who had had an unfortunate experience."

"What if I hadn't told you anything about it at all?"

"That would have been unfair of you," I said. "I don't know that I could have done anything about it."

"I haven't been fucking unfair!" he shouted. He was visibly angry with me. He trembled and one fist was clenched, with the other gripping his beer. "I told you more about me before I touched your hand than I know about you. You come out here alone, changing your life, leaving your friends, having no particular reason, and for all I know you could be running from the law. But *you're* having *me* checked out."

"Okay, look, I thought I'd get your side of the story. Nothing about this discussion feels good to me either. You asked me for a date right at the time I told a friend about you. Now, she called me with some information. She took it upon herself to research this. I wouldn't feel safe not listening to what she'd learned. I don't want to make trouble for you or hurt you."

"Why didn't you ask me for some of the details, then? Why'd you have me investigated? And if you're going to have me investigated, why don't you do a thorough job and get the answers? Don't you have any instincts about people? Can't you tell if they're decent people or liars?

"What happened is this—your law-firm friend can get it verified via the police reports. The man who was harassing me, whose voice was on the phone recorder after hours at my office threatening to kill me, was institutionalized at the time my wife and four-year-old daughter were killed. My whereabouts at the time were harder to establish because I was with a woman whose identity I didn't want to disclose. I was a suspect for a whole fifteen minutes until—scared to death—I gave them her name."

"And you told them who you thought killed them?" I asked.

"I told you that, too—Jason Devalian. Mental patient who is saner and smarter than you and me together. They wanted me. They didn't want the real killer; they wanted me."

"You said he was an inmate."

"At a minimum-security hospital. I believe he left for less than an hour; it couldn't be proved. Later he was charged with arson at a time when he was an inmate; and they managed to prove in that case that he sneaked out of the hospital, did his crime, and sneaked back in. I know he did it. He knows he did it."

"Why were you reluctant to use your alibi? The woman was married or something?"

"Shit, Jackie—where's your imagination?" he asked with a sarcastic sneer. I imagined tears in his eyes. His voice was lowered but no calmer. He behaved as if I'd uncovered a turd patch in his life. "She was a patient," he said more quietly. "It got me canned. Check it. It checks."

He hadn't opened his beer. He turned away from

me and went into the kitchen, where he put it back in the cardboard six-pack and closed the refrigerator door.

"I'm sorry I've upset you," I said. "I'll tell you again: I didn't have you investigated—the information came to me. I couldn't ignore it."

"Save your breath. You called back to L.A. and dug up the stuff; you had to have done that."

"No," I said as calmly as I could. "Not at all; I have friends who worry about me, that's all."

"I'm out of here," he said meanly. "I don't need this. You got your stuff now; you think you know what you have to know. You couldn't trust me; you couldn't handle it another way. What are you? A woman or an investigator? I thought our worries would be about one likes fish and one likes beef. I didn't grill you, for Christ's sake."

He wasn't hearing me, or chose not to believe me. "Why not? If you think there's more to me, why don't you ask me?"

"Because my mama told me to live and let live. Because I figured that if there's some personal stuff you want to share at some point, trust me with it, you'll let me know. Since I don't need to fix you, help you, or protect myself from you, I thought I'd enjoy your company and let you be. We haven't even kissed, for Christ's sake, and I don't usually pry for all the details of a personal life with people who are still new acquaintances."

"Are you saying that you think I shouldn't have asked you about this story? That I should have gotten to know you first? Is that it?"

"We've known each other a few months now. We're not steadies. You ought to have a feeling for whether you're afraid of me. If there's something scary about me, you never let on."

"I didn't have to be afraid of you to listen to what my friend had to say," I said truthfully. I wasn't afraid of Tom. He had made me feel safe up to now. My only reason for not letting him sleep on the couch the night I came home from L.A. was my penchant for privacy.

"I didn't expect you to be an operational, that's all. I suppose you want my medical records."

He had thoroughly pissed me off. "It's a high-risk society. I wouldn't mind."

"Well, you're outa luck, babe," he said, his voice calm now and his eyes clearly narrowed in annoyance. "I haven't been to a doctor in five or six years. See ya around, Jackie. I hope you're satisfied that I'm not a criminal, because Coleman would be a bad place to have that around."

"It was never my intention to spread gossip. I was told you weren't charged or indicted. I wanted the details and your side. If that can get you this riled up, you and I have nowhere to go from here."

"I guess not," he said. And he left.

His story checked further. He was investigated and suspended for having a personal relationship with a patient and never went back to work for the state. He must have been terminated for breach of ethics. And Jason Devalian did commit a crime as an inpatient—one that got him locked up a little tighter, in the state penitentiary.

For two years.

5

CAN we talk?" Tom asked me.

"About what?" I replied coyly. I resort to coyness only when so dismayed I don't know what else to say or do. I had not expected to hear from him. I was unsure of my feelings at this point. I knew I wanted him to let me off the hook; to absolve me of the crime of sneakiness, of investigating a friend. I secretly wished he could also make all this heavy-duty wreckage of his past life disappear. I wasn't prepared for it to be worse.

"About my thoroughly unreasonable behavior. I'm sorry about the way I reacted. I think it was the surprise, the way you hit me with it. You're a clever lady, Jackie. You did the right thing and you did it straight. I was an ass."

"Well, there. We've talked about it. Was that an apology?"

"It was the first half of one. I'd like to see you."

This threw me further off balance. "I thought we established that it's going nowhere. I don't hold a grudge. You're off the hook, I won't gossip about you, and I'm sorry about the way that conversation went. I never intended to broadside you. I didn't purposely investigate you and I mean you no harm. It was all a coincidence, my finding out."

"Okay, fair enough. I see how that scenario could happen. That seems to unhook us both."

"Good. Let's call it done—"

"Come on, Jackie, don't make me beg. Seriously, have you looked around Coleman lately? There aren't many single women and single men. Except for that one foolish display of temper, we get along okay; we like each other. Temper isn't a problem for me. On that subject, feeling cornered I guess, I got hot. You gotta understand—I'm not as screwed up as I was then . . . but I am still accountable."

"Maybe we could meet for a sandwich or something," I suggested. There's an old singles rule: Keep it simple and public till you're sure.

"We could, but I'd like enough privacy to talk. I'd like to explain myself, if possible. And I'd like to exercise my option of asking you about yourself."

"What do you have in mind?" I didn't respond to part two—I always had the option of saying, "None of your business." I wasn't afraid of my past; I was haunted. There's a difference.

"I'd like to make you dinner." I was silent for a moment that seemed to stretch out. "Listen, I don't want you to feel in any way vulnerable. You should tell Roberta or somebody that you're coming out to my place for a home-cooked dinner." Again, I didn't accept or decline. I said nothing. "It's pleasant out here, quiet and pretty; we can talk, and I'm a halfway good cook. I was once a short-order cook at a greasy spoon for about six weeks. I miss you," he said. I swallowed. "More than you, I miss the anticipation I had that we were going to be friends. See, Jackie, I don't think we had a personality conflict; it was a misunderstanding brought on by me. By my reaction to what you'd heard from your friend."

Well, I missed the anticipation, too. I had started thinking about having a relationship that involved movies, dinners, laughter, camaraderie, and touching. Not the least of which was touching. I am a healthy woman with a body that is not dead yet, though for a good eighteen months after losing my son, I suspected I was down to a half a brain atop a useless anatomy. I had slowly come back to life after that. I longed for Sheffie; I always would. I knew I was among the living when I recognized that I was longing for other things as well.

Also, a skeptic to the end, I'd checked his story out, and he was never charged with any crime. Although it hadn't been my intention to investigate him in the first place, it was in the second place, after his display of anger. I was not going to share that. "Okay," I said. "What time?"

"Seven?" he asked.

Seven it was. It gave me time to go home, drop off my homework, take a quick bath, and freshen up— a new ritual of mine since I shared an office with a smoker. I asked myself all that afternoon and during my preparation what it was I wanted from this situation. What I did was lie to myself in the way only a woman who has been a long time without a man will do. I do not mean that in the biological sense; it wasn't that I was craving sex.

I wanted to be hopeful, I rationalized. I was ready to restore some things to my life that I had learned to do without. I wanted someone like Bruce in my life: a good friend of the male gender. If Bruce had still been around when I started breathing again, I would have attempted to reconcile with him. Having someone is so good. I wanted to have someone to talk to about cases, something to look forward to, and the physical contact that lends reassurance and affection.

I had looked around Coleman. I couldn't help it that Tom kept crossing my path.

The appearance of his quaint and spotless home charmed me. I am tempted by men with feminine traits; rugged, masculine men who can do the things that women are expected to do. His house was a beautiful sculpture of woods and wools. His table was set with mauve placemats, a bunch of wildflowers, plates, and flatware. I could smell the aroma of a beefy dinner. There was Fifties music on the CD player.

"This is a beautiful house," I said.

"I better be staying in it a long, long time," he said. "It's a one-man house and everything in it is for one man. One of everything. I built most of the furniture, too."

He explained his building in a way that one would expect a painter to explain a painting. He built one large room on the edge of the hill and lived in it while he did the rest. The large room was the kitchen. There had been a wall and after he built the great room behind the large kitchen, he tore it down. The two rooms were now divided by shelves two feet thick, so that spines of books could be seen from both rooms. Where there weren't books, one could look through, which gave the already large rooms more depth. The open-beam ceiling was sixteen feet high at its peak and there were triangular windows on each side. The late-afternoon sun was lowering in the sky. The room would be equally bright at sunrise. The windows were meant to catch dusk and dawn.

The entire kitchen wall, in front of which our table sat, was glass. Sliding glass doors led to a wooden deck that was ten feet wide and surrounded the house on all three sides. From the kitchen you could see a beautiful valley through which an old train track was threaded. In the early morning, he said, there were deer and elk. An occasional moose would lose his way from the high country and wander there.

"When you're mad at the world," he said, "and you come upon a place like this, it settles your soul. You can scream obscenities at God . . . and he whispers back."

I was romanced poetic. He was good.

The great room had other built-in furniture besides bookcases. There was a desktop with drawers and a wood sofa and loveseat with wool cushions in lavender, mauve, beige, dark rose. Multicolored wool area rugs accented highly polished wood floors. The few decorator items were Southwestern—a bison skull, a sculpture of an Indian woman, woven baskets.

There was a large bedroom, again filled with built-ins, and a huge bathroom off the bedroom. The house wasn't built for entertaining or for a family or for resale. There were no doors that closed except on the bathroom—and those were double doors that stood open and, I would later see, could not be locked.

Beneath the house, under the kitchen and deck that hung out over the hill on reinforced stilts, was his workshop. I declined a tour of it. When I had driven into the clearing, I saw the corral and a small barn that was about the size of a two-car garage. The horses were in the pasture for the night, he told me. Two dogs barked their greeting as I arrived, and aside from Tom's "Down, Pat. Down, Sunny," I was not introduced. They appeared to be friendly mutts.

I had a chance to browse among the books while he chopped salad ingredients. I found myself reading the titles of psychology texts, lawbooks, works on social sciences, astronomy books, and a few hardcover fiction titles of the most popular writers: Michener, Clavell, Ludlum, and Wouk. He showed a preference for pop psychology as well; there were many popular titles in both hardcover and paperback. Everything was meticulously shelved, by subject and author, as though he took his library as seriously as his building. I pulled out a book of popular case studies and paged through it. It was heavily highlighted.

"What are you cooking?" I asked.

"Stroganoff. Red wine or white?"

"Ah . . . red, I guess."

"What are you reading?" he asked.

"I don't know. Psychology . . . of some kind."

"Don't read that stuff, Jackie. You'll think you're nuts."

I laughed. "Is that what happens?"

"For a while. Till you find out that everybody is a little nuts and it's only the degree of nuts that separates the counselors from the patients. Come out here. The sun is setting—you gotta see this."

I was reluctant to put down the book. My father was an English professor and sometime writer. He had a habit of counting books in people's houses; he was intrigued by where they were kept and was most impressed with people who had books in every room of the house. He taught me the art of discerning, after a short perusal and interview, whether the person owned books or read books. I wasn't going to be able to know for sure because Tom was going to make me see the sunset.

He was right that I should. It was breathtaking from his loftlike kitchen. He handed me a glass of wine, had one of his own, and stood beside me to watch it.

"I can see why you love this, why you'd choose this."

"Yeah. You can't take a sunset for granted here, either. Each one is different. The purple ones are my favorite. Glorious."

"You haven't left psychology behind. The books, magazines, and so on."

"Well, it was my life's work. I chose it because I was completely fascinated. I can't practice, but I'm still fascinated."

"Are you sure you can't?" I had to ask.

He laughed good-naturedly, indulgently, and turned away. "We'll save that topic for the next time, Jackie. It's the natural order of progression—and after tonight you're going to be more insistent about it, I'm sure. First, the salad."

"What's going to happen tonight that's going to make me insistent . . . ?"

He opened the fridge, took out two plates covered with greens and dressed, and indicated the table. I sat and was served.

"First things first. I was a jackass the other night. I'm going to attempt to explain, though I have no excuse."

"Listen, it's all right if—"

"No, I think I might have a reason. I've given it some thought. What I'm about to tell you I would have told you eventually, anyway. You were one jump ahead of me. Had my daughter lived and expressed an interest in someone like me, I'd advise her to do what you did—get the facts.

"Fact," he went on. "At the precise time of my life that I was being victimized by Devalian, I had myself so messed up that I was losing credibility in my practice and my family was slipping away by slow degrees. This is uncheckable. It is also true. I was having an affair with a very sick patient who needed me desperately and I was using cocaine. I was stealing money—not holdups or anything. I was taking kickbacks from treatment centers, taking gifts of money from clients, and was generally an asshole." He half smiled, albeit sheepishly. "A manipulative asshole who was dearly loved by one and all; coke addicts are extremely self-confident."

I lifted a forkful of salad to my mouth and chewed. I had once listened to a client extol his sexual abuse of his wife without letting my abhorrence show on my face. I was, if nothing else, a well-practiced lawyer.

"I had borrowed heavily from my parents; they didn't know about the drugs, though they were confused by my behavior, which was alternately euphoric and depressed. I conned my wife, who had come to understand I dabbled in drugs. I convinced her that my intellect prevented me from being like any other cokehead. I had lots of excuses for depression and lots of rationalization for the euphoria. I was unfaithful, a liar, a cheat, and only a good father when I'd had a hit and was on top of the world. Through all this I did not have the slightest notion that I was in trouble."

He paused long enough to eat a few mouthfuls and sip a bit of burgundy.

"I got started on this roller-coaster ride by being a fast burner and brilliant psychologist. I finished my dissertation at twenty-five and had published a dozen papers by twenty-six. I drew a high check from the state and was considered a gifted shrink. I accidentally got hooked on the power of it; I was invincible. I was never wrong—I read people like maps. Nothing got by me. No one got by me. I was almost superhuman at testing; I found things that other psychologists missed. I discovered a man diagnosed as a pathological liar and borderline personality who was only learning-disabled. It explained his whole dilemma—he was a highly paid computer lab technician who could barely read. He was deceptive, living a lie, his behavior was aggressive, and his M.O. was hostile. Anyway—"

He ate again and I found myself absorbed. Entertained. Among other things, Tom was a good storyteller.

"Do you know anything about addictive personalities? I never did have to own up to the dope; I managed to get into a treatment program after my wife and daughter were killed, and I told the truth there. To friends I claimed I'd gotten accidentally hooked on tranquilizers from the stress."

"Why didn't you tell your friends the truth?"

"Pride. And, the fact that the mess I'd left in my trail was going to cost me. It would have been expensive. I could have 'fessed up; there's a little thing in the twelve-step program about making amends when it won't hurt anyone. Some of my amends would have hurt. I destroyed my caseload, my clients, my everything. I have to carry around that I was responsible for what happened to my family; I wasn't paying attention anymore. I had begun to make serious mistakes. My brain was all tuned into my next hit—I was beginning to believe I was God. I was unafraid and had the delusion that I was protecting my family from any harm though I wasn't there. I lost everything at once. Damn—in my heyday, I was good."

"I'll bet. How is it you can drink?" I didn't know that much about cocaine addicts. I had a couple of friends who were recovering alcoholics and they were tuned into cross-addiction. My friend Bill, for example, didn't even indulge in caffeine anymore.

"I seldom drink, and alcohol doesn't appeal to me in the same addictive vein. Coke is an energy giver, confidence stimulator, upper. Till it's out of control, which in my case took a few years." He finished off his salad, picked up the plates, and began serving up the stroganoff, noodles, and small peas. "Are you wondering where you come in?"

I didn't wonder at all; I had forgotten this had anything to do with me. I nodded anyway so that he would continue.

"I'm not only ashamed of that part of my life, I'm also paranoid about it. I still worry that someone might find out how bad I really was, blame me for people being hurt or killed. I wanted to do something to make sure something like my family's murder would never happen to anyone else, and I went to Roberta about a lawsuit against the state. Then, wham! I realized I'd be drawing attention to myself and I dropped that idea fast. I'm waiting for the bill, I guess. What if someone finds out, contacts the state, asks me to give back thousands of dollars in kickbacks? Or what if I'm accused of having perfectly all right people put in treatment programs for the kickbacks?

"I wasn't wrong about Devalian—I was right about him. He wasn't the only guy in jail in those days who was angry with me; I was the state's witness. So, when he was leaving threatening messages on my after-hours recorder at work, I didn't warn my wife. I called the police, but they were unresponsive. I saved the tapes, which helped get me off the hook for killing them.

"I can be honest about my accountability now, but you surprised me, hit me off guard and I got off balance. I felt confronted because I was confronted. I reacted really defensively.

"Jackie, I like you. I'd hate to not even get to see you because I'm holding back, lying, or screwing up. You were right to check out my story; that was an intelligent decision on your part. You were brave to bring it to me; I can appreciate that now. I'm sorry. Maybe you understand my paranoia better now. I haven't used anything stronger than a beer or two in over ten years now."

"A little burgundy now and then," I added.

"I am sorry," he said.

"What about Oregon?" I asked.

"Oregon?" he asked, as if he were momentarily off track. He looked at me with confusion, as though he didn't remember telling me he'd lived in Oregon.

"You said you went there to practice for a couple of—"

"Yeah. Yeah. Well," he began, lifting his fork to his mouth and chewing as though thoughtfully. "I had trouble working. Recovering addicts go through that kind of thing. My mind was on my day-to-day recovery rather than the clients who needed my full attention. I had it in my head that I couldn't do it without drugs."

"You said it was about your family. You'd lost your ability to reason."

"I had. That had more to do with cocaine than my tragedy. Cocaine, guilt, remorse, and regret. Mostly, cocaine. Don't misunderstand—I was filled with grief, guilt, and all that stuff. If you understand addiction, you know that my drug killed my emotions and I didn't get to my grief for a long time. I came out of recovery with a short attention span and severe preoccupation. I discovered building, and I discovered I loved the mountains. In the end, I made a good choice for myself. From 'seventy-nine to 'eighty-six I did small things, like I was testing all sorts of odd jobs. I really was a short-order cook for a while. I was a dock worker, picture framer, produce stocker, chicken farmer—"

"Chicken farmer?" I laughed.

"You bet. I just roved for a while, unsure and unsettled. I changed my name; I did odd jobs. I might have gone through more than a quarter-million dollars on coke, and what a treat it was to discover I didn't need much money. You have any idea how little it takes to live? You have money, or what?"

"I don't have money. I have a retirement fund," I said, chewing his tender, highly seasoned stroganoff. "Getting Roberta to pay for that was the toughest part of my negotiation."

"Yeah," he laughed. "Yeah. Roberta and Harry have a retirement plan that's this: You don't retire till you drop dead."

"Right. Mine will all just go to some home, anyway."

"No family?"

"My parents are dead and I have no brothers or sisters. There are a couple of little-old-lady aunts I keep in touch with, though we haven't visited. Friends, though. I hadn't realized how special they were until I moved away from them."

"But you did. Why?"

"Are you exercising your prerogative of asking about me?"

"I am," he said, smiling. Then, as he studied my face for a moment and his warm brown eyes—I could see the contact lenses—gained seriousness and lost mirth, he said, "You don't have to. I didn't bring you here to make you trade. My stuff is free."

"I'd like you to know something—I'm not into secret-keeping, Tom. I don't have any dark stuff like trouble with the law or drugs. What I have is something that evokes pity and I can't stand it. I am pitiful, and I hate it."

"Look . . ."

"No, you're entitled. It's just that for all kinds of different reasons, I don't want to draw attention to this. It's simple and sloppy. I was married one year; the guy was a bum and a jerk then, though he's come a long way now. I had my only child and my parents' only grandchild four weeks before my divorce was final. I lived for this kid and all the things I did were for him—law school, hard work, savings. He was killed in an accident when he was eleven; he was hit in an intersection by an armored car. It was resolved that Sheffie was riding his bike against the light— freak accident and instant death." I paused. My appetite was gone. I had known it would be. I took a deep breath. "You're the first person who might understand how devastated I was, how alone I became. My friends fell into two categories. Invisible or oppressive. I came here because I felt I had to do something different. I couldn't live in our house anymore; I couldn't take the loneliness any more than I could abide the caretaking and pity of well-meaning friends."

I pushed my plate away. I saw sympathy in his eyes.

"See what happens? I can't eat; you don't know what to say. There could be a murderer on the loose around here and we're up here eating stroganoff and licking our wounds."

"Murderer? Around here?"

"That Porter woman . . ."

"I thought that was somewhere else."

"She lived here; she might have left here with someone she knew."

"No kidding? Is that what Bodge says?"

Did I dare say that Bodge might have gotten it from the Beauty Shop? "It's what Bodge guesses. There are no suspects."

"I bet it's her husband," he said, eating. "You hear about that. I can't think of one person around here who I'd suspect of murder." He chewed again. "Oh, wow," he said, looking surprised. "Did you hear what I just said? Guess I have no business knocking the narrow-minded, huh? Her husband." He shook his head. "God."

"It was my first thought, too," I said.

"Well, on the other subject—thanks, Jackie, for telling me about your son. I'm glad I know that. Is that why you were all screwed up the first day we met? When I measured for shelves?"

"Yes. You know, I had hoped not to tell it."

"It doesn't work, does it? Not telling? I mean it's okay not to tell strangers. When you feel close to someone, you have to open up. I'm sorry for your loss."

I was still hurting inside. It would pass soon—I knew this now. I still couldn't tell the story without the inevitable pain.

"I'm glad you trust me with it. I'll support you while you grieve that loss . . . if you can accept that from someone as messed up as I am." I was touched by both the offer and the humility. He went on: "We tend to miss our former lives, and when we think it's in the interest of our survival to keep it quiet and subdued, we deny a part of our identity. Despite your law practice and success as a woman, your fundamental and chosen identity was as Sheffie's mother. You lost your child and your job and your identity."

I was stirred by his insight. He was good. His assessment and reinforcement lulled me into need. He was cool in his support. I wanted his affection and the nurturing quality of his therapy. I wanted him. My ex had tried hard to comfort me and was clumsy. Tom was practiced.

"You're not so all alone, Jackie. I'm glad you told me a little bit. I understand now."

"What do you think you understand?"

"Are you always prosecuting? I understand why you'd want a change of people and scenery, why you'd want to keep that loss private, and why you'd be more self-protective than the average beauty-school dropout."

"Oh." I was always either prosecuting or defending. I was sure I couldn't change it. Or wouldn't.

"Why don't you enjoy the stars while I rinse and stack the dishes, and I'll join you."

"I'll help . . ."

"Not here. I'm serving you tonight. I'm only bothering with this mess because I've gotten fussy in my old age. Refill your glass and sit at the table outside. I'll be out there in three minutes."

Later, when he did come outside to join me, he quietly took the deck chair beside mine and touched my hand. "You know, I didn't pay enough attention to my daughter and I was her everything. I bet one of the things you miss is being someone's everything. We may have that in common. In therapy, I got to be the everything of some people's lives. Their anchor. We call it transference and have to be on the lookout that patients don't become too dependent. One of the things we don't talk about enough is how good it feels to be that object."

"No," I said. "Not meaning to be argumentative, I never did want to be anyone's everything. I raised Sheffie to be independent, as I was raised. I wasn't successful in my marriage, and in the relationships I had later I was constantly being accused of being too independent. No, I just miss him, that's all. I loved him, I was proud of him, and I miss him."

He squeezed my hand and wisely chose not to say anything. Which made me feel I should.

"That other part is right," I said, as if to make amends for disagreeing. "That business about losing my job, my child, and my identity . . . that's right. You're a good counselor; you know how to comfort. Maybe you should practice again."

He leaned closer and put an arm around me. "No, I don't think so. Tempting, but dangerous. I'd get myself locked into that power thing again. Maybe. Who knows. Who cares."

"But if you have a gift . . ."

"Then it's mine," he said softly, gently. "Mine. And I can use it for me in my life. Right?"

I admired this in him. This attitude of self-assurance, of self-acceptance, was something I aspired to in my own life. He was so genuine, seemed to rebel against preconceived ambitions and be true to himself. It also crossed my mind that he had told me what I was going to do and I did it. He had said I would suggest he counsel, and I had. Because, I reasoned, his gift had been noticed by others and it was, he said, the natural progression.

He leaned closer, lifted my chin with his hand, and

kissed my lips gently. He shifted in his chair a bit; that first touch had worked and he put a hand on my waist and pulled me nearer. His mouth on mine was seductive; the burlap of his beard scratched my mouth in an unforgettable roughness and I opened my lips to have more, to be deeper. His tongue, hesitant and cautious at first, gained power and fierceness until he was penetrating my mouth. He was insistent, possessed of a delicate pressure.

That old part of me began to respond. It must have been that desire was not so dormant, but quite close to the surface after all. My arms tightened around his neck and I held him closer. I liked the sound of our breathing, labored and serious. His hands moved along my back, my sides, my arms. We engaged in this for a while, minutes. It was hot, slippery kissing and I was aroused. I knew where we were headed, I just didn't know how it was going to happen. I know I was thinking that he could pick me up and carry me. He could pull me to my feet with one hand and I'd follow. Or he might take me down on the deck . . .

He broke away. "Oh," he moaned. "Oh, Jackie."

I was trembling. I didn't have to say anything. It is true what they say about the body closing off the mind. The trait reflected in that old joke about men thinking with the wrong head is not purely masculine. This is why teenagers and others get into trouble; when your libido gets fired up, you turn off all your good sense. You're not supposed to; you're supposed to be clear-headed and rational. I often tried to imagine good lovemaking that wouldn't carry me away and put me out of control. I never could. That feeling that I was as unstoppable as a freight train had always been my favorite feeling—and it didn't come all that often.

"If you have any sense, you probably won't get any more involved with someone like me."

"Why? Because of all you've been through?"

"Because in an abstract way, I actually brought on all I've been through."

"You didn't deserve what happened—"

"What do you want to do, Jackie?"

"I don't know," I said honestly. For a woman who usually knew precisely what she wanted, I was having trouble with the decision making now. I wanted to go to the bedroom, and my conscience, sounding remarkably like my mother, suggested I might like myself better if I waited for a few more dates, more talking, kissing, and petting.

"We're going to end up in bed eventually," he pointed out.

"I suppose."

"Do we need birth control?" he asked.

"No," I said.

"Does that mean you're using something or does that mean you're going to take chances?"

"I had a tubal ligation. I can't get pregnant. I can get infections, however."

"I don't have condoms," he said, "but I've only had one partner in four years and I've never noticed anything."

A doctor had said something like that to me once. He had been apologetic later for having been so sadly mistaken. For reasons logical or idealistic, I thought that had Tom been sleeping with all the women of Coleman, I'd have heard about it. There probably was only that one; surely it was all right.

"Want to?" he asked me.

"Yes."

It is still vivid, that night. The pictures still come clearly. He was an accomplished, hypnotizing lover.

He had a charismatic body and technique, and his canny verbal skills were as apparent in bed as out.

"There are no curtains" was the first thing I said when I entered his bedroom, holding his hand.

"The entire outside is lit and the dogs will bark if a rabbit runs by. Here," he said, flipping off the light. The room was still bright from the high floodlights around his house. He could sleep in a dusklike light if he left the outside lights on through the night.

He undressed me slowly; he touched my skin softly, seductively. He brushed his hands along my shoulders, elbows, breasts. He took my mouth with his while caressing my body. I did not require all this foreplay, but I was grateful for it. Fast lovers don't give you time to think; they rob you of the savoring; the savoring went on and on until I knelt, naked on his bed, while he undressed.

There was something about his control of the situation that made me a brave lover for the first time in my life. I had never been able to do that before— watch a man methodically undress and smile at him. It was like an erotic show, an artistic sexual act. I thought it was the beauty of his body; he was both well conditioned and naturally fortunate. When he walked toward me, his erect penis bobbed slightly because of its size, which was generous. Knowing how men feel about their penises, I was happy for him that he'd been lucky.

There was more caressing; fingers, tongues, nibbles. He seemed to have plenty of time, though I was running out. When he spread my legs and put his tongue on me, I was gone. It was an explosion of pleasure and my fingers dug relentlessly into his shoulders. I heard his moan, as though it had been his moment as well, and that made me want him more.

He raised himself up and touched my lips. Gently, as I shuddered, he nibbled at my mouth.

"Do I taste good?" he asked me.

"Oh" was my inspired dialogue.

"I have to be inside you, Jackie; I have to be inside you."

I was hot and tender after such an enormous shock, and he was slow and gentle, entering almost stealthily, moving rhythmically. It's like a hammock ride, that motion in coupling. Easy, but pitched. Smooth, yet demanding. He was patient, giving me plenty of time to recover. "Come again," he said to me. "Come again."

I stayed with him, having his mouth, his hands, his body in my body. We rocked and lurched. He moved more quickly, breathing hard. "Come again," he said.

I did. I had thought I was holding myself back, being patient for his sake, on his behalf. That I was quick was not nearly the disadvantage of a man being quick; I was still capable of returning the favor. There I was, two down and Tom still ready. I collapsed from equal parts surprise and exhaustion. He stayed inside, letting me rest, whispering that I was the most wonderful, sexual, erotic woman alive. He said that one thing that hooked me in: "I haven't ever had it like this; I haven't ever had a lover like you."

I abstractly considered my position; he was still ready. I could have slept. Maybe for a week. Instead, I stayed alert, conscious of my obligation to participate. He gave me another brief rest . . . and then began to move again.

It was not my participation that he wanted, however. Drugged by sex and sluggish of brain, I allowed him to move me about. I felt the debt; if there was a position that would give him satisfaction, I could cooperate.

A couple of times he held my hands in a viselike grip and I asked him not to. Once, behind my back. Once, over my head. Both times I said, "No, don't hold me down, please," and he stopped. Although he wasn't a huge man, he was strong and made me feel small. I'm not a big woman anyway; I was moved about easily and found him creative in his maneuvers. I was on my stomach, my side, my other side, sitting on his lap. He didn't stand me on my head, but if he had moved me into that position politely, I might have gone along.

I stayed on the edge; if I had an orgasm, he let me calm, rest, before taking me to the crazy edge again.

"Can I make you come a hundred times?" he asked me, whispering.

"No," I said, still astonished by his fortitude. "I don't want to be a pig about it."

"Once more."

"Don't wait, Tom. I don't have your stamina."

"It's okay. You'll tell me when to stop. Or I could keep you a prisoner and torture you with ecstasy."

In fantasies women want a machine like this, women think they want to spend a summer vacation like this; that is only in their dreams. In reality, two hours of lovemaking will almost kill you. In the end, exhausted and sore, I had to admit I couldn't be a good sport or the lottery winner any longer. I was past the point of satisfaction and getting to the point of saturation. Every woman who has had the multiple experience, and I suspect we are few, knows that when you've lost count, you've lost your craving and nearly your mind.

And I think women are all alike in this too: Unlike

men who say thanks and put on their pants and go home, we say, ⌐

"I'm sorry," I said. "I just can't. We have to stop."

"Nothing to be sorry about, babe. You're fabulous. Let me be still a minute, huh?"

That I could oblige. When he began to move again, as though he had ignored my request, I began to pull away with firmness. I said, "I can't anymore. That's it for me." Then he believed me. And I stopped apologizing.

When his breathing and mine had become normal, he withdrew.

"What happened?" There were a couple of times that by his breathing or shuddering I thought we had finally done it. I was wrong. He never lost his erection, never softened. Not for a second.

"Nothing happened, babe. Go freshen up if you want to."

"Tom—"

"It's okay," he said insistently, giving me a smile and a peck on the lips.

I washed up and borrowed a towel and washcloth. My clothes were still in his bedroom; I emerged from the bathroom wrapped in a towel and found him sitting up on the edge of the bed. Still naked.

"Will you stay the night?" he asked.

"Would you be terribly hurt if I said I'd rather wake up in my own bed?"

"No, Jackie, not if that makes you feel better."

"It would be easier for me to get a good night's sleep, get up for work, at home, and indulge all my morning rituals."

"I understand," he said very solicitously. "Thank you. You were magnificent. Can I follow you home, make sure you don't have any problems?"

I checked the clock and shook my head. It was

twelve-fifteen. I was a big girl; I had gone home late before. "I don't think I was magnificent enough."

"It's a medical problem," he said. "It's not a bad problem; I get some relief, if not often the big relief. It's still wonderful for me."

"What kind of medical problem?" I asked.

He chuckled, got that engaging grin and twinkle. "The kind a lot of guys would kill to have. It's the opposite of a premature ejaculation, except the hell of it is that there is enough of an ejaculation—several small ones—to get a woman pregnant. There's a surgery; I passed. This problem has good points."

"Is it painful for you?" I asked, which made him erupt in a short laugh. I braced myself for a clever comeback, but he did me the courtesy of resisting an easy joke.

"It's great for me; the benefits far outweigh the disadvantages. Believe me. Understand, it's not you. It's me. I'm okay about it now that I'm over my adolescent embarrassment."

Thinking of a sensitive young man trying to ask a doctor about this unique situation took my mind away from my concern. I imagined he was right; if he could sell it he'd make a fortune. Especially if he wasn't being robbed of fulfillment.

"It's amazing," I said, reaching for my blouse. "Maybe too virile."

"Thank you," he returned, pleased with himself. "I did a lot of screwing around when I was younger; I think I was in denial that I had a problem and always looking for the woman who could make me come. Can you imagine?"

Rhetorical question. He didn't want an answer, naturally. Wasn't I just thinking that I wished I could have? Not so that I could be the one to finally satisfy him. So I could have stopped him.

6

IT didn't feel right. It hadn't felt good.

That was my sobering and suspicious thought as I drove home. The cool night air scoured away any sluggishness; I was wide awake, and I knew something was wrong. I tried to figure out what. I wasn't breathless, dreamy, or desperate . . . things I should have been if I had visited paradise.

Modern women can be so ruthlessly misjudged. What I had done was not impulsive. Nor had I done anything naughty-yet-fun. I felt no shame or regret. I know, understand, and am comfortable with my own sexuality. I'm fairly pragmatic about it; I'm an adult and I am not promiscuous. That I've had more partners than I like to admit is a symptom of my inability to find an enduring relationship, not a problem with my morals. I'm trying, for gosh sakes, which is what modern women do.

This feeling that I had was not unlike the sinking, frightened feeling that overcame me the morning after I had slept with Douglas Jefferson Emory, the married partner. It's an "ugh" of the conscience. I had done something wrong and put myself in danger.

With Doug, my mistake was unpardonable—I had stepped into another woman's territory. I brought sex into my work and it could have cost me far more than it gave me. I was entitled to feel I'd done something bad, and I faced danger.

Tom was a different case. I'd known him for three months, he was an appropriate sexual partner, I knew his legal history—and still I felt, somehow, that I shouldn't have. I was aware of this niggling, nagging, ugly sensation that it wasn't right. It had nothing to do with the aforementioned coke addiction or his dramatic medical problem.

Tom was the type of man that I should be with: physically appealing, unattached, stable under an extraordinary threat to stability, and sensitive. He understood himself and his inadequacies. It's an attractive trait: humility combined with confidence.

As I drove home, troubled, I had this mental image that came out of a horror film. A young girl is chased by a handsome prince; she is laughing, running, and hiding, keeping ahead of him and hoping he'll catch her and kiss her. When he does, her giggles are wild and joyful. And before her eyes he turns into a monster, and her giggles turn to screams.

When I got home I checked the doors and windows; I had locked everything. I was plagued and felt followed. I didn't sleep immediately, so I mentally listed the things that bothered me.

I was seduced. This is what women think they want.

At several points I was tenderly told what I would do and then proceeded to do so. As though it were my idea. In telling him maybe he could counsel again and in multiple orgasms.

I did not believe him about the medical problem, but there seemed no other acceptable explanation.

And I didn't like him as much as I thought I should under the circumstances. I didn't love him.

There it was—as if I'm a moralist. I knew when I entered Doug Emory's hotel room—out of town on business, two drinks, dinner, the end of lots of hard work, a man I liked and respected—I knew I wasn't in love with him. Had all the circumstances been proper, I could have been. Yes. I would have allowed myself to become devoted to such a man.

What was it about tonight, then, that removed rather than intensified my hopefulness?

I felt that somehow I'd been tricked.

I dozed fitfully, and when my clock-radio alarm came on and the music began to rouse me, I was sluggish. Slowly I realized that what I was hearing wasn't the usual brisk early-morning pace, not harassment from the disc jockey to get up and get going. It was soft, late-night music that played. And it was still dark. It was dark because it was three A.M.

I sat up and turned on my light. I pressed the little button on top of the radio to see the time setting for the alarm: three A.M. I listened to the music; I opened the drawer at the bedside table and lifted the pink angora sweater. There she was, silver, shining, and upon inspection, fully loaded. Was she still my secret or had the same person who reset my radio alarm inspected my chest of drawers and discovered my gun?

There I sat, radio playing, knees raised under the covers, light on, and gun in hand, with my arms on my raised knees. In a relaxed position, I kept my eye on the bedroom door and my ears open. Hadn't I wanted to think about it? Now I could. I wouldn't be going back to sleep. My alarm was always set for six-thirty; the only time I had touched it was after unplugging the clock-radio some weeks before.

How interesting that I didn't shake. I didn't call Bodge Scully, though I intended to call him later. I made a mental note to ask him for his home phone number.

This wasn't the first time in my life I was dealing with a very big X factor, the ever-present missing link that haunts the practice of law. Which, incidentally, is not for sissies. It isn't strictly criminal law that takes courage. My instincts were charged with warnings and all I lacked was the facts. I didn't know what it was, who it was, or why I was experiencing this. I knew there wasn't anything I could do except proceed and figure it out. I had no option now. Somehow, this had come to me.

In the early-morning hours, when the sun had risen and the house was bright, I did my inspection, gun in hand. The doors and windows were secure. I looked in every closet and corner, walked around the backyard, went out to the front sidewalk to get the newspaper . . . yes, gun in pocket. I was thinking that if someone saw me he could have me committed. When I told people about this, they might suggest that I have regular visits to someone who could straighten me out. But what excuse would Bodge give me for the new time setting on my radio? Shorted wire?

Bodge was one of the first people I was going to check out. I said that prayer: Please, God, let him be okay. I didn't feel suspense—I believed Bodge was genuine and trustworthy. Roberta was sharp; Roberta trusted Bodge, and she was no patsy.

I took my shower behind a locked door with a gun on the toilet seat. I felt more scared than ridiculous.

I lose weight easily. I reminded myself not to become frantic; this was a slow upheaval and I was going to take care of myself, bolster myself, keep up my strength. I didn't know what I was up against or where it was going. Had I known, I would have fled.

Dressed, primped, and ready for work, I drove to the office and unlocked the door. The stale smell of old cigarette smoke and dust assaulted my nostrils and I became annoyed with Roberta and Peggy. I paused to remind myself I was irritable. I considered going back to cigarettes—no one would ever blame me. I did private counsel on myself to stop the panicked, erratic thinking. I needed both good sense and Roberta on my team.

Peggy didn't come in until nine, which gave me a little time. I picked up the phone to call Tom.

It was his machine. I pitched my voice carefully.

"Hi, Tom, it's Jackie. I'm at work and the client I rushed in here for is late. I thought I'd give you a quick call and thank you for the dinner. I would have called from home earlier, but I overslept . . . never even heard my alarm. I'll be tied up all day and most of tomorrow, so I wanted to be sure I thanked you. Later."

Done.

I called Chelsea. "Hi, doll-face," I said.

"Hey, the lawyer. How are you?"

"Fair. Is Mike already gone?"

"You want Mike?" she asked, laughing in disbelief. "You aren't trying to get him back, are you?"

"Yeah, sure."

"Hey, Jackie, you okay?"

"I have a stumper on my hands and I need a detective."

"Case?"

"Oh yes, a case," I said. A case of the heebie-jeebies. "Is he there?"

"In the shower. I'll go dry him off." The phone

went plunk as she laid it on the kitchen counter. I heard the girls in the background, talking about what was on the back of a cereal box. They were seven and eight years of age, a fun time of life with children. I leaned my head in the palm of my hand and fought envy; it hit me sometimes this suddenly—like the feeling I get in my stomach when I drive over a bump. The kind of feeling that would make Sheffie say, "Again! Do it again! Turn the car around and go back and do it again!" Except it wasn't good. Or fun.

I wasn't happy for Michael that he had a second chance. I wanted to be, but I wasn't. I was happy for Chelsea, though. She deserved a couple of sweet little girls. And I was pleased for the girls; they had a good mom and their good mom had somehow turned that jerk into a good dad.

"Jack," he said. "What do you want? I'm naked."

"You must look stupid," I said.

"I have on a towel; what do you want?"

"Go in the other room. I got a complicated problem and I need your help."

"My help?" he asked, filled with surprise. "Ohhh. My help?" I had, naturally, never let him into my life in any way if I could prevent it. He tried to be helpful after Sheffie died; I couldn't bear it, and pushed him away.

"You, specifically. And don't give me a hard time. I need you."

He was smarter than he looked. I heard the phone do that kitchen-counter plunk again, heard the girls, and heard Michael. "Chelsea, hang that up—I'll get it in the bedroom."

She would not be told what to do, which was what I loved about her. "What is this?" she said to me.

"Let me talk to Michael, doll-face. Maybe I can fill you in later. Okay?"

"Jack," Michael said. Chelsea's receiver clicked off.

"Okay," I began. "You know I'm tough."

"Come on, will ya. I'm cold!"

"Some funny stuff is happening to me," I said in a rush. "When I got back from L.A. that Sunday night, I found someone had been in my house. He didn't do anything except lie down on my bed and lift the toilet seat. One morning there was a bunch of flowers tied together with a shoelace on my back steps. Last night I got home late and my radio alarm had been reset to go off at three A.M."

There was silence for a long moment. "Yeah?"

"All the doors and windows are locked; nothing is damaged, missing, or upset. The first time, that Sunday night, the back-door dead bolt had been opened, possibly with a key. I have new locks now and it doesn't appear that anything was jimmied."

"Who are you seeing, Jack?"

Nuts. It would have to be, right? This was why I was calling, so why try to pretend it wasn't? I was slow to answer because I had spent so much time trying to convince myself that it couldn't be Tom, all the while thinking it must be. I hated the idea that he would be the most likely.

"Got a pencil?"

"Go."

"A guy named Tom Wahl who changed his name from Tom Lawler—spelling, L-A-W-L-E-R. Formerly of L.A.; a psychologist who was once terrorized by a man he testified against. His wife and daughter were strangled and he firmly believes it was the man, though the accused was a patient in a state or county hospital at the time. Tom himself was a suspect for a while . . . a short while. He was cleared. No indictments. Later, the same patient, a man named Devalian, was convicted on arson charges for a fire that occurred while he was hospitalized, which Tom believes proves he was able to get in and out of the hospital to do a crime."

"So? How does he seem?"

I was quiet for a moment. "I don't know," I said.

"Come on," he demanded, impatience in his voice. "Since when don't you know?"

"Too good to be true. I don't believe it; he's like a god—good-looking, smart, sensitive, somewhat manipulative, and—"

"Jack," he interrupted, "what does it usually mean when something is too good to be true?"

I stopped myself and took a breath. "It isn't true." My voice sounded tired.

"What do you want?"

"Some L.A.P.D. stuff. I got press stuff from Janice Whitcomb at the office, but I want some police stuff. Find out about this case. The cases."

"Jack, Jack," he whined. I pictured him, as I could remember so well. He was freshly showered and still looked scruffy; he could somehow look unshaven and tousle-haired fresh out of the barber shop. "You want me to go do file research on some guy because you found your alarm reset and your toilet seat up?"

"Maybe a photo?"

"A photo of the guy you're seeing . . . because why?"

"There's been a body found out here."

"Yeah? So?"

"The woman was youngish—twenty-nine—had been mysteriously missing for four years, and there were no suspects. Her best girlfriend thought her behavior indicated an affair. This is a small town,

Mike. Small; I mean everyone knows who's in bed with everyone every minute. She was strangled, buried fully clothed with her wedding rings on."

"Yuk," he said. I heard him thinking. "No motive?"

"None yet."

"You think this guy—"

"No!" Then I made this whiny sound. "I don't know if he lived here then. He told me it's been 'about' four years. I don't feel good about anything right now."

"Break it off with him; tell him you're out."

"There's nothing to break off. I had someone in my house before I had anything on, for God's sake."

"Oh really?" he asked, sounding surprised. "Really? Hmmm."

"He's charismatic; a gifted psychologist who isn't practicing and doesn't want anyone to know he's a doctor who's living the life of a carpenter."

"Oh, right. While all the other guys are pretending to be doctors when they're carpenters, he's playing a carpenter who is really a doctor. Neat-o. Let me jot that down; I have some friends who need a new line. What a hero."

"He can maintain an erection for hours," I said.

"Oh, Jack, Jack, don't be telling me this shit."

"He says it's a medical problem."

"Yeah, right."

"Ever heard of that kind of medical problem?" I held back from saying, "You sure didn't have that problem."

"Is it contagious? I could get the next plane out."

"Come on—don't you think this sounds strange?"

"I could get a fucking charter. L.A. Lakers, Congress, all of L.A.P.D., not to mention—"

"Am I crazy? Something's wrong here; somebody is messing with me and I don't know who. Something is wrong here. I wouldn't be riled except there's this body and no suspect and you don't know what it's really like to find your toilet seat up when you're a sitter."

"What are you going to do?"

"I don't know. I'm open to suggestions."

"Get a bladder infection."

"Huh?"

"Make an appointment with a local ob-gyn for a Pap smear and check-up. Complain a little bit about burning with urination—you might get lucky and have a quack who diagnoses you and medicates you without the legitimate infection. The visit to the doctor's office is the important part. Imply, how you do so good, that you spent a night with Superman. In case, you know, so the town gossips can back up that you were to see the doctor. Without telling any of your secrets, you let it out that you've been to the Olympics with this guy. Ask the doc about this here medical problem . . . no need to name names. Unless, of course, you want to name me . . . tee-hee-hee. Okay, then tell the guy with the medical problem you overdid—you're off limits for a week, ten days. He gets to feel like a champ and you get a break to think it out. Yeah?"

"And?"

"I'll have a look at L.A.P.D. and see what I can find. You can interview him."

"Interview him?"

"Well, Jack, do you want to figure this guy out or you want to escape? Sounds to me like you've made up your mind to figure out what's going on."

"That's the problem . . . I'm skittish and I want to be wrong. I'm scared of something, I don't know what or who. Mike, if I thought cooling it with this guy was going to make my problem go away, I'd do it. Unfortunately, I have a feeling it could get worse and leave me less protected. I think I have to face it. What bothers me is that there shouldn't be any reason in the world why I'm not begging this guy to marry me—and the fact that I'm not concerns me. Something is wrong."

"Good. That's good."

"What if I feel stupid about this later on?"

"Stupid and sure? Not a bad way to go."

"What do you think I should try to get him to tell me?"

"Nothing. If he's a wrong guy who's feeding you bullshit, he'll do most of the talking. Let him talk and talk and talk. Something is bound to be said that leads you to whatever next step you take."

"So, Michael, you think I ought to talk to the sheriff? He's like an overweight, chain-smoking Andy of Mayberry, but he keeps a real close watch on this town. He seems okay; I don't know how to check him."

"It's like this. A creep is usually someone you know; you know that much—you get the same stats I get. That's why you're on the line, right? Because you wonder if this woman who was killed knew her killer, and you've got weird shit, right?"

"Suspicions. That's all. The killer could be Andy of Mayberry, for all I know. And I've got a forty-five-year-old, brain-damaged, sweet lawn guy named Billy. And the local judge wears gold chains and winks at me. . . . Not in court," I was careful to add. "Out of court, he tells me I'm attractive and winks at me."

"Nothing new there, huh?"

"I guess not. Overly friendly judges haven't been a regular problem, though."

"One would be too many. So how long has the sheriff been sheriff? More than a couple of years?

Seems like if he was lifting toilet seats and resetting radio alarms and killing housewives, stuff like that would have been happening for a long time, huh? So here's what you do with the sheriff. You tell him what's happening, you tell him you aren't going to tell anyone else, and ask him what he thinks you should do. Let him give you some advice, and if he doesn't sound okay, cut him out of your problem and go somewhere else. You'll get a feeling for him after you work with him on this. You've got good instincts."

"I thought so. Till now."

"Why now? You're calling me because your instincts are screaming bloody murder. Your problem is you don't want to take this transmission. You're going to have to deal with that."

"I've got a gun."

"Well, don't shoot your goddamn foot off."

"I won't."

"Take a second shot. I didn't tell you that."

"You didn't have to." I'd tangled with him over the possession of firearms. He was opposed. Only the big, strong policeman could have a gun; these defenseless, nervous little ladies with guns were a danger to society. Why, without guns, they would merely be raped and stabbed; guns could get them shot. I took my ex-husband to the range and showed him. I told him that I would shoot and I might put in a second bullet to cancel out any legal technicality brought on by a wounded, but living, perpetrator who could build a case against me. I didn't necessarily mean that. What I meant was that the gun was for my defense—and I would use it.

"I gotta go," he said. "I'm freezing. Anything else?"

"I can't think of anything."

"Be careful, for God's sake."

"Aw. You care."

"I lost enough," he said.

"Me, too." The line was still for a moment. Mike and I didn't talk about Sheffie; we occasionally acknowledged our pain. Mike had gotten so much smarter since we'd been divorced. He went to some trouble to establish what we both knew: My pain was worse. "There *is* something else—a small favor."

"Yeah?"

"I have a couple of boxes of Sheffie's stuff that I've been keeping. They're stored in a spare room. Don't try to understand this—it's like he's in the room; I'm as protective of those boxes as I was of Sheffie. Let me send them to you until I feel better. You take care of them for me."

"Jack, you oughta talk to somebody. Really."

"Do it for me, okay?"

"Okay. I can tell Chelsea about this?"

"Let's not. You know how she worries."

"Awwww," he whined. "She's gonna be all over me."

"Don't."

"She's gonna be on me like a cheap suit."

"Don't call me. I'll call you. And thanks."

"Hey, wait. Be sure to let it out you're not all alone. Know what I mean? Get a lot of friends."

"Yes, I understand." Peggy was just coming in. "Hello, Peggy," I said. "Thank you and I'll get back to you later."

Going back to my house, even in the middle of the day, frightened me. I walked around inside with the gun in my hand. That I had to go through this made me so damn mad that I might have killed anyone I found in my house. Anger, once my enemy, was becoming my friend.

The house was secure, apparently untouched and not violated. I put mailing labels on my precious boxes, took them to the car, and went to the post office. In their place I put two boxes of sheets that I had used to cover some of the ground-floor windows before I had curtains and blinds installed. In Magic Marker I wrote "Sheffie's Stuff" on top of the boxes. It was a test of mine: How far would my phantom go to terrorize me? Would he open my special boxes?

I decided to get my nails done before going to the doctor's office. I had done a bad thing in insisting that Michael couldn't tell Chelsea what was bothering me. I loved the idea that he would try, however briefly, to keep a confidence and that Chelsea would, with the stamina of a salmon trying to mate, work him over until she got it.

I was tired. I'd been up most of the night and had a full day still ahead. Roberta had called and told Peggy she wouldn't be in. I looked at her calendar and didn't see anything; no client appointment, no court date. Anyone is entitled to have a day off or be sick. An explanation would have been appreciated; I fought the pettiness, bitchiness that would not serve me. I had to ask Peggy to manage the office alone, and she complained that she was supposed to leave by three.

I wanted Nicole to work on my nails for an hour. I wanted to hear what she was on today. She was temporarily off the murder and on one of the deputies, Sweeny, who gave her a ticket for sliding through a stop sign right after she had waved at him.

"The son of a bitch," she grumbled. "He's your best friend one minute and the next minute he's gotta be sure you know who's boss. I'm gonna plead innocent."

"You don't have to enter a plea in Traffic Court,"

I told her. "You tell the judge what happened, that's all. In your case, I don't advise you to tell the judge what happened or he'll tell you to pay the fine."

"Big asshole, that's what that Sweeny is. Honey girl, when you wave at him like he's your best friend, follow the traffic laws to the letter. He gave my boy Eric a ticket for going twenty-five in a school zone."

"How many kids do you have, Nicole?" I asked her. I found out there had been seven; now there were six. She was forty-six; the oldest child was twenty-nine, soon to be thirty, and the baby was sixteen. Her husband, Lip, a county lineman for the phone company, was one of the men who hung out with Harry and the guys every morning at the café.

I was getting the daily bulletin. This is how a beauty shop is—you take what you get. I was going to accomplish one thing I'd set out to do. I had a simple plan; I would throw a few people off by changing my agenda. I meant to throw a wrench in the secret-trading business. I had told Tom I didn't want the details of my son's death to be known. If I told Nicole, the secret would be out; it wouldn't belong to Tom anymore. I did not consider Roberta a player in the secrets game.

I scared myself a little. I had been thinking about Kathy Porter, and what Nicole had said. What was an "illegal" guy who could get a woman in a spot where she didn't even tell her best friend she was "interested"? A preacher or married man? Or . . . how about a sexual athlete who had a secret past that he didn't want anyone to know about? How about a guy who was a psychologist, with such a heavy-duty history that he just had to go low-profile? Would a woman who was lonely, vulnerable, tell him he was so good, so sensitive, he should go back to being a doctor? I was so unsure of Tom and of what was happening that I didn't rule him out of Kathy Porter's demise. This sweet and tender man with a medical problem. I worried that I would regret my obsession, but I proceeded.

"They're a hoot, these kids. Too bad you never married or anything."

"To tell the truth, Nicole, I did. I was married, briefly, and had a child. He was killed a little over two years ago. Hit by a truck in a crosswalk."

"Oh, baby," she sighed. "Oh, sweet baby."

I felt terrible. I had used Nicole. Nicole was the kind of woman a person felt like cuddling up to. I could fall into her ample bosom and take all her comfort—and all I'd done was put into action my plan to throw the secret sharing off balance. I was getting out of the game. I was going to own the past I said I couldn't bear to be pitied for.

"I wasn't going to tell anyone. I'm not over it, not nearly. There's nothing worse than pity. Nothing."

"Oh, angel, 'course there ain't. There ain't, you're goddamn right. I lost my Jeff when he was seventeen. Car accident, too. 'Course there was six others but that don't matter; I'll never get over it. I had the others. You got no one."

"Oh, not true," I protested. "I have wonderful friends in Los Angeles. I thought I'd come out here and start over, change my whole life. I visit them, they'll visit me as soon as I get a sofa bed, and we talk on the phone all the time. I'm getting some new friends here. I'm very lucky to have Roberta and Harry." Didn't I make it sound like we spent our evenings together? "And I've had a date with Tom Wahl—he renovated my upstairs bathroom."

"Yeah, Mr. Tom." She chuckled. "Now, there's a good-looking man. Used to be tight with Elaine Broussard. . . . She used to live here. I thought they was gonna get married. Been gone back some-where—Detroit maybe—about two, I don't know, over a year ago now. So . . . you and Tom hooking up?"

"No." I laughed. "No, not a chance. I'm not looking for romance." I shrugged. "Friendship is enough. He seems to have bigger ideas, though."

"He's sorta shy, ain't he?"

Tom? Shy? In my mind I practically had him convicted of murder. Surely they would put me in a rubber room for this. I was tired, and this vacillating I was doing was a symptom of what I would do for months.

"He doesn't seem shy," I said.

"He don't say much. Lip says he sort of keeps on the edges of things, doesn't get close to the men."

"Well, gee, Nicole, those men are a tight bunch."

"Yeah, and Wharton don't like him. Don't make no secret about it, either."

"Wharton? Do I know him?"

"He's in the café with the men every damn morning. We'd get overtime if Lip didn't hang out at the café mornings and Wolf's evenings. Wharton's quiet, cranky, someplace over sixty and hard-used. Smokes Camel no-filters, ranches in the valley, and has a big old house on the lower ridge. Got four kids, all grown and moved on, and been widowed six, seven years. Can spit on his place from Tom's road and I just bet that's what Wharton hates: having to share a road with anyone."

I hadn't seen a house.

"They're neighbors?"

"Well, sort of. From Tom's east end you can look straight down into the valley and see Wharton's ranch. They've argued over trash, fences, horses, roads, and whatever. Tom forked a road off Wharton's to get to his place and they share the road to Sixteen. Somehow or other Tom pissed Wharton off. I figure that's why poor Tom stays back from that crowd, 'cause Wharton is bound and determined to be his usual jackass self. Those that know Wharton don't take him serious. Tom, I think, takes him serious."

"It takes a while to get to know people here when you're a newcomer. Everyone is so established; everyone has their friends."

"People are cautious, that's all. Most of the people here have known each other all their lives and it don't take no work. Somebody new you gotta work on. Build up all this stuff. Know what I mean? You won't have no problem, angel. You're such a sweet little thing. Who'd believe you'd go and be a lawyer?"

Who'd believe the lawyer was now keeping a gun in her purse because her toilet seat had been left up, I thought.

"Nicole, you by any chance see Dr. Haynes for anything?"

"I've seen him, yeah. Don't like him much, though."

"Why not? Isn't he good?"

"We had Doc Rogers so long. . . . He delivered my babies and cured a couple of the croup and always had time to visit and take coffee before he left. This young one, I don't know, all business. Why? You sick?"

"No." I laughed. I tried to picture the old country doctor. "I think I'm getting a bladder infection, and if I'm right, I need antibiotics. Can't get those without a doctor; I want to catch it before it flares up."

"Yeah?" she asked. "How do you know?"

Nuts. I had hoped she was one of those poor women plagued by bladder infections after intercourse. I wasn't going to educate her and spill my guts all at once. This was only our second date, Nicole's and mine.

"Well, I've had them before. Some women seem to get a lot of them. I used to keep antibiotics on hand. . . . My old doctor in L.A. said I could tell the symptoms as well as anyone and shouldn't let it get bad. It's mostly a burning sensation when you go to the bathroom. If you don't jump on it, it can be unbearable and cause some kidney damage." I was working on memory. I'd never had a bladder infection; it was something talked about among my women friends.

"The yeast is what I get. I found me a douche that keeps me from getting the yeast. Angel, you let that get going and you got yourself big trouble. Nothin' worse than the yeast."

"Nothing, huh?"

She looked at her watch. "Gotta get you out of here before 'All My Children,'" she said. She put the cap on the polish and got up to turn on the television set. Her favorite soap; she was done talking. "You'll dry in a couple minutes," she said, spraying some fast-drying spray on my fingernails.

I found Dr. Haynes to be an affable and qualified replacement for the old country doctor, which further illustrated how resistant people can be to change. He was forty, perhaps younger. He was friendly and had a warm bedside manner and a good sense of humor. He seemed unhurried and thorough. I could easily picture him taking a cup of coffee after a house call.

He gave me my antibiotics. He listened to me discuss the rigors of letting a bladder infection get out of control and asked me if I'd ever taken prophylactic antibiotics on a morning-after basis. I was momentarily stumped. As I thought about this I realized that he could tell, from his brief examination, that I had had a rigorous night, yet there wasn't semen present. I was still touchy there. He asked me if I was sexually active and I replied, "Recently reentering." The nurse lifted an eyebrow and didn't make eye contact.

"Well," he said, "if you find that bladder infections routinely follow intercourse, some doctors have been trying prophylactic medication."

"I hadn't noticed my infections doing that," I said, blushing. I was going to have to practice this lying. I was lousy.

He did the Pap smear—nurse in the room—breast exam, and questionnaire. Here's what I hadn't figured on—but then I hadn't figured on going to the doctor. Part of every gynecological exam is the standard questions about childbirth and birth control. I had to tell about Sheffie; the nurse had to hear. The doctor was very sweet. "I'm terribly sorry, Miss Sheppard," he said. "I have children; I can't imagine."

I nearly wept. People tended to take this on themselves. It's something to which any parent can relate and feel sympathetic pain. I remember the good old days, when I shuddered to think of the possibility of a child's death.

After I was dressed and ready to leave I happened upon Dr. Haynes's open office door and feeling like a supersleuth, whispered to him, asking about this inability to ejaculate. He motioned for me to enter and sit down in front of his desk. He did not laugh or act surprised.

"Is it chronic?" he asked.

"I'm told it is," I replied, still whispering.

"I haven't treated anything like that. I recommend

the person see a urologist. Especially if there's any pain involved."

"He said it's an enviable problem," I put in.

Dr. Haynes didn't smile. "Sounds like he has a good attitude about it, but it's recognized as a form of impotence and most sufferers consider it a handicap. I was under the impression it's usually painful. Do you know if this person has looked for medical or psychological intervention?"

"No," I said. I noticed the pictures of Haynes's wife and kids on his credenza; I imagined him laughing over this at dinner.

"I would recommend a complete evaluation from a urologist," he said.

"Maybe I'll pass that on."

"You should if you're affected by the problem."

Who wouldn't be? I thought.

7

I GOT your message," Tom said. "Sorry I couldn't call you right back. I had to go over to Salida and pick up some lumber and I just got home. I've been busy as hell today. I sure feel good." I could almost hear his smile.

"And I am up to my neck. Roberta didn't come in today."

It was seven, the sun beginning its downward path as the days grew shorter, and I was home with file folders that required attention I was too preoccupied to give. I was waiting for Bodge Scully to come over.

"That's okay, Jackie. I'd love to see you, but I'd enjoy the time more if I could get some paperwork done."

"Paperwork?" I asked.

"You wouldn't think so, would you? Even a small business has its red tape. Receipts, contracts, ledgers. I'm going to make myself a sandwich, do some paperwork, and maybe later I can get this wood measured."

"I've got a mountain of paper to shuffle myself. And I'm really tired."

He laughed into the phone. "We'll have to find a

way to get together in daylight," he said. "More time, more sleep."

I shivered. Daylight dee-lite? With hours to kill, how long would he go? "Well, it's a good thing we're both too busy for the time being," I said. "I have a slight problem; a couple of things. I . . . ah . . . how can I say this?"

"Try saying it."

"First off, I did enjoy myself, and being of sound mind and body, can honestly say I knew what I was doing. But, Tom, let's not get too serious; let's take it easy."

"I disappointed you."

"No. I'm thirty-seven and set in my ways. I'm interested in having friends, not interested in a hot romance. This has nothing to do with your behavior; you were a perfect gentleman. I'm not seeing any other man nor am I looking. I am adamant about independence and freedom. I feel that our friendship is moving too far too fast. I need space."

"I'll try not to crowd you."

"I hope you can understand. I'm not ready to go steady. Besides, we enjoyed each other's company before, without the sex, and I want to be sure that that part of our friendship isn't lost."

"How could it be? 'Enhanced' would be better."

"And, also, I have a bladder infection and am temporarily off limits."

"No kidding?"

"No kidding. I might have overdone it a bit."

"I could have sworn *we* overdid it—I thought it was great. And I thought you thought so, too."

I noticed that his attention was focused on sex. I talked friendship, independence, freedom; he kept creating sexual innuendo. My regrets increased. "As I said, I'm not looking for a steady. Or a steady diet of sex either. It had been a long time for me and I think one should . . . ah . . . take it easy? Work up to it?"

"I'll take that job."

"Tom, please, this is a problem for me. I have to be careful. I'm too young to risk a life without kidneys. I'm sure the dialysis machine would get in your way."

"Jackie, I'm sorry. I hope I didn't hurt you."

"No, of course not. It's the bladder infection that hurts. And I've got a ten-day course of antibiotics to work off."

"Sometimes I don't know my own strength. Believe me, though, babe . . . I only want to make you feel good. I don't like possessiveness either. Want to make some plans for the weekend? It's not necessary. . . ."

"Let me cook for you," I said. "Since it's going to be a platonic dinner, would you like me to invite someone else? Roberta and Harry?"

"What for? It's not like we don't have anything to talk about."

"Okay, then let's make it Saturday night. I've got a lot of work to do and will have to work weekends and evenings for a while. We have a lawsuit pending. So let me get back to this and you go eat and measure your wood."

"Should I call you?"

"I'm going to be in court all day tomorrow. How about some evening later in the week?"

"Talk to you later, then," he said.

I wasn't sure how long I could carry this off. Duplicity was my enemy. There were certain things I had trained myself to do, like subdue my reactions in court or with a client. I could get information without appearing to dig or grill. I could pretend to be calm when I was afraid. What I had the most trouble with was pretending to like someone I didn't like or pretending to believe something I thought was a lie.

This was a wrong guy.

I picked up the phone. I held it for a few seconds. I thought of an excuse for calling him right back; I had heard sounds in the background of his conversation that I hadn't heard when I was at his house. It could have been his television or a radio talk show. It could also be he wasn't calling from home. Less than a minute had passed since we'd hung up.

Had I met this guy in L.A. and he'd given me these dubious impressions, I'd have canceled the next date. Got on with my life. Found another date. I could do that with Tom. I could decide, here and now, without telling him all the reasons, that I didn't want to see him anymore. I could pursue the mysterious clock-radio and lifted toilet seat with Bodge. This would all go away. I hoped I'd feel silly after trailing this to a dead end, anyway. I didn't get the right vibrations from the doctor of psychology turned low-profile carpenter, and I couldn't figure out my position in this.

I dialed. "Hi, this is Tom. I can't come to the phone right now . . ."

I hung up. He was going to make himself a sandwich, do paperwork. Would a reclusive carpenter who claimed to have only acquaintances and no real friends have any reason to screen his calls?

I bit on a pencil. When something like an abduction and murder happens in L.A. and you're filled with ghoulish curiosity, you read the papers more thoroughly. In Coleman you look suspiciously at the postman, crossing guard, and carpenter. I began to wonder about Wharton. He was, after all, an unusual character. And, undeniably, there was that business Tom mentioned of being trailed to Oregon by the psychopath. That thought sent shivers up my spine.

I waited ten minutes and dialed again. Again the recording came on. I have a recorder. If the phone rings several times followed by a disconnect and the caller keeps trying, I answer. Someone doesn't want to talk into the machine; they want to talk to me. The machine only kicks in for messages; it doesn't record the number of hangups. I tried a third time. Recorder.

I tried a couple more times and, checking the time, left a message. "Hi, Tom. You in the shower? Workshop? Screening your calls? I wondered if there's anything special you'd like me to cook Saturday night. Bye." He didn't call right back. Not in fifteen minutes, not in thirty.

Finally the doorbell rang. It was nearly eight P.M. I let Bodge Scully in.

"Hiya, Bodge. Thanks."

"I gotta admit, Jackie, I'm starting to feel like I work for the KGB."

"I'm sorry. It happened again. And this time I don't want anyone to know. I know you told Roberta about the first time; she wouldn't purposely set me up for another incident by talking about it. What the hell, you know the worst thing you can do is mention it to anyone."

"What happened this time?"

I told him about the locked doors, the clock-radio. And where I was for the evening. I was suggestive, implying intimacy without actually saying Tom and I had had sex. Bodge made the fourth person to know I'd been on a date with Tom.

"Listen, Bodge, can we have a conversation that is completely confidential? Without error?"

"We could try," he said. "Let me look at the door locks."

"Yeah, please. I bought some more new locks. I went all the way to Lincoln to get them—and I've got a tool box; will you put them on for me? I don't want to call the locksmith."

"Yeah, sure."

"So, how well do you know Tom Wahl?" I asked.

"Tom? Oh, hell, I know Tom pretty good. I had him help me add on the rumpus room at my house and he took a bunch of kids from the junior high on a trail ride last year. Two-dayer. He's a decent guy, Tom is. I see him a couple times a week in town, either buying or delivering or stopping at the café or Wolf's."

"How long has he lived here?"

"Ah, I dunno. Jackie, this lock looks okay to me. I'd have to bet on a key."

"Couldn't a good B and E man get in?"

"B 'n' E?"

I shrugged lamely.

"You just a lawyer, Jackie, or you with the FBI?"

I grinned and kind of rocked back on my heels. "Now, Bodge, that would be Bureau business . . . right?"

He got a chuckle out of that. "You said a few things that make me think you have a little police background."

It occurred to me to tell him that I had a little detective in my background. Tonight wasn't the right time to explain Mike. "All lawyers are investigators, Bodge. I've hired private investigators and worked with the police. Maybe that's why I'm so gritty on this—I know I'm not dreaming this up. It's spooky, especially since the Porter woman was found killed the way she was killed."

"What way?"

"With her clothes intact, her jewelry on."

"What's that mean to you?"

I offered up a silent prayer. Please, God, let Bodge be legitimate, trustworthy.

"That it wasn't a sexual assault and was probably premeditated," I said. "Someone took her a long way from home and he had a shovel with him. That implies a plan. Since she had taken her child to preschool and hadn't made arrangements for someone else to pick him up, she didn't know she was going far. But she went willingly."

"Oooo-weeee. Well. Motive?"

"If I knew the motive, I could hand you her killer, now couldn't I? Unless the motive was to kill her. Period."

"Meaning?" he asked. The look in his eye suggested he was prepared for my answer, perhaps also the only answer he had come up with.

"Meaning, her killer was looking for someone to kill, and that's about all."

"I hate the sound of that," he said. "But what we found makes it look possible." He paused, and his expression darkened. "You and Roberta are already on my list of people who know a few forensic details. I never thought to tell you to keep your mouth shut; don't have to tell Roberta. I reckon you know better than to talk about it."

"You bet. I wouldn't want to help inspire a copycat."

"Her hands were bound behind her back with twine; there was a clear plastic bag tied over her head. Her jaw was broken; I think someone knocked her cold before killing her. Now, that could've happened anywhere. Could've happened right in her house and she was carried to a waiting car; could've happened somewhere between Coleman and Canon City."

"Leah thinks she was having an affair with the kind of man Nicole calls real illegal. What kind of guy does that represent to you, Bodge?"

"Senators and priests." He shrugged. "Get your tool box."

"You bet."

We talked while he put the new locks on the doors and accused me of building a prison. I asked him about Billy; he said he thought Billy was square as a block and easy to watch should he, in the most extreme situation, become any kind of suspect. Billy, Bodge said, was incapable of such a complex crime—as he was incapable of breaking into houses and lying on beds. "If you knew the number of times we've had to get into his house for him or open his truck for him, you'd never even ask."

I asked about local law-enforcement people, local judges, and fast as a whip he said, "Don't you worry too much if Bud pinches your ass. Turn around and coldcock him once and threaten to call his wife; that'll fix him."

"You know about him?"

"Mrs. Scully offered to turn that stallion into a gelding with one shot; she ain't dealt with him since. He's harmless. Kind of hard to believe such a smart man could be such a fucking idiot. Oops. Sorry 'bout that."

I laughed in spite of myself; I might have been laughing to think of Bodge's wife getting pinched. She must surely be a female version of Bodge, over-weight, sloppy, and painfully homely.

Bodge was unprepared for my request that the windows on the ground floor be nailed shut. "Aren't you getting extreme here, Jackie? What if there's a fire?"

"I'm capable of breaking a window if necessary," I assured him. With my head, if need be. It was certainly hard enough.

I told him what Nicole said about Kathy Porter: falling off on her soaps, shopping alone, doing her housework at night. He grunted, nodded; he was up to date on that.

"You think there's a killer around here, Bodge?"

"If there's a murderer here, I don't know why I don't smell him. Kathy Porter's the only woman ever missing from this town found dead, and if we have a killer on our hands, he's a lazy one. Nope, Jackie, what bothers me is thinking someone passed through, chose Kathy as a victim in a random search, and we'll never get him."

"I didn't mean a serial killer; maybe a man who murdered a woman because she got in the way or she was going to tell something on him."

"Jackie, half the men in this town got a woman in the way or one who'll tell secrets. We can't call them all suspects."

"Well," I attempted, "then you have to find out who has the biggest secret. Or is the best manipulator and liar."

"Listen, Jackie, don't go stirring up Nicole or I ain't never going to get any work done. I'm sorry you got some strange stuff going on here, but I don't think there's any connection between what you got and what Kathy got. She could have been walking to the library, took a ride, and—"

I was shaking my head. Her car was in the driveway; she'd been keeping secrets about how her days were spent; she'd been growing discontented with her marriage; she'd lost some weight. "Bodge, she knew her killer. She had to. How many friends did she have out of town that she'd have gone off with on a whim while her kid was in a three-hour preschool?"

Bodge sighed. "I agree. She knew him."

"Why do you think that?" I pushed contrarily.

"Because she knew she was going. She got her housework all done first so she wouldn't have to rush around later. She had everything done and meat was thawing for supper. She thought she was going for a ride. A short enough ride to get back in time to pick up her son. And she took her purse. We never found her purse."

You should never underestimate a man's powers of deductive reasoning because he seems simple, ordinary. Bodge had the appearance of a dummy, to get honest. He was overweight, unobtrusive, and homely, and had poor grammar attached to a drawl. He seemed sloppy. These aren't usually thought of as characteristics of brilliance, of canny thinking. Bodge was canny.

"She knew who she was going with."

"I think so," Bodge said. "Unless there's some angle I can't dream up. I think about this all night, all day."

"You *are* looking for a killer here!"

He waited a moment to answer me, studying my eyes. "What're you after here?"

"I don't know. Relentless curiosity. I think you've got yourself a killer somewhere around here. He might be in the next town; he might be a hundred miles away. I have a nagging feeling that Kathy Porter found herself with a questionable character—someone whose dark side she didn't sense—and he meant to kill her all along."

"I'm looking around," Bodge said slowly.

"Have you checked around to see if there have

been any other murders like that one? Or any phantom-type invasions like are happening to me? Want me to check when I'm at the courthouse or state police—"

"Jackie, we got teletype. We aren't goddamn hicks. And no, we haven't found any connections yet."

"I didn't mean to insult you, Bodge. Never mind, I guess I ought to let you do your job. . . . Bodge, don't make a report on this visit, okay?"

"We have never had a problem with police reports before."

"You ever have one of your nice little housewives buried with a plastic bag over her head before?"

"I'm telling you, I think you're safe. I think you're safer with Tom around than you would be with me around."

This was the entrée I'd been looking for. "Want to know what I know about Tom? He checks and doesn't check. He says his name is really Tom Lawler; he says he's really a Ph.D. psychologist who came here to start a new life after his wife and daughter were killed by some psychopath he testified against in court.

"Every guy I've ever been involved with had connections to other people I knew and trusted. He worked with people I worked with or maybe was the cousin of my best friend's husband. Tom? He doesn't connect with anybody. And nobody knows about his trouble except me and Roberta. He asked me not to tell anyone and Roberta is silenced by attorney-client privilege. Now do you understand why I have the willies?"

"Jeez. Tom?"

"See? That's it. I actually feel sorry for him; it's a helluva thing. That hideous crime was not his fault, either, and no reason it should follow him around.

Oh, he feels it was his fault in the way that he wasn't paying attention, his work endangered his family . . . the way a cop might feel if the bad guy gets away and hurts someone. You know what I mean; he was probably helpless to prevent it.

"Or what if what he was put through really messed him up? What if he *is* off-balance? Huh?"

"You're going out with him; you aren't scared of him."

"I'm unsure about him. Some of his behavior is suspicious. He's very persistent, very possessive. I invited him to dinner Saturday night and I'm going to cook. I hope to convince him to give me more space, leave me alone a little. I don't feel good about Wharton, either. He's all alone out there next to Tom and he's an old fart; unfriendly, withdrawn, scowling all the time like he hates the world. He has a mean look in his eyes—you gotta admit that."

"Wharton? Hell, he's had that look in his eyes since I met him forty-odd years ago. He's just a pain in the ass, that's all. He's a good guy. Now, of that I'm sure."

"How do you know?"

"I knew his family; I've known them all for years. He's no different than he was in the fourth grade, and he isn't one drop mean. Wharton will help out a neighbor before I will."

"He doesn't like his neighbor now, I hear."

"Wharton gets like that sometimes; he's stubborn and narrow." He winked at me. "I keep my eyes and ears open. All the time."

"Me, too. And I'm always checking details. I guess that's why I'm already aware of Tom's bad past, Wharton's mean eyes, Bud's clumsy come-ons. Single women who are smart pay attention to the men who enter their lives."

"Well," he said, pausing to think, "you should, I

guess. Yeah, you should. You gotta understand, Jackie. I don't know squat about what it's like to be single. We got domestic trouble and I don't understand any of it. I arrest."

"Small towns are worse in the domestic-trouble department, I think, than big cities. That's my conclusion after a few months in Roberta's office."

"Nicole or Roberta tell you about the Tray family?"

"No."

"Roberta wouldn't. Roberta's the only woman I know who doesn't talk. Harry talks, so Roberta even quit talking to him. The Trays. He was a painter. They moved here from White Plains, New York, to be peaceful and have a 'natural' lifestyle with their eighteen-year-old daughter.

"Trays stayed isolated. They never really settled. They bought that big old run-down Millborn ranch on the south ridge and kept to themselves. My nose was working real good and I smelled trouble, but I didn't see anything. After about a year we had ourselves a murder-suicide. And it was her. Killed her husband and daughter. Left us poor folks a forty-seven-page suicide note." He wiped his forehead with his hand. "After I read it, I wanted to commit murder-suicide. Nothin' but bad stuff."

"What kind of bad stuff?"

"Bad family stuff: brutality, incest, pornography. The girl wasn't eighteen but fourteen. She didn't go to school. This letter the woman left was terrible, a chronicle. I knew something wasn't right about them. I felt odd about the way they acted, and I knew it was all wrong, and I was right, but Jesus. What could I do?

"Jackie—there ain't anybody in Coleman I don't understand at the moment. 'Cept maybe Raymond, my eighteen-year-old. He's a jackass if ever. At the jackass age, too. So here's the ticket—I'm not thinking about Tom or Wharton, because there isn't any reason to. I won't say anything about your locks or our talk, and I'm a humble man. You get me a murder suspect and I'll be very grateful. Just for God's sake be careful what you do and where you do it."

"Believe me, I will."

"You're locked up tight; I don't worry that this is going to keep happening. If you have anything valuable, I'd suggest a deposit box or vault."

"There's only me," I said. "Which is why, I guess, Kathy Porter's murder interests me."

"I don't know why you gotta get into this."

"Curious. Women aren't safe. The safest woman isn't as safe as the average man. Women, children, puppies: By being who they are they become victims. Somebody's going to a great bother to upset me, scare me. I'd like to know who and why, and I'd like to know what happened to Kathy Porter. I hope you're right, Bodge. I hope there's no connection."

I had a strong and deep sense of apprehension. I foresaw two possibilities. One, that I was diving into a private investigation that would yield me a feeling of foolishness and maybe find out some benign character—like a kid or a senile old man—had been in my house. Maybe it would simply stop with new locks. Or, second possibility, find out that the psychologist was off-balance, in which case he would be put away for a long rest.

At ten-thirty Tom called. He had changed his mind about the paperwork, had been in the workshop with the sander and saw running. He wanted to get all the dirty work done before his shower; when he did come upstairs to the house, he never looked at his machine—he showered, ate, and got started on paperwork. He was sorry to be calling so late. He felt terrible. What if I had needed him?

"Don't be so silly; what if I needed you when you were on your way to Salida or Colorado Springs? If I'm not capable of taking care of myself at this point, having you sit by the phone for my next urgent call isn't going to help me. So, what would you like to eat?"

"Anything you like, Jackie. It's your dinner."

My neighbor to the south was an elderly woman who lived alone, Mrs. Wright. She wasn't friendly. She opened her door just wide enough to show her thin face, pursed lips, and furrowed brow. I explained that a bouquet of flowers had been delivered and they weren't from a florist; I had a secret admirer and was curious whether she had seen anyone come to my house.

"I saw the police car there," she said.

"Oh, that was something else altogether," I said. "I should explain; I'm a lawyer and work for Roberta Musetta. You might see the sheriff now and then, bringing me paperwork or picking some up. There are things like restraining orders or subpoenas that have to be coordinated through the county sheriff. Sometimes we don't get it all done during business hours. . . ."

The neighbors on the north side, a couple in their thirties with two youngsters about ten and twelve, were friendly and wanted me to come in for coffee or a beer. Sybil and Matt Dania. Sybil worked in the cafeteria at the grade school and Matt worked for the telephone company. I went through the same drill about the flowers, explained they might see a police car for the reason of legal papers. They had seen nothing. They were apologetic about not getting over to introduce themselves; they gave the vibrations of potential friends.

Roberta missed work on Friday. She called Peggy and gave no explanation. Being self-absorbed at this point, I didn't contact her and ask if anything was wrong; when dealing with someone as tough and resilient as Roberta, one tends to think there are never problems. This time there were. They had nothing to do with me.

Saturday night had all my attention. The evening itself was okay. Tom happened to like talking about himself.

I handed him a glass of wine. "Your fingernails look pretty," he said.

"That reminds me of something curious I wanted to ask you. Nicole said you and Wharton don't get along. Isn't he that old man in the baseball cap who sits with the guys—scowling the whole time—at the kafeeklatsch at the café?"

"Wharton," he said with a laugh, nodding. "How'd that come up?"

"Accidentally. She was asking who I'd met so far in Coleman, and when I mentioned your name she remarked on how good-looking and shy you are. I said I thought you were about the friendliest person I'd met so far. Then, who do I have to compare you to? Roberta? Anyway, she decided maybe you were quiet around that group of men because Wharton makes it no secret he doesn't get along with you. She said you and Wharton have been fighting since you moved in."

He chuckled, shook his head, sipped his wine. "Wharton," he said again. "Hell, he made up his mind about me before I moved onto that lot. I bought the land he wanted, for starters. He's damn near the crankiest old coot I've met; I hear he's kindhearted underneath. You couldn't prove it by me. He hated me on sight."

"Well," I said, going back to the kitchen, beginning to move baked potatoes and salad and broccoli to my small dining room table while the beef brisket was under the broiler. "Have you tried to make up with him?"

"Aw, I tried doing everything his way and that didn't work; he keeps coming up with more problems he's convinced are my fault. His cattle got out once and he said I must've opened the gate. His fence got knocked down; he said it had to be me ran it down since I was the only one up that road, and he demanded I fix it. I was going to do it, too. Then he pissed me off. You ought to see him, Jackie. Sometimes when I drive by that fork that goes to Sixteen, he's standing there staring at me with a shovel or something in his hand. Standing there, looking mean." He laughed again. "I can't fix *him*, that's for damn sure."

"Keep talking," I said. "I can hear you and I'll get this dinner rolling."

"I understand Wharton has had a hard time of it the last few years. His wife died, his boys moved away when he was counting on at least one of them to take over his ranch. I guess this business about property gets to be a big deal to some of these people. Guessing from what little bit I've heard, I get the notion that Wharton's ranch is fairly pissant and his boys—men, actually—don't have any interest in taking it on. They moved away and I don't know that they've been back or that Wharton's gone to visit. Seems like he'd ask me or someone else nearby to feed for him if he went on a visit, and I never heard that anyone has.

"I figure Wharton is disappointed and working too hard for a man his age; protective of his land and animals and cranky because things aren't going his way. So, he's an ornery old man, working to keep it all going for no good reason except so he can have a place to die.

"Maybe I'm kidding myself, but I think I could be Jesus himself and Wharton wouldn't like me. I think he doesn't like many people and he's carrying around a big load of resentments. He sure is a pain in the ass."

"Well . . . what does he do? Call you and complain? Drive over to your place?"

"Oh, hell no, that would be dealing with the problem. He either waits for me at the fork and in less than ten words demands something—like that I use less well water. Or he says something snotty to me at the café. One day when I was getting a cup of coffee to go and said hello to the morning group, Wharton says, 'You mowed down that fence last night; you can put her up.' And I say, 'What are you talking about? Mowed down what fence?' And he says, 'The one after the fork to Sixteen.' And I say I didn't do that; I would have noticed something like that. And he justifies it by saying he didn't do it and no one else comes down that road. My truck is fine, I know I didn't mow down his fence, and he gives that stony look and announces that 'You and me both know you mowed down that fence. You gonna fix it?'

"Pretty soon all the other men get a little antsy and wiggle around and clear their throats and get up. Even the rest of them get tired of it. Not a one of them says, 'Now, Wharton, how do you know for certain it was Tom?' They just kind of let him go."

"And you said no?"

"I said, 'You prove I ruined your fence, I'll fix it. Otherwise, I want you to stay off my case.' That's the only way to handle someone like Wharton."

"Must be aggravating," I put in.

"That's all. Aggravating. He isn't bothering anyone but me, and if I let him get to me, it's my problem. He's a hurtin' old man underneath all that hostility."

"It's got to be hard to live next door to someone like that," I said when we were having dinner.

"Jackie, you've been to my place," he said, smiling. "I'd be a damn fool to ever complain. It's beautiful and comfortable, and when I'm at my house on top of that hill and watch the sun go up and down, I'm at peace. After Los Angeles, I'm grateful."

"I heard the bad stuff already," I said. "Tell me the other stuff about your life. Your family, your work, your education, all that."

"It's boring."

"No, I'd love it."

"The only thing about my life that isn't boring is awful."

"I'd still like to hear the boring stuff."

8

Tom Lawler had had an ordinary childhood. "The only thing that wasn't strictly average was that I got good grades from the very first and scored high on achievement tests. You remember way back then; there weren't a lot of 'gifted' programs for slightly above-average kids. I got a partial scholarship to the University of Illinois. Studied sociology. Got drafted."

"You were in the Army?"

"Well, it was 1970; no more deferments. I was lucky; ended up I didn't go to Vietnam, so I did two years of busywork in North Carolina and started applying to universities for my advanced degree. Columbia took me without a quibble."

Tom was the youngest of three boys, but he was the only natural son. His older brothers had been adopted. His parents didn't think they were going to have children and adopted two baby boys two years apart. Seven years after the second one, along came Tom.

To grease the gears, I talked about my own childhood, about making doll-people out of toothpicks and hollyhocks with my mom, going to the college library with my dad, learning to sew from my mom, disastrous prom dates, and the time I wet my pants in first grade and was humiliated for life.

He told me about his mother being like Edith Bunker, in the way she bustled around the house and had this high-pitched and naïve whine, fretting constantly about her husband and the boys. His dad was an untalkative mechanic; didn't have much to say but worked on cars with his sons like a surgeon. Tom talked about Little League, high-school baseball, and the problems of having older parents, to which I could relate.

"You keep in touch with your family?" I asked.

"Sure, though not as much as I could. To start with, we're not a real close family. My dad died a couple of years ago and my mom lives with my oldest brother, John. I call, I send a Mother's Day card, visit every couple of years. We were never that tight, and after I was in trouble everyone got nervous. They love me, I guess. My mom believes in me; she never thought I could do anything that bad. But . . ."

I felt that pain inside; that ache of feeling not good enough. Being blamed when you're innocent. Injustice could wring barrels of sympathy from me.

So what Tom told me he did was marry the girl back home before going in the Army; he took her with him to Columbia, where he was first noticed when he did a paper on domestic violence and became an expert. He was offered a good position by the state of California as a Ph.D. in the Department of Social Services. His primary job was evaluating inmates, criminals, and defendants. Testing was his specialty. Interviews and counseling evaluations were also part of the process.

"So you usually worked with people who were on the wrong side of the law?"

"Bearing in mind that not all of them belonged on the wrong side. I found a number of people who appeared to have been convicted on shabby evidence—had had inferior defense representation—and shouldn't have been locked up at all; some who should have been remanded to medical care; and some criminals. I continued to treat a few with counseling if the court would remand them to counseling. Testing was my gift. I was hot. Like I told you, that's when I started to get in trouble without getting caught."

I didn't want to hear any more about his trouble. I wanted to hear his other stuff.

"Do you miss anything about counseling, testing?"

"It's interesting, challenging, that's what I miss. I still have my credentials even if I did get canned. I've written a couple of articles for the hell of it."

"No kidding? For what?"

"For money."

"No." I laughed. "For magazines?"

"Yeah. I did four or five pieces on psychological evaluation and testing, and for a woman's magazine I did a commercial piece on getting a family member a psychological evaluation. You know, like if you think your husband is acting strange and don't know what to do to find out if he *is* strange. I listed behavior checkpoints and services."

"What was your most interesting case?" I asked. "I mean besides the bad one or the guy who liked to sit in people's cars."

"Oh, I don't know," he said, seeming to shrug it off while he chewed down on brisket. I gave him more wine. "I did have a nymphomaniac once and that was kind of fun."

I laughed. "Fun? Or tempting?"

"Not tempting in the usual sense, believe me. I

know I admitted already that I was kind of promiscuous back then myself, but I never was attracted to sex addicts. Imagine two sex addicts together, killing themselves slowly? Jeez. The impact of it was hard on me, pardon the pun. What was fun was this: I knew she was a sex addict right away, and after about four sessions I figured out that in counseling she had another place to experience her sexual exploits. She liked to talk about it. I had to make her stop telling me about sex."

"Aw. Was there anything left to talk about?"

"She was kind of neat. She was married, had a couple of kids, worked in real estate in L.A., and had no shortage of men or opportunities to screw. She would go out on calls to show homes, condos, and office space and show her panties." He laughed. He had me laughing in no time. "Her exploits were fun to listen to; she had all these outrageous near-misses. Like she was showing a house to a man while the owners waited on their patio, and she screwed the prospective buyer in the laundry room on top of the washer and dryer.

"Another time she did it in a fitting room in a department store, another time in a movie theater—not a drive-in, a theater. Now, try to imagine, I was about twenty-six, full of energy, charged up most of the time on those unmentionable illegal medications, and this woman was not only giving me graphic details of every little sexual adventure she'd ever had, she was blatant in her come-on to me. So, picture this, if you can: I'm not attracted and professionally I'm supposed to be objective, and I still have this little problem that my body doesn't remember I'm not aroused. I listened to these X-rated stories and I had to stay behind the desk or die of embarrassment. And I started to look forward to her appointments.

"I still had some ethics then; I gave her to a female colleague. Poor thing; she quit counseling. I often wonder what's become of her. Wonder if she's died of AIDS yet."

"I don't suppose you keep in touch with anyone from those days?"

"Sure, I have a couple of friends I keep in touch with. Remember, people were stunned by what happened. Then I dropped out of sight for a while."

He still had not mentioned names of friends or colleagues. No teachers, mentors, or bosses. He had only mentioned one brother's name. It was always "There was this guy" or "There was this woman." Nameless, faceless, rootless people. "So you went to Oregon. No one in Oregon was affected by your trouble in L.A. You must keep in touch with friends from Oregon."

"To Oregon to work for a private facility as a counselor. I drew the old twenty-two thousand a year as a first-year counselor who talked to codependent housewives, overstressed businessmen, alcoholics, people with eating disorders, and that kind of stuff. For a couple of years."

"Ordinary clientele?"

"Nothing is ordinary. Everyone has something to work out—doesn't always have to be in counseling. Some of these pop-psych books are good; twelve-step programs are changing people's lives. I think about some of the people I had as clients.

"There was a guy I used to see who, until the age of forty, had a charmed life. He managed to get himself to a position of importance in a big corporation, made lots of money, was under extreme pressure, had traveled widely; he had every social and economic advantage. All of a sudden he became disoriented—developed phobias and paranoias. Aside from lots of fears, he was feelingless. He didn't care about anything. He'd cry in my office and not know why. Here was a smart, good-looking man, suddenly chronically depressed.

"Well," Tom went on, "we had to get our M.D. to prescribe some antidepressants to get him going in therapy. Right away, on intake information, I found that there were large segments of his childhood that he couldn't remember.

"We had to move into family therapy for a while. Jackie, this guy was absolutely crushed over something. When I saw him with his family—wife and teenaged kids—he could barely hold it together. When I saw him alone, he came apart. I wanted to put him in the hospital immediately.

"We finally learned that he had had a younger brother who was severely handicapped, mentally and physically. He took up all his parents' time and energy, wore them out. This guy got nothing from his family; his folks were worn to nubs by the time their younger son died. My client somehow went into adolescence believing he had killed his brother to get his parents back. He spent his youth telling himself that it was his fault, that he had killed the boy, and then spent his early adult years trying to block what he had accepted as truth."

"How sad," I said. "And you're sure he didn't?"

"His brother died in an infirmary and there are records. My client's parents suffered a combination of grief and exhaustion and didn't help their surviving son in any way. The parents acted as though an ornery house guest had left; my client had all this grief and affection to deal with. My client had been neglected and was not exhausted; although his younger brother was in terrible condition, my client had spent time with him, loved him, visited him, and had developed a relationship with him.

"See what the mind can create and suppress? He developed a scenario in which he killed his brother, then suppressed the imaginary crime and became a success . . . and then finally his mind would not cooperate. He had what laymen would call a nervous breakdown."

"How did you treat him?"

"Hospitalization and antidepressants and intensive therapy. Added to that was family counseling including his mother, and finally outpatient therapy. The minute the pieces were put in the puzzle, he stopped being paranoid. Neglect and abuse are dangerous disease makers."

"Do you think about any other patients?" I asked him, pouring him more wine. "Want coffee?"

"Yes, to the coffee. You can't find this interesting."

"Of course I do. *You* find it interesting; why shouldn't I?"

I made coffee and went back to the dining room. I pushed him to tell me a couple more. A woman who had beaten her children and was attempting to gather up the family threads and make amends; a minister who was a religious fanatic and couldn't seem to hold a ministry together because sane parishioners rejected him; a man who suffered childhood abuse and was sociopathic and frighteningly brilliant.

"I can't even remember how this guy got into counseling—maybe a condition of employment, court order, something. I don't know if he was telling me the truth; he sure had a story. He went to school up to about the fourth grade, when his father arbitrarily decided to take him out. His father had a big piece of farmland and grew wheat. He had no brothers or sisters, he said ... that he knew of, he said. His parents worked him, this little kid. And beat and abused him. His mother was terrorized by his father; his father sexually molested him. His mother cooperated in the sexual abuse. He had fantasies about killing them both, which I thought was reasonable, and I didn't get the feeling he was planning to carry them out.

"He was in his twenties when I saw him. I gave him IQ tests prepared for the learning-disabled first, then regular tests. He had a photographic memory, advanced cognitive thinking; he could unravel complex story ideas. He had superhuman math skills after being taught some basic math concepts. Brilliant. And sociopathic."

"Sociopathic. Explain."

"No conscience. He couldn't make and keep friendships; he couldn't form positive relationships. He had a horrible temper and was always right; always. He wrote letters to editors that were filled with five-syllable words and beautiful prose—too hot and crazy to print. He'd misspell ... until being corrected once, and after that he'd get the words right every time. I suggested a GED and he told me it would be pretty impossible to go back and make up from third grade on, and, that he didn't need any fucking piece of paper to know how smart he was. He told me anything I wanted to know, with zero emotion. He told me about the temper; I never saw it. He was cool and controlled. . . ."

"I wonder about him," Tom ended.

"What kind of childhood abuse makes a sociopath?" I asked.

"There are a lot of theories. You can take one kid

who suffered neglect and abuse and he becomes a criminal, and take another one, similar circumstances, and he becomes a neurosurgeon. You tell me."

"You don't think it's environmental?"

"Well, could be. This guy had a mean old son-of-a-bitch father who raped him and worked him; that's not a role model for a conscience. And a mother who couldn't protect him. Then figure in his superior intelligence. Where does that come from?"

"Intelligence isn't connected to moral behavior," I said. "Hitler taught us that one."

Tom smiled. "Very good. You should get certified."

"What if you're so brutally abused that the only safe place is inside your head and survival means being smarter than your captors? Don't you ever wonder if he went back to the farm and killed them? His parents?"

"Yeah," said Tom. "Hell, *I* wanted to go kill them."

"What did you ever find out about Devalian's childhood?"

"Devalian was a psychopath; irresponsible, lack of remorse or shame, liar and convincingly so, compulsive criminal and antisocial behavior. He said he was in a gang; he left his family at a young age. I'm certain he was abused; I never ran into a sociopath or psychopath from a nurturing family. Thing is, they can't help it. Can't."

It was midnight before he was talked out. I indulged in only one glass of wine and then drank cranberry juice for my imaginary bladder infection. I calmed so much in listening to him; his stories were compelling and his delivery of them filled with feeling and compassion. I had begun the evening feeling tense. As he was leaving, he said he had noticed my nervousness and I admitted that I might be feeling pressured into a relationship.

"I wish you wouldn't be so suspicious of me, Jackie. It's such fun to have an intelligent woman to talk to."

"I want to live here a long time; I don't want to rush into a relationship without being sure and then break up, go through all the humiliation of being considered fickle and the embarrassment of looking like a woman on the make. Let's be friends for a while. No expectations."

"Okay by me. Will I be in trouble if I admit I liked the other night? I wouldn't mind more nights like that."

"I'm flattered. But that was too impetuous; I'd rather nights like that come after more nights like this, when our friendship is established and solid."

"Then you leave me a message when you want me to call. I don't want you to think I'm pushing you. I don't want anyone who doesn't want me."

"Okay," I said. "I'll give you a call."

When he was gone I cleaned up the kitchen and decided, for the twentieth time, that I had been ridiculous. There was nothing about him that should bother me. The idea that something had been happening in my house drifted far from my mind. I slept soundly and awoke rested.

Sunday morning I had coffee, turned on the stereo, read the Sunday paper for hours. It was noon before I noticed, as I passed the open dining-room doors, that there was something on the table. I walked closer and had a start.

A wineglass lay on its side and a bright red stain soiled the white linen tablecloth. Closer inspection told me it was cranberry juice. And the back-door dead bolt was open.

That's when Sweeny became my roommate.

9

LATHROP Munroe Sweeny, sheriff's deputy, is a six-foot-four-inch, strapping, twenty-eight-year-old boy who doesn't seem, at first, to be overly smart. One of my first thoughts upon meeting him was that I might be safer with just about anyone else. He was frowny, made do with grunting in lieu of talking, and he had those dark, hooded eyes that when brooding look mean.

It was Sunday noon when I called Bodge at home. A small female voice answered the phone and I asked for him. I told him what had happened and he asked me to drive over to his house and sit down for a talk.

Coleman has a downtown district, about eight blocks' worth, and residential streets around the town. From Wet Mountain Valley, in which the town is set, one can see foothills rising behind the populated streets that stretch for about four blocks each way. I lived on one of those streets. The houses resemble miniature Victorians, sixty or eighty years old. The sidewalks are cracked and the front yards are small. Huge elm, ash, and aspen line the narrow, potholed streets in town; Coleman looks, except for the hilly contours, like Mayberry.

Many of the residents of Coleman took advantage, as Tom and Bodge did, of larger acreage outside the town. The sheriff's office was in Pleasure, and Bodge had a place off the county road that led to his office. When I drove up I noticed a kind of bedraggled country look: A cyclone fence surrounded a side yard; the driveway was dirt; the lawn was sparse and had gone yellow. Behind the house was a garage or minibarn or large shed and there were three old cars that seemed to have been abandoned in the midst of restoration or repair. There were a swing set that had rusted and a couple of old oil drums; the lawnmower was sitting out and had a dog lead hanging over the handle; and there was what seemed to be a pyramid stack of coffee cans plus stray cans all over the place.

It looked like Bodge; tired and sloppy. I was unprepared for the rest.

The door was opened by a small, bleached-blond, and attractive woman who looked years younger than Bodge. She could have passed for thirty-five and I wondered if she was a second wife. Her makeup was heavy and impeccable, her hair was teased around her crown and long in the back, and her nails were long and bright red. She had a tiny, compact figure; narrow waist, full bosom, round but not fat hips. She wore her jeans too tight; her sweater came exactly to her waist. She looked like sex appeal was her motive. But I was about to become acquainted with a woman who was not overtly sexy.

"Hi, Miss Sheppard," she said, smiling. "I'm Sue Scully. Come on in; Bodge told me about you."

I stepped inside the front door onto polished oak floors. To the immediate left was an immaculate, beautifully furnished living room, done in French provincial, on a thick cream-colored carpet. To the

right, a shining formal dining room. I followed her
into a spacious kitchen done in doorless cupboards
with bright blue hanging pots. Fragile plates and
cups and crystal—hard to picture in Bodge's big
ham-fist—decorated these shelves. There was a
breakfast bar separating the kitchen from the family
room and a table in front of the bay window. The
curtains, white and blue, were fresh and crisp-look-
ing. The family room was more masculine; a patterned rug covered the beautiful floors. The TV was
crackling some sporting event and Bodge flipped it
off with his remote. He hoisted himself out of a
leather recliner. "Hi, Jackie. How ya doin'?"

"This is beautiful, Bodge. I thought you said you
were building?"

"His game room," Sue said. "Our room is that
way"—she pointed to the right—"and the kids'
rooms are that way, and he's been building a game
room on their side, off their hall, for six or seven
years now."

"Because Sue's on their case every second that they
can't mess up the family room, so I been working on
a game room."

"Except they'll all be gone before there's a game
room."

"For the grandkids, then," he said.

She grinned at me and shook her head. "We have
two grandkids already and only Raymond and
Trisha still live at home. Trisha's a sophomore this
year . . . so it isn't going to be long. 'Course, I may
never shed Raymond."

The family-room fireplace mantel was covered
with many years of family pictures. I was astonished;
Sue was obviously the mother of all four kids, two
of whom were adults, and she looked young enough
to be Bodge's daughter. Or Bodge looked old enough

to be her father. In any case, I never would have put the two of them together.

"Coffee?" she asked me. "I'm doing some ironing."

She had her ironing board set up and a bunch of sheriff's shirts hanging from the doorway molding. I accepted the coffee and had a flash of pity for her. As immaculate and impeccable as she was, as crisp and perfect as those ironed shirts looked, it must kill her to have her husband look so much like an unmade bed all the time.

"I been talking to Sue about this, Jackie . . ."

"Oh, Bodge, you promised . . ."

"Promises don't include Sue," he said, not the least remorseful.

"He tells me most things, and be glad," she said. "First, everybody has to have someone they can talk to, and second, I'm smart in some of the things that Bodge isn't. When it has to do with women and kids, you want me on his staff. And third, you can be sure it isn't Bodge who's giving you the go-around."

"Anyway, Sue thinks maybe you ought to have someone stay with you for a while."

"Who?"

"Sweeny," Sue said, giving the shirt she was working on a squirt of spray starch. "Lathrop Munroe Sweeny." She laughed. "Only a person who doesn't know Sweeny would come within a mile of you with him there. Bodge was telling me that whoever has been in your house isn't doing anything except leaving clues he's been there. Or she, who knows? You live next door to Mrs. Wright, and I've always thought she's dotty."

"You know Mrs. Wright?"

"Sure. I used to walk to school past her house. She doesn't keep things up much anymore. She used to have flower beds that she was digging in all the time and she gave the kids hell for getting near them. I swear, she hollered at 'em when they were across the street. I don't know where the 'Mrs.' comes from; I never knew a man ever to go near there and that's gotta be thirty-five years ago I walked past her house. She doesn't talk to anybody; she yells at dogs and kids. She's an old bitty." Sue made a face and lowered her voice. "I bet she's an old spinster."

"She must be seventy-five or more," I said. "Maybe she was married young and her husband died and she never remarried."

"My mother can't remember any husband, either. Back to you—you ought to have Sweeny stay with you a few nights, now that this bozo is going in your house while you're there. It's one thing for you to come home and find someone's been there, but while you're sleeping? That's too much."

"I don't think whoever this is means any real harm," Bodge said.

"That's what you know," his wife told him. Then she looked at me. "We haven't ever had anything like this before. It sounds dangerous to me. I can't figure it out. It's not the usual pervert stuff; it's a kind of psychological terrorism. I asked Bodge if he thought you were maybe trying to get some attention, but—"

"Sue!"

"Well, it's a reasonable question and has to be asked. But he said—"

"I'm not, Mrs. Scully; I could find a lot of better ways to get attention and sleep better at night."

" 'Course you're not, Jackie. Can I call you Jackie? And you call me Sue. No, Bodge says that he and Roberta, too, figure something is going on. You're new in town, living alone, and someone has decided to get a charge out of scaring you. You know, like obscene phone callers like to do."

"When did Bodge tell you about it?"

"Oh . . . I don't know. Right away, I guess."

"So what do you think about Tom? I cooked Tom dinner last night. He's almost the extent of my social life."

She shrugged. "I thought about Tom. Seems like this would have started happening right after you met him. That's when he was in your house all the time fixing, what was it, shelves and a bathroom? Well, why would he all of a sudden start creeping into your house after he's got an invitation to come? I don't know Tom that well, but it doesn't seem very logical."

"Does any of this seem logical?"

"Oh, sure, Jackie," she said. "Not to Bodge, because he sees things in black and white; it's legal or it's a crime. The logic in this is the same logic as in phone calls, exhibitionism, that sort of thing. Somebody likes the power of working you up. Pervert."

"Sue tells me that I don't understand crimes that victimize women; crimes like she said—obscene phone calls and flashers." Bodge shrugged and went to the coffee pot. "She's mostly right—I don't get the point. There must be a point because we sure get more of that stuff than regular old bank robberies. I can't figure out the payoff."

"Bodge doesn't have a perverted bone in his body," Sue explained. "The payoff is you get to live on the edge for a while, sneaking around and doing something bad, the danger of getting caught versus getting away with it sends off a shot of adrenaline. There's control—you get to watch someone run away or hear them gasp and hang up. You get to picture them not being able to sleep or pick up the phone without being nervous or scared." She stared at me and lifted one slim, light-brown eyebrow. "Power," she said.

"Like what's-his-name, remember, Bodge? That crossing guard who used to accidentally leave his pecker hanging out of his pants till they fired him?"

A bubble of laughter came out of me. "Who?"

"Aw, he's long gone. That was a long time ago," Bodge said, annoyed.

"Right here in Coleman?"

"Honey, Coleman isn't that much different than anywhere else except maybe people are more careful because it's easier to get found out in a place where everyone knows everyone . . . and their truck. We had a guy who stole undies off people's clotheslines. He's still right here—in church every Sunday, which is why I won't name him."

"What'd you do?" I asked Bodge.

"I told him if he didn't knock it off, he'd be wearing undies on his head. There are advantages to being a cop in a small town," he said, sipping his coffee. "Sometimes you get to make up the law, not just enforce it."

I looked back at Sue. "You almost sound like a psychologist," I said.

"Just a cop's wife," she said. "And I read magazines and novels. I listen to Bodge, read, and listen to Bodge some more."

"We don't have serious crime around here," Bodge said. "Haven't had a rape around here in . . . jeez, a long, long time."

"Yes we have," Sue argued. "Date rape, marital rape, and miscellaneous rape. Now that it's been on Oprah, a lot of women are realizing—"

"Let's not get on that," Bodge told his wife. "Here's what I'd like to do, Jackie. I want to print the glass at your house and send Sweeny over to sleep on your couch this week. Because I don't understand this, which means there could be more to it than I think.

Sweeny is a big boy, and he isn't married so he won't be putting anyone out."

"I'd go stay with you myself," Sue said, "but Raymond and Bodge would turn this house into a hovel."

"I wouldn't want to put you in a dangerous situation," I said. "And you're smaller than I am."

"Believe you me," Sue said, "I may not look big, but honey, nobody gets through me unless invited."

"I don't think you're in a dangerous situation, Jackie," Bodge said, shaking his head. "I don't, I mean that. I'm curious as hell about why you're getting this attention. I sure wouldn't mind catching someone."

"This time you're not suggesting that Tom be invited to protect me," I pointed out.

"Not because I have any notion that Tom's doing this to you, because I can't imagine why he'd do something as strange as that. It's because you don't seem too comfortable about it, so I gotta hear that. And Sweeny is just an idea—maybe nothing will happen while he's there. . . . I'm going to have him go over in his truck and park it down the block."

"If Jackie doesn't feel right about Tom Wahl, Bodge, you ought to have a closer look at him. There is nothing better than a woman's instinct."

I felt grateful and ashamed all at once. I felt validated by having someone support my instincts, and I felt guilty about drawing negative attention to a man who might be innocent of any wrongdoing. I smiled at Sue. "Thanks, Sue. Bodge is probably right; there's no reason to suspect Tom other than the fact that he's the only man I've dated. And I don't plan to date him anymore."

"Why?" she asked.

"This phantom stuff hasn't made me feel comfortable about dating anyone. When I think about it, though, that's not the reason. He's interesting; he's friendly and accommodating. And I don't like him." I shrugged. "I kept thinking I should. I don't. That's it."

"That's enough," she said.

I had a second cup of coffee and talked with Sue and Bodge for a while longer—blissfully, not about the crazy stuff going on in my house. I learned Sue was a housewife and had raised four children. Her oldest daughter, twenty-six, had two tiny children and lived in Aurora. Her second child, a twenty-three-year-old son, had just graduated from college, had gone into police work like his father, and lived in Santa Fe, New Mexico. Raymond, eighteen, worked on cars and nothing more. Trisha was fifteen and in a perpetual state of PMS, but a smart cookie, a cheerleader, and spoiled.

Sue Scully was active, intuitive, and down-to-earth. She was busy every minute; when the ironing was done she began chopping vegetables; she couldn't sit still. Getting to know her, finding I liked and admired her, was beneficial because I found a potential friend. The greater advantage was that I now trusted Bodge completely. I decided it would be impossible for him to be anything but a straight-arrow with a wife like Sue.

We said our good-byes and promised to stay in touch and Bodge followed me home. He had a fingerprint kit with him, but it was futile. There were no prints on the glass or the jug of cranberry juice. I threw out the cranberry juice. I was tempted to throw out everything in the refrigerator. The rest of my day was uneventful until eight P.M., when I met my roommate.

He held his ball cap in one hand and a large grocery bag in the other. He stood an easy and graceful six-foot-four, had unruly black hair, wore jeans, boots, and a plaid shirt. "Miss Sheppard?"

"Yes. Lathrop?"

"Sweeny, ma'am. Nobody calls me Lathrop."

"Okay, Sweeny. Come on in."

"Yes, ma'am."

"I appreciate this, Sweeny. I know it's an inconvenience, to camp out in someone's house . . ."

"Yes, ma'am. Can I borrow your refrigerator, ma'am?" he asked.

"Certainly," I said, and watched him unload a bag of groceries into it. He had hot dogs, cheese, buns, chips, frozen pizza, ice cream, a six-pack of soda, and a twelve-pack of little cakes, the kind you put in school lunches.

"I like a snack at night—if I'm careful not to make a big mess, do you mind? I could borrow the microwave?"

"Sure," I said, and gave him a quick tour of the kitchen. I showed him where the plates, flatware, glasses, pots, and napkins were stored. I assumed he was laying in his food supply for the week. When he returned the second night with another grocery bag, equally well stocked, I understood. Sweeny required a lot of fuel.

"Didn't you have time for dinner?" I asked him.

He came close to smiling. "I have dinner every night at the steak house, Miss Sheppard. Like a clock."

"Oh." My goodness, I thought. Raising a boy like that would be expensive. In twenty years, he would look like Bodge; a complexion gone to hell and a round, solid gut.

"What do you make of this, Sweeny? This business about someone coming in my house?"

"No telling." He shrugged. "I got a good nose, and

if he comes around while I'm here, I'll smell him."
He whiffed the air. "Sure would like to get someone."

"Bodge talks about smelling crime, too," I said.

"It's not the same thing, ma'am. I don't smell crime, exactly—I just know when someone is where they're not supposed to be. Bodge, now: He knows when someone is not *what* they're supposed to be. With me it's really ears and eyes. With Bodge it's like an extra sense." He punched the palm of one hand with the fist of the other. "Don't you worry about a thing, ma'am."

I felt a shudder. I was certain where Sweeny was coming from. He didn't seem wily enough to sneak around or dream up psychological games; he seemed like a big bully who might hurt someone while taking them into custody.

"You watching TV?" he asked.

"No. Go ahead. I thought maybe I'd take a long hot bath since I have someone guarding the house."

"You relax, then. Make yourself a big drink; I won't be taking anything . . . not even beer. Believe me, if anyone touches a door or window, I'll know it."

"With the TV on?"

"I got this knack, Miss Sheppard. From camping. I learned how to hear two places at once."

"Oh. Well, don't hurt anyone, Sweeny."

"No, ma'am," he said. "Unless it's necessary."

I made myself a big scotch. I momentarily felt more concern for my spook than I did for myself or Sweeny. I let go of that right away and chose to take advantage of having a big lug in my living room. I spent a restful, peaceful night.

Monday morning I went downstairs at six A.M. and saw Sweeny lying on the couch with his size twelves hanging over the arm, his mouth open, his head back, and an occasional snore coming out of his cavelike mouth. I quietly opened the front door, went out for the paper, came back in, and saw that he had moved, but not awakened. I showered and dressed, and when I had coffee brewing, he slowly came awake and sat up. He rubbed his eyes and looked around.

"Morning, Miss Sheppard," he said, sleepy.

"Morning, Sweeny."

"Quiet night," he said. Before we could discuss the side of beef and dozen or so eggs he would have for breakfast, he said his farewell and went home to shower, breakfast at the café, and report for a day's work.

I saw Bodge that morning and he asked me what I thought of Sweeny.

"He seems like a nice young man. Healthy appetite. Well . . . I don't know, Bodge—are you certain he could catch someone tampering around the house?"

"Yeah, I do believe he could. He's pretty remarkable in that particular regard."

"This morning I went in and out of the house, showered, and made coffee before he closed his mouth and opened his eyes." Bodge laughed, rocking back on his heels, and made that old tee-hee-hee kind of giggle. "What's so funny? He was dead to the world."

"What time do you usually get up, Jackie?" he asked me.

"About six. Why? You think he was awake all night?"

"Oh, hell, no; I suppose he shut his eyes around ten. How'd you like to check Sweeny out? See what he can do?"

"What do you mean?"

"Tomorrow, get yourself out of bed around four

thirty. Listen toward the downstairs. We'll see if Sweeny's still got his stuff."

Puzzled, I set my alarm for four fifteen. I heard an engine and looked outside. Bodge's police car came slowly up the street; the lights were killed and the car doors soundlessly opened. I thought I knew what was going to happen; Bodge and another man got out of the car.

I sneaked downstairs and leaned around the banister to see that Sweeny was in his usual position: feet over the arm of the couch, head back, and mouth open. I waited a minute; two minutes. And then I saw the most remarkable thing I've ever seen in my life. Sweeny suddenly rolled over onto the floor as silent as a cat; he crouched and moved along the floor toward the laundry room. I heard the dead bolt slide, the door open, and a shout almost all simultaneously.

I couldn't resist; I ran into the living room and through it toward the laundry room, and found Sweeny with his big grip around a young man's wrist.

"What the hell are you doin', Raymond?" Sweeny asked.

"Seein' if you're awake," Raymond replied, very good-naturedly.

"Boss? Why you keep doin' stuff like that? Huh?" Sweeny called that out into the dark predawn backyard.

"Can't help myself, Sweeny," I heard Bodge say. "It's the damnedest thing."

"Well, stop doin' that! Now let's get back to sleep. I got another hour at least!"

"Sure thing, Sweeny," the invisible sheriff called.

" 'Night, Sweeny," Raymond said, skipping down off the back step.

Sweeny closed and locked the door and turned around. It was as if he knew I was there; it didn't startle him at all to see me standing there open-mouthed, amazed. "You got another hour, hour and a half at least, Miss Sheppard."

"I've . . . I've never seen anything like that in my life," I stammered.

"I got a good nose," he said, looking at me.

"God, Sweeny . . ."

"Ma'am?"

I was going to be a long time in believing this had happened. I shook my head. "Will you marry me?"

"Aw, Miss Sheppard, don't be ridiculous."

Later I learned more about Sweeny from Bodge. It seemed that Sweeny didn't like to use his gun, so there had been no danger that he would start shooting and kill Raymond. It seemed he liked his fists, and one of the things he was still "working on" was his ability to make an arrest without causing a bloody nose. Sweeny, in fact, still had some fights, though he had made tremendous progress in his control since high school. And finally, Sweeny was not good at cognition and deduction; he would not have passed a large city's police-force detective exam. However, he had an uncanny intuitive sense for danger, threat, or wrongdoing. He would not glance at me going out the door for my paper, but a hand on the back door to my house—which he had sworn to protect—would pull him from a deep sleep with the instincts of a panther.

He wouldn't have made it on any other police force. One fight or proven instance of police brutality in L.A., for example, would get him tossed out. Bodge believed he had himself a good man with a few edges to be filed down.

This is the atmosphere, the intimacy, which I grew

to both love and suspect. That people could know each other in this way, that their assumptions could be correct. That Bodge could get Raymond, who he said was at that jackass age, to get up at four A.M. to do the Sweeny test. And they could trust Sweeny's behavior, what he'd do; that Sweeny wouldn't suddenly change and shoot Raymond's head off. And Sweeny would not be angry or resentful. He'd respond in his predictable way and be only mildly annoyed by their prank.

This was Coleman, where I was almost one of them. People knew each other in a complete sense, a family sense, in which assets were never overglorified, but taken in stride. And in which faults or flaws were understood and accepted. Not tolerated—accepted. "Sweeny? Oh, Sweeny's not punching people as much anymore." "Don't be getting Nicole on that murder or I'll never get any work done."

To have become one of them would have been good. That small-town trust and intimacy were never wholly mine. If you don't have the stamina to endure the years it takes to become one with the town, it helps to have been born there.

The next morning Roberta, again, did not come to work. By this time I had to call her; she said she wasn't feeling well. She sounded fine. The men had not been in the café in the morning and I realized it had been days since I'd seen them. At lunchtime I drove to Roberta's house for a showdown.

10

Tuesday, noon, I arrived at the Musetta home. Harry and Roberta had a large ranch style place on the eastern edge of the valley. Harry did farming that he called gardening; he specialized in herbs, summer plants, and strawberries, and had a modest orchard and a small flock of sheep from which he did a salable lambing each year.

Harry also had a few horses, a few cows, a few goats, some chickens. He wasn't an ambitious farmer; like many residents of Coleman, he was willing to live a less wealthy life in order to live *this* kind of life. This was why Coleman was blessed with good professionals like Roberta, Dr. Haynes, the dentists, other lawyers. The populace was small, the cost of living reasonable, and the town was postcard beautiful. In the beauty shop, I heard a part-time resident say that it was like living in Switzerland. Having never been there, I couldn't agree, but I could believe it. Coleman is healthy, natural, clean.

I had allowed myself to become agitated by Roberta's unexplained absences by the time I got to their place. I realized I wasn't Roberta's partner, but I couldn't function in an office in which there wasn't trust—and I couldn't imagine what reason Roberta could have for not going to the office and not making an attempt to contact me personally.

There were three trucks in addition to Roberta's Suburban in front of the house. I parked, went to the door, and heard the sound of men's voices inside. It took Roberta a long time to answer. She held a magazine and was wearing her glasses, which she immediately removed. "Jackie!" she said, taken aback.

"I'm sure I'm intruding," I said. "I felt I should come out here and find out what's going on."

Roberta sighed and looked exasperated, and I nearly fled. "Of course," she said. "Come in; you're entitled to some explanation, I suppose."

"I wanted to assure myself you're all right," I said.

"Don't bullshit me, dear. You're probably put out that I've been absent without cause. I can imagine."

"Well . . . I would have liked a phone call from you. When you just leave word with Peggy—"

"It's my office; it didn't occur to me to clear it with you that I was taking time off."

"Well," I said, moving inside the door to her house, "then let's talk about that. If we're going to work together and rely on each other—" I stopped when I heard a surge of laughter come from inside the house. It sounded as though Roberta and Harry were having a party.

"Oh, come in, Jackie. Let's not bicker. This won't take long to explain." She walked off ahead of me, her wide hips swinging under her double-knit trousers. I had never seen Roberta in stay-at-home dress. She usually wore a suit to work, and her sensible lace-up shoes.

I followed her into the kitchen, where I found a

lunchtime poker game. A cloud of stale smoke and laughter greeted me. Harry and Wharton, Lip and George Stiller were seated around the kitchen table, sharing a full ashtray, coffee mugs, Coke cans, and a plate of hastily thrown together bologna sandwiches, half gone.

"Hey, there's our girl," Harry said, half rising. "I guess you couldn't stand it without us, hey, girl?"

"Looks like you moved the party out here," I said.

"Yeah, for the time being. Just having us a little game; want to sit in?"

"No, I came to see how Roberta is doing."

"Berta? She's mean as a snake today, tell the truth."

Roberta was busying herself making a new pot of coffee. "I don't think I'm any meaner than usual, frankly. Harry, tell Jackie what's going on. That's why she's here. Tell her."

I looked at Harry; the three other men watched me. Harry was a man who I supposed had been handsome in his youth. Of the couple, Harry was the more physically attractive. He still had a solid physique, a good set of teeth, twinkling blue eyes, a full head of graying hair. He had a crepelike set of wrinkles around his eyes, on his forehead, and down his neck from exposure to the elements.

"Well, Jackie, it happens I had a visit to the doctor and I have a cancer. It's taken me and Berta a few days to decide just how we feel about that. Berta isn't sick; she's sick of me, I guess. Sorry if we worried you."

"Worried me?" I gasped. I moved closer, dropped my purse on the counter. "Harry! What kind of a cancer?"

"Well, guess," he said, grinning. "Aw, I'm sorry,

honey. I don't mean to be such a bad tease. It's lung cancer." He patted his chest. "Right here. Figures, don't it?"

"Why aren't you in the hospital?" I asked.

"Because I don't aim to be."

I was speechless. I stared at him; he sucked on a cigarette. "Harry! Put that out!" I shouted this as though he had lifted hemlock to his lips.

He didn't react. He blew out the smoke. "It's too late for that, now. I'd only die crabby."

I turned toward Roberta, a pleading look on my face. She held up her hands as if to ward me off. "I quit," she said. "I don't much like it, but I had a clean X ray and put 'em down. What Harry does is up to him."

"Jeez," I sighed. "What are you going to do? Have surgery? Chemotherapy? What?"

"Well, honey, I decided that I'm going to get all my wood chopped and sell off the lambs. Other than that, nothing."

"Harry, what does the doctor say?"

"The doctor says it ain't good, that's what he says. Now, the choices he gave me don't seem like good ones at all. Seems I have it spread already. I don't feel half bad, that's the thing. And we could try all these fancy drugs and X rays," which he pronounced "ex-a-rays." He tapped out his cigarette. "I got a cough, which I think I've had now forty years; I got a sore throat, which I think I've had twenty years. My legs aren't as strong, but I get around as good as ever. Thing is, I could try to beat it, except the odds are bad and the cure is worse than the disease."

"Maybe not, Harry. There's all kinds of wonderful stuff now; there's new drugs, special clinics, and psychotherapy, and positive thinking, and—"

He stared at me, unblinking, smiling indulgently. I gave up and looked back at him.

"Pull up a chair, gal," he said to me. I absently dragged a chair from the big bleached-pine table and took a seat. "You want a little nip? You can have a sandwich and coffee to sober you up before you go back to lawyering." I nodded. Harry dragged himself to his feet and got a glass, put in some ice, poured a little whiskey in it, and handed it to me. It didn't taste one bit good. I made a face.

"What is this?" I asked.

The men all laughed. "He ought to buy at least one bottle of decent whiskey before he goes," Lip said.

"Doesn't hardly matter now," Wharton said. "He's come to like the taste of that rotgut and would probably get sick on good whiskey now."

"You want to try something else, honey?" Harry asked. "I got some rum from a Christmas party we had one year."

"No. I'm sure this will work. Now, tell me this again."

"There ain't nothing to tell. There'd be even less to tell if I hadn't've got stepped on by that old mare; I should a put that mare down last spring anyhow. I meant to. She doesn't get by too good. Anyhow, she crushed two toes and they swelled all up and I went to see Doc Haynes. Once those doctors get their hands on you, you're done in. He takes a little blood, gives a little ex-a-ray, and next thing you know you're driving to Denver for more blood and more ex-a-rays, none of which I would've done except that Berta hounded me till I couldn't stand having her come home to supper." He chuckled a little. "You never trust those doctors. Doc Haynes is a sneaky son of a bitch. Called Berta at work and told on me."

"You didn't want to know?"

"What's the difference?"

"But, Harry, if you'd found it sooner—"

"I didn't, see. Wasn't anything wrong that I could tell, and it still doesn't seem like anything much is wrong. To hear these fancy doctors talk, I might not get to deal the next hand."

"I'm ahead," Wharton said, grinning.

Now, Wharton is an unhandsome man. He's stoop-shouldered, with a long skinny face, nearly bald, has deep-set and weathered eyes, a stubbled chin, a mole on his nose, and slippery false teeth. He's ugly. He's an old man who has lived a hard life on a ranch. Wharton, about seventy, would work till he died. When he grinned he looked downright friendly. He turned and looked at the coffee pot, pushed back his chair, and got up to refill his mug. He returned to his seat.

"So you've refused treatment?" I asked, sipping my drink.

"In a way. I got me some pain pills. They're doozies, too. I took one the other night. Shew."

"Are you in much pain?"

"Naw. I just wanted to try one out. I don't reckon I'm going to have a lot of pain."

"Really?" I asked, surprised. I knew cancer, especially lung cancer that had spread, to be horrendously painful. The men at the table chuckled. Roberta left the room with a coffee cup in hand. "I'll be in the living room, Jackie," she said while leaving.

"How's Roberta holding up?" I asked.

"Oh, hell, Berta's doing good. That's one good old girl. We've had some good years. Probably a good thing we never had children—we were old and set in our ways even when we were young."

"Isn't there any compromise, Harry? Won't you

even go back and hear what the doctors have to say about this . . . condition?"

"It's like this, Jackie. I had me a lot of tests, even stayed overnight in a hospital a coupla times. I got a second opinion and a third one. They all say the same thing: It's bad and the treatment is bad, too. And the odds are bad. And it's damn near the first bad thing's ever happened to me.

"I'm sixty-six and I've had exactly the kind of life I wanted to have. Not a lotta men can say that at my age. No one ever disappointed me, no one ever let me down or stole from me. I lived where I wanted to live, I had a good woman to live with. I was damned happy to see the sun come up every morning and I ended damn near every day pleased with the work I'd done. The only thing I regret is that I'll be leaving Berta on her own—but I couldn'ta been married to a woman who couldn't live on her own. Berta will be burdened, but she'll be okay. The boys here'll see to her."

I sipped my whiskey. It was terrible stuff, but at least it was working. I felt my insides uncurl and my head go soft.

"So now?" I asked. "You just going to have poker games?"

They all laughed. "We wanted to get this all settled among ourselves before it got around," Lip said. "We've been having coffee at the café and Cokes and beers at Wolf's about twenty years or so now. When things like this come up, we like to get it settled among ourselves."

"Things like this?"

"Barn raising," Wharton said. "Troubles among friends." He pulled a Camel no-filter out of the pack. "There's feeding to do here; there's orchards and some crops and chickens. We always figure out who's doing what. And when there's something needs doing, we get each other in on it. When Ellen died—that's my wife, Ellen—I called Harry to come before I called my kids. That's how we do things here."

"Does everybody do things that way?" I asked.

"Oh, hell no, gal," Harry said. "We're old-timers. When this wasn't too much of a town, we learned to rely on each other. We don't stand on ceremony, hon. We just get things done."

I felt tears come to my eyes. I blinked and bit my lip and I know that my nose got pink. I sipped.

"Now, women is another story. Women are hanger-oners. I imagine you're going to drive yourself crazy trying to think of some way to make this go away . . . try to get me to change my mind or something. I want you to forget about it. I figure if I go get one more opinion, they'll get their hooks in me. They wear you down with drugs and tests and pretty soon you don't have the strength to get up and get out. Next thing you know you can't even pee without help, and you sure as hell can't blow your brains out. And there you are, six feet long and sixty pounds, staring at the ceiling and groaning.

"If I stay right here, that isn't gonna happen to me. Hear?"

"What are you saying, Harry? Would you . . . you wouldn't? You don't mean to say you'd consider blowing your brains out?"

"Oh well, no. That'd make an awful mess."

"Thank God," I breathed.

"I got all these pain pills . . ."

"Harry!"

"Up to now, I never had any pills of any kind."

"Hate to see you try to kill yourself on that whiskey," George said.

"Or Milk of Magnesia," said Wharton.

"That's what's nice about the mountains," Lip said. "You could go right up the trail, sit yourself on the edge of Mount Sunshine, and kind of teeter off. No way you could live through that."

"Naw," Harry said. "I promised Roberta she'd have something to bury."

I put down my drink and covered my ears with both hands. The men chuckled. "You're doing this on purpose! You're teasing me and it's awful; Harry, you're full of it."

It got quiet for a minute. Serious. "No, I ain't, Jackie, honey. I got a cancer. I got a whole bunch of cancers. I'm not a vain man; don't make any difference to me if I get homely or lose weight. I don't care if I have to go easy—I been meaning to do some light work for a long time now. But I ain't gonna be six feet long and sixty pounds of moaning, groaning bag of bones. I'm leaving before it comes to that. The end."

My attorney's mind snapped to attention. "You've made us all accomplices," I said. "You've told a bunch of people you're going to do something illegal. Now we can't let you."

"I can," Wharton said.

"Me, too," Lip said.

"Ain't up to me to stop him or start him," George said.

Harry grinned. "You're going to drive yourself crazy if you think you can do anything with me. Hell, if Berta can't make up my mind for me, how the blazes can you?"

"What does Berta . . . ah, Roberta say about this plan of yours?"

"She says it's my life." He lowered his eyes in an almost shy fashion. "Oh, she says some tenderhearted things, too. Kind of hard to imagine, me and Berta, whispering tender things. We're tough old boots; we don't get too sentimental." He lifted his gaze. "I been married to her forty years now. We promised we could rely on each other in good times and bad. What that means to me is Berta will miss me, but she'll go along with me. She'll make her own decisions about what kind of life she wants to live . . . and respect mine."

I could feel that I would soon start to snivel. I took a breath and it lurched into a hiccup. I sniffed. Harry handed me a tissue. "I'm not going to allow a lot of this," he said. "If you think I'm going to let you make my last days miserable, you're dead wrong."

"I gotta go," Wharton said abruptly. "Gotta feed. See you tomorrow."

"Me, too," Lip said, pushing back his chair and standing. "I think a three-hour lunch oughta do it."

George rose without a word and the men moseyed . . . an easy, unhurried shuffle to the door. There were no showy farewells, handshakes, or emotions. They all said, "See you tomorrow" and didn't look back. The door slammed. I sniffed. "Good bunch," Harry said. "Want another whiskey? Coffee?"

I blew my nose and asked for coffee.

I didn't break down; I didn't lose it. I indulged my stunned sadness with some quiet sniveling and Harry comforted me with country tidbits like "A good, short life is better than a long miserable one," and "It's not a question of whether you die, just when and how." And how that damned old mare could have stepped on his head and saved him all this trouble. I dried up and Roberta came back to the kitchen. She filled her coffee mug, put down her magazine, and joined us at the table.

"I'm planning to go to the office tomorrow morning, Jackie," she said. "I'd like you to know that I'll be taking extra time here and there when I want to. I won't stick you with anything, I won't leave you stranded or in trouble unless I have a legitimate emergency. I want to keep my schedule flexible."

"That's good," I said.

"And," she went on, "I don't do this sort of thing well or easily, but I want to tell you that I'm glad you're in the office and I appreciate the way you handled this. You're right; you're entitled to demand an explanation from me about anything that concerns the practice. My unexplained absence affects our practice."

That was the first time she had said that—"our" practice. And that was as close as Roberta would ever come to telling me how much she appreciated me.

We didn't talk anymore about cancer, about death, or about saving pills. Roberta talked about an article she was reading on an ecosystem set up and lived in by an ecological scientist. Harry talked about getting a woman he knew named Gladys Hermosa to take his elderberries and make gourmet jam. And they both talked animatedly about the coming "Showing the Colors" town festival, which was scheduled for the weekend.

I learned that at the end of September every year, when the trees began to turn and the weather cooled, there was a huge town party; parades, booths, dances, food and drink, and many vendors and visitors from neighboring towns. The banners and posters announcing the event had started going up. I had been only vaguely aware of them in the way I was vaguely aware of everything. With Harry's sickness and the news of the immensity of this town fair, I became conscious of how self-centered I'd been, how suspicious and obsessed. I had thought of nothing other than the strange happenings in my house—though they weren't overtly threatening. And the four-year-old murder, though I could see no way it was connected to me or anyone I knew. My suspicions of Tom dominated my thoughts, though the only things I knew of to make me suspicious were things he had openly shared with me. I vowed to take notice of this: that people had troubles bigger than mine, that there were events larger than mine.

I asked Harry, "Why is it that Wharton hates Tom Wahl so much?"

"Says who?" Harry returned.

"Well, I've seen that Wharton doesn't have much chat for him."

"And who *does* Wharton have chat for?" Harry bounced back.

"Okay. . . . Tom says that Wharton hates him. Anything to that?"

"Hmmmm. He's pretty perceptive."

I glared at Harry and then Roberta. "Now I know where you get it. Come on, Harry. What's the deal?"

"It ain't that much a deal; it seems to be Tom wants to make something bigger than it is. See, Tom wanted his own road to Sixteen, but it would have cut across Wharton's pasture, and Wharton said no. Told Tom to grade a road from his house out to Wharton's road and they could share the road to Sixteen. They argued about that for quite a while; Tom wanted his own road—not to have to drive past Wharton's house all the time."

"Why not?"

"Who knows? He has to share maintenance out to

Sixteen with Wharton now; seems like that would be easier and cheaper than maintaining your own stretch." Harry shrugged. "Now, what Tom was stuck with was a straight shot from Sixteen that forks off—east goes to Wharton's and west goes to Tom's. Tom's got a big piece of land, but from Sixteen to his road is Wharton's, everything east of his road is Wharton's, and everything north of his road is Wharton's. Everything south and southwest is Tom's. He'd have to build and grade a seven-mile road to get out of passing by Wharton's. By forking with Wharton's road to Sixteen, Tom has a total of four miles to maintain, three and three quarters of which he shares with Wharton. Makes no sense to me that Tom needs a private road. So to start with, Tom didn't like that.

"Second, Wharton told Tom he was getting the dogs barking at all hours by driving up and down his road to the fork—and then some—with his lights off or dim. Tom said he was doing no such thing. Wharton said then it was his company or visitors and Tom says he doesn't have any, hasn't in a long while. Then the fence gets run down and Wharton ends up chasing half a herd of milk cows and by now he is furious. He spoke to Tom about fixing it, Tom swears up and down that he never got near it, they got into a row, and they haven't patched it up yet."

"Who do you think is right?"

Harry chuckled. "Well now, Jackie, you gotta remember that I knew Wharton a long time before I knew Tom Wahl. And I don't hold nothing against Tom—he seems a nice enough young man, and he's good with wood—but Wharton would cut off his tongue before he'd tell a lie, and if he says Tom or Tom's friends are running up and down that road with their lights off, then he saw it. Wharton says that Tom likes people to think he's some young hermit, except he's gone as much as he's there. I suppose if Wharton says that, it's because he knows it."

I leaned forward in my chair. "Why?"

"Why would he be gone? Oh hell, he might be out buying supplies, he might be out giving sermons, out drinking whiskey, or just plain out. He likes everyone to think he's some quiet kind of loner. . . . Don't ask me."

"Why would he drive up and down that road with his lights off?" I asked.

"Truth?"

"Yeah. Truth."

Harry half whispered: "Because it pisses Wharton off. That's the only reason in the world: Because it pisses Wharton off and Wharton can't prove it. See, it wouldn'ta hurt Wharton a bit to let Tom cut through a piece of his property; he's not grazing on it or anything. Wharton's an old-time rancher who believes you don't let anyone, not even your best friend, get a foothold on your land. You don't let 'em dig wells, put through roads, plant, or build fences. It's his land; it stays his land—which we old-timers respect. This younger generation thinks like sharecroppers.

"Wharton's dogs get barking and his cows got loose once and he gets himself mad as hell and looks like a damn fool. Now Tom, he stays just cool as can be, never lets his irritation show, and says to Wharton, 'Mr. Wharton, I will gladly build you a whole new fence and a whole new barn if you can dig up one witness or one piece of evidence that I damaged your property.' And old Wharton says it can't be anyone else; no one else drives that road.

And Tom says maybe it's kids. . . . Of course it ain't likely. Nothing out there but two houses. Once they got down to that fork, they have to go all the way to one house or the other."

"Harry," I said, "maybe that's how the fence was broken. Maybe some kids got out on that road and tried to turn around."

"No, Jackie, it's after the fork you got one lane. If you're going to Tom's house from the fork, you got one narrow road. If you're going to Wharton's, you got one narrow road. From the fork to Sixteen there's plenty of room for turning around, two lanes. No, Tom's probably doing it mostly on purpose. I told Wharton to shut up about it and it would stop."

"Has it stopped?" I asked.

"Hadn't heard about it in a long time. But then, Tom said something to you."

"Yeah. It was the same story, at least. Except for the part about the lights being off. And also, Tom says Wharton wanted that piece he built on."

"True. He didn't want it at that price, though. Can't have it both ways, can you?"

"I guess they're just at odds," I said. "Too bad they can't resolve it, help each other out. Tom doesn't have livestock, but he's got dogs and horses."

"He does?" Harry asked. "Hmm. I didn't know that. Usually hear when someone has animals; unless you're around twenty-four hours a day, seven days a week, you need a friend or neighbor to feed."

"I guess he is. There, I mean."

"Seems like he'd mention dogs and horses when the rest of us are talking about animals. Can't figure that. Oh, well, I never said Wharton was easy." He reached for Roberta's hand and gave it a pat, a sentimental if not romantic gesture that reminded me of what I had been thinking a moment earlier: People have serious lives to get on with.

We talked for a few minutes more, and then I left. Harry and Roberta both walked me to the car. "After we get this town party behind us, I'll cook you up a big pot of chili some night," Harry said. "Come out to the house and eat, maybe play some cards."

"Yes," I said. "I'd love that."

I went to my office for the rest of the day. When I went home, I longed for Sweeny's company for the sole purpose of having three nights' sleep in a row. Though I had been up once at four-fifteen to observe the Sweeny test, I still rested better that week than I had in a while. Some of these Coleman people— Harry, Roberta, Bodge, Sue, Sweeny, Nicole, even Wharton—were becoming generous with themselves; I was feeling accepted if not embraced. I didn't know if I had anything in common with any of them, nor did they know whether I had the makings of a good friend. They tugged at me a bit, inviting me to participate. And there didn't appear to be any strings.

There was one thing I didn't think about until I went to bed that night. It was something Harry had said that had meant nothing to me at the time, about Tom wanting people to think he's some young hermit. And there was something else he'd said that I had ignored, concentrating on the incident of the road, the fence, and the feud. Harry had said it irritated Wharton that Tom talked all the time about building his house from scratch, even the furniture. Wharton said Tom had subcontracted almost every step of the house and hadn't done any more than put up the shelves and paint. Wharton had seen the construction trucks and delivery vans. Tom, Wharton said, could make some passable, simple wood

things, but he wasn't an artist. He was just a handyman.

I wondered why Tom billed himself as such a
clever craftsman. Why wouldn't he tell the truth
about something like that?

11

THE streets of downtown Coleman had become so busy by three P.M. on Friday that we closed up the office for the rest of the afternoon. The banners were stretched across the main street between buildings, vendors and clubs were setting up their booths for Saturday, and a huge bandstand was erected at the end of the street for the Friday night kickoff dance.

Tuesday afternoon with the Musettas and five nights with Sweeny on my couch had changed my whole perspective. Not part of my perspective, all of it. Now, as the town was coming alive for the weekend of celebrating, I took the time to retrace my thinking. I went home, changed into jeans, grabbed a diet soda, and sat on my front steps. For the first time since moving to Coleman, I watched the children coming home from school and reminded myself that the world, even in this small town, is very big. Grade-schoolers were skipping down the street, easily distracted by a rock or tree or piece of trash in the gutter. They hauled their book packs on their backs, as Sheffie had done, shuffling along and daydreaming, or playing with others. Of course I missed him; always would. I was learning not to face every memory with only pain.

Older children walked in groups or rode their bikes, yelling at each other, laughing, calling out plans to meet later. High-school kids rode by in cars with tops down. It was like the afternoon before the homecoming game; there was a feeling of expectation and vitality in the air. Though I'd lost my child, I could still be a part of this, of life. I would have more and more friends with families; I would let them pull me closer.

The afternoon was sunny and cool, invigorating. The tree-lined street on which I lived was a colorfest in itself; the breeze made dried leaves scuttle along the street and gutters. I waved to neighbors I didn't know, talked with Sybil over the fence that divided our yards. It was, in fact, white picket. I shouted a greeting to bitchy old Mrs. Wright, who didn't respond in kind; she merely turned her head in my direction. I hadn't been around a resplendent fall like this in years; I had forgotten how cleansed it made me feel, how safe and warm. I believed I was coming to my senses.

Tom had called earlier in the week. He asked me how I was, whether I had been busy. I told him I was fine, busy, and informed him about Harry and Roberta. Tom expressed his shock and sadness; he talked about how much he admired the Musettas, how great a loss Harry would be for everyone. Through the week I had developed a deep sense of peace regarding Harry's illness and his decisions about how he would live his last days.

Then Tom asked if I'd like to join him at the fair and I said, "No. Thanks anyway." I told him I might wander around the fair later, at my leisure, and then again I might not. I hadn't decided. His surprise came in the form of silence.

"Oh," he finally said, then paused again. "Well, I could drive into town and take you."

"Town is only a few blocks away." I laughed. "My driveway is probably the best parking there is. No thanks. If you're worried about a place to park, go ahead and use my driveway. I've had a hard week; I want to have a quiet, lazy weekend and make no plans. That way if the music drifts up this way and I decide to stroll downtown, I can. I might just read a book, clean house, something. I appreciate the offer."

"Saturday? Or Sunday?"

"I don't think so, Tom. Thanks anyway."

"Well, okay then. Want me to call next week?"

"Call anytime," I said, and then, after a moment more of chitchat, said good-bye.

How simple. I didn't want to worry about him. I didn't want to "interview" him, as Mike suggested. I didn't want to date any more than I wanted a serious relationship. For a while a relationship had appeared an agreeable option; I can remember thinking it was what was missing from my life. Then the thing that was missing reappeared, and not in the persona of Tom or sex, but rather in Sue and Bodge, Roberta and Harry, the guys, even Sweeny. It was a connection with people that I longed for. I wanted to mean something to someone. When I did, I felt less alone, I felt less in need.

My association with Tom had been brief and complicated. Even if through no one's fault, it had been spasmodic with disquiet, with problems. My worries, uncertainty, suspicions. The best way to end that part was to end that part.

A car pulled up in front of my house and I observed

it with only passing interest. A white Mustang. The driver parked, opened the door, stood in the street, and looked at me—grinned at me. I nearly dropped my pop can. I slowly stood and squinted. He leaned on the roof of the car with that bad-boy grin on his stupid face. "Jack!" he said.

"Oh, shit," I said. "Mike."

He closed the door and walked up the steps toward me. He skipped, actually. He is loose and goosey; he has a swagger. He can move through a room and look like he's jigging around, cutting up in a goofy dance step.

"You say 'hello,' Jack. Not 'oh, shit.' That's not a proper greeting."

"What the hell are you doing here, Mike?"

"I came for a visit."

"Without calling? Without asking?"

"Aw, Jack, you would have said no. This was Chelsea's idea; she wanted me to check on you."

"Chelsea is demented. Doesn't she remember you're my ex-husband? Doesn't she worry that I was once in love with you? What is she thinking of?"

"Who knows," he said, smirking a little. "You figure out Chelsea; she knew I was getting some stuff together for you and said I should fly out, rent a car, make sure you're okay here."

"You're planning to stay here?"

"Come on, Jack. You think I'm out here to get in your pants or something? Gimme a break. You want me to find a hotel when you got spooks in your house? I'm a cop; I'm good with this stuff."

"You're a confident son of a gun, aren't you? What if I have plans? What if I have someone else coming for the weekend?"

"The sex maniac? I'd like to meet this champ."

"You are the most infuriating man I have ever known," I said, turning around to go in the house.

"I'll go get my stuff," he said, not discouraged at all. A minute later he was in the front door with a suitcase, hangup bag, briefcase, and grocery sack. "Hey, Jack, I brought a treat. Looks like I got here just in time for the party."

Inside, hidden deeply inside, I was thrilled to see him. For that split second I remembered what had originally drawn me to him and hooked me in until I couldn't take him anymore. His playfulness, his irreverence, his attractiveness. Not a big man at five nine and three-quarters, he was slender and lithe. He always seemed so comfortable in his body; he was overconfident and found it difficult to be serious. He always looked like he needed a shave; the hair on his head was coarse, light brown, curly, and uncontrolled. Both those traits had somehow come into vogue—the day-and-a-half beard, the nonconforming hair.

On the outside, I remembered a lesson hard learned with this man: Don't let him get away with anything. I put an unpleasant expression on my face and took his sack. "You've got nerve, that hasn't changed."

"It's my charisma, Jack. Admit it, you're glad to see me. Come on, you've been lonesome, huh?"

"I have not been lonesome." I insisted.

"Let's have a beer and reminisce," he suggested, dropping his luggage inside the door.

"I don't like beer. You have a beer."

"You still don't like beer? When are you going to loosen up, Jack? I brought you stuff on your carpenter-pretend-psychologist . . . or is that psychologist-pretend-carpenter? I can never get it straight."

I put his six-pack in the fridge and poured myself a glass of wine. I handed him a beer and pulled out a chair from the kitchen table. "Get it," I said. "What do you think of it?"

"Nice enough," he said, looking around.

"No, dummy. What do you think of the stuff on the carpenter that you brought me?"

"Oh, that," he said, going back to the front hall to gather up his briefcase. "I'm not supposed to have this stuff, you know. I had to register the copies I made and it's not supposed to go any further, so just remember that. If it wasn't you, I wouldn't take a chance like—"

"Tell me about him," I said.

"I think the guy could be fucked up, which doesn't make him a whole lot different from all the other bad guys. It's just that fucked-up guys can't be much fun, huh? You get anything new from him?"

"No," I said. "I decided this week that I'm taking your original advice; I don't need this. I'm not going to see him—date him, play friends with him, or get in the sack with him. He gets under my skin in a way I can't put my finger on. I'm cutting him loose. If he doesn't like it, he can lump it."

"Ooooo-weee, she's on the road again." He opened his briefcase and took out a file folder, pushing it toward me. He took his beer and popped the top and drank too much of it too fast. That was another thing that had sucked me in—his recklessness. In the simplest action, combing his hair, blowing his nose, eating a cracker, he could affect a sense of breakneck confidence. Even if you didn't trust it or enjoy it, you could be drawn to it. Bottom line, sometimes Mike was fun and funny. Dangerous, but not lethal.

I watched him while he gulped ten or so swallows

of beer. When he lowered the can, I called his bluff. "I *am* glad you're here," I said.

"Go on," he rebuffed. "But you'll put up with me to keep Chelsea off my back."

The old softy; he had a hard time being sentimental or serious. He could expend enormous energy trying to get you to say you wanted him . . . until you did say it. Then he'd become embarrassed, shy.

"Yeah," I said, pretending to admit it. "We wouldn't want you abused by mean old Chelsea."

"You know, I thought *I* was pigheaded till I married that woman. She's something else. You can't believe what she's like when she gets an idea of something she wants." I flipped open the folder and began to glance at the Xeroxes and photos. "Like when she was in labor with Tiffany—she wanted this certain doctor who had been called and was on his way to the delivery, and she said she wouldn't have the baby without him and she by-God would not have that baby. When he shows up and smiles at her and says okay, let 'er go, old Chels dilates and z-z-zip"—he made a slide with his hand—"she gives it to him like that." He finished with a snap of his fingers. "And I said, 'Chels, how'd you do that?' and she says, 'You can do anything you put your mind to, Michael, and you should remember that.'"

Every page was stamped CONFIDENTIAL POLICE RECORD. "How big a no-no is it to show a civilian like me records like this?" I asked him.

"Felony," he said. "There'd have to be some kind of reason, though. You gonna take it to the press or something?"

"Of course not, I just want to know."

"Then I'll take it all back with me and no one's the wiser. Except you—maybe you're the wiser."

"Gee, he's changed in twelve . . . is it twelve years?" I had an old newspaper photo in my hand—not clear, but good enough for a general likeness. He had been photographed coming out of the courthouse.

"Seventy-nine. Close. What's changed?"

"He's put on weight. He has a beard now, so that might be it. His face was rounder then, but he's thicker in the torso now. Interesting. His eyes look better now; maybe he'd been crying or not sleeping then. Plus, his hair isn't as light. I wonder if he used to dye his hair or something? It's darker now."

"Don't be a boob, Jack. He dyes it now. Gray."

"Oh," I said. "Sure." I held the page away. "He looks healthier now; he told me that although no one knew it at the time, he was into cocaine back when all this happened."

"That figures . . . if it's true. See," he said, reaching into the papers, "he entered a treatment center, but it could have been to avoid indictment. At least that's what the detective on this thought at the time. 'Course, it coulda been drugs, I guess. That would fit the scenario better than anything. This guy had a motive, a bigger motive if he was medicated, and it all came tumbling down. He was in deep shit with the cops, the state of California—his employer—the prosecutor, and a couple of ethics boards. So he did the sensible thing; he checked into a fancy-dancy dry-out facility."

I continued to scan the copies of reports. "What motive? Why didn't they indict him if they had a motive?"

"Motive: His wife was heavily insured and he was screwing around and building debt. He had a mistress. . . . He might've had an expensive habit. That debt . . ." he said thoughtfully. "I guess that goes with drugs. Wonder why Ramsey thought it was just an excuse. Hmm."

"That wasn't a mistress, that was a patient."

"No, Jack," he said. He fanned the papers a little and pulled one out. He pointed to the second paragraph. "That was a patient." He pointed to the first paragraph. "That was a mistress. He had at least those and probably a couple of other women, too. Now that you told me about his perpetual hard-on, I guess I can understand it. See, the shrink was a real shit and ran out of character witnesses. Somewhere in here there's a statement from his parents that they weren't sure what he was into. They were worried, didn't trust him, and had loaned him money."

"Why didn't he get indicted?"

"Not because he was squeaky clean, babe. He was dirty as mud, but there wasn't any hard evidence. That case is still open. I talked to the detective who handled it; he's gonna retire in a couple more years. Anyhow, the detective thinks there's a good shake he did do it."

I was stunned. I was holding a bunch of papers in both fists, reading, my elbows on the table, and I dropped my forearms flat with a huff. "His daughter?" I asked, incredulous

"Might've happened that way, Jack. Might've been he was telling you almost the truth—that he was in trouble, drugged up, and maybe he was out to kill his wife and had to do his little girl, too. Maybe she saw him or something. Wife and daughter were both in the wife's bed. Or it even might've been that he did 'em both in a state of drug psychosis. It might have been he was smoking coke, or doing a bunch of stuff together. Many possibilities here, one of which is he might've done it. I told you—it's pretty much established that he was one fucked-up cowboy."

I looked at the photo again. He didn't look crazy; he looked pitiful. His eyes were hanging, deep and dark circles around them; his mouth was slack and his complexion smudgy. Pocked? His cheeks appeared to be marred with acne scars. That wouldn't change . . . unless he'd had a facial peel. I hadn't seen him clean-shaven in a while; I would have remembered a pocked complexion. I read the description: brown eyes, brown hair, five ten and a half, 145 pounds . . . he'd gained a good twenty pounds since then. That broken nose. A burn scar on his left scapula. I had not seen his left scapula and wondered how that had happened. No mention of the pocked cheeks; maybe it was just a bad news photo.

"What about his contention that it was the patient, what's his name?"

"Oh, now *that* is good stuff," Mike said, pulling out the chair and sitting down as if he was getting down to business. "Devil something."

"Devalian. That's it."

"Now this is a badass. They lost this guy in the system at first. He turned up again somewhere else, can't remember where, and he's done about every crime there is plus he made a few up. He's been sought on kidnaping, manslaughter, fraud and mail fraud, extortion, rape, murder. . . . He is something else. They locked him up on an arson charge, if you can believe it. They'd have taken him on littering at that point because he is slippery as an eel. He changes his appearance sometimes; got a wallet full of ID, moves fast and invisible. Nothing sticks to this guy."

"So maybe he did the woman and child?"

"Except, not probably, because even though he did slip out of the hospital to start a fire somewhere, the circumstances were all different. At the time of the Lawler murders, Devalian was in a lockup facility undergoing the thirty-day court-ordered intake and he was shot full of enough tranquilizers to drop a cow. Later, before he did slip out, he had been moved to a minimum-security section of the same hospital, had done his intake and had been evaluated and was tagged manic or psychopathic or something, and was in group therapy. They'd dropped back his meds, so he was functional. He was noticed missing that time and somebody on the outside identified him in a lineup. The first time, when they checked the possibility of his doing the Lawlers, the hospital was doing hourly checks and giving him IM medication—it's not like he could hide his pills to stay alert.

"Your shrink buddy went after Devalian as a suspect because he had proof that Devalian had threatened him and his family."

"Phone tapes."

"Yeah. Something like that."

"So what happened to him? Devalian?"

"Dake Ramsey, the detective, he kept up with Devalian for a while. After he got out on good behavior for the arson gig, he broke parole, left the state and there was even some suspicion that he attempted to go after Lawler because he'd tried to nail him—then he slipped away. Ramsey turned him over to a federal agency. Not *him*, you know, because he got out of Dodge. His file, his stats. The file on Devalian after his two years in Los Angeles prior to the Lawler murders and two years in prison in California for the arson gig is about this thick." Mike showed a three- or four-inch measurement with his thumb and forefinger. "And your shrink buddy couldn't take the heat, left California with permission, and headed for someplace up north."

"Oregon."

"Something like that. And Ramsey said he heard from Lawler that Devalian actually followed him there or something. I don't know if that was ever proved; Ramsey said that's when he discovered Devalian had broken parole and left town. You should have seen this guy. . . . This guy was like a Charles Manson. He had thick shoulder-length hair, a strange thin mustache, these icy, evil light-blue eyes . . ."

"Did he get the insurance money on his wife?" I asked, more concerned with the first case than the others.

"Not for a long time; not until the police officially dropped him as a suspect. They wouldn't press any charges and wouldn't let him leave the area; wouldn't let him off the hook and couldn't reel him in, either. Made for some high-stress times for Lawler; he was a tenacious little devil, which is why there was this much stuff to get for you. He was determined to find the killer, which Ramsey thinks is all phony. Finally, after a couple of years, they told Lawler he could go if he stayed in touch."

I closed the file. I took a sip of wine, crossed my arms. "Mike. Tell me what he is."

"He's a man with an ugly past, whether he did it or not."

"From what you found here, is this a crazy, cold-blooded killer?"

"Jack, Jack, don't you watch '60 Minutes,' babe? There are crazy cold-blooded murderers who teach Sunday school. You've been missing too many movies of the week; successful, handsome, professional men kill beautiful wives; beautiful, perfect, happy wives knock off their husbands. Now, what this shrink is *not*, is a chronic criminal; this is his one brush with the law. He never did anything wrong even when Ramsey was on him like stink on shit, watching everything he did. He isn't, like, waiting in the bushes for teenage girls, I don't guess. He probably had it in him to do his wife and daughter, and after this many years I don't think we're going to know for sure. He knows.

"So how much in love with him are you?"

I took a drink. "None in love."

"You went to bed with a man you didn't love?" he asked in mock-incredulity.

I thought about telling him that that had happened once or twice in my life and I had divorced the first one. That would have been untrue, though fun. And . . . I didn't feel like playing all the time even if he did. This was serious.

"I hadn't made love since Sheffie died, Mike. I think I might have been vulnerable, easy to manipulate. I'm not saying I was manipulated; I'm still not sure. It was the first time I had considered sex and it was like I was almost alone; I wasn't thinking of anything except that my body was alive after all. Tom happened to be in my path when I became a runaway."

He listened patiently; he watched my face, my eyes, and didn't snigger or make a joke. "Back when Sheffie died, there was a guy . . ."

"Yeah, Bruce. Remember? What a good guy, too. I think he hung in there about six months . . . and it was a long, dirty six months. No, I shut down, body and soul. I—"

I stopped because the doorbell rang. Mike jumped up and skipped toward the door. "Michael!" I protested. "This is *my* house."

"That's okay, Jack. I'll get it. No problem." He could be so oblivious, yet he made a good detective from what I heard. "Yes?" I heard him ask.

"Where's Miss Sheppard?" Sweeny's voice, sounding unpleasant.

"It's okay, Sweeny." I laughed. "This unexpected visitor is my—"

"Friend," he said, glancing with his devilish smile over his shoulder at me.

I reached past Mike and opened the screen door for Sweeny. "He is not my friend, Sweeny. He's Michael Alexander and he's my ex-husband. He's been my ex-husband for so long that we not only get along, his wife is my best friend." Sweeny looked blank. He probably had not heard about what these wild and crazy California couples were into. "We were married for a year in 1975; we parted so amicably that Mike feels safe dropping in on me. Okay?"

Sweeny stared at Mike; he wasn't really following this. I decided that that wasn't because he was Sweeny—this scenario would be tough on anyone.

"I wondered if you heard about this, Miss Sheppard," he finally said. "Bodge and me, we just pulled this together yesterday afternoon and I didn't want to say anything until we knew more. It looks like you're not the only one." He handed me a newspaper, the Coleman *Courier*. There were a few paragraphs on page A-8. It seemed that a number of households in Coleman had reported an invasion of sorts; household items were rearranged, beds were mussed, one kitchen table was laid for dinner, a dishwasher cycle was interrupted. The reporter considered that there might have been more incidents, but that in households in which there were many family members coming and going these antics went unnoticed.

If I had one child living with me, of whatever

age, I would not have thought twice about a lifted toilet seat, an imprint on the bed, a spilled glass of juice . . . even had my child denied it.

"How did you come upon this?" I asked Sweeny.

"Seems like Bodge got a couple a calls on Tuesday; both women were sure someone had been in their houses while they were out. One said her baked beans in the crockpot had been unplugged and her underwear drawer turned upside down. The other one said that her garage door was put up when she knew she had put it down, and her trash cans were pulled in off the street.

"That made Bodge think this had been going on a while and no one noticed. . . . Then he got a couple more calls, and then today he made the police report and the reporter got it. I was going to tell you tonight, anyway. I don't guess you need me now." He looked at Mike, and if I'm not mistaken, he scowled. "If you're still scared, I'll come. I gotta work the fair first."

"No, Sweeny, I'll be fine. Besides, Mike's going to need your bed since there's no way he'd get a room in a bed-and-breakfast during the festival." I sighed. "Polite people call ahead and make sure you don't have plans."

"Hey, Jack! I wanted to be a surprise."

"Go ahead and keep the paper, Miss Sheppard. See you in town."

"Yeah, probably. Try and have a good time, Sweeny. And listen, thanks an awful lot. You were a great comfort to have around. I can't tell you how much—"

But he had said "Awwww" and lowered his gaze, like a big shy boy, and wandered down the walk.

"Jackieeee, he's smitten with youuuu. Yes he isssss."

"Oh, fuck off," I said, turning away from the door. "You are the biggest pain in the ass I have ever—"

"Now we can have some fun, yessir. We'll have another beer and we'll go down to town and drown our sorrows in chili dogs and barbecue chicken and pies. Oooooh, I bet a town like this has pies and cakes and ice cream and . . ." He was dancing around again; I've never known another person in my life who could have such a good time with himself. That was another thing that had attracted me to him— Mike could have fun anywhere, with anyone, doing anything. He could have fun at a car wreck.

He was taking off his nylon jacket and hanging it over the kitchen chair. He wore a shoulder holster with a .38. "Will you put that thing away, please?"

"Why?"

"In case someone comes to the door, like my neighbor, or someone."

"I'm registered to carry it."

"I don't want the whole town to know I used to be married to a cop."

"You weren't. I wasn't a cop then. I'm a cop now. I wouldn't have thought of it if I'd stayed married to you. You wanted something like an advertising executive or insurance agent, right? A CPA."

"I wanted a civilized man," I countered.

"Look at us," he said, grinning. "Just like old times. Ain't this great, Jack? I gotta call Chels."

I went into the kitchen to refill my wineglass and listened to his side of the conversation with his wife. It was the kind of talk that if I could delude myself for one second that I had anything that resembled the matrimonial gifts Chelsea had, I would feel a twinge of regret. She had somehow made this irreverent jerk into a devoted and dedicated husband without crushing his spirit.

"Hey, Chels, how you doin', babe? Oh, she's fine, fine. In fact her bogeyman sort of went away. Anyway, five minutes ago she found out that all kinds of people all over town have been visited by this phantom. Yeah ... yeah ... yeah, she says you're demented." Long pause. "I know, Chels. ... Yeah, Chelsea, I know. I will, I will. How're the girls?" Long pause. "Really!? You tell her that Daddy says that's wonderful. And Tiff? Oh, that's okay. I didn't need it. Yeah, Chels. Yeah, Chels. Oh, Chels, come on ... I know. No, we're not staying home. ... We're going to do the town, there's a big fair here that goes all weekend. No, Chels, I won't have fat or cholesterol. ... I know, me too. Monday afternoon. Okay. Me, too. 'Bye."

I handed him another beer. "There any fat or cholesterol in this?" he asked.

"She's good for you," I said. "Sounded like you were taking orders."

"Oh yeah, Chels has to tell me how to act and what to say."

"Well, someone should, I guess. Want to shower or something?"

He sniffed his armpit. What class. "Yeah, I guess so. You mind?"

I shook my head in exasperation. "Be my guest," I said. "And if you feel like it, we can wander downtown."

"Yeah! Fats and cholesterols!"

"You have some kind of a problem, like high blood pressure or something?"

" 'Course not," he said, going to the hall, beer in hand, to get his suitcase and take it upstairs to my room for his shower. "Chelsea is so nuts about me, she's trying to make me last."

12

Fairs and town parties have a tendency to give everyone present the feeling of being old friends. Friday night featured bountiful food, keg beer, jug wine, and a country-western band. Mike and I sampled all the edibles and danced till we wheezed. I could have predicted his behavior had I thought about it; Mike Alexander has never met a stranger. He circulated, introducing himself, shaking hands, making friends, and dragging me along as though I was in town for a visit.

It was Mike who happened upon Bodge; he ran down almost his whole life story so that by the time I caught up with him, Bodge wanted to know why I had never told him my ex-husband was an L.A. police detective.

"Bodge, Mike is such an ex I forgot about him. We were only married a year and have been divorced for twelve. Having him show up on my doorstep was the biggest fright I've had since."

"Aw, hell, she's thrilled to see me," Mike said, unabashed. "I'd love to see your shop, Bodge. Any chance you'd have time for a tour while I'm here?"

Bodge told him he couldn't during the party; if

there was time Monday morning, he'd give Mike a tour.

I found Roberta and Harry by myself and for a change got to do the introductions. Mike found Wharton, Lip and Nicole, my neighbors, and others. During a break, he met the entire band and invited them to Los Angeles.

"Jack, you don't know anything about this place! You know you have a Pulitzer Prize–winning author who lives here? And Blake Sillingston? He's a world-class biker—came here to train for a big international bike race that happened in Durango last summer and moved here for good. And you've got a retired attorney general from California, a retired brain surgeon, not to mention—"

"I know, I know." In truth, I hadn't known that much. I knew that many skilled young professionals had chosen the valley in the way our parents' generation could not. Modern young men and women followed jobs less, created jobs more. The valley was large and spotted with small towns; newcomers picked up expansive acreage for a song. I'd been isolated, trying to get to know the town slowly, taking my time in doing that.

Mike stumbled on Billy and his dog, Lucy. He shook Billy's hand and gave Lucy a nice pat on the head. "I take care of Miss Sheppard's yard," Billy said.

"Do you?" Mike replied. "I bet she's glad you do."

"Did she tell you I do a good job? Did you tell him I did a good job, Miss Sheppard?"

"I did, Billy. He does a beautiful job, Mike."

"I do a good job on Miss Sheppard's yard. Don't I, Miss Sheppard?"

This could have gone on all night with Billy. One

has to be firm and change the subject. "Yes, Billy. Now take Lucy to see some of the booths and we'll see you later. 'Bye, Billy."

And Mike said, "Whew. I guess he's not the phantom; he wouldn't be able to keep his mouth shut long enough to phantomize people."

"Plus, he's clumsy," I replied. "And he has no cunning whatsoever. Billy's definitely not our man."

While Mike was busy taking it all in, making all these acquaintances, I sat at a picnic table on the edge of the dance floor with Roberta and Harry.

"He's somethin', ain't he?" Harry asked.

"Something else," I said in good humor. I hadn't had fun like this in a long time. Mike spotted me over his shoulder, kept tabs on where I was, and sauntered back to us now and then to give us an update about people.

He danced Sue Scully around the dance floor for about three in a row and wore her out; she escaped to sit with us. "Jackie, that husband of yours . . ."

"Ex," I corrected.

Laughing, she exclaimed, "You have to sometimes miss him; he's a kick in the pants."

I thought about trying to explain; our ages at the time of our marriage, Mike's lack of sensitivity then, the fact that he'd become fun yet responsible when before he could be fun, but was cruelly negligent. I rejected all this. He was a friend now; I counted myself lucky and said, "He's busy wearing out his second wife."

"And she let him come out here to see you?" Sue asked, astonished.

"She insisted on it." Sue looked amazed. "Oh, it's a long story, Sue. I promise I'll tell you all about it soon. The bottom line is, Mike and Chelsea—his wife—and I are special friends now. Mike and I haven't been married in over twelve years. I'm more like a sister or cousin to him."

And suddenly, there was Tom at our table. He seemed to ignore Roberta, Harry, and Sue and focused on me. "How about a dance, Jackie?" he asked in a quiet, unpleasant voice.

I knew instantly that I'd done something wrong. I knew what he was thinking and feeling; his expression and rigid posture smacked of hurt. Possessiveness and jealousy. I consented to the dance, which was a country two-step, to get it out of the way.

"Why didn't you tell me you had other plans? Why'd you string me along like this?"

"Listen to me, Tom. I want you to hear this. I didn't have any plans when I talked to you. Mike is my ex-husband. His second wife—whom he's been with almost ten years now—is my best friend. That makes Mike and me better friends now than we were when we were married. He showed up. That's it."

"Why would he show up unless you asked him to? Or why would he show up at all unless he does that regularly?"

"He showed up because his wife, Chelsea, was worried about me. She knew I'd been having a problem; somebody was getting in my house while I was out or asleep. I talked only to Bodge about it and not to you and not to Roberta because the best way to handle stuff like that is quietly. And Chelsea wanted Mike to come out and make sure I was okay. They worry about me, Mike and Chelsea. They were with me when I lost my son."

"You had more of that stuff with someone in your house? And you didn't think you could tell me?"

"That's right. I was spooked and I didn't want to tell you. I don't want you to get the idea that you're going to take care of me, which you seem all too willing to do. Although I enjoyed our couple of dinners together and am grateful for your help on the house, this relationship of ours is not working out. A couple of dates and you already feel you have priority on my time. I want to make friends; I don't want a boyfriend."

"What did I do wrong?" he asked, sulking.

"Nothing at all. I don't want to pursue this. I like you fine; I hope we'll get along for years to come, but that's it. It's no deeper."

"You're telling me you're breaking it off."

"I'm telling you it didn't get started."

"I thought it got started and got serious."

"It didn't."

"Do you frequently have situations like this, where you spend the night in bed with someone you're not sure you want to see again?"

I wanted to slap his face. My instincts told me I didn't have to justify myself to him; I could walk away without offering an explanation. I tried, one more time, to draw a reasonable response from him. I preferred to exit this situation with a certain amount of grace, if possible. "I've been thinking about that," I said. "Since that's not my usual behavior, I believe there's a logical reason. You offered a very nurturing and supportive atmosphere; we shared some intensely personal information. We were both made vulnerable by the evening, the conversation. I think we reached out to each other. That's all. It wasn't wrong or bad, but it isn't what you think it is. We're not in love. We can be casual friends or not; it's up to you."

"Just tell me why."

"No chemistry. No other reason."

"Jackie, we started something special. . . ."

"This is utterly childish! People our age, having been alone and single for as long as we have, try sometimes to start something special. We aren't teenagers who are committed just because we went to the prom together. We're adults. If it doesn't work, we move on."

"Sometimes only one person moves on," he said in irritation.

"Look, I came here thinking I didn't want to date or get serious; I briefly considered changing my mind, and I was wrong. I knew what I wanted in the first place, and that's where it stays. I don't want to hurt you, Tom. . . . There just isn't any chemistry. Sorry."

"Sorry," he repeated. "You should be more careful of people's feelings, Jackie. You can hurt people this way."

"Don't make this hard on us both, please."

"It's because of all the trouble I've had, isn't it?"

"No," I lied. "We both have complicated lives; we both have had our sorrows. Let's not blame or accuse. Let's be friends and keep it simple."

"Hey, Jack!" Mike called. I looked over at him and saw that he was talking to a couple on the other side of the dance floor. He motioned me to come over and I smiled, waved a hand to indicate I'd go in a minute, and looked back at Tom.

"You don't want a boyfriend," he chided. "You're not so all alone. It's me. I think you don't trust me."

God, how I hate when someone lays that on me . . . as if I'm supposed to trust him. How and why? I don't know him, don't know what he's guilty of, innocent of. It's like an accusation of cruelty. Trust him? Hell, no, I didn't trust him! At that moment I felt like I was being the most generous person on the planet by not going straight to Bodge with the file that Mike had brought me. This man with whom I was doing the two-step might have killed his own family. He would have me feel cheap and superficial for not trusting him.

"This is strange behavior for a man who didn't want to apply pressure or be pressured. This is an unusual way for you to act if everything you told me is true, that you liked me and wanted to be my friend. It appears, Tom, that during the process of getting to know each other you made up your mind about what you wanted and left no room for me to make an independent decision. This is too possessive and too rigid for me. I had an indication of this in the week after I'd been at your house; you're too involved and your expectations of me are unreasonable. This is why I won't pursue a relationship with you. The end. Don't call."

I shed him; I withdrew from his grip without any resistance from him and went over to where Mike was talking to another couple. "Jack," he said excitedly, either not noticing or not commenting on my agitation, "this is Brad. Jack Sheppard, my ex-wife, meet Brad Krump, like Secretary of HUD. I used to work with Brad at LAPD and he left to go to the big time in D.C."

"It's Kemp," I said, beginning to laugh.

"No, Jack, it's Krump."

"The HUD head, dearest, is Kemp. Hi, I'm Jackie," I said, correcting Mike, who was the only person in the world who talked to me and of me as if I was one of the boys.

"Kemp, huh? Oh well."

Brad shook my hand, introduced me to his wife, Jennifer, and said this was the first time he'd made the "Showing the Colors" party. I asked him if he was a visitor and he said sort of, he was a newcomer.

He and his wife had a place up the road, right between Coleman and Pleasure, the county seat. He'd moved from D.C. to Colorado for those typical reasons I'd heard repeatedly: good place for the family; clean and healthy and beautiful. He did some consulting research for a government agency, he said. He could commute, doing the bulk of his work out of his home. Jennifer, he said, was a free-lance writer.

"Kids?" I asked.

"Two teenage boys . . . although they're going to boarding school this winter, not far from here. We seem to be running a halfway house for burned-out cops who want a little fishing."

"Sounds like fun. How *is* the fishing, Brad?" Mike asked him.

"Doesn't matter," Krump said, "as long as we're always having a good time."

Mike's eyes were twinkling, which was often the case, making it appear he had a perpetual secret. We parted company with the Krumps and Mike took my arm, walking me away and whispering in my ear.

"Oooooh, op-er-a-tive," he said.

"What?"

"I think my old buddy Krump is doing undercover crime work for the feds."

"Come on, you're nuts."

"No way, Jack. He wasn't married three years ago, and when he left LAPD, he went to the FBI." He giggled. "Consulting work, what a crock. Hey, was that guy the shrink?"

"Yes. He's all stirred up again. He's upset to find me here with you. He acted like the lover betrayed. That sort of thing really pisses me off. Who the hell does he—"

"Aw, ease up. Let's two-step."

We danced. We ate some more; we drank beer and wine. We told stupid jokes with the gathering at Roberta's table. We saw a fight, broken up by Sweeny; when Sweeny was pulling one of the thugs away, he accidentally gave him a left hook to the jaw, causing the poor man's knees to buckle. I heard Sweeny say, "Aw, shucks, did you trip there, Clyde?" We decided to walk back to my house at midnight, during which time Mike announced he had a bad case of flatulence. As we were leaving, an ambulance complete with lights and sirens drove out of town. "Uh-oh," my ex-husband said. "Too many corn dogs."

When I lay in bed that night, Mike crashed on the couch downstairs, I tried remembering the faces and names of everyone we met, everyone we talked to. I had, because of Mr. Energy, had a panic of fun and met some people who had potential as friends. I found myself in a whole new Coleman.

The next morning, this Coleman was overflowing with fairgoers. The day was long and gritty; there was noise, food, art, demonstrations, a parade, prizes, dancing troupes. The sculptures, paintings, woodworking, leatherwork, and metalwork were fabulous. Mike and I became noticed as something of a couple—I found myself hoping these people would understand my autonomy when he left, because I was already looking forward to his return this winter with Chelsea and the little girls.

And there were men. I was caused to remember the day that I considered there weren't any besides Tom. There were many unattached men moving through the crowds, some of whom I was introduced to by . . . oh yes, my ex-husband. Pete Salado was a painter who lived up on the eastern rim. Walt Mattingly, a nationally acclaimed long-distance runner, lived near Wellsville, a tiny town of 250 people twenty-five miles southeast of Coleman. He'd picked Colorado as a good place to train because of the altitude and hills. Buck Nording was a single chiropractor from Hartsel, a town on the north side of the valley, who was hooked on the Sierra Club, Greenpeace, and backpacking.

"And it isn't like you don't have your degenerates and crazies," Mike pointed out. We did; no question. An old chronic alcoholic called Indian Joe who was no more Indian than I was; he wore some mighty old feathers on his vest and lurched through town night and day. We had some homeless who could have been confused with campers; they lived in the woods as opposed to the streets. We had squatters; Bodge would occasionally have to run them off private property. We seemed to have something akin to a red-light district on the far edge of town, but it didn't seem as seedy as the big-city hooker-domes. I considered telling Mike about the crossing guard whose pecker kept falling out of his zipper and the churchgoing Protestant who almost had to wear women's panties on his head.

Instead, I let Mike tell me, show me. No wonder he'd become a good detective—he could root out everything and everyone.

At some point during the afternoon we learned from Bodge that the reason for the ambulance had been the shocking event of Tom Wahl cutting his pinky finger off at the second knuckle. The how and why was sketchy; he'd been helping someone clean up a booth and a dumpster lid had fallen on his hand; a sharp metal edge had sliced the pinky off clean. I felt a spasm of guilt, source unknown. I felt sorry for him, I guess. I wondered if what I'd said so upset him he'd been careless. I thought about visiting him in the hospital and then rejected the idea immediately.

It was late again when we headed for my place. We were not as tired as the night before and Mike fiddled with my stereo, finding music. "Jack," he called to me. I had gone upstairs to freshen up. "Any fat or cholesterol in scotch?"

"Good idea. Make two."

Patsy Cline was singing her greatest hits when I came downstairs and was handed a drink more darkly golden than I would have fixed for myself. One sip told me it was not watered. We each sat on one end of the curved sofa. He talked about the people of the town, the mountains, the air, the food. "Coleman's got potential," he said.

"Bring Chelsea and the girls this winter?"

"You bet; you did the right thing here, Jack. The change has been a little tough on you, huh? Don't worry about it. These are good people. Might be a guy here, too."

"How'd you find Chelsea?" I asked him.

"Come on, Jack; I couldn't find anything that good. She found me."

"So . . . how?"

"We had a blind date and I was an asshole; didn't pay her much attention and probably insulted her. So she did the sensible thing—she called me. She asked me to come to her apartment for dinner, and since I just couldn't believe it, I went.

"She told me I was a loser, I drank too much, I wasn't concentrating on my potential, I was probably going to fuck up my whole life. 'Course she didn't say 'fuck.' Then she gave me a good meal, one glass of wine only, and asked me straight out how many women I thought I could thoroughly piss off before I found myself all alone and miserable." I couldn't help it—I laughed; I believed every word. "I told her I wasn't sure how many. She said she wasn't going to be one of them.

"Now, I'm a long time in figuring her out, right? I left her place without getting lucky. For about a month I try to put this uppity bitch out of my mind. I mean, you've seen Chels! Is she a dish? No way; she's kind of round and soft and has the most beautiful skin and the deepest, kindest eyes. When you first meet her, you think she is absolutely the sweetest, most docile woman. . . .

"So I called her for a date and she said no. It wasn't that she didn't want to go out; she wouldn't go to a bar and restaurant with me and my friends. Dinner alone in a nice place, conservative drinks, that she would do.

"Again and again I punished her by not calling her. Again and again I caved in and had to get close to this woman who could be so tender and not take any shit. It took around six months before I said, 'Okay, I give up.' Now I'm forty years old, a father again . . . two little girls just as soft and pigheaded as their mom. And you know what the sweetest smell in my life is? It's that smell I come home to of steam and spray starch, Lemon Pledge, roast beef or tuna casserole, bathroom cleaner and crayons and paste. It's Chels, betting on me." He sipped his drink. "I don't know how it happened. I used to work so hard to avoid good breaks."

I listened quietly. The powerful scotch was bound to make me agreeable if not sleepy. In the background I heard Patsy sing of "Sweet Dreams."

"Us," he said. "I have to say a couple of things, Jack. I'm sorry I put you through what I put you through."

"It wasn't just you. I couldn't have done what Chelsea did; I wouldn't have known how."

"This isn't going to the bank or anything, but for my conscience I want you to know—I was tit over ass in love with you. I probably never said so. I was, though."

"No kidding?"

"No kidding. You're gorgeous. You're still gorgeous; those long legs on a tiny little rump; that golden, strawberry hair, those eyes, that grin. You're holding up good, too, despite all you've been through. You never did know you were a dish."

"I've never been a dish," I said.

"Oh, yeah, that's right. You're a lawyer. Come on, Jack; you were always the only one who didn't know you're smart and sexy. Don't waste your time on any schmucks; you're going to end up with a good man and be as happy as me. Maybe happier. Have a family."

"No," I said.

"It isn't too late."

"It is. I shut it off. When Sheffie was seven; I had my tubes tied. That's okay; I had never planned on children. Sheffie was a legitimate surprise."

"You're not running away from that because of the hurt, are you? I mean, I could understand, but are you?"

"It bears thinking about; another drink?"

He nodded and I took his glass to the kitchen. I wasn't sure this scotch and conversation was a good idea. I hadn't been alone with him in years. He talked while I was in the kitchen. He was saying things about Sheffie, about taking him places, about having him help polish the car. Oh, I didn't want to do this.

When I brought him his drink, he pulled me down

beside him. He remembered how proud Sheffie was that he could ride a two-wheeler. He took his dad to elementary-school open house and showed him all his artwork—some of it was awful, but Mike made a big deal. Sheffie wanted to know how many sets of grandparents he totally had. . . . Could he call Chelsea Mom too?

I felt a lump grow in my throat. "Did he call her Mom?"

"No, because Chels said she could love him that much, take care of him that much, and spank him that much—but only you were his real, true mom. . . . So they made up a special name for Chels that meant 'mother.' He called her Madre. The girls started calling her that, too."

"God, she's something," I said. "It's as if she's the most secure, confident woman in the world, with no ego. She's an old soul; she's wiser than people who've been dead a thousand or so years."

"If I hadn't been this lucky, Jack, if I hadn't had two great women in my life, I couldn't have gotten this far. I wouldn't have known my own son. I wouldn't have a good life. I wouldn't be here with you now."

A couple of tears spilled over. I attempted to drink my scotch. My swallow became a gulp and Mike lifted the glass out of my hand, putting both our glasses on the coffee table.

"I can't do this," I said, crying. "I can't talk about him like this."

He put his arms around me and let me cry onto his shoulder. "I'm not doing this to you to be mean, Jack. Even though a whole bunch of people cried at the service, it was me and you who lost him. We managed not to talk about that too much; I had

Chels, see, and the girls. But he was ours. It was me and you who lost him."

He laid his head down on mine, he stroked my back, and he also cried. Not as dramatically as I did; he sniveled and let his face get wet. I gasped and snorted. In addition to crying, we talked through tears. We talked about my parents, his parents, Sheffie's foibles and accomplishments, the funeral, the accident.

I still felt rage. I told him how dark, how black, those days and weeks and months had been. I told him about how furious I was that people worried I would commit suicide—I thought it was my private prerogative and no one, no one, had the right to try to change my mind. I told him about the times I couldn't get out of bed, couldn't drive the car, couldn't move. I talked about the long days of crying without stopping, taking only brief respites to gather enough strength to go on crying. And then the days of what felt like absence of feeling; a blank, cold, hard wall between my mind and reality. I told him how my body had died for a while; my soul had become dull and suspended and had no pleasure, no hope, no life. I had been sure it would never pass.

There were things I hadn't known. Mike had been so angry and overwrought, he tried to hunt down the driver of the armored car. Chelsea stopped him, though he wasn't sure how. He wanted to sue; there simply wasn't a lawsuit in there. He was afraid, for a long time, to let me know how hard it hit him; he thought he would appear self-pitying and ungrateful since he had a wife and other children. He had experienced the black days, too; helpless crying, an explosive temper, some drinking binges. Chelsea took him off to counseling and made him sit in group therapy.

"Did it help?" I asked.

"I don't know. For a long time all I could think about was how bad I wanted to take his place. You know, I took two bullets on two different occasions and barely got hurt. Then my boy goes across the street when it says 'Don't Walk'—and my life feels as if it's over."

"Mike, does he stay eleven in your head?"

"Yeah," he said, surprised. "Does he for you?"

"Yes. When I want to imagine him at thirteen, fourteen, I can't."

"That's one of the things we lost, Jack. We don't get to see how we did . . . how he did."

"Why are you doing this with me?" I asked him.

"It's the last stop, the breaking point. We never talked about him, about it. I want you to clear it all out and get on with your life. You've been through the shredder; I know you'll never stop missing him and neither will I. I wanted to tell you how grateful I am for those few years I had him; I wouldn't have if you hadn't been so damn good about it. After the way I ignored him when he was a baby, I didn't have the right."

"Thank Chelsea," I said. "She set it up."

"I did thank her. I didn't thank you. You let me be his dad; you had every right to tell me to fuck off."

"I do usually find an opportunity."

"Don't joke; you never have done that to me seriously. You're just kidding around. . . . It's our ex-joke that you call me an asshole and I call you a frigid bitch. We don't either one of us—"

"You call me a frigid bitch?"

He shrugged and pulled the drink napkins off the table so we could wipe and blow. "I never mean it. Seriously, I thought you and me should have a chance to get this out . . . about us, about Sheff, about where we're going."

"Chelsea made you do it."

"Well, yeahhhh . . . She said since I was here I should tell you some of my feelings and listen to some of yours. This is the first time we've ever been alone together since the day you told me we should get a divorce."

"We were alone together in the hospital once."

"No. Sheff was there."

"That's right," I said, and I snuggled up to him. He held me. I held him back.

"I want you to know that I love you. Not like a sister or a wife or a lover. I love you for being the woman who let me have a son, helped me be a dad, and was with me when we lost him. I love you, and I want you to be okay. Whatever you need from me, you got it." He kissed my forehead.

"I love you, too," I said.

"You don't have to say that."

"I know. And thank you, too."

"What for?"

I looked up into his wet eyes. "For giving me Sheffie. And for turning into a sweetheart."

We were quiet. Patsy Cline had stopped singing. There was only one lamp lit and the ice in our scotches had melted. We held each other.

"I thought of something, Jack."

"What?"

"I think maybe Sheffie would be proud of us."

Maybe he would. He couldn't grow up . . . but we had. Hard as it was.

13

SEPTEMBER held for me one more act of horror, one more brush with hysteria. I might have packed and left then. I was somehow persuaded, or persuaded myself, to stay. I think it wouldn't have mattered—I don't think running away would have worked. I'll never know.

Sunday morning I cleaned up after Mike while he showered. There were glasses and dishes, shoes and dirty socks. Disorder was his natural state and Chelsea had been picking up after him. I started the coffee, wiped off the counters, and went out for the Sunday paper in my bathrobe. Far down at the end of the street I could see cars already circling the main streets looking for parking places for the last day of the fair, and it wasn't yet seven A.M.

My newspaper was always folded in half with a rubber band holding it together. I had tried giving the paper carrier a generous tip and he still couldn't get it to the top step; I had to walk almost to the sidewalk to retrieve it.

I put it down on the kitchen table and poured myself a cup of coffee. I sat down, got comfortable, and hoped Mike wasn't going to talk nonstop all morning. I liked slow, indulgent Sunday mornings. I popped off the rubber band and unfolded my paper.

I began to scream. I pushed away so hard that my chair fell over behind me and in backing away, I was shoving a felled chair across the kitchen. I screamed again and again. In the fold of my paper was a withering, bloody finger.

After a few seconds of paralyzing horror, I ran to the stairs. Mike was coming down, holding the towel at his hip, and by now I was shaking and crying. "The paper!" I said. "There's a cutoff finger in the paper!"

Mike ran past me and looked at it. He was stunned speechless for a moment. "Jesus. Jesus Christ. Maybe it isn't real," he said in a breath.

"Don't touch it!" I ordered.

"This is sick," he said in disgust. "Calm down. I'll call what's-his-name."

"Bodge," I said, tears in my eyes and on my cheeks. "The number's in that book under 'Bodge.'"

"That son of a bitch is crazy," he muttered while he dialed. "I've heard of jealous lovers, but this is unfucking-believable. Don't they sew fingers back on now? What do they do—give it to you like a pulled tooth and—Bodge Scully, please? Oh no? Well, can I reach him at home? This is important. Mike Alexander. Yeah, Alexander. . . . I'm at Jackie Sheppard's and it's important. Thank you."

"Why would he do this to me, Mike? Why? I can't believe that anyone would do something like this!"

Mike stared at the finger, about an inch and a quarter of it with protruding flesh on the end. It looked like wax; the fingernail was clean and perfect. He scratched his head. "Wonder what law he broke? Littering? Illegal disposal of body parts?" I thought I might be sick; if I hadn't been so scared and upset,

I could have been sick. Mike kept muttering. "Harassment, that would work. Too bad there isn't a law against being fucked-up. This guy is gonzo."

"God, is this happening?"

"Oh good, you have coffee," he said.

"You're kidding, right? You could drink coffee?"

He went to the kitchen and poured himself a cup. "I drink too much coffee, you know? Maybe I associate coffee and corpses. I got desensitized looking at dead bodies; they almost never bother me anymore. Well, they bother me when they're—"

"Stop! Don't tell me what kind bother you! If that . . . that . . . *thing* doesn't bother you, I don't want to hear about it!"

"Yeah, okay." He wrapped his towel around again, securing it. He shivered. "I got the carpet wet," he said.

"I almost got the carpet wet, too."

The phone rang and he picked it up. "Hello? Hiya, Bodge. Got a finger here wrapped up in Jackie's newspaper. I know, I know . . . far out, huh? Okey-dokey." He hung up and looked at me. "He's coming right over; can I throw some clothes on?"

"You aren't going to leave me alone with that thing, are you?"

"Well, Jack, I'd say come upstairs with me, but to tell you the truth, I think you ought to guard it. This shit is so weird it wouldn't surprise me if you went to the toilet and came back and it was gone. I don't get it. I don't get it at all."

"Well, I get it!" I raged. "I damn sure get it—he's playing with my mind! It was him all along, getting in my house. Think about it—he asks me to come out to his place for a date. He calls me at work so he knows I'm not home. He might have called me from here for all I know. And then he plays with my radio alarm so the music would come on in the middle of the night. He asked me to spend the night with him; he must have had that fright in mind for me if I refused and came home! And if I did stay, it would get me the next night. You know, your radio-alarm only plays for an hour and then shuts itself off."

"Look, I'm going to get some pants—"

"And he just happens to call me the Sunday night I get home from L.A. He calls after I've been home about an hour so he knows by then I know. Wearing me down, making me feel unsafe so I'll do the sensible thing and ask him to move in and take care of me, protect me."

"Jack, chill out till I get some pants—"

"Then he gets me in his grip and decides we're going steady; that's right. So if I won't play his game, he's going to let me know that he's a bad, bad boy who can always get to me and scare the living shit out of me even if I have a bona fide cop staying in the house." I stopped for a moment. "Why don't you get some pants on?"

Mike paused only long enough to throw the bolt on the front door before jogging up the stairs. I continued to rage silently downstairs. If I had seen Tom Wahl's face in the window, I would have found my gun and put a bullet in his head. I was convinced that this lunatic was somehow, for some reason, after me. He wanted to scare me to death, drive me insane, something. I knew in my heart that he was crazy.

And I felt I had to nail him. It was a survival instinct.

By the time Bodge arrived, I was roaring with anger, indignation, and a shuddering fear that made me furious. I was outraged at the injustice of this; why would someone do something like this to me, a woman alone who was trying desperately to start over after losing an only child? To do this at all was cruel; to do this under such circumstances seemed to me inhuman.

"It's Tom Wahl, and you can't convince me otherwise," I said. "I know all about this bastard. I checked him out before I ever accepted a date with him, and he didn't check great. There's more to him," I said. I handed Bodge the file that Mike had brought.

"Aw, Jack, you shouldn't—" Mike began to protest. "Bodge, you gotta understand, she's distraught, and I pulled all that stuff from L.A. and you know how it goes with police reports. I'm not supposed to have that stuff here. If it wasn't Jack I was helping out, I wouldn't . . ."

"I understand, Mike," Bodge said. "Let me have a look; this'll go no further."

"Yeah, look it over," I urged. "Bear in mind that the case is not closed. While he's been playing the polite, reclusive carpenter around here, back in the big city they still think he could have murdered his wife and daughter. He wasn't indicted, but they haven't found any other suspects either. He's a son of a bitch, Bodge. I just know it."

"Take it easy, Jack," Mike said to me.

"I can't take it easy anymore, Mike. I was set up and used. I danced with him Friday night, Bodge, right before he had his 'accident.' He gave me a lot of grief for being at the fair with my ex-husband, told me he didn't believe I was really alone. He was pouty and sulky; he talked mean and avoided everyone else. He never said hello to Roberta and Harry and Sue. And then this. He was mad at me because I wasn't going along with his game plan! He's nuts."

"We'll check it, Jackie," Bodge said. He said it

smoothly; authoritatively. The tone of his voice made me feel that I'd been frantic, out of control. I started to cry.

"She's upset, Bodge. Why don't you take that thing out of here and see what you can find out. And call us later."

"I'm upset, not *wrong*," I argued softly. "Ask Wharton about him; Wharton insists that Tom drives up and down the road to Sixteen with his lights off. Wharton doesn't trust him—I'll bet Wharton thinks there's something wrong with this guy."

"That business about the fence?" Bodge asked.

"Yeah, how about that?"

"That was a long while back, Jackie. I don't know if it got resolved, but it went away. That doesn't have anything to do with the rest of this stuff. And I'm pretty damn sure that Tom isn't sneaking in people's houses shutting off their dishwashers and unplugging their crockpots."

"How can you be so sure?" I demanded angrily.

"Because I don't think he has the time; because a lot of people know him and someone, somewhere, would have seen him or his truck. I can't say for sure. It doesn't make sense. I don't think it would be him."

"Well, I think maybe it is!"

"Anyone would be upset by this, Jackie," Bodge said.

He took that disgusting appendage away. It took me a couple of hours to calm down at all. I was wanting to talk it to death; I couldn't get off the subject for five minutes.

During that morning, while I followed Mike around the house ranting and raving, he occupied himself with some police-type busywork. First of all, he found a dormer window upstairs that was unlocked and could have been used by someone to enter and leave my house. A ladder would be required, and I had one in my unlocked garage. There was nothing in there I valued, so I hadn't locked it. I didn't park my car in it, detached as it was from the house. My yard, though not huge, was fenced, surrounded by thick shrubs and tall trees and concealed from the neighbors' view. Anyone could wander around back there without being seen.

"This is it, Jack," he said, then explained as he walked me around the yard. Any kid could come down through the backyards at night or right up the unlit driveway to the back gate without being seen; anybody with an imagination could open the side garage door, use the ladder, climb in the unlocked window of my spare room, and sneak out the back door, put the ladder away, and leave as quietly as he came.

"Except it was him, not 'anybody.' "

"I don't know, Jack. Wait and see."

"Too bad he didn't try it when Sweeny was on my couch," I said. I would have loved the sight of that. The feeling of not being able to catch the bastard created an anger in me that was hot and irrepressible.

"Bodge thinks it's a couple of kids doing the phantom act," Mike said.

"During school?" I asked, unconvinced.

"Well, I guess those days of playing hooky to go fishing are over."

"You don't think it's him, do you?"

"Regardless of what I think, there is no convincing evidence, Jack. There wasn't enough evidence in L.A. to indict him for a murder in which he was the only suspect. You can't make assumptions like this."

"And the finger?"

"Yuk," he said. "Really sick."

Here's what Mike had in mind. He was going to spend Monday morning putting on some more locks. He knew of a couple of types that could be used from the inside only: a hinge lock and a bar lock. They would secure the house in such a way that entry without breaking down a door or breaking a window would be virtually impossible. At least I would be safe while inside.

Then he surprised me with a fingerprint kit and taught me how to lift prints. For myself. He said it would take a police computer to run them, but I could gather them and mail them to him if I wanted to.

"What for?"

"Well, for starters, Lawler's prints are on file even though he wasn't booked or charged. He did do military service. And if this funny business keeps up, you might as well be able to lift a print. Doesn't sound like Bodge is going to print him. I brought it so you could have it; I forgot about it when Sweeny came to tell you this stuff was happening all over town. Now, I guess, you ought to have it even if you never use it."

"I hope I'll never use it. God, how I wish I could get a look inside that guy's head. He's had me up and down since the day I met him. I think he's swell, then I think he's trouble, then I decide I overreacted and he's perfectly normal, then I'm convinced he's a lunatic. I'm ready to pack up and run for my life."

"You can do that, you know," he said. "You can pack a bag and come back with me. We could get your stuff later."

"Do you think I'm in danger?" I asked.

"Logically? No. There just isn't anything worse than being scared witless. But there isn't any reason you have to stay here. It's a great place and all, but life's too short to put up with this crap. You wanna leave? Leave."

"And quit? Before I understand this? Before I know what this is about? No. I'm staying. He's not running me off with spilled cranberry juice and a chopped-off finger."

"Just remember, Jack," he said, "you can change your mind any time. If you feel like you ought to get out of here, don't think about it for long."

After playing with the fingerprint kit for a couple of hours, drinking coffee, and talking, we ran out of things to say and do. I put the recorder on in case Bodge called and we walked down to the fair.

The Sunday afternoon was quiet and so was I. I saw some familiar faces, but since I didn't feel it would be prudent to tell anyone how I'd spent my Sunday morning, I didn't chat much. We took Mexican food from a street vendor to my house, where Mike ate with gusto. My appetite had not yet recovered. There was no message from Bodge on my machine.

"I'll stay longer than I've planned if you want me to," Mike said.

I was exhausted, frustrated, and angry. "No, Mike, you have to go tomorrow. This isn't your job anymore."

"If you need me . . ."

"If I need you, so what? You have a wife, kids. This isn't your bone to chew on. Anyway, I get the feeling that both you and Bodge think I'm overreacting. I hate that. From a woman's point of view, it's so much worse. Women are always being accused of being hysterical—and I'm not hysterical."

"Maybe a little hysterical."

"Not!" I insisted.

One thing a woman hates to be accused of is hysteria. Or jumping to conclusions, which is what Bodge said I had done. He called at about nine that night. The coincidence was again bizarre, again indisputable.

"There was a break-in at a mortuary and the body of an elderly man, which was embalmed yesterday, was violated. Someone or several someones cut off two fingers and two toes. So far three of these appendages have turned up around town—tucked inside the Sunday morning newspaper. The finger is not Tom Wahl's."

"How do you know for sure?" I wanted to know.

"Several ways, though I'm planning to have the lab match these up for me. We have recovered Tom's amputated finger from the hospital lab, two fingers and one toe from the corpse. Jackie, I'm sure. The hospital had iced the finger Tom lost. They talked briefly about taking him by ambulance or Airevac to a hospital where a specialist could try to sew it back on—but Tom scrapped that idea.

"The body at the mortuary was in one piece Saturday afternoon, the break-in was Saturday night, and Tom was hospitalized at that time. He wasn't in good shape. He was in pain and full of pain medication.

"He was discharged this morning. I drove him home from the hospital and Sweeny followed us in Tom's truck.

"Jackie," he said solemnly, "it just wasn't him. And I know before the lab tells me, it isn't his finger you found."

"You're sure?" I asked very softly.

"I'm sure."

"Who is doing this to me?"

"I don't know, but you haven't been singled out. It's being done to some other people, too. Much as you're going to hate the sound of this, I believe it is random and not linked to any other crime or crimes in this area."

"Random?"

"Like random vandalism, random anything. Like someone happens to think you're in a good 'hit' house; maybe your yard isn't well lit or it's been noticed that you're not home much. Burglars tend to be able to spot unlocked doors, dim passageways, concealed entries . . ."

"Random," I said aloud.

"I took the opportunity to interview Tom. I'd better tell you this. He believes that the information about his former life in Los Angeles came through you. He would think that, of course, if you're the only one he's confided in."

"What did you say to him, Bodge?" I asked weakly, sitting down.

"I asked him what this business in L.A. was about and he didn't miss a beat. Told me the whole thing from start to finish. Everything he says matches everything in that file. He knows for a fact that he is still suspected."

"And what do you think? You think he's innocent, don't you?"

"Doesn't matter, Jackie. There's nothing on him as far as I'm concerned. Even if I had an instinct about this, which I can't say I have, there's nothing on him. He hasn't so much as run a stop sign in my town. Now it's time to let it go."

Let it go, he said. Just like that.

"I can't see the good it'll do to keep working this in your head. Get you some good, strong locks, keep an eye on things, avoid him if you don't feel right about him. . . . There isn't anything else to be done."

"And don't call you if my toilet seats are up or a wineglass is turned over on my white linen table-cloth?" I asked emotionally.

"Jackie, you call me for anything at all. I want you to understand, I do not consider Tom Wahl, or whatever his name is, a suspect in these incidents. And you might be relieved to know that he asked if there was any reason he couldn't leave town for a while. He's decided to get away, by himself."

"Why?"

"Pressure, maybe. If I recall, he takes a winter vacation sometimes anyway. He's talking about closing up his shop and house and leaving for the winter. He asked me to check on his place from time to time to be sure it's okay."

I was deflated. I didn't know at the time if I felt embarrassed, relieved, or still frightened.

"I got a lot to do, Jackie," Bodge said. "That husband of yours still around?"

"Ex-husband, Bodge. Yeah, he's here."

"Tell him to come out to the station tonight or tomorrow morning and I'll show him around."

"Sure. Bodge? Why didn't they try to sew his finger back on? Isn't that an option now?"

"Yeah. The chances of it working are around seventy-five percent. Tom has no medical insurance. He lives from job to job. He has a few thousand dollars saved, and that wouldn't even get him the emergency ride to the surgeon. Too bad, huh?"

"Too bad," I said.

Another double-scotch night for me and Mike. I felt so stupid, so unsettled. How could I be so certain about the guy, and then be so wrong? Mike said I hadn't had enough practice; he's been through that sort of thing more than once. He'll get a guy he's so sure is dirty, he gets himself all worked up and convinced that the problem is not that he's innocent, but that they just couldn't nail the bastard. Then, sometimes almost by accident, the criminal turns up. Plays havoc on these instincts that you want to be on target. Sometimes, doubting your instincts, you let a bugger get away from you because you're working too hard at trying to get the wrong guy. That might have happened twelve years ago in Los Angeles, he said. Maybe it wasn't Lawler or Devalian who killed the woman and child.

"That's why we work on evidence, Jack," he said calmly. "You can get yourself so damned convinced that you got the guy that you don't look any further. And then what happens? The bad guys slip away. Might be old Mrs. Wright wandering into people's houses—"

"And cutting digits off corpses?"

"Naw. When something about someone bothers you, you give 'em a wide berth. In this case there isn't anything more you can do."

That night I had trouble sleeping for another reason; I felt guilty about what I'd done. I didn't feel I was wrong to do it, I felt bad that I had had to. Had I been ignored in the creepy digit distribution, I would not have hurled that file at Bodge. I would have walked away from Tom Wahl, his suspicious history, my feelings of unease.

On Monday I told Roberta I planned to hang around home until Mike was ready to leave town, which he planned to do in midafternoon for a night flight back to L.A. from Denver. I had slept later than usual and was at least rested.

Mike went to the hardware store and bought the kind of locks he believed would do the trick: padlocks for the garage and bar locks and hinge locks for the downstairs doors and windows. With his hardware in his trunk, he dropped in on Bodge, had a quick look around, and came back to my place. He was not in a good mood. He was quiet and grumpy as he puttered around my house. Then I asked a favor.

"One last thing, and if you think it's stupid, you have to tell me."

"Shoot," he said.

"I want you to go with me out to Tom Wahl's place. I want to look him in the eye and tell him that I'm sorry he's upset, that I was scared and that's why I told Bodge about his past. I want to look him in the eyes when I tell him, for the last time, that we aren't going to be friends. We're going to be polite in public and call it done."

He thought about it for a second and then said, "Yeah. That's a good idea. Let's do that."

14

Mr. Happy-Go-Lucky was in an intense mood on the drive out to Tom's. Since I was no jovial companion myself, I didn't question or examine him. I was concentrating on what I was going to say, and how to say it. I saw Wharton out in his field in his little truck, loading up hay or counting cows or whatever ranchers do, as we neared the fork. I could see Wharton's dilemma about the fence; from the fork you could see the roof of Wharton's house. Cars coming and going down that road at night could be heard; barking dogs would increase the irritation. Who else could it be? As in my own case, I couldn't find any other answer. Even with my imagination at its wildest, I could not envision that on the same night I'd had an argument with Tom he would accidentally cut off a finger and an unrelated finger would be wrapped in my newspaper. I understood Wharton's quandary; it matched my own.

I was surprised to find Tom outside in his drive between the house and barn. It appeared that he was attempting to load a trailer attached to his truck. A few boxes and large garbage bags were lying around, plus large metal chests that I assumed to be big toolboxes. I was relieved that I didn't have to go knock on the door. He stopped whatever he'd been doing in the back of the truck, closed it, and stood beside it.

He wore a big, thick gauze bandage around the finger and hand. It was wrapped up around his wrist and held in a sling. He stood there, an intolerant look on his face, the thumb of his good hand tucked into his pants pocket. I got that feeling again: I was going for a ride. Which Tom would he be today? I knew before he spoke that he was going to sound convincing and sincere. Intelligent; filled with the righteous indignation of the greatly wronged.

He looked past me and eyed Mike. He stiffened slightly; he shot his eyes back to me after a mere glance. Mike was wearing his tie and sport coat, his loafers, and his gun. I don't think Tom could see the gun, however. I thought it was Mike he was reacting to.

"I'm sorry about your finger," I said tentatively.

"What do you want from me, Jackie?" he asked. "Just tell me what the hell you need to know. We'll get it over with once and for all."

"Take it easy, buddy," Mike said. "She came to explain."

"Explain? Look, let's stay clear of each other from here on. I don't get it, what you're doing to me. You're inviting me to dinner, you're avoiding me, you're talking to me about your problems like I'm your best friend, you're sending the sheriff out here to interrogate me. Listen, I don't know what the hell's going on with you, but I can't take this. This is getting to be too damn much."

"Tom, I'm sure Bodge told you what I found in my newspaper, didn't he?"

"You could honestly think, for one small second,

that I'd chop off my finger and drive it over to your house, stick it in your paper, and leave?" His voice rose an octave, became filled with incredulous wonder. "Even if you thought I was sick enough to do that, how did you think I physically could?"

"I don't know. I was scared. Things kept happening after I was with you, after we'd talked. The night after we'd had dinner together at my place, sometime after I went to bed, someone came in my house, filled a wineglass with cranberry juice, and tipped it over on my table."

"And you decided it was me? Why? Did I say something during dinner that got you thinking I'd like to spook you? What did you think my motive would be?"

"I don't know," I said, shaking my head. I had thought I had a motive, then I lost it. 'Round and 'round. I was stumbling, trying to make some amends or at least get a feeling for what he was about. "There's all this terrible stuff in your past—"

"My mistake, Jackie. I thought I owed it to you to be completely honest about that before we got any more involved. Maybe I shouldn't have told you anything. That's not the way I operate, but in this case the truth from my own lips didn't do any good, did it? You still had to see what you could dig up, see if you could ruin me."

"I wasn't trying to ruin you; I was only trying to be safe."

"You said it the other night at the dance. You said you weren't going to let me move in and take care of you, which I seemed all too willing to do. Well, I'm not that damned willing, Jackie. I was trying to be thoughtful. But you fixed me, Jackie. It'll be a while before I'll be considerate again."

"Bodge tells me you're going away."

"I'm going to Florida," he said with impatience. "A change of scenery, a little warmth."

"What about your pets?" I asked. He gave me a perplexed look, as if he didn't know what I was talking about. "The horses? Pat and Sunny?"

"Were you going to offer to feed them? They're taken care of; the horses went to a stable and the dogs are in new homes. Don't worry about my business, all right?"

I cocked my head; I didn't believe him. I didn't think the dogs were his and I didn't believe he'd ever had horses. It was just another lie. "Look," I said, "I don't think Bodge is going to bandy it about that you had trouble in L.A., that business about your wife and child. I knew all about it and you scared me. Your behavior at the dance was outrageous; you were hostile."

"I wasn't hostile, Jackie. I was disappointed. You came on real strong; you backed off abruptly. You avoided me, told me you weren't going to the festival—then you showed up with a guy. So I wasn't delighted. Sue me. But I wasn't hostile. I felt screwed."

He had been hostile; he made it sound as if I had overreacted to his behavior, too. "Tom, I felt I had to share what I knew because I suspected you. I work in law, Tom. That simple."

He made a sound, a vibration in his throat that combined a groan with a rueful laugh. "It doesn't bother me so much that you checked me out. It doesn't upset me that you felt compelled to tell Bodge Scully my whole damn life story. But do you have any idea whatsoever what it's like to relive that again and again? And I never told you, did I, that they never believed me."

I shook my head; there were tears in his eyes.

"That I'd kill my own family; that I'd strangle my four-year-old daughter and put her in her mommy's bed? Jesus. I found them, you know. I will never be able to get rid of that picture!"

I blinked my eyes hard against threatening tears. I'd been to the morgue to identify my dead son. No one knew better than I. "I'm sorry for that," I said softly. Sincerely.

"Do you have any idea how hard it is, how painful it is to be considered guilty for no reason other than the fact that there is no other viable suspect? My own family is not yet convinced of my innocence."

"I'm sorry that happened to you."

"I'm surprised they didn't find a way to lock me up. It happens, you know. They can't let their only suspect get away; they have to find a way to make him guilty. So I didn't go to prison . . . but they damn sure locked me up! Screwed up my whole life! They make sure that anyone who asks gets told they still believe it was me! And it wasn't me! There's proof, damn it! There is proof that that guy—" He broke off. I knew what he meant: If Devalian could get out of the hospital to set a fire, he could get out to commit murder. That angle hadn't worked then, and it couldn't work now. "Forget it," he said. "I'm talking to myself."

"I only wanted to explain," I said. "I don't know what else to say."

"How about saying you're sorry?" he demanded, his eyes cold and narrow.

"I have. I did. I'm sorry you were upset. I'm sorry for any pain and inconvenience. I'm sorry you're hurt. I did what I did, telling Bodge about you, because I was upset, in pain, inconvenienced, hurt, and mostly scared to death. I would do it the same way again. Much as you'd like to, you can't run away from it—as long as there's a record, it's going to come up from time to time. Maybe it's better that it did; there isn't any mystery anymore."

He laughed, shook his head. "I don't *believe* you. You think it's better that it's out? You know what it's like to have people who liked you, trusted you, start to think you're a killer? Not an ordinary killer, but the kind of sick son of a bitch who would kill his wife? His baby? God. You're something."

"Tom—"

"I came home at four in the morning once and found my family dead! My front door standing open and my family dead! And if it wasn't enough that I had a killer stalking me and had lost the people I loved most in the world, I got some hotshot cops who couldn't get him, so to look good they went after me! And to make sure I never forget, to make sure I never have a day of peace, they keep it open; they keep me as the only suspect!

"Now you tell me something, Jackie. Do you have the slightest understanding of why I'd like to keep that to myself? Can you even begin to understand what it's like to have no one believe you? Do you know what it's like to go to bed with someone, make love, get happy . . . and have that person join the other forces in making your life hell?"

"Come on, Jack," Mike said. "That's enough."

I turned to go. I might have hung my head; I could imagine Tom's anguish.

"Stay away from me, do you hear? Stay the hell away from me and mind your own fucking business!"

The ride back to Coleman was quiet. Glum. Mike was driving his rental car and would drop me off at my house and then head for Denver to fly home. We drove for five or ten minutes before he spoke.

"How do you feel about it now, Jack?"

"I feel awful. You?"

"Me? I have my doubts, but then I usually do."

"What doubts?"

"Didn't you notice? You're the bad guy now."

"Oh, I noticed," I said. "That's the game we've been playing. He tells me he wants to share the truth with me because we're close, then he's furious because I got my own information, then he's contrite and needs to be forgiven and gives me even more information, then he's mad as hell because I know that stuff. Mike, I did not come on to him."

"Let me ask you something, Jack. What if you'd been accused of murder . . . stinky murders like those. And what if you were innocent, but no one believed you? So, what if that was so terrible for you, you went somewhere to start over, changed your name and everything. So, would you tell anyone? I mean, if you want it to go away, would you tell anyone?"

"No. It is possible he was trying to be fair by telling me himself before we got involved."

"Well, maybe. . . . And what if he hadn't?"

"I could have found out."

"How?"

"Roberta knew. There was a short case file; it's probably ready to be tossed out by now since we don't keep things for long that don't go to court. He went to see Roberta a couple of years ago about filing a suit against the state of California because the alleged murderer had been an inmate at the time of—"

"Why would he do that? Huh, Jack?"

I thought for a moment. "Well, there wouldn't be any case, would there? Since they never had any grand jury or indictment or arraignment or anything. He'd have to prove the other guy did the killing before he could prove the state of California mishandled him."

"So?"

I shrugged. "So, I guess Roberta would have told him that and he dropped it."

"Kind of think a smart guy like that would know that much, wouldn't you."

"What are you getting at?"

"There's only one thing that doesn't fit together. If he's so goddamn insistent that no one know about this trouble he has, and if it's so goddamn painful for him to be a suspect, then why would he ever tell anyone anything? Why would he go to an attorney in the town where he wants to start over and be anonymous, and tell that attorney that all this shit went on in his life? That's not a logical move."

"Client-counselor privilege. Roberta was sworn to secrecy."

"Aha. So *he* told you."

"Well, I'm in the office and had access to the files. He might have felt that since he wanted to date me, and since I would find out anyway, he should tell me his side of the story before I found out on my own. Wouldn't that be sensible?"

"If you could make it sensible that he went to Roberta in the first place, then the rest would follow. If it were me, though, I'd go to a lawyer in Denver. I don't think in a case like that one or in a deal like that one I'd go to a small-town lawyer right where I don't want anyone to know. But there's no accounting for judgment. Unless . . . I did want someone to know."

"But why?" I asked him. "You can't have it both ways; you can't have a secret and then tell it."

"Unless you think admitting you're a bigshot psychologist gets you in someone's pants. Or gets you some special compensation, like respect. Or maybe he wants it kept a secret but at the same time can't handle keeping all that in his gut. Beats me. I think he brought it all on himself and can't blame you for anything."

"Thanks. I guess."

"You feel better that he's leaving town?"

"I feel sorry for him," I said. "That's what I've hated about this whole thing since the first day I met him; I would feel suspicious of him, then I'd feel he was misjudged, then I'd think he was a murderer, then I'd feel sorry for him. I can't figure the whole thing out."

"I think you've been used, Jack. I think the guy is a class A manipulator and you started to get sucked in. I think you gotta stay away from him. As in far."

"No other choice," I said. "At least he's leaving town. Maybe he'll stay gone."

"You still determined you want to live here? There's crime here."

I sighed. "There's crime everywhere, Mike. I'm one of the few women I know who hasn't been robbed, mugged, or raped. L.A. is more scary than Coleman; the chances of being a crime victim are greater in L.A. than here."

"True. True." He began to whistle. "Look at all those hills, all those trees. It goes on for miles and miles and miles. You could wander around out there for days and not see another human being."

"There are lots of hikers, trail riders, backpackers, and campers in Coleman."

"There's also something else out there, Jack. It's

going to be press before long and I asked Bodge if it was all right to give you a heads-up on this." He had my attention. "There seems to be some link between the Porter woman's death and some others. Looks like a serial killer somewhere around here in Colorado. Somewhere in the big valley."

"Here?" I asked, dreading the potential answer.

"There haven't been any bodies found in the area surrounding Coleman. The fact that Cathy Porter was taken from Coleman, maybe from her house, isn't giving Bodge any comfort. And, of the bodies they've found, she was one of the first to be killed that way."

"Oh, God," I said. "How many?"

"So far? Eight that look like the Porter murder. There're some similarities; I am not on the need-to-know list and I'm grateful in a way. Long and short, the bodies have been found in wooded areas outside of small towns. And they've been buried with their clothes and rings and jewelry on."

"Hands bound and bags over their heads?" I asked.

"I wasn't told. Is that how the Porter woman was found?"

"Yes," I answered with a shudder. "And who knows what else." I asked him to tell me what Bodge had said. They had leads that went nowhere; there were only a few common forensic details, but Mike was careful to point out that similar executions of crimes—modus operandi, forensic prints, behavior prints—might tie one killer to many crimes, but might not be the extent of his crimes. He may have committed murders that don't match his usual pattern. If the police thought they had one killer, they had found some traits in common. Eight women, between the ages of eighteen and forty, strangled and buried in their clothes, seven of them suddenly missing from their homes.

One woman in Gunnison, a small town southwest of us, saw a man in a suit go to her neighbor's door. She couldn't identify him or what he'd been driving; he appeared to be on foot, like a door-to-door salesman. Her neighbor's body was found in a wash fifty miles away. A gas-station attendant saw another woman who was missing leaving town with a priest in a small white Datsun. Another victim had been seen at a truck stop and was assumed to be hitchhiking; she was the youngest one. Her body was found thirty miles from the place she was last seen.

It was because the police had found two bodies, recently killed and buried, that they had something. Two women, killed in late spring, had been found in deeply wooded areas; their bodies had not decomposed enough to make forensic pathology impossible. Now they had forensic detail. I wasn't sure if it was information Bodge had given me—the twine, clothing, plastic bags—or new stuff that I was not privy to. Only the investigators—and the killer—knew certain things. It was part of the confidential information that could allow the police to arrest and charge.

"It appears," Mike said, "that the victims have gone with their killer willingly. That doesn't mean they knew him. Just about anyone would get in a car with a priest or police officer."

I swallowed; I might get in a car with a priest. "You're starting to make L.A. sound good."

"The per capita crime rate is higher there," he said.

"What's Bodge doing about this?"

"While investigating the Porter murder and looking for links, he used the state police. When he found links, he notified them first. They notified the feds. I didn't have the balls to ask him if Brad Krump was working on this. I figure he might be, but it's a state operation now, with federal help. What they do is try to link up details and trail these events. All that Hollywood shit aside, it's tough to catch one of these. They change ID, change personal appearance, stay on the move. They don't always do this Hollywood stuff, like leaving a lipstick kiss on their victims' foreheads. Or secretly wanting to get caught. The killer is about killing, not playing tag with the cops. Some of them can be linked to so many murders that it gets incomprehensible. Like hundreds. And the methods vary with the circumstances. Only thing is, this burying victims is unusual when there are so many. Hiding them like that takes lots of planning. Taking them far away and actually digging a hole. Mostly, victims are left where they drop if the murder is a spontaneous act."

"Blllkkkk."

"Of the eight women whose bodies were found, only two came from the same town. And that was Leadville, which isn't far away. So, one thing Bodge is doing, is almost done doing, is checking whether these towns ever experienced any of this crazy shit like missing digits, phantom prowlers, and that stuff. He wants me to be sure to tell you that so far, nothing like that was going on. And he also wants me to tell you that he doesn't have any reason to believe the killer is in Coleman; more than likely it's someone from a bigger city, where he can come and go a lot, remain anonymous to his neighbors, and get his hands on a variety of different vehicles."

"So, you don't take rides and don't open the house door too fast. Right?"

"Right," I said.

"And . . . now this might seem goofy, but if you can afford it, get a cellular phone."

"What for?"

"Safest invention we've come up with yet," he said. "You can carry it in your purse, phone from the middle of nowhere if your car breaks down, phone from behind a locked bathroom door. You might have some trouble with reception when you get in the mountains, but it should work most of the time."

"You're giving me the creeps."

"And don't tell anyone you have it; get it for backup protection. Take it with you on long trips, like when you're going home from the Denver airport and you have to do that long stretch."

"What are the chances I'm going to be able to make a phone call when I need to? What are you saying? That you think I'm a potential hit for this guy?"

"Noooo, noooo, not that. Don't be lazy or ignorant, that's all. You've got good locks, you've got a gun. . . . You shoot that thing lately?"

"Not lately. It's been a year."

"We'll do that before I go. I asked Bodge where we could do that."

"Look, I have a strict rule about no one knowing I have a gun and you went and—"

"Bodge said there's a range out of town off Forty-four; plenty of people around here practice-shoot. Besides, Bodge won't tell anyone and he taught Sue to shoot a long way back. You'd like his attitude, which is not the same as my attitude; he has no doubt Sue would unload a whole barrel into someone if she needed to. He's glad you have one."

"Does Chelsea have a gun?"

"No way. I lock up my service revolver when I'm at home. I've taught the girls all about it and they're never to touch it. Not only that, it's out of their reach at all times. I think door locks, cellular phones, yard lights, and a barking dog are the best way to stay at home and enjoy the evening."

I listened to all this and when he'd worn himself out, we finished the drive in silence. Finally, as we turned into town, I spoke to him again. "Now that you've loaded me up on advice in fending off the serial killer, you're on your way. Right?"

"Gotta go, kid. First, let's shoot your gun and make sure you're okay on that. We'll stop by your house and pick it up."

"I've got it," I said. I patted my purse.

"Jesus, Jack! You carry it?"

"Only because I wouldn't want anyone to steal it. I used to hide it at home; now that I've started to get company, I keep it in my purse."

"Well, Jack, if you're going to go it alone in this little town, you're going to have to be prepared to take care of yourself. And a little better than you have been. No more unlocked upstairs windows, no more dates with funny-bunnies, and don't take any chances. This place is not Nirvana. They get the same cross-section here that they get anywhere." He made a couple of turns, taking us out the north end of town to a range. "Don't be naïve."

"I'm never naïve," I said.

"Don't be innocent; be cynical. Be tough."

"I am."

"Good. Let's go shoot. Then I'm outa here."

Later, about an hour and a half later, I hugged him at the curb in front of my house. I became teary and sentimental. And I said, "Thanks, Mike."

"Hey, Jack. No problem."

15

THE phantom did not visit me again; within two weeks the incidents ceased altogether. With my house secured by a professional, there was only one mode of entry when I was not within, without breaking wood or glass, that is: the front door. A long time ago I'd seen a movie in which a spy arranged a hair or thread across his door so that he could tell if it had been opened in his absence. This wasn't feasible on an outside door; I chose a small piece of tape. I experimented for a long time, trying several brands, until I found a cheap brown tape that had to be licked to stick and wouldn't pull off wood finish or paint when removed. It wouldn't stick again once it had been pulled off. This assured me my space hadn't been violated while I was at work.

In addition to that, I checked all the doors and windows when I got home; I inspected each one closely. Nothing was ever moved, changed, or adjusted. This kind of thinking will make you a little insane and your memory has to be perfect. A glass moved from one side of the sink to the other can consume far too much energy until you remember that last late-night sip of water.

Hearing from Bodge that there had been a few more complaints gave me perverse comfort. It made me feel less exclusive—less targeted. Knowing these invasions continued after Tom's departure from town let him off the hook, in my mind. Then even the phantom gave up. It appeared that the press coverage in our Coleman *Courier* and the escalated neighborhood-watch programs discouraged these peculiar acts.

The paper also covered the murder of Kathy Porter. She was officially placed among the number of women killed by another kind of phantom. Although there were eight bodies, other women reported missing under similar mysterious circumstances had not yet been found. The articles set up a scenario of young wives and mothers vanishing from shopping malls, car pools, homes, and so on. It was never said how many women vanished; it was said that in some of these instances the women might indeed have run away. It was akin to hearing of missing children and asking if there was any custody dispute. It would be equally frightening and tragic for a mother if her ex-husband abducted their child—but it made the rest of us mothers feel safer. Such were the unanswered questions about the missing women: Was there a boyfriend? Was there abuse? Was this woman abducted and killed or did she exercise her prerogative and escape? And, I wondered, are we talking about eight women . . . or eighty? The stories ended when the press exhausted its information. There had been a memorial service for the departed Mrs. Porter soon after her remains were found.

A sad piece of news regarded Billy. It seemed that the implement used to remove the fingers and toes from the corpse was a common yard tool, a clipper, the type that could be used on small trees. It was found among Billy's collection of lawn equipment in his truck. Billy was never a suspect; Bodge immediately assumed that the pranksters stole Billy's clipper and replaced it. The incident upset Billy greatly; he was seen by all of us shaking his head and crying. It was good that there would soon be snow, as he could barely do his minor chores.

As the fall air became colder and the trees began to lose their magnificent artwork of color, Coleman became restful. The streets were quieter, we were between sets of visitors. One night I ate chili with Harry and Roberta and some others they invited to their house. I had my cellular phone, and on the way home I had a flat tire. The roads are ill traveled out Musetta way and behind me by a few minutes was good old honorable Bud.

I was staring in frustration at my flat when he pulled up behind me. Although I had opened my trunk and looked at the tools, I had absolutely no idea what to do with them. I had always meant to back up my fierce independence with knowledge and practical experience. Ha. In Los Angeles, you wait for a highway patrol or call a towing service.

"What luck," he said, getting out of his car. "I've been praying since the day I met you that I'd find you all alone on a dark country road."

I jumped in my car, locked the doors, and used my phone to call Harry and Roberta. Bud was stunned. He began knocking on the window as I listened to a busy signal. I thought about dialing the sheriff. The wait for a patrol car to come out here could be long. I mouthed a few fake words into the phone, hoping to give Bud the idea I had relayed my emergency to someone. "Jackie, hey Jackie," he kept harassing.

Bud Wilcox is not a scary man. I was afraid none-theless. Women die when they talk themselves out of instinctive fear, when they try to be polite and agreeable so no one gets their feelings hurt. What this brave, intelligent woman did was point a gun at a Superior Court judge and order him to change my tire.

Yes. I did. Bud stumbled backward and muttered, "Jesus Christ, are you out of your mind?"

"Someone around here is killing women and you're glad to find me stranded out here," I said, getting out of my car, phone in one hand and gun in the other. "Change the tire, Your Honor. And don't give me any lip."

He did. He swore a lot. He sweated on his gold. He lost all lust for me that night. I suppose he could have had me arrested or something, I don't know. Two weeks later in his courtroom, I approached the bench and he scowled. He granted my motion and peered at me. "And I trust you are unarmed, Miss Sheppard?"

I felt like a fool for a long time. I don't know what else I might have done. Someone was killing women. Bud showed up at the wrong time with the wrong choice of words. The experience did render one ben-efit I might not otherwise have had. When I told Roberta what I'd done, she laughed so hard that tears ran down her cheeks and she held her sides. I hadn't seen that before and I haven't since.

I began to sit for a while in the café with the boys before taking my Danish to the office. I drove out to an orchard with Sue Scully to pick a bushel of apples and learned how to make and put up applesauce. And I hostessed a backyard barbecue for my neigh-bors, feeding six couples and their kids. I invited mean old Mrs. Wright, but she was a no-show, never bothered to respond. I laid a plan to plague her with friendliness until she succumbed. That was one of the many plans I was ultimately unable to carry out while in Coleman.

Then the town changed and lost its peaceful and quiet atmosphere as the hunters arrived. October is elk season; elk are huge and beautiful beasts. Shooting them seems so horrible to me and the town is divided on the issue.

The hunters bring revenue; they murder gorgeous elk. The hunters are having sport; they are dangerous. Schoolchildren and their parents are warned to be cautious, to stay out of hunting areas, because stray bullets and accidental shootings and fires are a fact of life in hunting season. The sheriff's department works as hard as the fish and game division and the highway patrol; patrols are set up everywhere. Licenses are checked, rechecked. Camp sites are patrolled, alcohol consumption is closely watched.

It's a shocking transition for a sleepy town surrounded by the magnificent natural wonder of God's own handiwork. Suburbans, campers, trucks, and jeeps converge on the town; men in red suits and hats, toting enormous and powerful weapons, are everywhere. The roads out of town that rise above valleys are lined with vehicles, hunters standing about with their guns ready, waiting for elk to come into a pasture or drink from a stream. My closest friends hunted or didn't, and everyone met this season with ambivalence. Harry, Bodge, and Sweeny liked to hunt, but the last two seldom had the time as they were needed to monitor hunters. Bow-and-arrow hunting was big with others. Still others were opposed to hunting with anything other than a camera. It surprised me that the arguments were not more heated, more volatile.

I thought of hunting season as an invasion of my town. All the people became edgy. The streets had been crowded with visitors who came to enjoy the bounty and beauty; now our visitors were arriving to kill something of ours and take it away. I found even the gentlest, handsomest, most polite of the hunters scary. I guess I'll never grasp the pleasure factor. I'll never understand that feeling of domination and conquest that hunters yearn to have.

Hunting season culminated in a tragedy when, less than ten days into the season, Wharton was shot and killed. He was in his pasture at dawn, dressed in his old brown work clothes and brown baseball cap, when a stray bullet from a Winchester .270 hit him in the back of the head at one hundred yards and killed him instantly. The circumstances of the accident made it worse than a misfire or careless shot, because it was a desperately messy homicide and was never resolved in any conclusive manner.

The gun was registered to a man named Robert Roper. He was with six other men in a large party of hunters who were camping on the eastern rim several miles from Wharton's ranch. When they rose before dawn to begin to hunt, Robert Roper's rifle was missing. The men looked in various sites for the gun as though it were possible that Roper had left it behind; all claimed they didn't believe that possible, but went through the ritual anyway. That whole business of "looking" became significant when they sauntered into the sheriff's office to make a complaint.

Trouble was, their complaint was late, as was their

luck. By the time these men made their appearance at ten A.M., Wharton's body had been seen by other hunters and Bodge was at his ranch. From the way he lay and the appearance of his wound, the shot was deduced to have come from within a thick patch of trees. There, lying on the damp, mossy ground, was the abandoned gun.

In the days following the death of a dear and beloved man, controversy roared. The hunters who had "lost" the gun had consumed considerable alcohol the night before. That much they would admit. How much other drinking had gone on, they would not say. They denied having drunk anything during their hunting—yet, according to Sweeny, who did not touch spirits of any kind, the men had an aroma of the brewery when they came to report the missing gun. They insisted they had not gone near the Wharton ranch during any of their hunting.

Had they truly lost the gun? Had Roper's gun been stolen by someone? Had Roper himself made a mistake and fired on Wharton's cows and hit Wharton? Had Roper or any of the hunters in that party attempted to shoot game that had wandered into Wharton's pasture despite the fact that it was a restricted area? Had they been negligent? Incompetent? Criminal?

During the few days of debate and investigation, the seven men in the party served as seven witnesses to one another's whereabouts—and Bodge could not cite Robert Roper with manslaughter or murder. He had to charge them or let them go, so he tagged them all on disorderly conduct, hunting while under the influence, illegal disposition of firearms, and trespassing. Seven hunting licenses were revoked. All of this he had to reach to get. There were fines, suspended sentences, and Bodge escorted the men out of town. Once they were at the county line, he pulled over and spoke to them.

"We don't do business around here like you fellows like to do business. We don't get loaded up and load up. Now get out of here and if you ever somehow manage to get another license, stay the hell out of my county." I got this third-hand. Maybe there were more expletives; maybe not. It sounded like what Bodge would say.

Now, the boys had a rough time with losing Wharton. In the end so did I, because seeing Lip, Bodge, Harry, George, and a few others struggle with the pain was the most excruciating thing imaginable. These were easygoing, brave, callused, rough-and-ready men. They all did difficult physical work and covered their emotions with laughter and teasing. There wasn't a bad temper among them. They took the shooting hard.

Bodge's chin quivered at the graveside. He almost didn't get through the funeral. George Stiller broke down and sobbed on his father's shoulder, his wife holding up his other side. Lip and Nicole, along with all six children, saw Wharton off together, and poor Lip, well, he needed them all there to keep him from going to pieces. Maybe Harry had the hardest time of all. His eyes were red-rimmed and glassy; his mouth turned down at the corners and twitched. He was silent and stoic. And when they lowered the casket into the ground, Harry turned to me and with tears coursing down his cheeks, said, "Wharton, that old son of a bitch, never in his life let me do anything first."

I remember wishing for Harry that he'd be able to really let go and cry, but I never saw him do it.

Roberta was steadfast at his side; I had her figured for a woman who found showing emotion difficult. It occurred to me that before long I would be standing beside her when Harry took his final rest. That combination, watching Wharton go, seeing Harry's tears, was all that was needed to take me apart at the seams.

I must tell about the aftermath, which was enlightening and endearing for me. It is true that hardship can bring people together; in the sadness of Wharton's death, many of us were bonded.

Had I listened only to Tom Wahl, who spoke of Wharton with scorn, I would have known only an angry, resentful, and tired old man. This was not who we buried. Wharton's three grown sons and one daughter came home to his ranch for the final goodbye. They were a proud and formidable group. They held a buffet at their father's ranch, which, filled with their unity and their children, became a thriving and beautiful home. Two members of Wharton's household surprised me: Pat and Sunny were Wharton's dogs. Now they would be placed in new homes; I couldn't imagine why Tom had been deceitful about that.

Brevis Wilhelm Wharton was his given name. He was seventy when he died. His eldest son, Wilhelm or Will, was a forty-eight-year-old dentist with four grown children of his own. Wharton's second-eldest, Mitch, was a divorced architect with adult and nearly adult children and an ex-wife with whom he was friendly; she, too, was there to see Wharton off. June, the third child, a homemaker married to an executive, was there with teenagers in tow, and Mark, the baby of the family at around forty years old, was a commercial pilot, married, with three children. Some of Wharton's grandchildren had children. It was a noisy, close, happy family, even on this grievous occasion.

The house in which Wharton had lived alone was large, with every room standing ready for family. According to the stories I heard and the plentiful photos, the children and their children and their grandchildren gathered every summer and some winters. Wharton had not been a lonely old man, but a man with a full life, a good family, and much to be thankful for. It happened, at that time in his life, that he lived alone most of the time.

Wharton's ranch was warm with homey touches, decorated with quality—albeit not chic—items. There were quilts, prints, ceramics, and linens that had been lovingly purchased or created by his late wife. It was not the house of a man who had no interest in such things, nor of a man who had let things deteriorate following the death of his wife.

He had had his good friends and chums, his land, his work, and his way of life. He hadn't been the kind of man who would ever have asked me out for coffee or cake, but he was not as solitary as he had seemed.

The eulogy, given by his kids, painted a picture of a tough and compassionate father, a quiet, sensitive man of great strength. They told stories of his aid given to others, his softness toward the land and wildlife, his generosity, and his loyalty. It had never occurred to me to ask about Wharton's family, yet the family that gathered for the funeral was well known to all the folk who attended. If Wharton's offspring and friendships were any testament to the success of his life, he had succeeded as much as a man can.

The Wharton heirs told their Coleman friends that they had been left the acreage that Wharton ranched.

They offered to divide the livestock and plants among Wharton's friends. The land would be sold after at least a year of considering how to sell it. They exercised uncanny wisdom in asking Wharton's friends to think about this and write to them with their ideas so that no one would be offended, slighted, or in any way inconvenienced by the transaction.

We laid to rest a man I knew and respected more after his death than I did in his life. I was sorry for that. I was grateful to have known this Wharton at all.

People who have been close for decades seem to have few long-lasting resentments or unresolved conflicts. Wharton had few legitimate enemies; none was apparent at his funeral. His friends carried on admirably. The café was unnaturally quiet those first mornings, but it picked up the usual steam before many days passed. From these people I came to love, I learned one of the most profound lessons of my life. They did not have time for self-pity or duplicity. These were not done. Not used. That seemed to be why their lives worked so well. Perhaps, despite what he'd told me, Harry *had* been let down, stolen from, lied to—but because he lived as he lived, he wouldn't have taken notice. Maybe every one of Harry's days hadn't begun with a perfect sunrise or ended with a good feeling at sunset, but because of the way he lived, he did not feel the impact of an imperfect day.

At Thanksgiving I stayed in Coleman and ate turkey at the Scully household with family, friends, and neighbors in attendance. The Scullys' was one of a dozen invitations I received and I accepted because it was first. I was invited by many of my neighbors, none of whom could stand to see me alone. I was invited by Nicole, by Roberta, and by two clients, and I was invited to L.A. I had a loud, fun, fattening day with the Scullys.

The snow hit, the ski season began, and although we weren't a ski town with a resort or lift, we still had skiing traffic and plenty of winter visitors. The nearest good downhill area was thirty miles away and made for an excellent day trip, and right in Coleman there was terrific cross-country skiing. I did ski, took some beginner lessons, had plenty of company from L.A. all through the season. I had Mike, Chelsea, and the girls for a busy, lovely five-day stint over Christmas school vacation.

I took a big risk on Christmas. I was afraid of what I was about to do, but forged ahead with hope: I stayed in Coleman and I stayed alone. Since losing Sheffie I had feared Christmas mornings and insulated myself by filling the day with friends. I didn't put up a tree for the first two Christmases.

It had been two and a half years and I was in a new place, becoming a new person. My friends were having Christmas parties, Christmas open houses, and there was an atmosphere of hospitality, celebration, giving. I put up not only a tree, but plentiful decorations. I damn near broke my neck stringing lights along the drainpipe on the front of my house; thankfully, Matt Dania came to my rescue.

I knew it would be my last Christmas with Harry; he was still good with the jokes, but his health was in rapid decline. His skin had a grayish pallor that was giving way to yellow, and I suspected liver involvement. He'd lost weight and his eyes were beginning to look dull. He had always had a bit of a stoop; now he stood bent. Illness was becoming a burden for him; he must have been having pain. He was seen in the café and at Wolf's less and less. I admired his courage, for his sense of humor was intact; he had spark and mischief.

I shopped for a gift for him that would knock his socks off without appearing like the gift you'd give to a dying man. I finally found an Austen sculpture of a cowboy bent over a lamb, and when I brought it to him, his eyes filled with tears. Which only served to make me cry.

I held my breath through the entire season, in wait for the demons grief and memory, but they had not been invited. I went to seven parties around town; I went to four open houses. On the Sunday after Christmas I staged my own—a leftover party. I invited twenty couples to bring their leftover turkey, pie, soups, breads, and cookies—risk food poisoning and get rid of the fattening junk before the new-year diets began. I sent out my printed invitations, built a fire in the fireplace, lit candles, and played music, and my first real party was a success.

It was the best Christmas I had ever had. I felt almost disloyal to Sheffie as I thought that. I was given gifts by many—not big fancy gifts; clever, thoughtful ones from people who didn't feel obligated. I was given tapes to listen to, books to read, wine to drink, a robe to wear around the house, a wreath for the season, homemade treats to eat, and accessories for my house. Someone made me a set of place mats and matching napkins at her own sewing machine. Another friend baked me a generous basket of cinnamon rolls. The mysterious Krumps whom Mike had known came to my leftover party and brought me a stuffed bear in a Santa suit. Better still, Brad told stories of my ex-husband's early years at LAPD. After laughing over Mike and his antics, I felt that everyone in my home both understood and accepted our strange postmarital friendship.

I noticed that Bodge and Brad spoke quietly a couple of times, and at that moment I began to believe Mike was correct: Brad was here undercover, possibly for reasons connected to the murders. He did not speak of work, past or present, with the exception of saying that he had been in law enforcement when he was a young man and found that one burns out quickly on chasing crime.

In the first three months of the year, I came to realize why Roberta would want an experienced family-law attorney. The work in small communities like this is primarily seasonal, and the economic dislocation of such income takes its toll in winter.

We filed for more separation agreements, restraining orders, divorces, and property settlements in January, February, and March than in the other nine months combined. Men out of work from November to spring; loggers laid off, construction and road-work gangs out of work, many family men on subsistence, created domestic problems in higher numbers than I'd seen before.

It's too simple to say the men collected unemployment, sat around the house, drank beer, and began to beat their wives come January, but that seems to be what happened. Or the wives gang up on them. Either way, we kept Bodge and his boys busy with domestic battles and papers to serve.

At this time my practice of post-office and grocery-store law escalated to such proportions I didn't want to be seen in public. I'd be pinching tomatoes and hear, "Jackie, you know what that bastard's gone and done now?" Roberta, even with her personal problems, took this in stride better than I. I stopped going to the beauty shop altogether. And when the snow began to thaw, the craziness seemed to ebb. Men began to work again, slowly. The knowledge that some of them were going back to work seemed to give the rest of them stamina and patience.

It was as though Harry hung on through the worst legal period of the year: We lost him in March. Maybe it's more accurate to say that he went away. There was little fanfare in his passing. His condition had deteriorated and it was becoming obvious that his pain had intensified, though he didn't complain. No one complained much in Coleman.

The first week in March, Roberta came to the office, went through all her work, passed me a bit of it, and cleaned her desk. In her brisk and official way she said, "Harry's not doing well. I'm going to stay home with him for a couple of weeks. I don't believe there's much time left. Anything you can't handle, pass on to Matthew St. Croix or Rick Padilla," she said, naming two other attorneys in town.

"What can I do, Roberta?" I asked.

"Well, Harry really likes those cookies with the candies in them that you made over Christmas," she said. "Bake him up a batch if you feel like it."

Uncomfortable as I was with a situation like this, I dashed home, baked the cookies, and drove out to the Musettas' first thing the next morning with a huge box. I had another lesson about how people like this cope; it appeared that despite the emotion, Harry's death was accepted as a part of the human condition. His passing seemed a slow, easy, uncomplicated slide.

I gave him his supply of cookies and asked him how he was feeling. His pallor was dreadful, his body had grown thin; he was lying back in a deep chair with his long legs propped on a hassock and an afghan thrown over him. He had glasses half full of juice, water, and pop on the little table by his chair and held the remote control to the TV on his lap. He flipped it off when I arrived and told me he felt punk.

"Well, honey, I feel punk, but that's to be expected. These will sure taste good, though. Tell the truth, Berta likes 'em as much as me."

"How's your appetite?" I asked him.

"Ain't bad. Ain't bad. Jackie, you're a young gal. Don't be worrying about me too much. It wouldn't do. Anyhow, just what they got on TV in the daytime is enough to make the hereafter look good." I chuckled in spite of myself. "Berta always said she went to law school because there wasn't anything else to do. . . . I imagine she meant there wasn't anything good on TV."

I didn't stay long; it seemed that Harry had a hard time with small talk and he looked so uncomfortable that I got ready to leave soon after I'd arrived. I bent over and kissed the top of his head and said, "Goodbye, Harry."

He said, "I'll see you later, honey."

That stopped me for a moment. I knew he had meant to say that, and we both knew he wasn't going to be around for long. I got some tears in my eyes and said, "Harry, did Roberta ever tell you that I had a child once? That he died?"

"Yeah, I sure was sorry to hear that. You're a strong gal. That's a tough one, losing a child."

"Harry? Look in on him, will you?"

"You bet, honey. And I'll tell him he'd be right proud of you."

Despite the fact that I cried all the way back to the office, I felt a kind of glow growing within me. As I sobbed, I fantasized that Wharton and Sheffie and Harry would go fishing in heaven, as preposterous as that sounds, as far from my own spiritual beliefs as that is. I couldn't help thinking, though, how safe and secure Sheffie would be with them.

Dr. Haynes wrote "heart failure" on Harry's death certificate. If anyone wondered about the pills he'd collected or whether there'd been any conspiracy between Harry and Roberta, no one asked or speculated. We sent Harry off in much the same way we marked Wharton's passing. There were tears, remembrances, embraces, and laughter.

"This town sure has changed," Bodge said, wiping his eyes.

That I know of, no one heard a word from Tom Wahl all winter.

16

THE winter had been hard. Roberta took two weeks off following Harry's death. His passing had softened her; she was more sentimental. I remember hugging her and telling her she was tough and unbreakable; she told me we shared that. Our bond was now deeper; we had each buried loved ones and were left behind, alone. She could speak candidly about how quiet the house had become, about missing "that old fart," about not knowing what to do with the lambs and wishing at least Wharton was still around, because he was best with animals. But she soldiered on—which is what my new friends were so good at doing.

Over the winter I had opened up about Sheffie and my loss. The story came out while picking apples with Sue Scully, while drinking a beer with the Danias, when signing a petition for a traffic light near the grade school that one of my clients brought to my office. I found that my life with Sheffie and even my grief for him was not something I wanted to hold quietly inside me. I wanted to share all of that with the valley people who were letting me know they cared about me.

The early signs of spring teased Coleman. There were a few sprouts and buds, then another snowfall. Even with fresh snow on the ground, we could feel the rush of warmth heading in our direction. In the spirit of spring cleaning, of renewal, I decided to hang wallpaper and replace old curtains with blinds. The best place to order this stuff was from a little store called Finishing Touches owned and operated by a woman named Beth Winters.

I hadn't done much on my house through the winter. Besides buying and hanging a couple of prints, setting up twin beds in the spare room for company, and adding accessories to the bathrooms and the kitchen, I hadn't taken on any major renovation projects. I wanted to extend and enclose that back porch. A sun room to enjoy through summer would be uplifting, yet I stalled, putting off any plans. I didn't want another carpenter in my house. I made do with superficial improvements.

I went through books, samples, and fabrics. I was down to a few choices and having trouble with a final decision. I had a picture from a magazine that I had coupled with my fabric and color samples for my bedroom.

"Beth," I asked, "are you a decorator?"

"Yes, of course."

"I'm having trouble making up my mind here. Any input?"

"Would you like me to come out to the house, take a look at the room, the light, what you already have in it, and give you an opinion?"

"Perfect," I said. Beth Winters is an agreeable, dependable, amiable, and businesslike decorator. She has only one helper in her store, her teenage daughter, Sarah. There were times, she told me, that she had to close the shop in order to go to a client's house during business hours. She kept very little stock for sale as hers was primarily a special-order business and the decorating she did in Coleman was not a huge concern.

Beth and her husband and children had come to Coleman a few years earlier; Bob Winters was an area manager for a savings and loan that had branches in several Colorado towns and cities. Traveling from town to town made for long days for Bob, and Beth's small business kept her from boredom and loneliness.

After she looked around my house, gave me her suggestions, and I made my selections, we had a cup of coffee together and talked about the town, her kids and the schools, her husband's job, my job, and various other ordinary stuff. It was when I went into her shop the next morning to give her a deposit on the orders and pick up my receipt that something occurred to me.

"Hey, I wonder if you ever knew that other decorator who left a couple of years ago. What was her name? Eileen something?"

Beth's face immediately seemed to close up and she covered a look of irritation. "Elaine Broussard," she corrected. "She was my partner."

"Oh," I said, stopped by her hardened expression. There was obviously ill will between them. "Where was it she went?"

"I have absolutely no idea," she replied sourly. "It turned out that she left no forwarding address."

I gathered that I wasn't invited to ask anything more. And I didn't, at that time. I'm cursed with a relentless curiosity, however. When the first of my orders came in, Beth offered to drop the blinds off at my house on her way home after she closed up her shop. The grim look on her face was gone since the ex-partner's name hadn't come up again. She offered to have the blinds installed for me, but I was capable of doing this much. I invited her in for a glass of wine. I had no premeditated strategy to get information out of her, but once we'd drunk the first half-glass, a question slipped past my lips.

"I hope this isn't too forward. You aroused my interest with the way you reacted to my question about Elaine Broussard."

"That name tends to do more than arouse me, Jackie. Elaine and I parted on unfriendly terms and I haven't talked about it much. If I could find her, I'd have her arrested."

"Is it personal? Can you talk about it?"

"I can. I seldom do. I'm still angry and it gets me going. Why would you be interested?"

"Oh . . . besides morbid curiosity, you mean? I had a few dates with Tom Wahl last fall and he mentioned her. Apparently they were steadies and I got the impression, well, that he'd been hurt by her in some way. I'm not dating him now."

"Poor Tom—I imagine he was hurt by her. She turned out to be a thief and a liar. She fled in the dark of night and took the shop's bank account with her."

Beth Winters had been living in Coleman less than a year and had some decorating experience when Elaine Broussard came to town and began establishing a decorator service out of her home, which was a rented house on the east end. They met through that connection because Beth was trying to order some supplies to refurbish her house.

"She was generous with her time and her commission on the things I ordered—everything from paint to wallpaper to custom-tailored spreads and valances. Bob and I aren't all that social, and I hadn't yet made many friends, although I'd met a few people. Besides volunteering at the schools for the kids, and shopping, I was occupied with decorating my house. I had worked for a decorator in Richmond when we were there and I did have secret, unspoken ambitions of opening a store.

"Elaine and I became close too fast. We were inseparable in weeks—both of us starved for friends, I thought. We began talking about opening a business. We both had to commit money to the venture, of course, and we both agreed that our own homes should reflect the kind of tasteful and reasonable decorating we were trying to sell. So we began to work out of her house, keeping all the samples, books, and receipts there until we could move into a shop.

"We advertised, circulated brochures, took photos, published coupons, did the legwork, and finally had a few clients. In order to do that, we had to borrow, and Bob not only approved our business loan, he cosigned. We put all our money into our own decorating and the store stock. Things like upholstery fabric that we bought on the shop's books, we could put into our own homes because we used all that stock to get clients. It kept our income looking like zero while we were building a clientele and we were spending our earnings on ourselves. Because it was shop money, not divided fifty-fifty between us, all the furnishings of Elaine's house were dually owned, as all my intake was half hers. Neither of us drew a salary that first year."

A year after they opened their shop, Elaine started dating Tom Wahl and Beth was pleased for her. The shop used Tom as a repair man, carpenter, Mr. Fix-it. He could install doors, hang blinds, and do other things for clients. Because of Beth's family responsibilities, Elaine was often alone. Until Tom.

"I didn't realize until she had gone how little I knew about her. I thought her family was in Milwaukee, but I was never able to find any there. I thought she was getting serious about Tom Wahl and I learned later that they'd stopped seeing each other weeks before she left town. Elaine and I started to argue about things like charges for clients, wholesalers we were ordering from—that sort of thing. The reason Elaine gave me was that she needed a larger income. I was able to live on my husband's salary; she was not. I think we each cleared about twelve thousand dollars that first year we had a shop. While my money went into extras, hers was supposed to keep body and soul together. Elaine became more and more irritable and impatient.

"She said she wasn't making it financially and had sunk her entire savings into our store and our stock. She mentioned that she might have to go back to Milwaukee to work. I remember saying that I thought she was so happy in Coleman, with Tom, and she corrected me instantly. She said she liked Tom fine, but there was no future with him. She asked me not to say anything to anyone about her situation with Tom and that she'd fill me in sometime. He was not marriage material; they were only friends.

"She told me she would have to go north to work and she'd give up her half of the business. She said she wouldn't need to be reimbursed for her share of the partnership immediately, but if she could just have a small portion of the bank account to get started, she could be patient. We made up a long list of the money we had used in our own houses and planned to count her possessions against the final tally."

So Elaine, I was told, was going to take a couple of weeks off and go back to Milwaukee, which she did. She returned, packed up her stuff, and told her clients she was moving to Milwaukee, where she would work.

She had rented a truck that she was going to drive herself, towing her small car behind, which was how she'd arrived in Coleman. On this end she had friends to help her load; on the other end she had friends who would help unload. The only problem was, on her way out of town she stopped to withdraw all the money from the Finishing Touches account and had not terminated the lease on her house. More than half of that money had been deposits made by customers—money needed to make final payments on the materials ordered. The rented truck turned up empty, not in Milwaukee but in Des Moines, having never been leased to Elaine Broussard. Some man named Kyle something or other had signed the lease.

"You were robbed," I said.

"And left with a big payment on a business loan that we both signed. I'm not sure if it was a scam from the start or if it was something she thought of after her cash-flow problem emerged. I'll never know for sure.

"I asked Tom about her and he was angry, too. What happened to him was similar to what happened to me. Elaine got all hot and heavy and involved with him, never told him she was having money trouble of any kind, and later told him that there was a man in Milwaukee she had lived with, broken up with, and was going back to. Good old Tom, he even helped her pack up and get out of her house so he could stay on good terms to the end."

"That was an awfully generous thing to do," I said.

"He felt terrible about everything. He even offered to loan me a few thousand dollars because he had no idea Elaine was cleaning out the bank account and sticking me with debts. He said he felt partially responsible; we never talked to each other at all. I mean, if he'd come to me and explained some of the things Elaine had said to him versus what she'd said to me, I might have been warned.

"What she did, whether she'd planned it from the start or thought of it later, was so well organized. My husband's home office is in Denver and he drives over about once a week. About two years after Elaine was gone, Bob brought home a lamp with the Finishing Touches sticker on the bottom and inside the shade. He's a garage-sale junkie; he got it at a garage sale. The rose color was in tune with the shop decor and the decor of Elaine's house so out of curiosity he lifted the lamp up and found our sticker. When he asked the lady where she'd gotten the lamp, she said a couple had sold a whole truckload of furniture and accessories at a flea market in Denver. Elaine dumped everything on her way out of town."

"So there was a guy somewhere, in the deal with her?"

"Near as I can tell. I told Sheriff Scully about all this, but to tell you the truth, she got away clean and quick. I didn't even know where to look. Kyle Somebody rented the truck with a Colorado driver's license and when we researched that through DMV we found it was expired and there was no current address on him.

"As we compared notes, Tom began to wonder if she'd planned it all along. I doubt it. She was with me just about all the time and got away with about forty thousand dollars, total, for two years' time invested. I would think a real con artist would need more than that to get by. No, I think there was a man in her past and he came up with the idea."

"Did she do any damage to Tom?" I asked.

"Emotional damage," Beth said. "He told you about it?"

"Only that he had been dating her, didn't know she had anything else going, and then they broke up."

"There's more to it, never mind what he says. He was in love with her. He was going to ask her to marry him," Beth said. "They were inseparable; spent all their time together. He's such a sweet, sensitive guy. He helps me out without charging me half the time because he feels bad about what happened with Elaine. She used him, too. To what end, I don't know."

"Why would you say that?"

"She needed an ally here to help her get out of town. It didn't seem sudden at the time, but in retrospect, it was pretty abrupt. It was all happening at the same time—her gradual edging away from me, the business, everything. She became silent, tense, worried. I thought she was upset about finances; Tom thought she was upset about another man. I guess that's when she was plotting her getaway. That would explain her behavior."

"What do her other friends say?"

"What other friends? She didn't get close to anyone else that I know of. Me and Tom . . . the injured she left behind. Oh, there were acquaintances—and there was Nicole, whose theory was that Elaine was not the genuine article. Nicole called her a hoity-toity floozy. I asked around for a while, but the only thing that was really clear was that she suddenly got a hot notion to leave and then left quickly. From her first mention of going, it was less than a month."

I leaned forward. "Beth, surely you could have this investigated if you really wanted to. You could get the answers."

"Bob and I considered that. We even discussed the details with Sheriff Scully. I've already lost about forty thousand dollars in this deal and I would have to get a detective and then file a civil suit after finding her. People who are dodging debts tend to slip away after they're served by the court and finding them can get complicated and expensive. I decided to take the forty-thousand-dollar lesson. You know how it is—even hungry for justice, I thought it was better to satisfy the clients who were left hanging, do a good business, and get on with my life. But, Jackie, I'm going to take my anger over this to my grave. I can't get over it."

Beth and I were not destined to be good friends, there was no chemistry. It was no loss for either of us. She was a good decorator, a nice lady, and I was sorry that she had suffered through losing a friend and a sizable chunk of money because of her involvement with Elaine Broussard. I could have offered to help her track Elaine down—I'm good at tracking people. I could have offered her a break on legal fees. I didn't do any of that.

There was something in her telling of the story that got me thinking about Tom again and began an interesting quest for me. Despite my early-warning signs, I set out to investigate him in earnest. Before getting very far, I was seized with a new goal. I thought I could prove, with enough evidence at my disposal, that he had not killed his wife and child. This odyssey required help from Mike, and time.

When I considered doing more checking, it never

occurred to me that I would resume any kind of relationship with him. I didn't contemplate even a casual friendship. It wasn't that his absence softened his image in my mind. I remembered clearly that contact with him and events in which he seemed centered, were fraught with indecision, disquiet.

I didn't pursue this because I desired Tom. To the contrary, I wanted him out of my life. Over the winter, with all the gatherings and happenings, I'd met men I liked better, men who didn't give me any signals that there was danger or complication ahead. There appeared to be no pressure of any kind. There was cross-country skiing with a group of people that included the painter, and I met the world-class cyclist at a political meeting. The possibilities for companionship were wider than I originally thought.

I wasn't sure whether I would tell Tom what I found. What I wanted to do was have a sense of closure on that portion of my life. That month with the phantom, the finger, and the eerie feelings I had struggled with still held a nightmarish quality in my mind and I wanted to be past it. I wanted final, resolved peace of mind.

Roberta, only a month into her grief, talked about closing the office for a couple of weeks, perhaps a month, before the intrusion of summer campers and vacationers hit town. There were plenty of things at home she had to finalize after Harry's death. She wasn't about to go on keeping chickens and cows. She wasn't going to continue to pay someone to look after animals that Harry had bred and cared for.

I was glad to have the time. I locked up the house and went to Los Angeles for a long visit. This time I bravely stayed with Mike and Chelsea: Mike and Chelsea and their pictures of Sheffie around their house. Sheffie and me. Sheffie, Tiffany, and Jessica. Sheffie and his dad; Sheffie, Chelsea, and Mike. It was time to see these.

"How many women come home for a visit and stay with their ex-husband and his wife?" Janice Whitcomb asked me.

"Not many, I'm sure. Think of how effective it is. I can't possibly fall in love with him again when I get a first-hand view of how sloppy and lazy he is."

"Think of his poor wife! What must she feel like, having you there under her roof?"

"Chelsea?" I laughed. "Listen, Chelsea is the only thing in the world that makes this possible. If Mike and I had been smart, we *both* would have married her. It would have saved us a divorce and we each would have gotten the best wife there is."

I told Mike that I was still interested in the Lawler murders, that I wanted to take a closer look at that period, that case, and see what I could find. It isn't hard for a lawyer to get access to files, research data, and DMV and phone records, even when working on an inactive case. What is hard is getting good stuff that's twelve years old.

The first thing I did was go to the library and cross-reference this guy. I found his articles, some of them on microfilm. I found a brief biography in an old scientific journal, and in the Columbia yearbook I found his degrees and awards. Some of this information was repeated in newspaper accounts of the crime. I found his name in a scientific *Who's Who*. I had already seen the newspaper photos; there was a picture in the University of Illinois yearbook, twenty years old. He was a fresh-faced youth, though unsmiling.

Thomas Patrick Lawler, Ph.D., was born in Chicago in 1947, the third son of Joseph and Rosie

Lawler. He graduated from college in 1970, attained his Ph.D. in clinical psychology in 1975, and had published several papers before 1978. I read them. They were scientific and verbose but, I thought, comprehensive and insightful. He wrote about psychological testing, which, as he'd told me, had been his specialty. The case studies interested me, for they mirrored some of the stories that Tom had told me. There was a long paper on obsessive-compulsive disorder that seemed to be the story he had told me about the man who fantasized he had killed his handicapped brother.

The man who wrote about this and other clients he had seen in therapy had to be patient, disciplined, intelligent, and compassionate. But the articles I could relate to more easily were those few that had been published in women's magazines. Here again, I was impressed by his handle, his sensitivity to these issues. I absorbed the warmth I knew him capable of and reminded myself of his other, more callous side.

One long piece was intended to help people detect mental illness in someone they loved—a friend or family member. The energy in his writing was devoted to removing the stigma of mental illnesses, comparing them to other physical conditions and limitations; he explained the brain chemistry of chronic depression, schizophrenia, manic-depression, senility, and Alzheimer's. Then he set about giving a list of interventions the readers could employ to get the necessary help for their loved one. And finally, he wrapped the article up with a supportive finale and established a goal for our society: to treat these diseases with the same aggressiveness we use on more socially acceptable illnesses like heart disease and cancer. Included, as a sidebar, was a list of support organizations for people who had to deal with a close relative or friend who had a mental illness or disorder.

It was comforting to read. This man did seem to know his stuff. His articles were authoritative without being intrusive or bullying. The magazine article about identifying and helping the mentally ill had been published in December of 1986 and the bio called Thomas P. Lawler "a research psychologist who studies and writes in his Oregon home." Well, I figured that was fair enough—he claimed to have come to Coleman in that year; it didn't seem strange to me that he'd keep an Oregon location for the public. Had the article said he was practicing in Maine, I would have been very suspicious.

So I wondered, was he still doing some research? I don't mean complicated all-consuming scientific research, but was he perhaps still studying, still collecting some data, even if he wasn't doing much field work? He was still doing some writing, he had told me. His collection of books was impressive. The ones I had picked up were heavily underlined and highlighted; notations were made in margins. He did have a personal computer, on which he did his price and materials lists for building work. He must also be doing some writing on it.

Finally, I got to the feature stories from newspapers and news journals about the crime. Here I was confronted with pictures—terrible pictures. Pictures of him crying while a policeman wrote down details. Pictures of him at the funeral, his head in his hands, and an elderly woman, I suppose his mother, touching his back in comfort. A profile photo of him at the graveside. A picture of him emerging from the police station with a briefcase-toting man walking beside him: his lawyer. I wrote down the lawyer's name; he might still have a practice in Los Angeles.

I read the article about the Lawler murders and an account of Thomas Lawler being briefly questioned as a suspect. This article said there was another possible suspect, but the police wouldn't elaborate. That was when I had to go back into court reports and police files, and pay a visit to the nearest maximum-security psychiatric hospital.

That was when I had to look at Jason Devalian through my own eyes.

17

WHILE I researched, Tom's voice rang in my ears. "There's proof, dammit!" There was. It didn't take long to be convinced that Tom was right: Jason Devalian had threatened Tom and his family, then killed Janet Lawler and little Lisa. He probably meant to kill them all.

A good attorney or law clerk gets what she needs right away and doesn't get absorbed in meaningless detail. So, I went directly to the Department of Motor Vehicles . . . or should I say I took my buddy the badge with me. Mike and I looked for the address of Jason Devalian at the time of the slaying in March of 1978, twelve years before. We found that he had been issued a notice of a driver's license suspension due to unpaid fines, and his mail had been sent to the maximum-security hospital, which, according to court records, was his residence. The next notice was sent to a minimum-security facility because the first had been returned. This immediately made me wonder where he had been held.

I had time and I was suffering from an obsessive desire to know everything. So, knowing I was frittering away time I could spend with my friends, I

started at the beginning. I read the court records
from the coroner's inquest in the death of one Pauline Renee Zappalla. It seemed she was picked up at
a bar by the accused, moved in with him, spent three
short months in cohabitation, and died from injuries
sustained in a beating. Jason Devalian was picked
up, booked and charged; he retained the services of
a public defender who requested an evaluation from
a psychiatrist.

The state also produced an expert: Tom Lawler.

When the two experts disagreed on the disposition
of the defendant, the court required a third. The
defendant's expert said the accused was a multiple
personality; the defendant required hospitalization,
medication, and long-term therapy. He estimated
that the defendant was only lucid and responsible
fifteen percent of the time. Devalian's "other" personality was psychotic—hallucinating a good share of
the time and helpless to control his mind or know
right from wrong. This personality heard voices and
orders from God and could not be controlled. He
was not responsible by reason of insanity.

Dr. Lawler also examined, tested, and interviewed
the defendant. He found Devalian to be lucid, highly
intelligent, manipulative, and sociopathic. Lawler's
intake information pointed to substantial early-
childhood sexual abuse, lack of formal education,
and an unsupervised adolescence, as the defendant
had fled his abusive parents at the age of thirteen.

I saw the similarity between this description and
one that Tom had given me of one of his clients.
Either he had evaluated many sociopaths with similar case histories or he had been describing Devalian
without naming him.

Devalian had a long list of priors ranging from
assault to petty theft to vandalism and destruction

of property. And, while he put on a show of hearing
voices and changing personalities, Dr. Lawler was
convinced it was an act. Whether Devalian wrote his
tests as himself or as his alleged alter-personality,
the results were either identical or comparable. That
was not in keeping with what is routinely understood
about multiple personalities, Lawler testified. All
personalities have individual traits, histories, and
abilities. If, as an example, a thirty-eight-year-old
man is experiencing the personality of a ten-year-
old, that ten-year-old writes the test. In some cases
alter-personalities are blind, deaf, or in some other
way incapacitated.

Dr. Lawler's recommendation was that the defendant was competent to stand trial and that any court-
ordered psychotherapeutic intervention could be accomplished either privately or in a state penal insti-
tution. Dr. Lawler said that Mr. Devalian admitted
to slaying the deceased woman, that he knew what
he had done and had a reason if not a motive, and
that he was a dangerous man.

A third expert witness was called into camp. Even
from my distance, years and miles removed from
this case, I could see the critical flaws. By the time
the court ordered a third evaluation, Jason Devalian
had heard the previous testimony. In his new tests
he functioned as a multiple personality who was psychotic. Tom Lawler had given Devalian a diagram in
his own testimony on how that could be done.

I needed a court order to examine the records at
the hospital; fortunately, I have an acquaintance
among the judiciary in Los Angeles. I went to His
Honor Sy Resselman, explained the whole situation
in ten minutes or less, and got not only a court order
but an invitation to dinner. Sy was a fifty-five-year-
old widower whom I'd seen in Family Court many

times over the years; while there never was anything romantic between us, we liked each other. Dinner and the court order were both gratefully accepted.

The reading I did at the hospital was both intriguing and upsetting. I hadn't seen any photos of Jason Devalian yet. Considering them illustrated how drastically a judgment can change with appearance. When arrested for the murder of Pauline Renee Zappalla, Jason Devalian was an awful-looking character. His arrest photo showed a long, thin nose, thin lips, masses of stringy, oily hair, a disheveled appearance, and a narrow mustache; they caused him to look sinister, like a character out of a comic-strip lineup. His cheeks were sunken; his chin jutted out; he had a sickly pallor and wild-looking blue eyes.

His hospital admission records included an improved photo, because he had been cleaned up by his public defender. There never had been any newspaper photos of him; the case of a poor woman killed by her boyfriend in a poor neighborhood didn't get any press attention. When I looked at the photo of the new, improved Devalian, even I hesitated to see him in such a criminal light. His hair was styled, he had shaved, his eyes were calm; his face didn't look as long or grim. And, unmistakably, there was a small smile on his lips.

I read through his intake information. He'd been raised by his father after his mother abandoned them both and he had suffered through sexual abuse by his father. He told the intake counselor that his mother conspired in the abuse; she didn't protect him. She was likewise severely abused by Devalian's father.

His father isolated him from society, kept him a prisoner. He lived on a large farm in Nebraska at which there were a number of hired hands. Most of them were transient in nature and no one got close enough to the family for any intervention. There was no family life, school life, or spiritual life.

Jason Devalian was educated only to the fourth grade, but had somehow developed his reading and math skills beyond that level. Though they were simple skills, not to include things like training in linguistics, algebra, or the like, he could still hold his own in a written test. He had been on his own since the age of thirteen, earning money in a variety of ways both legal and illegal. He had escaped his father's abuse by running away with a transient farm laborer.

There was no longer any doubt that I was reading about one of the cases that Tom had described. I knew that Tom would have remembered who he was talking about and so had withheld the identity from me, saying he couldn't remember how the man came to be in counseling. But I excused his duplicity: On the night we had the discussion, I had been firm in telling him I didn't want to hear any more about his traumatic past but was interested in knowing more about his life, his profession, his family. His unemotional description of this particular case history continued to confuse me, however. I wondered how he could do it, so coolly narrate the psychological history of the man who had killed his family.

I read on. Devalian was heavily medicated during the first weeks of his stay in the hospital, but judging by his attendance in group therapy, in the dining room, in card games and chess games, it appeared that he was functional. The nurses, counselors, and psychiatrist wrote rather glowing attributes to his behavior while he was there. He was said to be remorseful, penitent, and determined to turn his life around. He was recommended early for transfer to a minimum-security facility.

And that's where the evidence lay.

The Lawler murders took place on the fifteenth of March. The documentation of Jason Devalian's transfer to a minimum-security facility was officially dated the eighteenth of March. It looked certain to me that the document was originally printed with the number thirteen and corrected, or altered, to become an eighteen. This could mean that Jason Devalian had been housed in a minimum-security unit on the night Lawler's family was killed.

"Tom Lawler didn't do it," I told Sy at dinner that night. "Tom, who is impossible for me to understand anyway, *did* have a psychopath on his hands."

"What about the alleged threats?" he asked.

"On the message tapes? According to the police report, after the Lawler murders there was one tape preserved for the police department. Lawler claims that when you work exclusively in criminal courts and the prison system, it isn't unusual to get threatening stuff over the phone. That was his explanation for not doing more than he did at the time. For instance, he said he didn't warn his wife or stay close to home."

"And what did he do at the time?"

"He telephoned the police, made a complaint, and was told what he was told at other times—there wasn't too much they could do about it. He said he'd had threats from prison inmates; it isn't as though you should put them under surveillance if they're already incarcerated."

"Did you track down the transfer record?"

"Oh, it was signed by the attending psychiatrist, that's for sure. When the date was altered and by whom remains a mystery. It could have been a staff member—or the doctor himself, when he realized there was a crime and he could be held responsible. Besides that, there are medical notes on him right up to the eighteenth, but that could be a fancy deal, you know. Like how we list our car expenses after the taxes are filed. Maybe someone went back in after he was transferred and made a few notes about his behavior, his medication, that sort of thing. There hadn't been a visit with the doctor during that questionable five-day period. I thought about the possibility of Devalian himself altering the date and adding to the daily reports up to the eighteenth, but patients are locked in wards and have no access to the nurses' station.

"Devalian was an animal, a wild man, when he was picked up by police after the death of his girlfriend. He had to be subdued by four officers to get him handcuffed. To read the staff reports on the same guy while he was an inmate, you'd think he was Prince Charming. It's possible he manipulated some staff member and managed to get his transfer out early."

"All things being equal, when should he have been transferred?"

"Sy, you're a judge, you know the beauty of indeterminate sentencing. After his thirty-day intake and diagnosis, he was left to the discretion of the attending physician. If they thought he was crazy and dangerous, they kept him. If they thought he was mentally deficient yet manageable, they could do anything at all with him. They could have let him go unless the court tagged a specific time commitment on him, which wasn't done."

"And wasn't done," Sy said, "because it was a domestic crime and the couple were dangerous only to each other. With one of them dead, the state of overcrowding . . ."

"Happens every day," I said, knowing only too well. There was no one to file a civil suit on behalf of the dead woman, no one interested enough to press for prosecution. Nobody was involved in his case; nobody cared.

"And then," I told Sy, "the frosting here is that from minimum security he did a crime. He put an orderly's jacket on over his jeans and walked out of the hospital, went to a bar and had a couple of beers, chatted with some of the patrons and the bartender, took a bus to a residential area, broke into a middle-class house, stole some jewelry and money, and lit a fire in the family room to cover the theft. The arrival of the fire department created enough of a scene to allow him to wait for the bus four blocks away without arousing suspicion. The house was badly damaged. The staff found the stuff on him and the police found witnesses who had talked to him while he was out on this little self-oriented leave. He was supposed to be in ceramics. Ceramics. He had signed out of his ward to go to ceramics." I drank my wine. "Whatever happened to basket weaving?"

"What are you going to do about this, Jackie?"

"I went after this information to reassure myself. I started to date this guy, Tom Lawler. Then this stuff from his past began to complicate and confuse the relationship. By the time we stopped seeing each other, I thought he was a madman. He seemed to have personality shifts and mood swings; bizarre things were happening to me.

"To give you an example, we had a pleasant evening together, shared personal things, talked of how neither of us was interested in a serious or committed relationship . . . and then I discovered someone had been in my house while I was asleep—a glass of cranberry juice, which I'd been drinking that evening, was spilled on my tablecloth. Next, he'd call and put the pressure on me to go somewhere with him. He'd tell me he understood and respected my desire to remain unattached, then become hostile if I declined an invitation. He saw me at the local town fair with Mike and became jealous and agitated. Later, when I took the trouble to try to explain myself, he turned the whole thing back on me and accused me of playing games with him and trying to ruin his reputation. I'm through with this guy. It comes as a relief to know that Tom Lawler didn't kill his wife and child; I was praying I hadn't been involved with a murderer. I won't mention this to him, however. It might make him want to resume the friendship. He may be an innocent victim, but he's also screwed up. Strange."

Sy chewed thoughtfully before commenting. "Crime victims can have long-term psychological and emotional problems; surely you know that."

"Of course."

"Paranoia, phobic reactions, anger, all sorts of things. If the guy is innocent and was a respected professional before his family was killed and is now strange, it doesn't strike me as improbable. Perhaps it's taken its toll on his ability to socialize. That certainly doesn't obligate you to any friendship."

"Sy, the guy has me so confused that I can't risk friendship with him. I felt justified in asking Mike to get me some police stuff, then I felt guilty as though I'd purposely set out to ruin an innocent man, then back to anger and defensiveness. . . . I'm too confused to think clearly. I just wanted to settle this one thing in my mind."

"Then don't say anything to anyone. Take your proof in your head back to your little practice in Colorado and write this guy off. It's not as though he's facing a prison sentence and you're the only one who can save him."

"And if this is following him around and he's still, as he claims, being blamed for, if not charged with, some awful crime that he didn't commit? Shouldn't this be brought to someone's attention in the interest of justice if nothing else?"

"You could write an anonymous letter, but you know how much attention that gets. You could try to track down his lawyer. You could go to the police here and try to give them the information without giving your name. You could maybe have Mike take care of it for you."

In the end, that's what I did do. Before I got to that point, however, I did a little more looking into Jason Devalian's records following the arrest for breaking and entering, theft, and arson. He was paroled after serving two years in prison, broke parole, and drifted off.

While he was in prison, he was again the model inmate. He was only in the infirmary twice: once when he'd been beaten and once for appendicitis. Either his recovery on both occasions was miraculous or he hadn't been very sick. In prison he had suffered from severe peritonitis associated with his appendectomy, and must have been one sick puppy. He was treated with heavy antibiotics and large doses of Demerol and Valium. Yet he went back to the cell block four days after surgery and the results of his postsurgical checkups were noted as favorable. In the battering he suffered a broken nose and jaw, two lost teeth, two fractured fingers, and marked bruising. He was not hospitalized and was treated with aspirin for the pain. This pattern had an interesting parallel in his earlier hospitalization. These reports attested to the fact that Devalian could withstand severe pain, just as the earlier hospital reports suggested he could function physically and mentally while heavily medicated.

The model prisoner was an incredible physical specimen and an intellectual anomaly. Although he was lacking in formal education, he studied everything from astronomy to law while he was in prison. He wrote long letters to experts and received answers to all his questions. He ordered books and taught himself to speed-read. In a work program he learned how to operate a computer and how to repair air conditioners, refrigerators, and small appliances. He read copious fiction as well. To do all he did he must have been a paragon of concentration, dedication, and endurance. He also must not have slept more than two hours a night.

He was reported in one evaluation as being manic sans depression. He behaved as though he couldn't manage inactivity. He resorted to body building on the recommendation of the visiting psychiatrist. That physician noted that tranquilizers had little effect on him; barbiturates did not help him sleep.

And they all loved him. He had many privileges while he was in prison; he got soft jobs and plenty of time off. As the hospital had reported, the man was cooperative and determined to turn his life around. Reading all this, of course, put it into perspective for me: He was intelligent and a manipulator. When he came up for parole he had a job lined up, a parole officer waiting to take over, and a deep and sincere goal of making something of himself. He walked out of jail and walked right out of the state, perhaps out of the country. That's where they lost him.

His multiple personality, incidentally, was never treated or mentioned again.

I felt compelled to speak to Dake Ramsey, the detective who had worked on the Lawler murders. We arranged to meet in a coffee shop near the police department. I got the impression he was going to turn me down until I mentioned that my ex-husband was Mike Alexander. He was reluctant and irritable.

When I asked him what he remembered about the Lawler murders, he hesitated; he thought for a long time before answering. It seemed his memory for detail was fuzzy, but that wasn't the worst of it.

Dake was fifty-eight, and for reasons I will never know, he was bitter and angry. He remembered that he couldn't pin anything on Lawler and remembered being convinced Lawler had done it.

I told him about the evidence, the altered transfer record.

"That's no secret," he replied, flip. "We saw it right away. It was a flubbed record, a typo corrected by the typist at the time it was done. There were plenty of witnesses to the fact that he was there."

"What witnesses? Like doctors and nurses?"

"Staff, yes," he said. "And other patients."

"Did you look at the intake records in minimum security? Had you noticed their failure to record his transfer? There is no intake there. None. They have nurses' notes after the eighteenth; no transfer or intake document. I think it was taken out. It's possible that someone removed the transfer and intake information and the first five days of nurses' notes from the minimum-security file and added five extra days of records to the maximum-security file."

"Now that it's been twelve years, it looks like it was

taken out," he said, very sarcastic and impatient with me. "At the time we talked to everyone on staff and he was in a tight mental unit during the murders, in a minimum later. Look, why you doing this?"

"Didn't Mike tell you?"

"Tell me what? He got some stuff on this, but he didn't tell me nothing."

"I met Tom Lawler. He's still haunted by this thing, and the worst of it is that he's never been charged, so he's never gone to trial, so he's never proven his innocence. It still follows him around; he can't do his work, he can't live a good life."

"Lady, if you're getting yourself involved with this guy, you're as crazy as he is. Lawler may not be mentally ill, but he's goddamn conniving and sneaky. He got everything he ever wanted, and when he got tired of it, he got rid of it. Now, if I was you, I'd rather spend my time with someone certifiable instead of some evil, sneaky bastard like Lawler."

"What is it with you?" I asked him. "You act like you hate him for some reason. You were supposed to find a killer, not take a personality inventory on a man you had no evidence to connect to a crime."

He leveled his stern, rheumy gaze on me for a minute. "I got no time for fancy shrinks, lady. Tell your boyfriend he isn't getting any trouble from LAPD; we haven't pursued him in five or ten years now. He can't make a good life, it's his headache, not mine."

"He isn't my boyfriend," I said.

I was frustrated though not surprised by the lack of decent paperwork on the case. I was annoyed by the fact that people just don't change their minds. Here they had seen what could, best case, be enough circumstantial evidence to get an indictment on Devalian and clear Tom. No one was interested anymore. I questioned my stake in this; I cared about justice more than I cared about Tom.

My last attempt to reach someone failed. The lawyer whose picture appeared in an old newspaper clipping with Tom was named Charles Nielson. And he was on vacation.

"So Mike," I said, "this one last thing. He'll be back in about a week. Call him for me? Please? Or better still, drop in on him some time soon and tell him what we found."

We were having dinner, Chelsea's famous chili made with ground turkey rather than beef. And Mike said, "What's this 'we'? You got a mouse in your pocket?"

"Come on, you helped me with this—let's finish it. Maybe it's a good thing that Nielson wasn't in town. I'd like to see this thing solved once and for all. If Tom Lawler Wahl is going to get some good news, I'd rather it didn't come from me. I plan to have less traffic with the guy."

"Maybe he won't even go back to Coleman. Maybe he'll move on. He's a moving kind of guy, isn't he?"

"He's got property there, a house. I'd love to hear he's selling it and leaving for good, but I'm trying to prepare myself for seeing him around town again."

"You know, Jack," he said, pointing his fork at me across the table, "I got it figured that you think you ought to like this small-town jazz, and it isn't exciting enough for you. Who else would develop a whole case out of a few little pieces of information and a lifted toilet seat?"

"It's exciting enough," I argued. "Especially since we have a killer somewhere in the valley. I had this insidious doubt about Tom. I wanted to be sure. Maybe I'll tell Bodge."

"Do yourself a favor; let this one go once and for all. Drop it, forget it, and don't say anything to anybody. Let the doctor pretend to be a carpenter, and butt out. You might somehow be keeping this whole issue alive by working it to death. Bodge can take care of himself. Anyway, Bodge has got the Mod Squad to help him out with the killer."

"The what?" I asked.

He ate, chewed, and talked with his mouth open. "I'd bet my left nut that Krump is in Coleman working on this. It all adds up to him being there for a reason. Him and about ten others scattered around. Now, what did he tell me? Yeah, yeah, he got burned out on police work after making about a dozen of the best busts in the country and shooting around as many people. The guy got drafted, for Christ's sake. And now he wants a good place to raise the kids ... which he didn't have before and they're already like teenagers. And they're in boarding school. Yep. That's pretty convenient."

"So he married a woman with kids?"

"And he says he feels like he's running a retreat for burned-out cops who need to get away, smell nature, camp and fish a little. This is a guy who never knew from fishing when he lived here, I can tell you that."

"Well, everyone knows he used to be a cop, so he doesn't have much of a cover if he's undercover," I argued.

"That is his cover, Jack. He was a cop, he's retired and does consulting, and that's how he can justify having so many of 'the guys' visit him. That way if anybody makes one of his house guests for a cop, it washes. Huh?"

"I think," I said, "that your imagination is more dangerous than mine."

18

I RETURNED to Coleman still ambivalent about what to do with my information about Tom Lawler, so I did nothing. I didn't tell Bodge or Roberta what I'd done in L.A.

The end of April brought a spring that was refreshing, renewing, and I was feeling stronger and more confident every day. I believed my mental health had greatly improved as a result of having done my own research on Tom's brush with the law. I had clarified for myself that he was not a criminal. I felt I could face him with more self-assurance now.

I went to Finishing Touches to pick up the custom-sewn quilted bedspread that would match the blinds, curtains, and wallpaper I'd purchased, and as if to challenge my position, I found Tom in the store, chatting with Beth. Beth stood behind the counter and Tom leaned on it, blocking her.

I almost withdrew. My feelings were a mixture of embarrassment, resentment, and fear of his reaction to me, mine to him. When Beth leaned to the side to see who had come into the store and let out a cheery "Well, hi, Jackie," Tom turned to smile in his shy, reserved way. He gave a nod.

"Beth," I said. "Tom. How is everyone?"

He muttered something that sounded like "Fine" and Beth said, "Great, and I've got your spread."

There was the business of paying and getting a receipt; when I reached for the bulky plastic-wrapped cover, Tom stopped me. "Here," he said, grabbing it. "I'll be glad to put it in your car for you."

"I can do it," I protested, but he ignored me and took it through the door, tossing it in the backseat of my BMW. After which I could only come up with a lame "Thanks."

"You look like winter agreed with you," he said.

"It was my first snowing winter," I said. My eyes were drawn to his hand and the missing finger, then back to his face. "And you?"

"Good. I'm glad everything worked out like it did— I needed a change of scenery, a little perspective, and the ocean is calming. I guess you remember. . . . I needed calming down."

I ignored that. "The Florida ocean?"

"Yeah. I traveled around the state, camped, and took short-term jobs here and there. Checked out the Everglades. I keep being drawn back here for some reason; I can't give up these wonderful hills and valleys. I don't have to be tied down. I can move around as much as I please. Live out of a truck and trailer. My life is uncomplicated."

I had to be careful not to roll my eyes in disbelief. Uncomplicated? This was the most complex man I had ever known.

"You have a house and work here. That's a big draw, too," I said, wishing I hadn't made any excuse for more small talk.

"I pick up work everywhere. Everyone needs a handyman, carpenter. I have to relearn that lesson all the time, about how little I need. I used to be attached to money, material things that are meaningless. Listen, Jackie—"

I braced myself for what was coming. I sensed he wanted to make up. I was willing to smooth things over. Those aren't the same.

"I don't know how to say this. I'm sorry about all the trouble. It wasn't your fault and I think I might have acted like I thought it was your fault."

"I know it wasn't my fault. Not your fault or mine. I was doing what I thought was best at the time. That's all. I don't blame you for being upset, I don't blame me for being upset, and neither of us could help any of it."

"I know. I acted like an ass."

We had already done this number once. It began a whole series of me being applauded, then chastised and blamed, then forgiven, then criticized. It wasn't unlike what a battered woman goes through; being rescued by her own attacker. After a few rounds of this, you're perpetually off balance. You never know whether what you're going to do will make him mad or garner his praise. I was at once conscious of this and refused to let it go on.

"Water over the dam, Tom. No problem. Let's forget about it and press on, huh?"

He smiled then, with teeth. "I'd like that, Jackie."

"Good. I gotta run; I have a busy calendar."

"Sure. Maybe we can—" He stopped himself right there. "I guess that would be a mistake, huh?"

"How long have you been back?" I asked.

"A couple of days."

"You heard about Wharton?"

"Yeah. Godawful; poor guy."

I thought about correcting his impression, telling him he'd been all wrong about Wharton. I held my tongue. I also knew now, after just moments in his company, that to hear from me that I'd further investigated his situation was too much—he was already making those noises about being friends, going out, whatever this was about. I refused to believe he was that uncontrollably attracted to me. We'd been trouble for each other. That wasn't a one-way deal; I was trouble for him, too. He shouldn't want to be involved with me any further.

"Well, I have to run," I tried again. He opened his mouth as if he was going to say something, and I opened my car door. His hand on the door stopped me and I felt chilled. Apprehensive.

"Beth told me she told you all about Elaine."

"Yes," I said, nodding. "Beth said it was a mess; both you of you were hurt. Terrible. Well . . ."

"So," he said, "maybe you understand now why I'm a little—I don't know—skittish and inexperienced with women. I've been through a couple of tough events with them. I'd like a chance to prove I'm not like that all the time. What do you say, Jackie?"

I put a hand on his forearm and felt his muscles tense beneath my touch. I looked into his eyes; his pupils contracted and his eyes narrowed, though the change was barely perceptible. I was thrown off kilter again; he didn't like me yet pursued me. This was a game and I couldn't fathom the motive. I used my firm, sincere voice. "You don't have to prove anything to me, Tom. I don't think there's any more explaining or apologizing for either one of us to do. Let's drop it. Now. That's what I want."

He slowly withdrew his hand and frowned. I could sense though not see his anger. He was rigid and glared at me.

"Jackie, I'd like to—"

"No," I cut him off. "We're not going to talk about

it again. I have to get to work. Now." I frowned right back at him.

"We'll be running into each other," he said.

"Fine." I physically nudged him away from my car, carefully and slowly. I got in, started the engine, and smiled at him. I gave a little wave and said, "See ya," at the closed window. He stood there, watching me leave, scowling. I watched in my rearview mirror for a while after I pulled out and saw him staring after my car until he was out of sight.

By now I was sick of this. Sick and confused. I couldn't understand what was happening, what he was about, what was going on. My instincts were screaming bloody murder, and my logic—and, indeed, my own sophisticated investigative prowess—had shown again and again that he was merely a man who had had a bad run of luck.

He was not okay. This I knew. And he seemed in no way to be experiencing the unfortunate side effects of being a victim of violent crime. This wasn't guilt, paranoia, phobia. His behavior was controlling and manipulative—which, unmistakably, is more typical of the criminal than of the victim. Wouldn't a guilty, phobic guy retreat and withdraw in feelings of victimization? Tom became agitated and angry when I refused to date him. I experienced another shuddering spasm of fear and suspicion.

Then, as in the past, after a few quiet days and no contact with him, my screaming instincts calmed and I once again talked myself into believing that for some reason I did not understand this man. And that that didn't make him bad.

Then Mike called me one morning at the office.

"Sit down, Jack."

"Oh, God. What now?"

"Well, kiddo, I don't know how to tell you this. . . . I went to see that guy, what's his name—Nielson. The lawyer?"

I braced myself. My heart picked up speed and my palms got instantly wet.

"It turns out that this guy, Tom Wahl, is not Tom Lawler."

"What?"

"He's not Tom Lawler. He's an impostor. A fraud."

"Well, who the hell is he?"

"No telling," Mike said calmly. "Could be he's Tom Wahl. Seems like this whole story is a whole story."

"He looks like Tom Lawler," I said. I began to tremble.

"I know; there's a strong resemblance between your carpenter and the younger Lawler. The carpenter looks like he could have changed a bit in the twelve years, huh? The real Lawler has changed ever more. Did I ever tell you about that cop who wasn't a cop? I cannot figure out these people, these frauds. We had this guy who was supposed to be a transfer and it turned out all his stuff was made-up, bogus, forged stuff. He wasn't a cop at all, had no education, no training, and—"

"Forget about that!" I snapped. "What the hell is this? How did you find this out?"

"Well, I did what you asked me to do and now I'm sorry I didn't get around to it sooner. I went to see the lawyer and asked him if he had once represented this Ph.D., this Tom Lawler, and he said he had. And so I laid it on him about how I knew someone who knew him and believed that he was still feeling that everyone thought he was guilty, and after looking at the evidence through police sources, I for one didn't feel one hundred percent sure he was guilty. I said I thought he was innocent.

"So this lawyer lets me talk and talk; I told him about the transfer, the records, the dates, the nurses' notes, all that and he finally says that I have some old stuff. They found it all a long, long time ago and that was one way Tom Lawler had avoided an indictment. He also said that we missed a couple of things—it turns out that Tom Lawler, working for the state and being a hotshot psychologist, could have himself gone into that maximum-security unit and played with the records if he'd wanted to. He could have changed that transfer record from the eighteenth to the thirteenth if he wanted to. Or he could have made it look like it was changed from the thirteenth to the eighteenth by pencil-whipping it.

"This lawyer says he didn't do that, and before the police even thought of it, Nielson took statements from everyone on every shift that they didn't see Lawler near the place."

"So how does that mean—"

"Nielson asked me what got me interested in this. So I told him, sort of. I told him my ex-wife began dating Tom Lawler, who is now living under a different name in Colorado, and merely wanted to assure herself that this guy was not capable of killing his wife and child. And Nielson looks at me and says, 'This must be quite a burden for Tom's wife, Megan, who believes herself to be happily married to a man who lives in another state.'"

"Megan?" I asked weakly.

"Yeahhhh," Mike said in a way that caused me to envision him stretching. "Dr. Lawler stays in touch with his lawyer, strictly professional relationship. Couple of calls a year to see if anything new has surfaced on that old case. Lawler remarried and has a child. Then Nielson drags out this box of Christmas cards; he hadn't thrown them away yet—always means to read through them. He picks through the cards and pulls out one from Lawler, complete with family photo. Jack, Lawler's hair is still a lighter color, what there is of it. He's chubby, he wears glasses, and he looks preppy."

"Jesus." It was truly a prayer. "Where is he?"

"Lawler? Oh, he's in Oregon. He went there, began doing some private counseling, did some teaching, some writing, and he's still got a business going. He's respectable.

"Nielson added some insights that were never passed on to me at work. Dake Ramsey, Nielson said, had a boner for Lawler; he's prejudiced against shrinks. Hates 'em. Hates the whole insanity clause. It was Dake who created the innuendo about mistresses and drugs and debts. Nielson claims it was established that Lawler was on an emergency call to see a female patient who was not a mistress; an unstable woman, not a lover. His treatment was for tranks and booze, almost a year after the murders, and his debts were legitimate. He spent too much money on credit."

"I thought Lawler lost his job over screwing a patient?"

"He was suspended with pay pending an ethics investigation. He was too sick to go back to work until after treatment. The next time he worked again was in Oregon. The real Lawler is legitimate and he's not worried about being cleared. He's worried about the murderer never paying for the crime. There's a big difference."

"What did Nielson say when you told him I thought I knew Lawler?"

"He said it's impossible. He said it's either a mistake or you got yourself a fraud. Jack, there ain't no mistake. Your man looks like Lawler, says he's

Lawler, and has exaggerated his story from printed information available on *the* Lawler. He's made it more dramatic, more exciting. There is a worm in the potato."

"Why would anyone pretend to be someone with Lawler's past? It's so shocking. So grim—"

"Gets so much pity, so much petting. The poor man, innocent and falsely accused. Maybe this guy just picked Lawler out of the L.A. *Times* and thought, 'Wow, what a great story. And I even look like him.' The first time I heard that psychologist-pretend-carpenter story, I thought it was a get-me-laid line. Did I ever tell you about that guy who pretended to be a general?"

This imposture couldn't all be for sex. For dates. It was more serious than that.

I couldn't think. I kept shaking my head. I'd been used somehow and I knew it, but I did not know what the payoff could possibly be. I'd been tricked. Duped and manipulated. He must be damned good, which made him damned dangerous in my mind. Hadn't I known all along that he was a liar? That he was not honest and did not tell me the truth? That he was odd, the kind of odd that made me shiver and be afraid, though in a subtle way that never made sense to me?

Now I couldn't ignore what was happening. Now I couldn't convince myself I had overreacted or that my not understanding him didn't mean he was bad. I was only unsure about how bad.

"Jack?" he was saying. "Jack, you there?"

"I feel helpless," I said weakly. "I'm the only person who gets bad vibes from this guy. Everyone loves him to death out here."

"Maybe I should come out there again—"

"I have to know who he is. Don't come, not yet.

Just the sight of you makes him ornery. He's got his eye on me. Here's what I didn't tell you yet. He's back in town and I ran into him at the decorator shop. He played his game with me again; he's sorry he was an ass and of course he understands that I was only doing the sensible thing and it wasn't my fault. Then the very next thing, after he forgives me, is he'd like me to understand just why he is so weird with the chicks, huh? Oh damn, when he doesn't piss me off he scares me to death. He's had these peculiar things with women; these bad breaks. He'd like to show me he isn't like that all the time. Mike, I watch his eyes when I say 'No thanks' and I think he hates me."

"He threaten you at all?"

"No. I had to physically move him away from my car, and he had that expression on his face again—that poorly concealed rage. Listen, I want to know who this asshole is and what he wants with me. And I want to know as soon as possible. How can we do that?"

"Well, Jack, there are some ways that are slightly outside the law to get stuff on him, like going into his house and going through his private stuff, huh? That is not a smart thing for a skinny little strawberry blonde to do, even if she has a gun. So, I have this idea . . ."

"I hope to God I like this idea," I said, and again, it was a genuine prayer.

"Okay, it isn't bad. You know that fingerprint kit I gave you? Get me a print, okay? If this guy has ever done time or military service, we'll get a match off the NCIC system."

I sighed. NCIC pronounced "nicees," is the National Crime Information Center. My prayers, I believed, had not yet been answered. That match would take a long time, and getting a print without going into his truck or house was not going to be easy.

"What do you suggest I do?" I asked irritably. "Perhaps I should invite him to spend the night and get the print off my boob? I don't want to get close to this guy! I'm not going to invite him to dinner and print the wineglass!"

"Will you calm down? You better stay cool, Jack, since we don't know who we're messing with here. Get the print off something glass or metal. Steal his coffee cup from the café. Or get him to push somebody's car. Maybe you could talk to Bodge about this; you better, now that I think about it. I don't know if Bodge would print him for you; he hasn't done anything wrong. Lying about who you are isn't a crime unless you defraud someone or set up a con."

At that moment Wahl's truck drove slowly past my office. The door is half glass and I didn't spot him quickly enough to see whether he looked in.

"He drove by. He's probably going to the coffee shop or the hardware store. I don't like being on the same street with him."

"If you get a print, come back to L.A. and sit it out."

"Maybe."

"I might call Bodge myself; I just don't know how he'll react to me helping you play detective on this guy. He might get exasperated, tell me to mind my own business."

"I'll tell Bodge. Listen, Peggy is just walking in. Can I call you back in a little while? Soon as I have something to say? An idea or an update?"

Peggy waddled in with a six-pack of cola and a bag of chips. I looked up and smiled a hello while on the phone. She walked past my desk to the back room to put her soda in the refrigerator.

"Be careful, Jack. If you don't get any support from Bodge, try Krump. Maybe he'd help. Don't take any chances at all with this guy."

"Don't worry. I won't."

I hung up and sat there, stunned. He wasn't Tom Lawler. Everything about him was a lie; he had never given me any history that didn't apply directly to Lawler.

My desk faces the street; Peggy's is right inside the door. She walked from the back room to her desk, picked up a magazine, and went to the back again. I heard the lavatory door click. Peggy was going to sit down for a while.

The storeroom behind our desks holds a sink, a counter for coffee and a microwave oven, some cupboards, and a small toilet closet. I heard the fan in the bathroom whirring, blocking out noise for the person who sat behind the closed door.

I got up and leaned against the door to look down the street and could see the back end of Tom's truck parked at the café. There wasn't any traffic; there weren't people on the sidewalk. There was a big file box that I was supposed to take to Roberta's house later because she wasn't coming in—she was in court all day.

I had an instant plan. I picked up the file box in my arms and smashed it against the window. The damn glass did not break. I tried it again. The box made a loud thunk and I froze, listening. I didn't think Peggy would have heard, not with the bathroom fan running. The glass was tough as iron. I leaned the box on Peggy's desk and picked up Peggy's ceramic flowerpot, which had a sad-looking geranium in it. I said a prayer: Please God spare this pot or I am cooked. I whacked the glass and the window popped. Ahhh, tempered glass. It cracked, it broke, and it snowed to the ground.

For effect I said, "Damn it!" I was ecstatic. The glass would have to be replaced before close of business; Tom was handy and obviously not overbooked today or he wouldn't be loitering in the café. Peggy was a slob and wouldn't clean the glass and I would get a print. I would worry later about how to dust and lift it with the tape without being seen by anyone.

I was standing beside my desk when Peggy emerged with her magazine in hand. "You will never believe what I've done," I said. "Look at that."

"What the heck happened?" she asked.

"I was trying to get out the door with that big file box Roberta wants and I guess I bumped the glass too hard. And I've got to leave. Listen, do this for me—run down to the café and ask George or Lip if one of them could possibly replace that glass for me before they get to work this morning. It's gotta be nine by now . . . neither one of them ever heads out before nine-thirty. Ask someone pretty please. I'll happily pay for it; I'll give whoever does it time and a half. I'll sign a check before I go.

"Oh," I added, as an afterthought. "Don't mention that I had to leave."

"Why not?" she asked.

"Because . . ." I began, knowing I couldn't tell her that Tom would eagerly fix the window if he thought he'd run into me. That was my assumption, since he'd been pursuing me again. "They like any excuse to tell tales. I'll be the incentive; they know I'm a good ear for gossip. If you say I'm out, they'll all turn too busy."

Peggy frowned, insulted. Had I just implied one of the guys would fix the window for me and not for her? Hardly anyone joked with Peggy; she didn't have much of a sense of humor and wasn't one to pal around.

"I mean . . . you know . . ."

"Forget it," she said. "I'll get it fixed."

I left then, carting that big box out to the car. I took it home instead of to Roberta's house. I picked up my little field kit and put it in my briefcase. When I got back, the exact thing I had hoped for had actually happened.

"Did Lip fix the glass?" I asked Peggy.

"No," she said, sipping her diet pop. "Tom did it. He was right there and said he had the time and could use the money."

I looked at the glass and disappointment surged through me. My heart nearly broke. "It almost looks like he cleaned it."

"He did. He has Windex and paper towels in his truck. He always leaves a job cleaner and better than he found it."

Damn, damn, damn. The dustpan, I hoped. "He swept up the glass?"

"Oh no, I did that before he even got down here."

Peggy, for the first time in her life, did something tidy to our office. Figures. "How thoughtful. Thank you," I said, hiding the sarcasm.

"He's so sweet, Tom is. He's always asking about Warren and the kids. He only charged ten dollars' labor, and it took him an hour. He had to take off the molding, scrape out all the old putty, get George to cut the glass at the hardware store. It seemed like it took all morning."

I slumped into my chair, disappointed and tired. You'd almost think he knew I had a fingerprint kit in my briefcase, I thought. "What a peach of a guy," I said, lethargically.

"He asked about you. Asked if you were seeing anyone."

I perked up. Cheeky bastard, wasn't he? "I hope you didn't divulge anything personal."

"Of course I wouldn't," she said, mocking an insulted tone. "But you aren't seeing anyone, are you?"

"Certainly not."

"That's what I told him."

"Peggy," I said patiently. "It's not only none of his business if I'm seeing someone, it's also none of his business if I'm *not* seeing anyone."

She looked at me with a wrinkle between her eyebrows that told me she was confused by this logic. I sighed, got to my feet, and headed for the back room. I'd be a hundred years old by the time I knew something for sure about this guy. I decided a diet soda would help, and then I saw it: Sitting in the sink, not rinsed out by my one-time-only-tidy secretary, was a coffee mug. I stuck my head out of the back room.

"What was the total Tom charged?" I asked.

"Seventeen-fifty," she said.

"Well. I hope you gave him a cup of coffee at least," I said.

"Sure I did," she replied.

I lifted the mug by putting a pencil through the handle, placed it in a plastic bag with as much efficiency as Columbo, put it in my purse, and ran water in the sink as though I'd been doing dishes. Then I had to leave the office again. At home I dusted the cup and lifted three good prints with tape—a thumb and two fingers, I think—put the tape on the glossy side of the index cards, wrote on the back "Tom Wahl, coffee cup," and Express Mailed them to Mike Alexander.

* * *

I rang the bell at the Scully house at three o'clock. Sue came to the door and must have known from one look at my face that I was on the verge of panic. "Jackie! I didn't hear your car. Something's wrong."

"I need your help," I said. I had run into skepticism from Bodge on the issue of Tom's mysterious past, his suspicious behavior. Sue, I believed, wouldn't blow this off.

She put on coffee, though I could have used something stronger. Sue knew about my reaction to the finger incident: blaming Tom and telling Bodge about his past. Now I explained that I had conducted my own investigation in Los Angeles and had come to the conclusion that Tom Lawler was innocent of any wrongdoing—though that research had not helped me explain away his unpredictable and questionable behavior toward me.

"I don't think you ever mentioned that he talked to you that way," she said. "Setting you up like that, coming on to you and making you feel like you wronged him."

"I told Mike, I told Bodge, and I felt they believed me. Neither of them knew what to say besides, 'So, stop seeing him.' I left Mike with one final chore when I left L.A. I wanted him to see Tom's attorney and pass on what I'd found, the substantial evidence suggesting Tom is innocent. When he did that, he learned Tom Wahl is not Tom Lawler at all. It's all a lie."

"What?" she said. "Now, what?"

"Tom Lawler is a practicing psychologist living with his second family in Oregon. Mike saw a picture of him; there's more of a resemblance between our 'Tom' and the young Dr. Lawler than between the young Dr. Lawler and himself twelve years later. He's gained weight, he's balding, he wears glasses."

Sue reached for the phone on the counter and picked it up. "This is positively the case?"

"Mike's a police detective, Sue." She dialed. "I don't want Bodge called on the radio to come here to see me," I warned. "I don't want anyone to know I'm talking to anyone about anything. I'm nervous."

"No problem, Jackie." Her voice was calm. "Hey, Sylvie," she said cheerily. "How you doin'? Great. Great. Do me a favor, Syl? Let me talk to Bodge. Oh? Okay, sugar, then radio him and tell him his mama dropped in and would love to see him. Be sure to tell him not to run the siren or his mama will have a stroke." She laughed into the phone. "Yeah, he should call if he can't run by the house. Thanks, Syl."

She hung up and shrugged. "It's a code. If I need him but I'm not in any danger, his mama drops in. If I'm in trouble or scared, his aunt Bertha drops in."

"What if his mama really does drop in?"

Sue made a face. "Bodge's mother lives in Hartsel and drives Bodge crazy. She's seventy-five, speeds because her son is the sheriff, and criticizes him constantly. He wouldn't want to be called home to visit with her."

"What's Bodge going to say about this?" I asked. "I've told him some strange tales about Tom and he acts as though he wishes I'd drop it, get off it already."

"That may be how it seems. It isn't that way with Bodge. It's more that he's prudent. He may tell you he can't make an arrest if that's the case. He'll tell you he doesn't have evidence if he doesn't have evidence. Don't ever think Bodge ignores what you say. His mama and Raymond are the only two people Bodge brushes off. He's thinking all the time. This town may seem like a speck on a map, this county a little old mountain valley, but Bodge isn't backward or dumb. He's a damned smart professional."

"Tom is slick," I said. "He hasn't crossed himself up once. Now I'm scared."

"You know why you're scared, Jackie?"

"He wants me for something. I can't imagine what."

When I heard the car I went to the window. I saw Bodge hurry toward the house. He wasn't frantic in his pace or looking frightened. He was efficient. Comical, too. He held his sidearm so it wouldn't bounce. His pants crawled up his inner thighs toward his crotch and his belly strained at a button on his shirt. His hair, as usual, was sticking out from under his hat in uncontrollable wisps.

He saw it was me when he opened the door. He stopped short, stared at me for a second, then said, "Damn it all. It's Tom Wahl again."

"How did you know?" I asked, wondering if he had just stumbled on some information of his own.

"I don't hear a worried sound out of you all winter and a few days after he's back you're upset again."

Bodge told me that he'd seen for himself that I wasn't one to overthink things. He didn't judge me as the kind of woman who liked to complain or stir up trouble. He'd been watching and remembering since that finger business; Tom seemed to single out one person at a time to aggravate . . . and he was careful that no one ever witnessed it. Like with Wharton. Tom was sweet as could be in front of the boys, but Bodge had never known Wharton to get himself in such a dither over small problems. My case was similar; I had these confusions and irritations to report when no one else in Coleman had ever seen or heard Tom be anything but cooperative and helpful.

Bodge listened to my details. I wished he'd taken notes, but he did stop me to ask a lot of questions. About our conversations, about Tom's mood swings, about his description of what he'd done last winter, about talking to Beth, about his dogs and horses, the road, Wharton, his "cases." Everything.

"I slept with him," I said. "That 'apology dinner' at his place. He got down on the gut level about this horrendous murder of his—I mean Lawler's—family and I reciprocated. I told him about Sheffie's death, how awful it was, how broken I'd been. He comforted me and seduced me. I wasn't forced and I didn't feel coerced at the time. It's clear to me now that he laid a good trap for me with his 'problems.'"

"Anything about that you think I should know?" Bodge asked.

I felt as if I were talking to my old gynecologist. Bodge and Sue had this nonjudgmental way about them; the way they never gasped or oohed made me feel I could bare my soul easily, safely. "Yes, since you asked. I'd nearly forgotten, or tried to put it out of my mind. He's an Olympic lover; he has some kind of sexual dysfunction and he never has orgasms. Ever."

"Oh Jesus," Bodge groaned. "Anything else? Anything kinky?"

"Nothing else; believe me, that was enough. I think you should know—I printed him. I Express Mailed prints to Mike."

"Why'd you do that?"

"I was afraid you'd just tell me that pretending to be someone you're not isn't illegal and you wouldn't want to do anything like print him. Mike brought me a kit last fall when I was having that phantom stuff. He taught me how to use it. He said he'd send the prints through NCIC for a match, but it would take a while."

"You think you got good prints?"

"Three good ones off a ceramic cup. A thumb and two fingers."

"Um. Jackie, let me tell you something. Your ears only. I'm putting Sweeny back on your couch until I feel I've taken a good enough look at old Tom. He's harassing you—that's reason enough to protect you. I'll see if I can get some help in speeding up NCIC. Give me Mike's number and I'll call him. We have a group of state police and federal people in the valley."

"Brad Krump," I said.

"He's a consultant. He's part of a federal task force working with the CHP and us locals on these serial murders. Any suspicious character is going to get some fast attention right now; these boys are hungry for tips."

"You going to offer up Tom as a possible serial killer?" I asked, a shiver running through me.

"Everybody in the valley is a possible—particularly those people with irregular behavior. You still worried about making trouble for the poor boy?"

I lifted my chin a notch. Damn right I was worried, but not about making trouble. I was afraid this would be another fruitless exercise. "I believe Tom, or whoever he is, is the one making trouble."

19

Brad Krump's home in Pleasure was a task-force command post from which law-enforcement groups studied the Wet Valley murders. Krump had computers, facsimile machines, several phone lines, copiers, and printers. I learned this from Bodge; I never saw the inside of Krump's house. I imagined maps that showed the victims' residences and the location of the bodies. All the dead women had been carried twenty to sixty miles from where they were last seen alive.

The task force was federal, the state police headed the investigation, and local law enforcement participated. I asked Bodge if he felt ignored in the process and he smiled in response. "I keep a tight fist around my county, Jackie. And my town."

"Do they keep you informed? I had always heard that when the big guns move in, the local guys get shoved aside."

"That may seem so," he said. "There's hardly anything that feds can tell me about Coleman or Henderson County that I didn't know first."

"Maybe I should ask if you keep them informed."

"I do, because I'll take all the help I can get. And

fast. Near as I can tell, there hasn't been a murder in the valley in a year. If something doesn't turn up— a suspect, evidence, something—we may lose the feds and the state."

"Do they have *anyone* they're watching?"

"A few possibles have been checked. You have to realize how tough it is to put someone who lives on forty acres and travels deserted country roads under surveillance. It's easy to watch someone in a New York apartment, someone who drives crowded freeways and wouldn't know he's being followed. Out here? You watch from a distance. No one has been targeted."

"What if it's him, Bodge?"

"That would be too good to be true. The only thing we're looking at is that he isn't who he says he is. There isn't a single other curious thing about him. Except why. To kill women? If that was it, you probably wouldn't be sitting here talking to me right now."

If Sweeny knew why he was back on my couch, he didn't say anything. Unlike the first time, I didn't feel so snug upstairs in my bedroom. Before, when I was worrying about a lifted toilet seat or a spilled glass of juice, Sweeny's presence gave me confidence. At this point I wasn't sure what I feared. A liar? An obsessive man with an unnatural determination to have me for a lover? A murderer?

I felt as though I were holding my breath. Mike had submitted the prints to NCIC and the process of making a match had been given a higher priority by the local investigation. Three days after lifting and mailing those prints, I wondered how long I could stand the wait. I was edgy and tense. I hadn't talked to anyone but Bodge, Sue, and Mike about this. Roberta had no way of knowing what was eating at me. Mike and Chelsea wanted me to sit the wait out in

L.A. It was a tempting thought, until I considered pacing around their small house waiting for a phone call that would tell me it was all a wild goose chase; he was a liar and opportunist and nothing else was wrong with him; he was someone named Arnold Horowitz from Chicago, bored and boring, who added this edge to his existence with a dramatic twist on a life he borrowed. I wanted to be in Coleman for the news.

On the third day of this high-strung wait, when Peggy walked down to the café to buy snacks and Roberta was out meeting a client, Tom came into the office. "Hi, Jackie," he said cheerfully.

I felt like running out the back door and I couldn't let on. I had to try to be my usual self, whoever that was. "Hi, Tom. What can I do for you?"

"Wondering how you've been."

I was miserable; the room began to feel close and stuffy. I tried to continue writing, not giving him any power by dropping my work to focus on him. "Like, have I read any good books lately?" I asked.

He leaned a hip on my desk, invading my space. "Yeah, like that."

He was close enough to touch me; I put down my pen, stood, picked up my coffee cup, and wandered away from him. "Not lately." I realized it was useless to behave in a friendly, cheery way. I wouldn't be fooling him.

"I've been working a lot. Summer is busy for me. I get calls from all over the place—from hardware stores and decorator shops. Do busywork when I'm not building. Got another cup of coffee?"

"I don't have time to chat, Tom. I have to work."

He stood and walked into the back room. I heard him rummaging around for a cup, talking all the while. "All work and no play, Jackie. You know what

they say about that. You ought to take time for fun."
He came out holding a cup of coffee. "You work too
hard; you're too serious."

"I have a lot to do; why don't you tell me what I
can do for you so I can get back to work."

He laughed. "Cranky today? Well, I did have a
reason for stopping by. How about dinner? My
place?"

Cool, I told myself. "No thanks, Tom." No excuses,
no plans, just no.

"Why not?"

"I don't want to," I said.

"You seeing someone?"

"Tom, don't push this. We decided, you and I, sen-
sibly, that we're not going to date or see each other.
That's for the best; that's what I want."

"*You* decided," he said.

"My prerogative," I returned.

"You're being too hard on me," he said. He didn't
say so meanly. "You're avoiding me, I think."

"Not at all," I lied. "I can't think of a single occasion
that would throw us together."

"I want another chance," he said. "I'm a good guy,
you're a neat lady. I want another chance."

"Don't be unreasonable, please. I've decided what
I want and I don't want to argue."

"Why? We were so good for each other. This is a
lonely place, Coleman. Have you looked at the available men around here?"

"I'm not lonely; I'm not scouting for available men.
I'm going to say this one more time. I don't intend
to date you. That was last year, Tom. Let it be."

"It was more than dinner."

"I'm not going to apologize for that. I'm not going
to change my mind because of it."

He sipped his coffee and looked around the cluttered little office. He looked me straight in the eye. "It was about the best sex you've ever had."

My eyes widened and my mouth tightened. "I think you'd better go."

"Wasn't it? Wasn't it the best sex you've ever had?"

"Tom, I want you to leave. You're making me very uncomfortable."

"I can do that for you, you know. No strings attached; me and you and fabulous sex. Pretty soon you'd like me again."

"Go," I said firmly. I reached out for his coffee cup but he moved it out of my reach.

"Come on, Jackie, why do you make it so hard on me? Why do you act like you don't want to? I know you want to—you're scared to let yourself go and enjoy it. I could show you some things; trust me."

"Get out and don't come back here. Don't bother me again."

"Aw, Jackie, you just—"

I reached past him and picked up the phone. I made a power show I didn't feel. "I'll call Sweeny," I said. "I mean it; you can leave or I'll call the police."

"For what? Going to register a complaint that I asked you to dinner? That isn't against the law. Maybe you wanna tell 'em that I can fuck your brains out all night and never stop." He laughed; his smile was menacing. "You had so many orgasms; that ought to be against the law. You can tell them how you hated it." Then he laughed again. Cruelly.

I started to dial and the door opened. Peggy came in, a bag of Chee-tos in one hand and a six-pack of diet soda in the other. "Hi, Tom," she said cheerfully. "How you doing?"

"Good, Peggy—never better. How's that boy of yours doing in Little League?"

"Well, you won't believe this: They're winning. And

Davey's had some homers, but they still don't play him as much as the bigger boys."

He eased off my desk and I replaced the receiver. He moved toward Peggy with his mug in his hand.

"I used to have that problem, Peggy. I was small for my age back then; they always left me for last. I was a good hitter, too."

"You think I should talk to the coach again?"

"Oh, yeah. Keep after him about it. First off, it's good for Davey to see that you're on his side about this, and second, the coach needs to be fair—sometimes you have to push for justice. Huh?"

He continued talking, asking questions about her husband, her kids, her house, leisurely sipping his coffee. I glared at his back; he was a smoothie. As the conversation between them continued over several minutes, I sat down again and pretended to concentrate on my work.

It was a test. He gave a good ten minutes to it. He finally said, "Well, I better shove off. Plenty of wood to chop this time of year."

I refused to look up from my desk.

He returned his coffee cup to the sink in the back room as if he owned the place. His presence seemed to fill the office. "See ya láter, Jackie," he said. I didn't respond. "Jackie?" he asked. I looked up. "I'll see you later."

"I have work to do, Tom."

"You work too hard, Jackie. Ought to play a little more."

"Not likely," I said, looking back at my papers.

"Lawyers," he said to Peggy, chuckling conspiratorially. "She's gonna be like Roberta." And Peggy joined him in the joke, laughing and teasing.

He finally left and I had to fight the shaking.

"What was that all about?" Peggy asked. "You were rude to him."

I picked up the phone and dialed. "Just get to work, okay?" I said. I heard her huff and grumble. "Sue, hi, it's Jackie," I said. "You know that legal problem we've been discussing? I have something I'd like to run by you and I could use some fresh air. Mind if I drive out?"

"What is it, Bodge's mama or his aunt Bertha?"

"If there's any connection," I said, "it could be both."

"I don't know why I never thought of it," I told Sue. "I could kick myself—I know the reason. Because I had these dark instincts about this guy and I worked so damn hard to talk myself out of them. It's what he does for a living! Even Wharton said Tom likes to pretend he's this great craftsman and carpenter, claims he built his house from scratch, but he contracted almost all the work. He's a handyman. He leaves his name and number with all the hardware stores, decorator shops, stuff like that. He installs curtains, blinds, shelves. Makes minor repairs. He's probably got a schedule; he drives around to the small towns in the valley."

"Doing jobs for housewives."

"Whom he seduces."

"And kills?"

I couldn't say it yet. "Do you know if Bodge has thought of this? It should have been obvious. It should have bit us in the butt."

"We'll find out," she said, picking up the ringing phone. "Hello? Yes, your mama's here and she's really anxious to talk to you. Where are you calling from? What are you doing out there?"

Sue passed me the phone and after asking Bodge if it was all right to talk to him on that line, I told him the same thing I'd told Sue. I also described Tom's visit to my office and the way he had harassed me.

"Do you know the towns he's worked in?"

"No. All over the valley, I suppose. When we were keeping in touch last fall, he mentioned Salida and Pueblo, but those aren't small towns. He kept his business to himself; he was never specific about anything except his past as Tom Lawler. Have you learned anything yet?"

Bodge expertly evaded my question. "I don't have any evidence that would allow me to make an arrest. I will tell you, though, it isn't going to take more than another day or two to get an ID on this guy, unless he's never done time or military service."

"And if he hasn't?"

"It's going to take longer."

"Are you going to check on this, Bodge? See if there's any connection between the deaths and Mr. Fix-it?"

"Yes, ma'am. I am."

"I'm scared."

"You don't have to stay in Coleman."

"I know. I don't know what to do."

It was then that it hit me. At that moment I believed I had been targeted by a killer. I was too frightened to cry, too shaken to plot an escape. My knowledge of the legal system didn't offer me any comfort; there was the question of evidence, enough suspicion to obtain an arrest warrant or search warrant. There might not be any evidence; it was unlikely that he kept a supply of rope and plastic bags under his bed. He might have done small jobs for every woman who had been killed, and that might not be enough.

"Bodge, is anyone watching him yet?"

"Much as we can. I told you; that's hard to do in the country. It's more accurate to say we're keeping tabs on him."

"Do you think I'm safe here? He's got his eye on me, I know it."

"Jackie, I'm about to tell you something that isn't going to sound encouraging, but you gotta listen. I'm taking a close look at this Tom character; I'm trying to find out who he is, what he's up to. I'm investigating. And I don't know if I'm looking at a two-day investigation or a two-month investigation. I could get a call from Krump or Mike or NCIC tomorrow with a make, a connection, and enough information to do something—or I could get disappointed. In conditions like this, Jackie, I can't do any more for you than let you stay with us or put Sweeny on your couch.

"That's not the problem, see," he went on. "You can do anything you want. You can close up shop and get on the next plane to L.A. You could go to Alaska and hide out. What you can't do is tell anyone what's going on. If this guy is who I'm after and he gets tipped off, I might never get him. You understand what I'm saying?"

I sighed and closed my eyes. I felt the ache of tears in my throat. "It would be best if I could follow my daily routine and hide my terror of this, of him."

"You can do anything you want. If you can act normal, we have a better chance of following up on this. Don't allow yourself to be vulnerable. Stay in public places or behind closed doors with Sweeny."

"My office? What if he comes back to my office?"

"We're going to keep a county squad car in Coleman; the presence will be reassuring without being suspicious. I don't want any CHP doing overtime in Coleman. That would be unusual. I'm guessing, but I don't think this guy would try to abduct you from your office in broad daylight. Don't go in early or stay late. That's the best I can do."

The act of walking through the following days without showing the emotions that set off internal fireworks in me was exhausting. I jumped every time someone walked in the office; I jerked my head up from my work to see who walked by. Roberta didn't notice; she was singleminded about her work and concentrated on that, not me. Peggy said, "My goodness, you're flinchy. And grumpy."

"PMS," I said, not elaborating.

Part of my routine was to go to the café before work, eight-thirty every morning, buy a Danish and a large coffee to go. The pot in our office was never prepared before I got there and I always had my cup while I waited for the next cup to brew.

How I longed for Wharton and Harry when I walked in that café in the mornings. Lip and George and a few others still had their coffee there and always welcomed me. To test my acting ability and composure, I had to face Tom. He sat, as usual, at his own table just inside the door, close enough to talk to someone at the end of the other table, not a part of them and not alone. I had to walk past Tom, then walk past the long table seating six men. A round of "Hiya, Jackie" came from the long table.

"Morning, boys," I said as cheerily as possible. I didn't move closer to chat; I went straight to the counter, where the waitress was already pouring my coffee in a Styrofoam cup. I looked at the pastries under the glass, wishing I didn't have to buy one. It was my routine. I selected one, and while the girl wrapped it, I turned around and looked at Tom.

He was watching me. I had known he would be. His face was calm; he wasn't leering or sneering, just watching me with a pleasant look on his face. He could look so normal, handsome. He was wearing jeans, and a plaid shirt rolled up at the sleeves. He wore laced work boots and a wide belt. He still had the beard, though spring was getting warm.

"Here you go, Jackie," the waitress said.

I turned back toward the counter and began to dig for the right change in my purse. I shouldn't have been caught staring at him; I was afraid he'd follow me back to the office. I slung my purse over my arm and couldn't get out of there fast enough.

"Bodge was in here around eight," the waitress said, stopping me. "He asked if you'd been in yet. I told him you come in around eight-thirty or so."

"Oh? Thanks, I'll give him a call."

It was a perfect excuse to hurry out. I left without looking at anyone or saying good-bye. I kept my head down and my pace quick; I hoped I looked efficient rather than frightened. My hands were shaking as I unlocked the front door to the office. As I shouldered the door open, I felt the weight of the door ease and with a gasp I realized that Tom was behind me, closer than my own shadow, pushing the door open.

I gasped and jumped so that I almost dropped my coffee.

"Hey," he said pleasantly, laughingly, "take it easy. I didn't mean to scare you, Jackie."

My insides quaked. I was as furious as I was frightened. "You *always* mean to scare me!" I accused. "I told you to leave me alone, stop harassing me. Now get out of here!"

343

"Aw, Jackie, come on. Come on. Relax."

I backed into the office, setting down my burden of coffee and Danish on the desk. I kept my purse strap on my shoulder but dropped the keys. He did not advance on me; arms akimbo, he gave a helpless snort of a laugh.

"Jackie, Jesus . . ." he began. "What's the matter with you? I just wanted to say hello, see what's going on."

"I asked you to leave!" I ground out slowly. He shook his head with a light laugh as if he couldn't understand my distress, my insistence. I lifted the receiver of the phone; then a noise behind me caused me to jump again.

"Hey, folks," Bodge Scully said, emerging from the little back room. He held a cup of steaming coffee in one hand. "Didn't mean to give you a start, Jackie. I had this old set of keys Roberta gave me years ago . . . let myself in to wait for you. I put on the coffee."

"Bodge, I could have had a heart attack," I said, feeling a lot better with him there. "It must be urgent."

"Ain't anything around here that's all that urgent. I just didn't want to have to drive back into Coleman since I was out this way now." He nodded to Tom.

"How you doin', Bodge?" Tom asked good-naturedly.

"Tell the truth, I been working too damn hard. How you been?" Bodge asked, taking a couple of steps past me so that he stood between me and Tom. Through the glass of the front door I saw two highway patrol cars pull up to the front of the office. Tom was looking at me, at Bodge, his back to the closed door.

"Been real good, Bodge," Tom said. "Haven't had

much fun since I came back from Florida; no fishing or anything."

"I'm glad I ran into you," Bodge said. "I've been wanting to talk to you. Ask you something."

"Shoot."

"Seems like you've been giving Jackie a hard time. Seems like you just won't take no for an answer."

Tom chuckled. "Well . . . I don't know . . ."

I couldn't believe my ears. I could feel my heart pounding in my temples. I backed farther into the office, parallel to the back-room door so I could dive in there if necessary. Four CHP officers approached the glass door.

"Seems like being a handyman put you in touch with a lot of housewives," he said to Tom.

Tom, amazingly, remained cool, detached. "What're you talking about, Bodge? What's going on here? Jackie tell you I—"

I have no idea what he was about to accuse me of. Bodge interrupted him. "Jason Devalian?" he asked. The front door opened and two officers entered behind Tom. He turned his head quickly from side to side, seeing them. The one on the left placed a firm hand on Tom's left shoulder, grabbing his left hand; the officer on his right managed his right side in the same way. Bodge said, "You are under arrest for the murder of Katherine Sullivan Porter. You have the right—"

He screamed. It was a wild, animallike wail. "Noooooo!" My hair felt prickly against my neck and I braced myself against the rear wall of the office. Tom—Jason—tried to free his arms but he was slammed up against the wall by the two men, his arms pinned and cuffed. His struggle went on; he swore and growled and cursed. One cop hit him in the back of his knees and brought him to the floor, where they pinned him flat. When he started kicking, he was rewarded by having his head smashed into the floor. He thrashed around a little less, but he was by no means giving up. Though his hands were cuffed behind his back, the cops continued to hold him down.

Both CHP officers were panting; he was a formidable prisoner. Bodge turned and looked at me.

"Jason Devalian?" I mouthed, almost no sound coming out.

He gave me a nod and looked back to the police and the prisoner. The front door opened a crack. A cop, with gun drawn and pointed skyward, peeked in. "How we doin'?" he asked.

"We got him," Bodge said. "You keepin' back the nice folks of Coleman?"

"You betcha; everyone's inside. Let's keep him in here till he's shackled. Need a little help there, Sam?"

"We got him," Sam replied, breathless, his knee pressing against Devalian's back, holding him firmly against the floor. "Let's take it easy, dickhead," the officer advised Devalian. "Easy does it now. We got all day. We can always go get the tranquilizer gun we use on loose elephants." The assisting cop chuckled.

When they began to shackle him, he started thrashing again. "Noooooo!" he wailed, though one cop had a fistful of his hair and was pushing his cheek into the floor. "Get your hands off me!" More grunting, snorting, growling. Bodge watched. Bodge was completely calm, one hand in a pocket, rocking on his heels now and then. He stood squarely in front of me so that I had to lean over to observe this violent arrest. I might have thought Bodge was being too sedate for this situation except that I noticed two things: The snap of his holster was popped and he didn't smoke. He might not look all that ready, but he was.

This went on for as long as ten minutes; I was so fascinated by Devalian's fight, by his incoherent screaming, that the fear began to drain out of me. Of course the presence of several armed cops, and Devalian's position facedown, cuffed and shackled, helped ease any sense of panic. It seemed an eternity before they were ready to drag him to his feet. When they pulled him upright and he began a renewed struggle, he got a brutal CHP elbow to the gut and doubled over with a groan. He straightened slowly.

He looked at me.

"You," he said, his voice soft and raspy. "You wanted to make me suffer. All along." The voice was calm enough to make me tremble.

The police pulled him from the office and he began shouting again, cursing and struggling. They loaded him into the back of a squad car with an officer on each side of him. A short parade of police vehicles backed away from the curb and drove slowly down the street. I followed Bodge to the front of the office, onto the sidewalk, watching them drive away. In front of the coffee shop were a couple of men I didn't know, in quilted jackets; they began walking toward Bodge and me; undercover police, surely. It was not until the cars were around the bend that Bodge spoke.

"Don't let that bother you, Jackie. He don't seem to be in any shape to hold a grudge."

"He knows it was me; I picked him as a killer."

"With a fella like him, there's only two ways it can go. You can get him or he can get you. At least you got him. I owe you an apology on one account. You knew all along; all you were lacking were the facts. He was all wrong, but he had most of us good and fooled. If it hadn't been for those prints and that conclusion about the handyman work, we wouldn't have him now."

I wouldn't be here now, I thought. "When did you find out?"

"I got a call from Mike around seven A.M. with a make; I needed a warrant to go with that, so Krump gave me a coupla guys to sit on Devalian. Those guys from the coffee shop," he said, pointing. "We were on him tight until CHP could wake up a judge, get us a warrant, and take him in. We were all just too damn busy to call you and explain before we could pick him up. I'd give my left nut for one deputy as good as you. Jackie, we got you to thank."

I sighed weakly. "Sure, Bodge. Any time."

The police had obtained arrest and search warrants based on a few shreds of circumstantial evidence. No one had seen his crimes; there was no physical evidence prior to the arrest. Seven of the eight women had had Tom Wahl do minor repairs or installations of decorator items for them. One woman, younger than the rest, had been hitchhiking. Bodge told me he was praying they'd find some evidence in Tom's house to link him to the murders. His likeness—there was no current photo available—had been identified by store owners, shopkeepers, neighbors, and family members of victims.

Bob Porter remembered that Kathy had hired Tom to fix the garage door and the fence, and that he painted the living room. She got his name and number off an index card that had been tacked to the bulletin board at the grocery store. She got her babysitter and her carpet cleaner the same way. His work for her had preceded her disappearance by five months. Bob hadn't seen any connection at the time.

In the hours following the arrest, hours I spent at home alone, the story began to fall into place for me. He'd had his nose and jaw broken in jail, altering his appearance. He wore colored contacts—and might have had plastic surgery; there were six years unaccounted for between his release from the penitentiary and his arrival in Colorado. He had had his chin squared off and his cheeks filled out; he looked more like the Tom Lawler of twelve years before than the Tom Lawler of today.

It was Devalian who could play chess and attend group therapy, functional even though he was shot full of drugs; Devalian who could manipulate a transfer from a maximum-security hospital. I had studied that character and hadn't made the connection. When I learned that Tom Wahl was not Tom Lawler, I never considered that Jason Devalian might imitate the very man he'd victimized.

I went to see where they kept him. He was in the county jail in Pleasure, his captivity maintained with earnest caution. He was watched by an armed Colorado Highway Patrol officer outside his cell. The door to the cell area was locked. He was also wearing cuffs and leg irons. Sue had driven me there; she and Bodge and I were going for a drink later—a big one. She was with me when I saw him. He sat on a cot behind bars. He was looking at his feet, unresponsive, subdued. I peeked at him through a square glass window in a locked door. His guard said something to him and he didn't move or reply. He continued to stare at his feet. The sight of him, the knowledge of how close I'd been and all he'd done, made me feel physically ill.

In the office outside the cells I shook hands with Brad Krump. "How's the fishing?" I asked weakly.

"Sheriff Scully kept me informed on your significant contributions to this arrest, Jackie. You've got a good head. You must have been frightened."

"That doesn't touch it," I said. "How long are you keeping him here?"

"Just long enough for an arraignment and a high-security vehicle for his transportation. The state is going to pursue his conviction; we'll transfer him to Denver."

I had decided earlier that day that I couldn't stay in Coleman. I was exhausted and disillusioned. I agreed to take a short leave of absence from the office before selling my house and moving away. I was going to spend that leave in L.A., where Chelsea and Mike would help me recover.

Bodge and Sue and I sat at Wolf's. We took a booth and drank and talked. "I called Mike," I told them. "He's coming out tomorrow; he wants to watch some debriefings and get from you, maybe from Brad, whatever information you can share. Bodge, do you have anything at all you can use for conviction?"

"I can't talk about anything that's being held for discovery, you know that. I'm not worried about putting him away; if we can get him on one tenth of what he's done, he's a dead man."

"He's behind bars, that's all I care about. I hope the prosecution isn't looking at using me as a witness; by the time this gets to trial, I'm going to be long gone. I hope Mike is ready to leave with me tomorrow. We're going to drive back to L.A. in my car; I'm picking him up in Colorado Springs at noon."

I was home at midnight. I tossed my purse on the couch and put my cellular phone in the base I kept plugged in, in the kitchen. I went to my bedroom and got out suitcases and piled clothes on top of my dresser. Then it hit me hard. The hands that had touched my body had choked the life out of women, had murdered at least one child. I began to cry hysterically and could no longer hold back the sick feeling.

I don't know how long I was in the bathroom bent over the commode, sick. I kept thinking of that night he used my body; his voice in my ears kept coming back. *I could keep you a prisoner and torture you with ecstasy. Come again. . . . Come again.* I cried and heaved. I couldn't control my insides or my mind. When I got in the shower, I experienced another frenzy and began scrubbing myself; that he had touched me was suddenly unbearable. I shampooed four, five times.

All this took over an hour; it might have taken two. I was weak from vomiting, crying, shaking, scrubbing. I dried my hair and pulled on a long nightie. I could hardly stay on my feet and believed, at that moment, that I might never recover from the dirty, tainted, violated feeling I had.

When I opened the bathroom door the steam rolled out, but still it was the first thing I saw:

There was an imprint on my bed. An impression on the new, thickly batted quilt ran from the pillow to the foot; it was smudged.

I stood in the bathroom doorway, mesmerized by the horror. How could this be? I asked myself. Someone else. The phantom is back. He is the phantom. I am possessed.

The phone rang. I walked toward it in a daze. I picked it up but did not speak.

"I think you've been too hard on me, Jackie," he said. Tom. Jason. His voice was as it had been on those other occasions when he was in control, when he was the man I was trying to rationalize into a boyfriend.

I said nothing. I listened.

"I'd like a chance to show you I'm not always like that. I think I overreacted. Give me another chance?"

I placed the receiver gently on the hook. I thought, then, that he had been in my house. It was impossible. I'd seen him in cuffs and shackles, behind bars. Just hours ago. He was guarded; he was caught.

They wouldn't let him call me from jail. I knew that. I needed my gun. I ran for the stairs and flew down them, holding the rail with one hand and lifting my nightgown off my feet with the other. I knew he was after me and couldn't think past protecting myself. I grabbed the newel post at the bottom of the rail and whirled around the stair toward the living room. He slammed me up against the wall before I even saw him. With his shoulder he rammed me against the wall again, knocking the wind out of me. After bouncing off the wall, I slid weakly to the floor, unable to take a breath.

There he stood, grinning, holding my cellular phone in one hand. He'd called me from inside my own house. He'd come in while I was showering or drying my hair. He'd been there, right outside my bathroom door, while I was at my most vulnerable.

I stared up at him from the floor, stunned and breathless. I remembered one thing I might use as a ploy to survive. I had no defense; the only thing that had kept me alive this long was that I had refused to play his game. I didn't like him, I didn't pity him, and his story got him nowhere. I reached up and turned on the light in the front hall, causing him to wince.

"All along," I said. "It was you all along. In my house; in everyone's house."

His contacts gone, I was faced with those wild blue eyes. His eyes sparkled, glistened. He gave a short nod, glaring down at me. He thought he had me now. "Till you locked the place up. I don't know what you were so scared of. It wasn't anything to be so scared of."

It only took me a second to assess his disheveled appearance and I knew his escape had been painful and daring, another real challenge of endurance. His wrists were smeared with blood, his pants legs still wrinkled at the ankles from the leg irons. He was glistening with sweat and breathing fast and hard.

He stared at me and, very slowly, began to smile. He tossed the phone to the floor and reached behind him, withdrawing a razor knife. The blade popped out. "I hid this in your backyard months ago. Months."

He reached out and grabbed my wrist, yanking me to my feet. He dragged me toward the living room and kitchen; all the blinds and curtains were tightly drawn but there was glass on the floor underneath a dining-room window. He had broken in while I was in the bathroom, shower and hair dryer running. I could feel the blade against my throat. I thought, Dear God, don't let him stumble. "Aren't you going to tell me how you got out? You're usually proud of your feats; how'd you get out?"

He pushed me into my small kitchen. "They always think they can hold me down," he said. "It's like they know all about me and haven't learned anything. It's because they're stupid pigs."

"But they had you this time," I said, trying not to whimper.

"I got sick," he said. "Puked and puked and puked; I was choking and someone had to come in when I turned blue. I got real blue. Stupid shits. They act like they never had a prisoner before. It's the oldest trick there is."

"And they let you get away?" I asked.

"The hardest part is getting your cuffs off while you're holding someone as a shield. I had him in a lock around the neck so one snap would do it. The cop who comes in the cell doesn't carry a gun. . . ." He started to laugh as though it was a funny story. "The prisoner might get his gun. Like they don't know about a prisoner's hands, arms. We walked right out. I took him right up to a Suburban with the keys in it. Jesus, don't people know better than to leave their *keys* in their cars? I drove it right into an open garage three blocks from the station. I had to hot-wire the second car I took. I only had to kill one asshole cop. Short night." And then he laughed.

"Did you stab him?"

"Don't be asking me questions. I broke his neck. I left him in the parking lot. Everybody knows I'm out and thinks I have a Suburban. They'll figure this out pretty soon. They ought to be coming here. It would be easier if we could leave before they get here."

"Are you planning to hurt me?" I saw car lights streak the wall and ceiling, but he seemed unaware of them. Or didn't care. I heard engines that stopped. They were out there. I just had to be careful for a little bit longer.

"It doesn't hurt that much," he said. "It isn't supposed to hurt; it can be over in about one second."

"Why do you want to hurt me? What good will it do you?"

With an almost sane look in his eyes, he said, "It makes me feel better, that's all."

"They're looking for you. You have time to get away. Take my car. Run."

He laughed at me. "Tell me the truth first. Wasn't it the best sex you ever had in your life?"

I could feel the taste of vomit at the back of my

throat. I nodded, my eyes filling with tears. And he drew back his hand and slapped me so hard I fell to the floor.

"Lying bitch," he said, his voice like a growl. "You going to make me knock you out or cut you up? Or you going to do what I say?"

I was rubbing my jaw, too stunned to cry, and nodded up at him.

"Well, what, bitch?"

"What do you want?" I managed.

"I want a ride," he said. "I'll go out to the hills. Once I get in the hills, I can go for days with just my blade and my brain. You'll drive me. They're probably out there, you know. They'll stay back just long enough to see what I'm going to do. They can't see in here. You'll be on the other end of this knife and we'll walk out and drive away. Simple, huh?"

"Why didn't you just go? You had a car."

He grinned at me and reached out a hand to help me to my feet. "Without you, Jackie?" he asked. "We're good for each other."

I let him help me up. I was almost sure he would strike me again, and when he pulled back his hand to do so, I cowered away and squealed. That caused him to laugh loudly, almost happily. "Get me a jug of water," he ordered. "Use a Thermos or something."

I moved toward the cupboard in a daze. I pulled out the four-quart picnic Thermos and turned on the tap, filling it up. "Why Tom Lawler?" I asked him, not looking at him. That knife was pointed at me and he stood two feet away. "Why not pretend to be someone else?"

I turned off the tap and looked at him. "Lawler was good," he said. "He was the only one I ever met who understood me. No one ever nailed me; I could fool anyone. Lawler was the smartest man I ever met. It was all his psychology—he's a head-shrinker."

"You killed his family!" I whispered this hotly, unable to believe it.

"Outsmart the smartest, my old man used to say. Beat the best. After this is over, maybe I'll go see him. Pay him a visit like I did before. Drop in and let him know I'm still out here."

"You set us up. From the start. Me and Roberta."

"I decided when I was in prison; I started reading there. I read all his stuff and everyone else's. He was the perfect one—the one person I would be least likely to impersonate. Perfect. I fooled everyone. Even you—and you checked me out. I let you prove to everyone who might ask that I was Tom Lawler. Let's go."

"God," I said in a breath. "That's why. You *meant* for Roberta and me to investigate you, prove you were authentic. You look like him. You knew his background, his—"

"You got a little too serious, though. You were supposed to feel bad about causing me trouble after you knew who I was. What my problems were. I don't know what got into you, Jackie. You should have been trying to *help* me. C'mon. Let's move it."

I handed the Thermos to him and he shook his head. "Uh-uh. I need my hands," he said, tossing the knife back and forth. "I have to hold you and the knife, and I have to walk. That's enough. Get your purse."

I looked at him in shock for a second. He motioned for me to hurry. He wasn't going to hold on to me while I walked the four feet to the sofa to pick up my bag. I shook, but moved as quickly as I could. I heard people outside my house; I heard a sound at the back door. Before he could change his mind, I picked up my purse. "Keys," I muttered, as if to myself. He stood in the kitchen doorway, just a few steps from me, ready to go.

"You take your purse because you know you're going," he said somewhat absently. "That's how that works. She knows she's going because she took her purse, so she wanted to. Right? You just wouldn't let me be nice to you, would you? I tried to give you some good times first, you know, before I had to do this. But you were such a bitch. I got so I hated you more than I ever hated. I usually don't even bother with *hate*. Slows you down, makes you act stupid."

I picked up my purse and turned to face him. I put the purse strap over my shoulder, lifted the flap, and reached inside. He just watched me; he thought I was digging for car keys. "Hurry up," he said. Please, God, I said to myself. I felt the safety on the gun and flipped it before I pulled it out.

"You'll play it my way now," he said. I pointed and fired.

I saw the look of surprise on his face for less than a second. I heard a distant siren as I fired; I heard his breath whoosh out.

One, two, three, four. Two bullets went right into his chest, one into his abdomen, throwing him backward. I saved one shot in case I had missed and needed another chance. He flew into the kitchen, hit the refrigerator, clutching his chest, and the knife bounced out of his hand. One bullet grazed his temple and left a streak of dripping blood. His eyes were open, his chest still, and his hands pressed to his chest wound. I stood, frozen, staring at him, pointing the gun.

I heard the screeching of tires. There were shouts and running feet outside. I heard my back door as it was forced open. I was vaguely aware of people coming in—two men. The front door was crashed against, then smashed into the wall as it flew open. If I could have found the strength to stay in the room ten seconds longer, if I had been alone for five more seconds, I would have walked over to his body, pressed the muzzle of the gun to his forehead, and fired one more time. It was too late; two men kneeled beside him, looking at him. I couldn't look at those unblinking eyes. I couldn't stand the smell of his blood and sweat.

I backed out of the living room, backed through the laundry room and pantry. I turned and went out the back door and down the steps to the driveway. In my pink sleeveless nightgown and bare feet, I walked past my parked car, past running men. There were at least six cars in front of my house. Bodge and his deputies were at my front door while men who looked like hunters or lumberjacks, carrying automatic weapons, ran up my drive.

I held the hot gun pointed down, and walked slowly toward the street. No one stopped me or confronted me or tried to help me. The neighbors were out in their yards, the static and chatter of the police radios was hyper and angry. A couple of red lights flashed and I noticed that orange tape was pulled across the street on each end.

Brad Krump unsnapped the thumb break on his holster as he walked toward me.

"You made a mistake," I told him. "He can get out of anything. Anything."

"He's a dangerous man, Jackie," he said. "He might be the most dangerous man I've encountered. I'm sorry."

"He could have killed me. He had a knife. He had time."

"Thank God you knew what to do; thank God you

did what we failed to do." He pulled a Ziploc bag out of his pocket and held it open. I dropped the gun into it. I wanted to slap his face: Why hadn't he rushed in, him and all his cops? How could they have let him trick them? "Are you all right?" he asked.

"I will never be all right again," I said. I kept expecting to collapse; I don't know what mysterious force kept me on my feet. That was when I heard the words that will have me sick and terrified for the rest of my life.

"He's still alive!"

Then I fainted.

20

JASON Devalian somehow resisted my bullets. Had they penetrated his heart and he had survived, I would have believed he was a devil. *The* Devil. Although it was difficult to accept, he was a human being and he had survived. Mike assured me the authorities had learned their lesson regarding this man; he spent even his time in intensive care, in a Denver hospital, handcuffed to the bedrails. I couldn't quite believe it.

The morning after I shot him I left Coleman. I met Mike's plane in Colorado Springs and gave him my house keys and car keys. I told him about the night before and knew, before he told me, that he would stay in Colorado and talk to the authorities. I wasn't willing to stay another day. I went to Chelsea.

Chelsea nurtured me while Mike spent a week in Colorado obtaining as many details as possible about the crimes, the arrest, the status of the state's case. He wanted to be assured of my safety; Chelsea wanted to help me recover. These two have loved me and cared for me with unimaginable devotion.

When Mike returned to L.A. after spending a week in Colorado, the three of us went through the boxes

of Sheffie's memorabilia. We bought a cedar chest
to hold the things; ribbons, school photos, drawings,
papers, report cards. A favorite stuffed toy he called
Chippie. His baby blanket; his L.A. Lakers jacket.
When I relocate, I will keep the chest near me and
never part with it again.

Mike's detective logic didn't do as much for my
recovery as Chelsea's tender care and homemade
soups. "Jack, you fingered one of the most dangerous
criminals in America! Fifty cops and a bunch of hotshot feds didn't figure him out, and you did!"

"He victimized me," I said. "He terrorized me."

"And he didn't *get* you. You got him. Feel strong!"

The feeling of strength and superiority may never
come to me. I can't help feeling lucky. If you think
you fingered someone like Devalian through genius,
perhaps you can feel powerful. I was still asking
myself if I had been more clever than he, or just
fortunate.

Devalian suffered a collapsed lung, had to undergo
a bowel resection that left him with a colostomy, and
lost his spleen. He spent nine hours in surgery and
two weeks in intensive care. He was moved to a
locked wing in the psychiatric ward of a county hospital; an armed officer stayed outside his room at
all times, with another officer monitoring his every
movement and sound on a closed-circuit television.
Inside his room there was no weapon for him to
steal. Another two police officers, the typical staffing
for a lockout ward, were on the floor of three wings.
Private-duty male nurses attended him. He was
cuffed and shackled. I wondered if that would do it.

Three weeks after I had shot him, I went back.
With Mike as escort.

"Are you sure you want to do this?" he had asked
me a dozen times.

"I'm sure. I have to." I was going back to Coleman anyway, to retrieve my belongings. Since I couldn't sleep and had trouble holding food down, Brad Krump had agreed to show me where they kept him. He hoped it would give me peace of mind, help me give this up.

The police had started talking to him. He was sick and weak and had refused legal counsel. He hadn't answered many questions, but he was talking more each day. Brad Krump and others were questioning him while he lay handcuffed to his bed, a tape recorder running during the interrogation. I was going to be allowed to see him, though he wouldn't see me. I could get some detailed information from Brad Krump about the interrogation. They didn't foresee using me as a prosecution witness because they now had obtained hard evidence. Devalian wouldn't know I'd been there. Then I was going to have my household goods moved out of Coleman, say good-bye to my friends, and never look back.

"There are about three ways something like this could go, Jack," Mike was telling me as we drove from the airport to the hospital. "Sometimes a guy like this accepts his fate and talks. He generally refuses counsel. Sometimes he denies to the end, gets a good lawyer. Sometimes he goes for the insanity plea. Devalian is doing a little talking; he might be giving up."

"He won't give up," I said. "He's sick right now. That's all. He's going to change his mind about all of this talking when he feels better. He'll say he was coerced. It could hurt the state's case."

"I know you don't have any confidence in Krump and his boys, but Bodge wouldn't let you down. This time I think they've got him. I don't think anyone will ever take him for granted again."

I hoped so. Mike told me that so far they believed Jason Devalian had killed twenty-eight women. A search of his house had not turned up any direct evidence, but there was an invoice for an annual payment on a storage unit in Denver; that search produced a locked metal trunk filled with purses. He kept their purses. In Kathy Porter's purse was the index card containing Tom Wahl's name and phone number. At the top of the card was typed "Handyman." That was why he told me to take my purse. It was more than an obsession, it was his trademark.

Elaine Broussard's purse was in the trunk. As was Jason Devalian's mother's purse.

There was other stuff in the trunk, too. Stolen IDs, a CHP shirt, a clerical collar and jacket. His disguises and accessories.

Mike and I met Brad Krump in the hospital coffee shop. I shook his hand and asked him how it was going, what he knew about this guy so far.

"It goes slow. Our research indicates he's a native of Nebraska, who ran away from his father's wheat farm when he was thirteen. His father was found dead at the bottom of a well when Jason was nineteen years old and his whereabouts unknown. He was next seen in his hometown nearly seven years later to collect his inheritance, the proceeds from the sale of the farm and equipment, and his father's savings, after debts were cleared and taxes paid. He let it all sit in a CD in a bank until he was nearly thirty and out of prison. Then he played with the money, transferring it around into various accounts under different names. He has about a hundred thousand dollars at his disposal."

"Did he have plastic surgery?"

"The examining physician says he did, but we don't know when or where. He's confessed to killing a police officer in his escape from the Henderson County facility, and he admits to having known some of the female victims. He tells us he doesn't need a lawyer and that he won't talk . . . but he always says something. He reacts; he can't help it. His reaction to questions about his neighbor's death leads us to suspect he shot Mr. Wharton. We know he stayed in the area after he was supposed to have been gone; he camped and blended in with hunters while he continued to play his little game of going into houses. Since he's a liar, our investigation focuses on separating his lies from the truth." He paused. "He told us about his finger."

I felt my back become rigid. I waited.

"It was an accident. It made him furious. He doesn't want scars or distinguishing marks that make it easy for people to remember him. He was so angry, he said, that he sneaked out of the hospital, drove to Coleman, 'borrowed' Billy's clippers, and broke into the mortuary. He meant to pay you back with that finger. Then he smiled and said it was perfect, that you looked like the idiot you were and you apologized."

I shuddered as though chilled. "My God," I muttered.

"He had to steal a car to do that. He took a hospital staff member's car and returned it. He said he doesn't think anyone was ever aware of it."

"Are you beginning to see how slick this guy is?" I asked. "What are you going to do to keep him away from the rest of the human race?"

"He has the highest-level restraint and detention we're capable of. That means—"

"It means nothing!" I snapped.

"It means," he continued calmly, "that he could be killed for eating his oatmeal wrong. He's in a very vulnerable position right now. He's regarded as highly capable of escape even under the most extraordinary circumstances and no movement from him is taken lightly. If it appears anything is amiss, weapons may be fired. I hope nothing like that happens before I find all the connections to what he's done. I want to know the extent of his crimes before he gets himself killed. I have missing women out there, Jackie, whom he may have killed. Those families deserve my best effort. I want to *know*."

He took a breath, slowed down. Brad Krump had no reason to feel personally endangered by Devalian, but he was trying to convince me of his dedication to Devalian's incarceration.

"I have to go back upstairs. You want a tour?"

"We're waiting for Bodge," I said. "I'll see you later."

"Maybe you'll calm down after you see the precautions we've taken. Just don't hang around, all right?"

"Why would I want to hang around?" I asked.

"Brad, we're grateful for this," Mike said hastily. "No kidding, thanks for giving Jack here a chance to quiet her nerves. We'll take a quick look and we're out of here. Thanks."

Krump looked at me, ignoring my ex-husband's rare politeness. "Look around, then go for a walk. Have something to eat. Get past this."

I just looked down into my coffee cup as Brad began to walk away. He turned back to me. "Jackie, I know you think we all failed you. I'm not going to make any excuses; I feel I've failed any time someone gets hurt. I failed to be fast enough, smart enough, cynical enough. The bad news is that this element, the psychopathic killer of above-average intelligence, is hard to catch. That's why there's a task force, people who dedicate their lives to studying these crimes and apprehending these criminals. I'll do my best. That's all I've got." Then he walked away.

Mike swirled his coffee. "It's not like he fucked up, Jack. His best is better than what a lot of people get. You can call him every day for the rest of your life to find out Devalian's status if it makes you feel better."

"I might," I said, a long way from feeling secure.

"Whatever it takes, Jack."

We sat silently for ten minutes when Bodge Scully walked into the cafeteria and bought himself a cup of coffee. He didn't see us sitting there, so Mike went over to greet him. Bodge suggested we go up to the ward, look around, get it over with.

"You come here often?" I asked, after giving him a hug.

"I spend too much time here. I don't rest easy anymore. I guess it'll pass, but for now I feel better when I can check in, see how it goes. You think this is going to help you, Jackie? Seeing where they keep him?"

"I don't know. I hope so. I had to come back here to get my things together, anyway. And . . . I can't sleep yet. Or eat."

"You'll come out to the house tonight? Have dinner and stay with us?"

"Thanks, Bodge. We'll stop by; we're staying the night at Roberta's. I'll never sleep in my old house again."

The elevator left us outside the locked ward. Bodge and Mike showed a police officer their IDs and vouched for me; we were allowed inside. The hall was long, sterile, and wide. There was an officer leaning against the desk at the nurses' station with a Styrofoam cup in his hand; he had a view of the entire hall. At the far end of the hall another officer leaned his chair back against the wall. He sat right outside a hospital room. The door was cracked.

Bodge spoke with the officer at the nurses' station. He was not on the Devalian job, but was assigned to the psychiatric floor. He pointed down the hall to the nurses' lounge. Bodge thanked him, indicated we should follow, and we walked to a room. Inside was another officer, armed, teetering on the back legs of his folding chair while watching a little television set. He looked over his shoulder and waved. "How ya doin'?" he asked.

"Good, Jim, good," Bodge replied. "Anything happening?"

" 'Fraid not. Same old stuff."

"Explain this contraption to my friend here. Jackie, here, she's the one put the clamps on our boy."

"No stuff?" he said, apparently impressed. "I'll be. Well, what we have here is a two-man ring of protection. One armed officer outside his room, one armed watching the monitor. His bed is centered in the room and we have two closed-circuit sweep cameras at perpendicular angles in operation. This gives us real-time data; everything is taped. Mr. Krump there," he said, pointing to the set, "has his own tape recorder—reel-to-reel—for his questioning. It hasn't been too interesting yet. Listen, Sheriff Scully, could you spell me? I've had to pee about an hour. Sorry, ma'am. Could you?"

"You bet, Jim. Go on ahead."

The patrolman left Bodge, Mike, and me alone. I looked at the monitor. The man in the bed, Jason—Tom—had lost thirty pounds. He was frail-looking, drawn, weakened. I wasn't fooled by this; I knew he was dangerous, powerful. I knew he would recover and become his tenacious self again.

"There he is," Mike said. "There the fucker is."

I saw a dial and turned it, recognizing Brad's voice. He held a brown grocery sack.

"You sure you don't want to talk about it? I'll get you anything you want first. You want something? Maybe a drink of water? Pain pill? Urinal?" There was no response. Brad went on. "Maybe you could tell me about this. You know what this is?"

Mike and I watched, exchanged glances. I was hearing this with my own ears. Mike pulled on my arm. "Jack, we don't want to be hearing this shit. Let's leave. Huh?"

"Want me to show it to you? What is it? You know what this is?"

He held an old, dirty purse. I felt my heart lurch. Devalian said nothing.

"What is it?" Krump asked. No comment from the bed. "You don't want to talk about it? I can get rid of it?" Nothing. "Maybe I'll burn it, then." Nothing. "Okay. It isn't really evidence, so no big deal if it disappears. I'm gonna burn it." He turned as if to leave the room. "Bye, then."

"A purse," came a low, weary voice. It didn't sound like him at first. I looked at the monitor, knew it was him, but his voice was far away, tired and whipped. "It's a purse."

"Whose purse?"

There was a long pause. "My mother's purse."

"Did you kill her?"

"He killed her."

"Who?"

"I don't want to talk."

"Who killed your mother, Jason?"

"My father, that's who. He didn't *murder* her. He just killed her. He punched her and choked her to death. He did that a lot. . . . And that time she died."

"Did you see him?"

"I always saw him. I was there. I was always there."

"Why did he beat her? Why did he kill her?"

"Because she was weak. Because she was useless."

"Did he beat you, too?"

The sound of laughter came out of him, a low, rumbling chuckle. He looked near death. He never moved his head. Sound came out of him, but he didn't move at all. "Yeah, he beat me, I guess you could say."

"With his fists?"

"Oh, sure, and everything. And his dick. And his mouth, and sticks and stones and belts. Leave me alone. I'm tired."

The voice I heard was beaten. Pitiful and wasted. Maybe he had given up. I just wouldn't believe it.

"How old were you when your father killed your mother?"

"I dunno. Five."

"And who buried her?"

"He did. With her purse and her clothes. She's right there on the farm."

"But you have the purse."

"I got it out. I dug her up and got out the purse after I heard what he said to the police. He said, 'She run off, that's all she did. Run off with some hand. She took her clothes and her purse and left the boy.' "

"Why did you dig up the purse?"

"I don't know. To have it. To give it to the police so they'd know she didn't run off, she got killed. By him."

"You wanted him to be caught?" No response

came. "You wanted him to be punished for killing your mother?" Still no response. "Did your father molest you? Sexually molest you when you were a boy?"

There was the sound of a snarl. "Did he fuck me when I was two? Three? Four?" he angrily replied. "Yeah."

"And when your mother was gone, there was no one to protect you?"

"She didn't protect me," he said. "She held me for him."

Mike gave a sharp tug on my arm. I turned my head and looked into his eyes. "They were mostly young mothers, Mike. Even me. I'd had a child. He killed the mothers . . . I bet he killed the mothers of little boys. . . . Oh, God. . . ."

"Come on, let's get out of here."

I turned back to the monitor. "Your mother participated in your father's sexual abuse?"

"Oh, fuck you," he said. "Who the hell cares? So *what*?"

"And you hate women? You brutalize women?"

"If only she'd liked me."

"Your mother?"

"No, man. Jackie. Jackie Sheppard."

"If only Jackie had liked you?"

No response. I was mesmerized. I felt Mike tug at my arm, but it was ridiculous to think I'd walk away while I was being discussed. He must have known that, because he didn't try again.

"Why did you want Jackie to like you?"

Again no response.

"You liked her?"

"Sure. Sure I did."

"You wanted to settle down? You wanted her to like you so you could settle down?"

He started to laugh. It was almost a giggle. "I just wanted her to like me. That's all."

"And if she'd liked you?"

No response.

"If she'd liked you, you would have settled down, started a new kind of life?"

I saw his head come up. His piercing eyes bore through Brad Krump. "You cops are such idiots," he said. "If she'd liked me, she'd be dead now."

"So, you only kill the women who like you?" Krump said, unruffled. Because my name had been mentioned, I had momentarily forgotten this was an interrogation. I was struck numb; Krump went on trying to get the facts.

"That it? You only kill the women who like you?"

"I ain't talking. Go home, Krump. I'm tired."

Mike was right; that was all we could take. I turned away from the monitor and walked out of the room, toward the locked ward doors. I stood there and waited while Bodge caught up and the officer on our side used his key to let us out.

I believed I understood. It was incomprehensible to me that a baby, a two-year-old boy—or younger if we could know the facts—could be terrorized this way. I found it unimaginable. But I'd read of such things. I knew it was so.

After we left the hospital, we went to the CHP headquarters, where Bodge and Mike wanted to ask a few questions about the case. Mike wanted me to talk to a professional who had been studying the Devalian case since his arrest. I let a psychologist for the state, probably a man like Tom Lawler, explain what he understood about Jason Devalian's mind.

This was what built him: A mother who held him for his father to rape. Years of hideous abuse and psychological terror. He kept their purses as souvenirs. Or maybe he did it to prove to himself that his victims went with him willingly.

Killing was Jason Devalian's job. He handled it like full-time work. He stole a little money now and then, but not because he needed it. Stalking and killing were a big operation, the way he did them. He wasn't much of a carpenter; he didn't take difficult jobs. He was more a handyman, Mr. Fix-it type. He'd get real friendly with the housewives, seduce them, give them secrets to keep, take them away. The women all had their clothes on; they never had a purse or wallet. The cooperation of his victims was important to him. He isolated them from their other friends and lured them into an intense, secret, sexually volatile liaison; they always went with him. The last bit of forensic detail was the presence of semen in the corpses. They had all probably had intercourse with Devalian, a man who was typically impotent. The psychologist suggested postmortem rape could explain the pattern. Devalian's was a psychosexual dysfunction that brought him ultimate relief through murder.

He liked to challenge his body, his mind, his capacity for pain, his proximity to danger. He liked the lies, the edge, the manipulation, and the win. He was not capable of normal social relationships or normal sexual relationships. The only thing that had kept me alive was the fact that I didn't like him. He'd have had to kidnap me, but his high wasn't as good unless he had a believer. The cooperation and submission of his victims was terribly important.

"He's crazy," I said to the psychologist.

"I think so."

"He could get the insanity deal again, couldn't he?"

"I don't think so. Do I think he must be insane? Yes. Can he help it? Maybe not. Does he know what he's doing? Every second. He is not acting out of psychosis. He fully comprehends his actions, his behavior. He knows it's wrong and punishable, which is why he was so careful to keep from getting caught. He is driven by something else. An evil created in him. That doesn't meet the definition of mental illness or insanity within the law. He will probably get the death penalty."

I wondered what it would take to kill him.

Further details regarding the commission of Devalian's crimes will keep coming as the interrogation and investigation progress. My questions are all answered. My clothes are packed and my house is full of boxes, which the moving van will pick up tomorrow. Mike and I will drive my car to Los Angeles. I said good-bye to the Danias; I will have dinner with Sue and Bodge, then drive out to Roberta's for the night.

This ordeal caused Roberta to make changes of her own. She decided it was time to close up her practice for good. She doesn't need the money or the work. She's sixty and widowed and hasn't seen much of the world yet. She'll travel, she says, keeping her ranch as a base and making L.A. a frequent stop. She offered me the practice. I was touched by her generosity, but I'm through with small-town life.

I'm going to visit an old aunt in Connecticut—haven't seen her in twenty years or so. I'm going to visit a college friend in Baltimore. Mrs. Wright, the cranky old next-door neighbor, never did talk to me, but I found a bunch of flowers from her garden on my doorstep with a little note. It said, "What a brave girl." I'm going to cherish that commendation, visit friends, take my time, get my life back. Devalian had possession of me for long enough, though he doesn't know it—never knew it.

I'm going to see if I can learn to sleep. And if I sleep again, I'm going back into family law, domestic law. Maybe my old firm will want me back. I'm going to do what I can to get closer to domestic crisis and child abuse. I'm going to see if I can cause any legal intervention where there's violence and abuse—and maybe, just maybe, I can prevent the building of just one psychopath.

But that's if I can sleep again someday.

If.

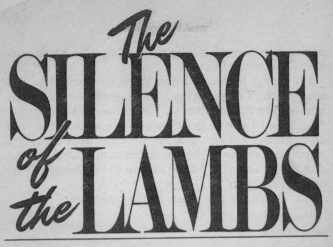

The SILENCE *of the* LAMBS

THE ELECTRIFYING BESTSELLER BY
THOMAS HARRIS

" THRILLERS DON'T COME ANY BETTER THAN THIS."
—CLIVE BARKER

"HARRIS IS QUITE SIMPLY THE BEST SUSPENSE NOVELIST
WORKING TODAY." — *The Washington Post*

THE SILENCE OF THE LAMBS
Thomas Harris
_____ 92458-5 $5.99 U.S./$6.99 Can.